MIRANDA
Lee

IT STARTED WITH A PROPOSITION

Discarded.

IT STARTED WITH
COLLECTION

October 2015

November 2015

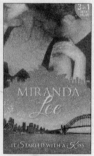

December 2015

January 2016

Miranda Lee is Australian, and lives near Sydney. Born and raised in the bush, she was boarding-school educated, and briefly pursued a career in classical music before moving to Sydney and embracing the world of computers. Happily married, with three daughters, she began writing when family commitments kept her at home. She likes to create stories that are believable, modern, fast-paced and sexy. Her interests include meaty sagas, doing word puzzles, gambling and going to the movies.

Published in Great Britain 2015
by Mills & Boon, an imprint of Harlequin (UK) Limited,
Eton House, 18-24 Paradise Road, Richmond, Surrey, TW9 1SR

IT STARTED WITH A PROPOSITION © 2015 Harlequin Books S.A.

Blackmailed into the Italian's Bed © 2007 Miranda Lee
Contract with Consequences © 2012 Miranda Lee
The Passion Price © 2004 Miranda Lee

ISBN: 978-0-263-91744-4

011-1115

Harlequin (UK) Limited's policy is to use papers that are natural, renewable and recyclable products and made from wood grown in sustainable forests. The logging and manufacturing processes conform to the legal environmental regulations of the country of origin.

Printed and bound in Spain
by CPI, Barcelona

BLACKMAILED INTO THE ITALIAN'S BED

MIRANDA LEE

CHAPTER ONE

GINO stood at the hotel room window, his hands shoved deep in his trouser pockets, his dark gaze fixed on the city streets below.

The snarled traffic moved along at snail's pace, and the pavements were filled with office workers spilling from their buildings, all eager to get home for the weekend. Wherever home might be.

He wondered where *her* home was. And if she was married.

His heart missed a beat at this last thought. As perverse as it was, he didn't want her to be married.

But of course she would be. A girl like that. So beautiful and so intelligent. Some smart man would have snapped her up by now. It had been ten years, for pity's sake. She probably had a couple of kids as well.

His cellphone ringing sent him spinning away from the window. He glanced at his watch as he hurried over to where he'd left his phone, by the bed. Five-thirty. Hopefully it would be the detective agency and not Claudia. He didn't want to talk to Claudia right now.

'Gino Bortelli,' he answered, with only the faintest of Italian accents.

'Mr Bortelli?'

Gino almost sighed with relief at hearing a crisp male voice on the other end.

'Cliff Hanson here, from Confidential Investigations.'

'Glad to hear from you,' Gino returned, just as crisply. 'What do you have for me?'

'We believe we've located the Ms Jordan Gray you're looking for, Mr Bortelli, although it's not as uncommon a name as we'd hoped. But there's only one Ms Jordan Gray currently living in Sydney who matches the age and physical description you gave us.'

'She's not married, then?' Gino asked, trying to keep the excitement out of his voice.

'Nope. Still single. With no children. And you were right. She's a lawyer. Works for Stedley & Parkinson. It's an American-owned legal practice which has a branch here in the Sydney City Business District.'

'I know it,' Gino said, stunned by this news. He'd been in their offices this very afternoon, signing a contract. Hell, he might have walked right past her!

'Word is she's the up-and-coming star of their civil litigation section. Took on a big insurance company recently. And won.'

A wry smile spread over Gino's face. 'That'd be her.'

Jordan had absolutely hated insurance companies. Her parents had had an insurance claim rejected after their home had been virtually destroyed in a storm, with the insurance company hiding behind some loophole in the small print of their contract. Her father had tried to fight them through the legal system, and it had cost him every cent he had and some he didn't. After he'd lost his final appeal he'd died of a coronary, brought on by stress, leaving behind a destitute wife and a daughter.

'Do you have an address and home phone number for me?' he asked.

'An address. But no home phone number as yet. Lawyers like Ms Gray usually have unlisted numbers.'

'Give me the address,' Gino said, striding over to sit at the writing desk which contained everything a businessman away from home might require, including internet access.

He picked up the complimentary pen and jotted Jordan's address down on the notepad. It was an apartment in Kirribilli, one of the swish harbourside suburbs on the north side of Sydney, not far from the bridge. He ripped off the page and slipped it into his wallet.

'Does she live alone?' came his next question, his throat tightening.

'We don't know that yet, Mr Bortelli. We've only been on the job a few hours. We need a little more time to fill in the details of the lady's love-life. There's only so much we can find out via the internet and phone calls.'

'How much more time?'

'Possibly only a few hours. I'm having one of my best field operatives tail Ms Gray when she leaves work this evening. We've been able to secure a recent photo, courtesy of her driver's licence. He's currently staking out the exit to her building.'

Gino winced at this invasion of Jordan's privacy. 'Is that really necessary?'

'It is, if you want to know the lady's personal status tonight. Which you said you did.'

Yes, he did. He was booked on an early morning flight to Melbourne.

When he'd flown in to Sydney yesterday Gino had had no intention of hiring a private eye to find Jordan. But during his taxi ride from the airport to the city the memories he'd been trying to bury for the last decade had resurfaced with a vengeance.

The need to know what had become of her had over-ridden common sense. He hadn't been able to sleep last night with thinking about her.

By morning, his curiosity had become a compulsion. A call to a police friend in Melbourne had soon provided him with the number of a reputable Sydney investigative agency. By ten this morning he'd set in motion the search for the first-year law student he'd lived with for a few idyllic months, all those years ago.

And supposing you find out there's no man in her life? What do you intend doing with that information?

Gino grimaced.

You were going to ask Claudia to marry you this weekend. You've even bought the ring. What in heaven's name are you doing, chasing after an old flame who probably hasn't given you a second thought in years?

He reassured himself. *I just want to see her one more time. To make sure that she's happy. Nothing more.*

What could be the harm in that?

'Keep me updated every hour,' he said brusquely.

'Will do, Mr Bortelli.'

CHAPTER TWO

JORDAN glanced up at the clock on the wall and willed the hands to get to ten to six, at which time she could reasonably excuse herself and go home.

She was attending the happy hour which the practice provided in the boardroom every Friday afternoon from five till six. It was a tradition at every branch of Stedley & Parkinson, introduced by the American partners when they'd begun their first practice in the United States forty years ago.

Employees who either didn't come—or left early—were frowned upon by the powers-that-be.

Normally Jordan didn't mind this end-of-week get-together.

But it had been a long and difficult week, both professionally and personally. Making small talk seemed beyond her today, which was why she'd taken her glass of white wine off into a corner by herself.

'Hiding, are we?'

Jordan looked up as Kerry angled her way into the same corner, carrying a tray of finger-food.

Kerry was the big boss's PA—the nicest girl in the place, and the closest Jordan had ever had to a best friend. A natural redhead, she had a pretty face, soft blue eyes, and fair skin which freckled in the Australian sun.

'I didn't feel like talking,' Jordan said, and picked up a tiny quiche-style tart from the tray. 'What's in these?'

'Spinach and mushroom. They're very nice, and not too fattening.'

Jordan popped the tart into her mouth, devouring it within seconds. 'Mmm, these are seriously yummy. I might have another.'

'Feel free. So what's the problem? Other than Loverboy having flown off home today, leaving you alone for two whole weeks?'

Jordan winced at Kerry calling Chad 'Loverboy'. Yet it had been his office nickname from the first day he'd waltzed in, with his wide, all-American smile, film star looks and buckets of charm. There wasn't a single girl in the place who wouldn't have willingly gone out with Jack Stedley's only son and heir—Kerry included. But it had been Jordan he'd zeroed in on, Jordan whom he'd been dating for the past few months.

'Come on, you can tell me,' Kerry added in a conspiratorial whisper. 'I'm not a gossip like some of the other girls around here.'

Jordan knew this was true. One of Kerry's many good qualities was her discretion.

She'd also been round the block a few times, with one marriage and several boyfriends behind her—the last having broken up with her only recently. Yet she maintained a sense of optimism about life which Jordan admired and often envied.

Jordan looked into her friend's kind blue eyes and decided to do what she very rarely did. Confide.

'Chad asked me to marry him last night.'

'Wow!' Kerry exclaimed, before shooting Jordan a speculative look. 'So what's the problem? You should be over the moon.'

'I turned him down.'

'You *what?* Wait here,' Kerry said, and hurried off to give the food tray to one of the other girls to distribute, sweeping up a glass of champagne before rejoining Jordan, a stern look on her pretty face. 'I don't believe this. The Golden Boy asked you to marry him and you said no?'

'I didn't exactly say no,' Jordan hedged. 'But I didn't say yes, either. I said I wanted some time to think. I said I'd give him my answer when he gets back from the States.'

'But *why?* I thought you were mad about the man. Or as mad as a girl like you is ever going to get.'

'And what does *that* mean?'

'Oh…you know. You're super-intelligent, Jordan, and very self-contained. You're never going to lose your head over a man, like I do.'

Jordan sighed. Kerry was right. She wasn't the sort to lose her head over a man.

But she had once. And she'd never forgotten him.

'What is it that's bothering you?' Kerry persisted. 'It can't be the sex. You told me Chad was good in bed.'

'He is. Yes, he is,' she repeated, as though trying to

convince herself that there wasn't anything missing in that department.

In truth, she wouldn't have thought anything *was* missing if it hadn't been for her relationship with Gino. Chad knew all the right moves in bed. But he simply could not make her feel what Gino had once made her feel.

No man could, Jordan suspected.

'What is it that you're not telling me?' Kerry asked gently.

Jordan sighed a resigned sigh. That was the trouble with confiding. It was like throwing a stone in a pond, causing ever-widening circles. Kerry was not going to rest now till Jordan had told her the truth, the whole truth and nothing but the truth.

Or at least a believable version.

'There was this guy once,' she began tentatively. 'An Italian. Oh, it was years ago, during my first year at uni. We lived together for a few months.'

'And?'

'Well, he…he was a hard act to follow.'

'I see. Obviously, you were madly in love with him?'

'Yes.'

'And what you feel for Chad doesn't compare?'

'No.' Not Chad, or any other boyfriend she'd had since.

'Was this Italian guy your first lover?'

'Yes. He was.' The first and by far the best.

'That explains it, then,' Kerry said, with satisfaction in her voice.

'Explains what?'

'It's impossible for a girl to completely forget her

first lover. Not if he was good in bed. Which I'm pre-
suming he was.'

'He was simply fantastic.'

'You know, Jordan, he probably wasn't as fantastic
as you think he was. The memory can play tricks on us.
For ages after my divorce I thought I was a fool for
leaving my husband. But then I ran into him one night
at a party and I realised he was nothing but a sleazebag
and I was much better off without him. I'll bet your
Italian boyfriend dumped you, didn't he?'

'Not exactly. I came home from uni one day to find
a note saying that his father was seriously ill. He said
he was sorry, but he had to go home to his family, and
he wished me well in the future.'

'He didn't promise to write or anything?'

'No. And he didn't leave me a forwarding address.
I didn't realise till he'd gone how little I knew about
him. He never talked about his family. Or called them.
At least not whilst I was around. I guessed later that he
was probably out here from Italy on a temporary
working visa and never meant to stay.'

'That's another reason why you find it hard to forget
him,' Kerry told her. 'He's unfinished business. Pity he
had to return to Italy, otherwise you might have been
able to look him up and see for yourself that he's not
nearly as fantastic as you thought. If truth be told, he's
probably fat and bald by now.'

'It's only been ten years, Kerry, not thirty. Besides,
Italian men rarely go bald,' Jordan pointed out, recall-
ing Gino's luxuriantly thick, wavy black hair. 'And
Gino would never let himself get fat. He was right into

physical fitness. He worked on a construction site during the day, and went to the gym several nights a week. He's the one who started me on the exercise kick.' Jordan jogged a couple of kilometres most mornings, and did weights three times a week.

'Worked as what on a construction site?' Kerry asked.

'A labourer.'

'A labourer?' Kerry repeated disbelievingly. 'You prefer a labourer to Chad Stedley?'

'Gino was very smart,' Jordan defended, 'and a darned good cook.'

'Well, bully for him,' Kerry said dismissively. 'Marry Chad and you can go out to dinner every night. Or hire your own personal *cordon bleu* chef. Look, I don't care if this Gino was Einstein and Casanova rolled into one! You have to move on, girl. You can't let some old flame spoil your future. And your future is becoming Mrs Chad Stedley. If you want my advice, as soon as Chad rings you tell him you've thought about it and your answer is yes, yes and triple yes!'

Jordan scooped in a deep breath, then let it out very slowly. 'I wish it were that easy.'

'It *is* that easy.'

Was it?

Jordan could see the sense of Kerry's arguments. Regardless of what she'd felt for Gino, he *was* past history. If you looked at things logically, to let her memory of him spoil what she could have with Chad was stupid.

Jordan was a lot of things. But stupid was not one of them.

'Yes, you're right,' she said firmly. 'I'm being silly. I'll do exactly as you said,' she decided, and felt instantly better.

Hadn't she read somewhere that any decision was better than no decision at all?

That was right. It was.

Kerry rolled her eyes. 'Thank goodness for small mercies. The girl has finally seen some sense. Look, everyone's starting to leave now. It's not my turn to help clean up, so how about we go have a celebratory drink together somewhere swanky? I don't fancy going home to an empty place just yet.'

'I'm not really dressed for swanky,' Jordan said. Unlike Kerry, whose red woollen wrap-around dress would look just as good in a nightclub as it did in the office.

'You can say that again,' Kerry said drily, as she gave Jordan's navy pin-striped trouser suit the once-over. 'Next time we go clothes shopping together I'm not going to listen to any more of your "I'm a lawyer, I have to dress conservatively" excuses. Still, if you take down your hair and undo a couple of buttons of that schoolmarm blouse, you just might not stick out like a sore thumb. We'll pop into the Ladies' and fix you up when we get there.'

'Get where?'

'How about the Rendezvous Bar? That's less swanky since they refurbished it.'

Jordan's top lip curled. 'It's also gaining a reputation as a pick-up joint.'

Kerry grinned. 'Yeah, I know.'

Jordan's eyebrows lifted skywards. 'You're incorrigible, do you know that?'

'Nah. More like desperate.'

'Oh, go on with you,' Jordan said. 'A girl as pretty as you will never be desperate.'

Kerry beamed. 'I do so love spending time with you, Jordan. You always make me feel good about myself. Want to go clothes shopping tomorrow?'

'Sorry. No can do. I have to work.'

'On a Saturday?'

'More like all weekend.' She still hadn't finished her closing address for the Johnson case. Not to her satisfaction, anyway.

Kerry wagged a finger at her. 'All work and no play makes Jordan a dull girl.'

'Which is why I agreed to go for a drink with you,' Jordan replied as she took her friend's free arm. 'So stop picking on me, woman, and let's get the hell out of here.'

CHAPTER THREE

GINO clicked off the phone, amazed by what Cliff Hanson had just told him.

Apparently Jordan had left her office building at ten past six and walked with a female friend towards Wynyard Station. The man tailing her had presumed she was going to catch a train home. Instead, she and her companion had turned into the Regency Hotel and they were, at this very second, sitting in the bigger of the two hotel bars, having a drink.

The amazing part was that the Regency was where Gino himself was staying.

For the second time that day fate had placed Jordan on a path which could have crossed with his.

This time, however, he wasn't in ignorance of the fact. Which was why he'd ordered Hanson to tell his operative to sit close to the door and keep an eye on Jordan till he could get down there.

Adrenaline coursed through Gino's veins as he swept up his wallet from the bedside table and slipped it into the breast pocket of his leather jacket. For a split second he hesitated, worried over what would happen when he confronted her after all these years.

Would she be pleased to see him? Or not?

Impossible to gauge how she might react. She'd loved him and he'd hurt her, no doubt about that.

Jordan was not a girl to easily forgive and forget. That he did know.

At the same time, their love affair had been ten years ago—a long time to nurse a broken heart or bitterness.

Gino scowled as he whirled and headed for the hotel room door. He'd cross those bridges when he came to them, because nothing short of death was going to stop him from going down there right now and talking to her.

Still, he was glad he'd had time to shower and change from the sleek Italian business suit he'd been wearing earlier today. Casual clothes were more in keeping with the Gino Jordan had once known, not the Gino he had become.

Which is what, exactly? he asked himself during the lift ride down to the ground floor.

A man who's forgotten what it's like to have fun, that's what.

A man weighed down by responsibility towards his family.

A man about to ask a girl he doesn't love to marry him.

An Italian girl.

If only he hadn't made that rash promise to his father on his deathbed.

But he had, and there was no going back.

Those last words echoed in Gino's head as he stepped from the lift and headed for the bar in question.

No going back.

What he'd once shared with Jordan was gone. If he was strictly honest, it had never been real. He'd been living a fantasy. A sexy Shangri-la which had disappeared the moment he'd received that call about his father's illness.

All that was left was a guilty memory, plus the ghost of pleasures past.

Tonight he would face that guilty memory and hopefully lay its ghost to rest.

A bouncer stood at the door to the bar, giving Gino a sharp look as he approached, but not barring his way inside.

The room was huge, with a dark blue carpet underfoot, disco-style lighting overhead, and a glitzy central bar. There were several different sitting areas, but most of the bar's patrons were clustered near the far left corner, where a three-piece combo was playing soul music.

Only a smattering of people were sitting at the tables in the area nearest the entrance, which was currently designated a no-smoking section.

Gino located the operative without any trouble—an innocuous-looking guy of around thirty, who'd blend into most crowds.

'She's over there,' he said, as soon as Gino sat down, nodding towards a table located on the edge of the dance floor.

As Gino stared through the faint smoke haze at the girl who'd once captured his heart he realised he probably wouldn't have recognised her if he'd walked right past her! Not with her glorious blonde hair scraped back up in that severe style, and certainly not dressed in that mannish trouser suit.

What had happened to the feminine girl he'd known? She was thinner too, her face all angles.

Yet she was still beautiful. Beautiful and sad.

Both moved him: her beauty and her sadness.

'I'll take it from here,' he said gruffly to the operative. 'You can go home.'

'Are you absolutely sure?'

'Absolutely.'

The man shrugged, swallowed the rest of his beer, and left.

Gino sat there for some time, watching Jordan. She glanced repeatedly at a redhead in a red dress, who was dancing cheek to cheek with a tall, good-looking guy. Clearly this was the female colleague she had come here with. Also clearly, Jordan wasn't happy with being left to sit alone.

As soon as the band stopped playing the redhead returned to the table, accompanied by her dancing partner. After a brief conversation with Jordan, the redhead and the man headed for the exit, arm in arm.

When Jordan started downing her almost full glass of wine with considerable speed, obviously intending to leave also, Gino decided it was time to make his presence known.

The distance from his table to hers seemed endless, his chest growing tighter with each step. Just before he reached the table Jordan put down her empty wine glass then bent to her left, to retrieve her bag from the adjoining chair.

She actually had her back to him when he said, 'Hello, Jordan,' the words feeling thick on his tongue.

She twisted back to face him, her chin jerking upwards, her lovely blue eyes widening with surprise.

No…not surprise. Shock.

'Oh, my God!' she exclaimed. 'Gino!'

Shock, but not bitterness, he noted. Nor hatred.

Relief flooded through him.

'Yes,' he said with a warm smile. 'It's me. Gino. May I join you? Or are you here with someone?'

'Yes. No. No, not any more. I—' Jordan broke off, a puzzled frown forming on her small forehead. 'You've almost lost your Italian accent!'

Trust her to notice something like that, Gino thought ruefully, as he sat down at her table. She'd always been an observant girl, with a mind like a steel trap.

When he'd first met her he'd not long been back from a four-year stint at the university in Rome, his Italian accent having thickened during his extended stay.

This reunion was going to be more awkward than he'd ever imagined. For how could he explain her observation without revealing just how much he'd deceived her all those years ago?

He had no option but to lie.

'I've been back in Australia for quite a while.'

'And you didn't think to look me up?' she threw at him.

'I couldn't imagine you'd want that,' he said carefully. 'I thought you'd have moved on.'

'I have,' she said, and tossed her head at him.

A very Jordan-like gesture, but it didn't have the same effect as it had when her hair was down.

'You became a lawyer, then?' he asked, pretending he didn't already know.

'Yes,' she said.

'Your mum must be very proud of you.'

'Mum passed away a few years back. Cancer.'

Another reason for her to look sad and lonely. 'I'm so sorry, Jordan. She was a nice woman.'

'She liked you, too.' She sighed, looking away for a moment, before looking back at him. 'So what are *you* doing nowadays?'

'I'm still working in the construction business,' he replied, hating himself for keeping up with the deception. But what else could he do? This wasn't going to go anywhere. It couldn't. This was just…closure.

Yet as he looked deep into her eyes—such lovely, expressive blue eyes—it didn't feel like closure. It felt as it had felt the first day he'd met her.

The temptation to try to resurrect something here was intense. So was his escalating curiosity about her love-life. Okay, so she wasn't married. That didn't mean she didn't have a lover, or a live-in boyfriend.

'You're not married, I notice,' he remarked, nodding towards her left hand, which was empty of rings.

'No,' she returned, after a slight hesitation.

Gino wondered what that meant. Had she been married and was now divorced?

'And you?' she countered, her eyes guarded.

'I might get around to it one day,' he said with a shrug.

'You always vowed you wouldn't marry till you were at least forty.'

'Did I?'

'You very definitely did.'

Gino decided to stop the small talk about himself and cut to the chase.

'What are you doing here alone, Jordan?'

'I wasn't alone,' she returned sharply. 'I was with a work colleague, but she ran into an old boyfriend of hers and he asked her out to dinner. They've just left.'

'You didn't mind?'

'Why should I mind? We only came in for a drink. It's high time I went home, anyway.'

'Why? It's only early. Is there someone special waiting for you at home? Boyfriend? Partner?'

Anger flared into her eyes. 'That's a very personal question, Gino. One which I don't feel inclined to answer.'

'Why not?'

Her eyes carried exasperation as she shook her head at him. 'You run into me by accident after ten years and think you have the right to question me over my personal life? If you were so interested in me, then why didn't you look me up when you came back to Australia?'

'I've been living in Melbourne,' he said, by way of an excuse.

'So? That's only a short plane trip away.'

'Would you have really wanted me to look you up, Jordan? Be honest now.'

Her face betrayed her. She *had* wanted him to. But no more than he'd wanted to himself.

'You could have written,' she said angrily. 'You knew my address. Whereas I had no idea where you were, other than in Italy.'

'I thought it better to make a clean break—leave you free to find someone more…suitable.'

She laughed. 'You were being cruel to be kind, then?'

'Something like that.'

She stared at him, her eyes still furious.

Gino had forgotten how worked up she could get when she thought someone wasn't being straight with her. Jordan had no tolerance of lies—or liars.

Gino conceded he'd dug a real hole for himself all those years ago. Not that it mattered what she thought of him. What mattered was whether she was happy or not.

The evidence of his eyes was troubling. She looked tired, and stressed, and frustrated. If she did have a live-in lover—or a boyfriend—he wasn't making her very happy.

'So there's no special man in your life right now?' he asked.

She glanced away for a second, then looked back at him. 'Not right now. Look, I—'

'Would you dance with me?' he asked, before she could bolt for the door.

The band had started up again, a bluesy number with a slow, sensual rhythm.

Jordan stared at him. But not so much with anger now. With a type of fear, as if he'd just asked someone scared of heights to step with him to the edge of a cliff.

Maybe she thought he was coming on to her.

He wasn't. He just wanted to find some way to get past her defences, to have her open up to him about her life.

She was a good dancer, he knew, but so was he. They'd loved going dancing together.

'For old times' sake,' he added, standing up and holding his hand out to her.

She stared at it for a long moment, as if it was a viper about to strike.

Finally she rose, taking off her jacket and draping it over her bag on the chair before placing her hand in his.

How soft it was, he thought as he drew her onto the polished wooden dance floor. Soft and pale, with long, elegant fingers and exquisitely kept nails.

She'd always had a thing for painted nails, he recalled. Both fingers and toes. Her favourite colour had been scarlet, but she'd had bottles and bottles of nail polish, of every imaginable shade.

Tonight her fingernails were painted a deep cream, matching her blouse.

Now that her jacket was off, he could see she still had a lovely figure, despite being thinner: her breasts were still pert, her waist was tinier than ever, and her stomach athletically flat.

His mother would have said she didn't have good childbearing hips—the way Italian girls did—but Gino had always found Jordan's slender shape extremely attractive. He loved her tight little butt and her long slim legs, loved her blonde hair and her pale soft skin.

Naked, she looked like an angel.

'Put your arms up around my neck,' he suggested, after he swung her round to face him.

'You always were a bossy man,' she replied, but did as he wanted, her fingertips like velvet as they slid under the collar of his leather jacket and settled on the sensitive skin at the nape of his neck.

Gino swallowed when he started to respond. This was not what he'd intended when he'd asked her to dance. But he seemed powerless to stop himself from becoming excited.

Planting his hands on her hips, he kept his lower half a decent distance from hers—not an easy thing to do once she started swaying to the slow, thudding beat of the music.

His good intentions, Gino suspected, were doomed to failure.

'You are real, aren't you?' she said suddenly. 'Not some figment of my imagination.'

'I'm very real,' he said drily. Just as his arousal was.

Her head tipped charmingly to one side as she looked up at him.

'Amazing,' she murmured. 'And you're not fat at all.'

He tried not to laugh. If only she knew…

'Why would I be fat?' he asked.

'Lots of men gain weight after they turn thirty. What are you now? Thirty-five?'

'Thirty-six. You've *lost* weight.'

'A little.'

'You're still very beautiful.'

Her eyes stabbed his with reproach. 'Don't, Gino.'

'Don't what?'

'Don't sweet-talk me.'

'You used to like me sweet-talking you.'

'I used to like you doing a lot of things.'

He wished she hadn't said that. Her words were sparking memories which would have been better kept buried.

And they in turn sparked something he'd been trying to deny all day, struggled to control ever since he'd asked her to dance. Which was that he still wanted her—despite the years which had passed, despite everything. He wanted to take her upstairs to his hotel room right now and strip her of those sexless clothes, wanted to take down her hair and just take her, as he had ten years ago.

She'd been a virgin back then, a fact he hadn't realised till it was too late. Her innocence had shocked him at the time, but her passion had quickly banished any qualms.

That passion was still there: he could see it in her blazing blue eyes and flushed cheeks.

And it was still overriding his conscience.

'Some things don't change,' he growled.

'Everything changes, Gino. Nothing stays the same.'

'Is that so?'

His hands shifted, one sliding up her spine, the other downward to her tailbone, giving him the leverage to press her close.

As their bodies made more intimate contact a wave of dark desire ripped through Gino, obliterating what little was left of his conscience.

'*This* hasn't changed, beautiful,' he whispered huskily.

CHAPTER FOUR

JORDAN stiffened, then tried to stop dancing altogether. But he would have none of it, keeping her body jammed tight against his as he moved his hips from side to side.

Impossible to ignore his arousal.

Gino was impressively built. Her mind flashed back to the first time he'd made love to her. Or tried to. She'd never forgotten the shocked look on his face when he'd realised she was a virgin. She'd begged him not to stop, and he hadn't, his initial penetration punching a pained cry from her lips.

She'd gloried in the experience, impatient to do it again as soon as possible. Afterwards he'd run them both a bath and lain her on top of him in the warm water, caressing her body. Then he'd dried her and carried her back to her bed, where he'd made love to her again, not stopping till she'd fallen into a deep sleep.

He'd given her tender body time to recover from his initial onslaught. Next morning, when he'd entered her, she'd welcomed him with a wild, wanton need. She'd climaxed swiftly and noisily.

After that, she'd always come whenever he was inside her.

Feeling his rock-hard flesh pressing into her stomach reminded her of how that felt: Gino being inside her.

Jordan suppressed a groan, burying her head under his chin to hide her flushed face from his eyes.

'I'm up here for the weekend,' he murmured, his lips in her hair. 'I'm staying here at this hotel.'

Jordan's head jerked back, her eyes disbelieving as she stared up into his darkly handsome face. 'You're staying here? At the Regency?'

'It is fate, is it not?'

Jordan shook her head. 'I don't believe in fate. Things are not predestined, Gino. People have free will. And choices.'

'And what would you choose, Jordan, if I asked you to come up to my room with me?'

Jordan's lips fell open. The arrogance of him! And the presumption!

But, oh…the passion. It blazed down at her from his beautiful black eyes, reminding her of his extraordinary virility and amazing sexual stamina. When they'd lived together it had been nothing for Gino to make love to her for hours on end, with only the shortest of breaks in between. He'd claimed he couldn't get enough of her, and his actions had backed up his words.

Gino had never been the first one to go to sleep. She'd been the one who usually pegged out, exhausted but happy.

'What for, exactly?' she snapped, even as she quivered inside at the thought of going up to his room with him. 'An old-times'-sake shag? Sorry, but I don't do one-night stands, Gino. I never did. You must remember that.'

'I remember *everything* about you,' he said, his voice vibrating with the most seductive emotion. 'And I'm not after a one-night stand. I want you to stay the whole weekend with me. I also want the opportunity to talk to you. To explain why I didn't come back for you all those years ago.'

Jordan's wildly galloping heart skittered to an unsteady halt. 'You...you wanted to come back for me?'

'Of course. I loved you, Jordan. Never doubt that.'

The last of Jordan's resistance began to crumble right then and there.

'Don't get me wrong,' he added. 'I don't want to talk tonight. Tonight is for us, Jordan. You and me together again, as we once were. Don't say no. Say *si. Si,* Gino. As I taught you all those years ago.'

Jordan's head whirled. That was another way she'd been different with Gino than with any other man since. The way he'd been able to make her submit to his will. Not like some whipped slave, but willingly and wantonly. She had wallowed in the role of being his woman. Wallowed in his possessiveness and his protectiveness. With him she'd always felt safe and secure, and totally, totally loved.

She'd been devastated when he left, devastated and despairing. That year she'd failed her exams and had to resit.

She hadn't had another boyfriend during her remaining years at university. Then, when she had eventually started dating again, she'd gone out with sweet, gentle men who were, perhaps, just a little weak. Men she could dominate and dump, once things got too serious.

Because she wasn't going to marry any of them. How could she, when she didn't love them?

Then Chad had come into her life. Smiling, charming, successful Chad, who'd impressed her with his intelligence and sophistication.

Sex with him was quite good.

She'd thought she loved him—till he'd proposed and she had suddenly been faced with a lifetime of sleeping with him.

If she were brutally honest, there was something irritatingly clinical about Chad's lovemaking—as if he was following a textbook on sex. Sometimes she faked her orgasm, so that he wouldn't ask her if she'd had one.

Gino had never asked her. He'd *known* she had.

Jordan trembled at the thought of how many times she would climax if she went up to his hotel room with him.

'Come on,' he decided for her. 'Let's go.'

Taking her arms from around his neck, he grabbed her left hand and began pulling her towards the exit.

'My things!' she protested, and indicated the table where, hopefully, her bag and jacket would still be on that chair.

They were.

He scowled as he watched her draw her jacket on. 'Why do you wear such unflattering clothes?'

Her eyes flicked over his outfit. Tight black jeans, a white T-shirt and a black leather jacket. He'd always been a jeans and T-shirt kind of guy. They suited Gino's tall, macho body.

'Female lawyers wear clothes like this to work,' she said. She didn't add, *Especially ones who looked like her.* The law was still a man's world, no matter what feminists liked to think. Even women clients preferred a male lawyer.

'You look better in a dress,' he returned, taking her elbow and steering her towards the exit. 'Or at least a skirt. You should never wear trousers, Jordan.'

Heat flooded her body as she recalled how, after Gino had been living with her for a while, he'd forbidden her to wear underwear. She'd fought him over that. At first. But he'd managed to convince her, and she'd started going round with nothing on under her clothes. Which was why she'd worn dresses and skirts back then, and not jeans or trousers.

Oh, heavens, she felt hot, so hot.

Thankfully, the air outside the bar was much cooler. Jordan scooped in some calming breaths as Gino urged her along the marble-floored arcade which led to the hotel foyer proper. If she was going to do this she would rather do it with a clear head, not because she was mindlessly turned on.

But it was no use. She *was* mindlessly turned on.

She tried warning herself that he might have become a heartless womaniser, was just spinning her a line to get her into bed for the night.

But she wasn't convinced. He'd seemed so sincere just now. Sincere and very passionate.

At the same time Jordan was desperate to find the answers to all those questions about Gino which had plagued her for the last ten years.

He'd promised to explain everything in the morning. Meanwhile…

It was the meanwhile which was sending her into a spin.

Was she really going to do this? Go to bed with Gino within ten minutes of running into him again?

Her heart fluttered wildly as her eyes raked over him. He was everything she remembered. And more…more handsome, more mature…and even more masterful.

She would not have believed herself capable of being seduced so quickly these days, even by Gino.

But seduce her he had, in no time flat.

Jordan knew that if she spent the night with her wickedly sexy former lover then it would be Chad who'd be history. She'd had a slim chance of forgetting Gino when he'd been safely consigned to the past. No way could she forget him now.

Still, maybe she wouldn't have to forget him this time. Maybe they really could take up where they left off.

Oh, she hoped so.

'What are you doing up here in Sydney?' she asked, almost running to keep up with him. 'And why are you staying here? This is a very expensive hotel.'

'Don't ask questions, Jordan,' he returned, his tone impatient. 'Not right now. Leave it till the morning.'

She opened her mouth, then closed it again. In truth, she didn't want to talk. But she didn't want to think, either. And silence encouraged thinking.

Thinking brought doubts and worries. She could

imagine what Kerry would think if she saw her now. She's say she was insane!

When they reached the bank of lifts, one of them was empty and waiting. Gino took no time steering her inside, inserting his key card and pressing the tenth floor. The moment the doors closed he pulled her forcefully into his arms.

'I can't wait another second,' he growled, his mouth already descending.

What was it that made one man's kiss different from another?

Jordan had once tried to analyse this when other men's kisses never did for her what Gino's had done.

Now she knew: it was not just a matter of technique, or the sensual shape of his mouth. It was the passion behind those kisses, that all-encompassing hunger which came not just from his lips and tongue, but from his whole body.

Jordan was panting by the time he wrenched his mouth away.

His black eyes blazed down at her. 'I should never have left you,' he said. 'Never!'

The lift had stopped by then, and the doors slid open. Two couples were waiting there to get in, all glammed up for a Friday night on the town. The women glanced at Gino as they exited, the men at Jordan.

She cringed a little when she saw her reflection in the mirror on the wall opposite. She looked dishevelled—some strands of hair falling down, her mouth devoid of lipstick, her eyes dilated and glittering with desires as yet unsatisfied.

Gino enfolded her hand in his and drew her along a carpeted hallway, stopping in front of room number 107.

As he bent his head to insert his key card again, Jordan noticed that his hair was shorter than he'd once worn it. She wondered if he was still a construction labourer. Maybe he was a foreman by now.

Another thought popped into her mind as he opened the door and waved her inside. Surely he must have a girlfriend back in Melbourne. Men like Gino didn't live celibate lives.

As jealous as this idea made her, Jordan held her tongue, not wanting to spoil the moment with any upsetting truths. All she needed to know for now was that he wasn't married and that he still desired her. As she still desired him.

But do you still love him? came the intriguing question as Gino followed her into the hotel room, kicking the door shut behind them.

Jordan was no longer a romantic teenager. She'd learned in the decade post-Gino that falling in love did not come as easily when you'd seen more of life. And of men.

When Gino curled his hands over her shoulders and leant her back against him Jordan realised she didn't care if she still loved him or not. Her desires had moved past the point of no return. She was Gino's woman again. At least for tonight. No, for the whole weekend.

An erotic shiver rippled down her spine as he eased her jacket off her shoulders.

'Do you wish to go to the bathroom first?' he whispered.

'No,' she choked out.

Her jacket gone, he turned her round and began unbuttoning her blouse. When her nipples tightened within her bra, she closed her eyes.

'Open your eyes,' he commanded.

She obeyed him, if a little reluctantly.

'Now keep them open. I want you to see that it is Gino making love to you.'

'You think I wouldn't know it was you, even with my eyes closed?'

His smile was almost smug. 'You have not forgotten me?'

'I remember everything about you, Gino,' she said, echoing his words down in the bar.

His eyes smouldered as he stripped the blouse from her body, then her bra.

'Then you will remember I am not always a patient lover.'

Jordan's mouth went dry.

Sometimes, when he'd come home from work, he'd lifted her skirt and taken her swiftly, standing up. No foreplay. Just his flesh filling hers whilst he told her how he'd thought about doing this to her all day.

His impassioned words had excited her as much as his actions, sending her over the edge within a shockingly short space of time.

She shuddered at the thought that this was what he was going to do to her now. Though he couldn't, could he? Not with what she was still wearing.

'You should not cover your beautiful body with clothes such as these,' he told her, as he unzipped her pin-striped trousers and pushed them down over her hips. When they pooled onto the floor she stepped out of them, leaving her standing there in nothing but cream cotton panties, beige knee-high stockings and sensible black pumps.

'Ridiculous,' he growled, his top lip curling at the sight of her. 'Get them off. Get everything off!'

She might have done as he ordered if he hadn't started undressing himself, tossing aside his black leather jacket and reefing the white T-shirt over his head in a flash.

The sudden baring of his chest kept her rooted to the spot, her heart thudding as her eyes washed over him. He was leaner than he had been ten years ago—leaner, yet still utterly gorgeous.

'Do you want me to do it? Is that it?' he asked as he unzipped his jeans and shoved them down, taking his underpants with them.

Jordan swallowed. 'What?'

Gino shot her a frustrated glance before sitting down on the edge of the bed and yanking off his shoes and socks.

Once totally naked, he remained sitting there, his dark eyes narrowing as they travelled up and down her tautly held body.

'You *are* thinner,' he said.

'So are you,' she countered, desperate to find some strength to fight the wave of weakness which was washing through her. 'And your hair's shorter.'

'Is yours?'

'No.'

'Then take it down.'

She just stood there, willing herself not to blindly obey him, as she once had.

His dark eyes glittered. 'If you don't, then I will.'

Jordan's hands lifted to pull out the pins which anchored her French pleat, her hair spilling down over her shoulders.

'Now come here,' he said, and moved his knees apart, drawing her gaze to those parts of his body which she'd been trying not to stare at.

Jordan stiffened. What did he want her to do?

'Put your right foot up here,' he said, patting a small area of the bed in front of him.

Relief loosened her frozen muscles, and she moved forward to do as he suggested.

He slipped off her shoe and tossed it aside, then peeled the short stocking down her leg, his fingers caressing her calf as he did so. Then her ankle, and then the sensitive sole of her foot.

'Mmm,' he said, once her leg was bare. 'Cream nail polish on your fingers, scarlet red on your toes. I wonder if your work colleagues know the real you, Jordan? The other foot, please.'

'And who is the real me?' she said, struggling to keep her voice steady whilst he gave the other foot the same erotic treatment.

'You're a closet exhibitionist. And a sensualist.'

Jordan grimaced when he pulled her foot towards him, pressing her toes into him.

'Rub your foot up and down on me,' he said.

When she did, a raw groan broke from his lips.

'You see?' he said, grabbing her ankle and depositing her by then unsteady foot back on the floor.

She saw nothing, her mind having tipped from reality into that wildly erotic, heart-pounding world where desire ruled and pleasure beckoned.

'Come closer,' he commanded.

When she did, he dragged her panties down to her ankles, then bent forward to kiss her stomach.

Jordan's belly tightened under his lips, her hands lifting to rake through his hair. She groaned when he swirled his tongue in her navel, gasped when his hands slid between her legs, whimpered when his fingers slipped inside her…

His head suddenly lifted from her stomach. 'Don't let go yet,' he warned her, even whilst he continued the most intimate exploration of her body.

'Oh, God, Gino. I can't. I… Please… Please…'

'Now *you* are the impatient one. I like that. Would you like me inside you now? Tell me how much. Tell me,' he urged, his eyes like shining black coals as they gazed up at her.

'Stop tormenting me,' she cried.

'But I find I am enjoying it. It makes me feel good to see you this desperate for me.'

'Just do it, for pity's sake!'

She was on the bed and under him before she could utter another word. He hooked her ankles over his shoulders, then drove into her. Deep.

'Is this what you wanted?' he muttered as he pounded into her.

'Yes,' she panted. 'Yes.'

'You can come now,' he growled, just as she splintered apart in an orgasm which blew her mind even further than it was already.

Dimly, she heard him cry out, her senses no longer her own. She was lost, drowning in the heady sensation of his hot seed flooding her womb, exulting in the feel of his flesh pulsating in a rapturous tandem with her own.

It wasn't till some time afterwards, when their bodies had finally become as quiet as the room, that Jordan's brain kicked back into gear, her stomach somersaulting at the realisation that Gino hadn't used any protection.

Not that this was a total disaster. She was on the pill. But her own lack of thought in that regard—and, more to the point, *his*—was a real worry.

'Gino,' she said, her hands pushing at his shoulders.

'Yes, yes, I know. I'm heavy.'

'It's not that. I was just thinking…you…you didn't use a condom.'

He levered himself up onto his elbows and stared down at her.

'Are you saying I could have made you pregnant just now?'

'No. Pregnancy's not my concern. I'm on the pill.'

'I promise you I'm no risk to your health,' Gino reassured her. 'Look, are you hungry? I am.'

'I'm starving,' she confessed.

'The Room Service menu's over there, on that desk. In a leather folder. Check it out while I go run us both a bath.'

'Wait,' she said. 'I need to go to the loo first.'

'I'm not stopping you.'

'But I don't—' She broke off, thinking how she would have died rather than go to the bathroom in front of Chad. Yet when she'd lived with Gino they'd hidden nothing from each other.

But she wasn't living with Gino any more, came the timely reminder. She was living by herself. An independent, grown-up woman who liked her privacy.

'I'm sorry, Gino, but I'd prefer to use the bathroom alone.'

He stared at her in surprise, then shrugged. 'Whatever.'

Jordan hurried, feeling slightly silly at her stance. She'd just let him touch her in very private places, let him strip her and have sex with her. Let him see her come.

Now she had suddenly gone all shy and precious with him. It seemed they couldn't exactly take up where they'd left off after all. Ten years had gone by. She'd changed, even if he hadn't.

Gino was waiting outside the bathroom door, totally naked, whilst she'd drawn on one of the hotel's bathrobes.

'All yours,' she said, and bolted past him, not wanting to start staring again.

The Room Service menu was where he'd said it was.

And so was a plane ticket, lying next to it on the desk.

Jordan stared at it for a long moment.

Then she picked it up.

CHAPTER FIVE

Gino found himself humming as he watched the tub fill, the bath gel having turned the water a pale green as well as providing some fragrant bubbles.

For the first time in years he felt light-hearted. And happy.

All because he'd found Jordan again.

It was as if the last ten years had been wiped away. He felt young again, and invincible. Jordan was still his woman—had been since the first day he'd set eyes on her.

She'd been working as a waitress back then, at an Italian restaurant not far from Sydney University, just across the road from the building site where Gino had been employed.

Although he'd been trying to opt out of everything Italian at that particular time in his life, the mouthwatering smell of his favourite pasta dishes had kept beckoning, and he'd finally given in to temptation and gone there for an evening meal.

Fate had sat him down at one of Jordan's tables.

The sexual chemistry between them had been instant and electric. He'd stayed on, eating more than he needed, just so he could keep talking to the beautiful blonde waitress who hadn't been able to take her eyes off him any more than he could her. He'd openly flirted with her, and she'd served him with a degree of attention which Gino had found both telling and seductive.

When she'd confided over his third cup of coffee that her flatmate had decided to drop out of university and go back home to live, leaving her to find the rent alone, Gino had grabbed the opportunity, saying he'd been looking for a place to live and asking would she consider having him as her flatmate?

His eyes must have told her that he wanted to be more than just her flatmate. So when she'd agreed to his moving in the next day, Gino had been a serious state of arousal even before he'd set foot in the place. He hadn't lasted more than half an hour before he had kissed her. One thing had quickly led to another, with Gino thanking his lucky stars that he'd come into that restaurant.

His discovering that Jordan was only nineteen—and a virgin—had been a huge shock. But subsequently a huge delight.

She'd become his perfect fantasy lover—her youth and inexperience allowing him to live out his own fantasy role as the masterful older male. He'd been thrilled by her falling for him despite thinking he was just a labourer, wallowing in her acceptance of him as a man in his own right. He'd revelled in the sexual power he'd held over her. What man wouldn't have?

She was an incredibly beautiful girl, with a brilliant mind and a strength of character which was formidable.

Yet, in his arms, she was all sensual submission.

Not passive, though; Jordan was too passionate for passive.

He hadn't been able to keep his hands off her back then, quickly becoming addicted to the primal feelings she'd evoked in him. It seemed that hadn't changed. He could not wait to carry her into this bath and for their lovemaking to begin again.

A loud rapping on the bathroom door had Gino whirling round, his heart lurching with instant worry.

He snapped off the taps, then wrenched open the door. There she stood, the object of his desire, her lovely face coldly furious, her hands jammed into the pockets of the white towelling robe.

'I know I agreed that explanations could wait till the morning,' she snapped. 'But that was before I saw this.'

Gino's stomach rolled over when she pulled her right hand from the robe pocket and held out his slightly crumpled plane ticket.

He'd forgotten that he'd left it on that damned desk, having emptied his suit pockets before changing clothes late this afternoon.

'This ticket is for tomorrow morning,' she swept on before he could say a word. 'Very early tomorrow morning. Which rather puts paid to your claim that you're up here for the weekend.'

'I wasn't going to take that flight, Jordan. Not after I ran into you. I was going to ring up and change it to Sunday.'

'You still lied to me, Gino.'

'I just twisted the truth a little.'

'Twisted the truth?' she repeated, with a caustic gleam in her eyes. 'And how would you describe giving someone a false name? Because this ticket is made out to a Mr Gino Bortelli.'

'Jordan, I—'

'I take it that's your real name?' she interrupted savagely. 'Bortelli? Not Salieri, like you told me ten years ago?'

Gino tried to keep calm, but a very true panic hovered in the wings of his mind. 'Salieri is my mother's maiden name. I took it temporarily when I came to Sydney for reasons of privacy.'

'Reasons of privacy?' she repeated scathingly. 'Like, people might recognise you as what, exactly? A rock star in hiding?'

'No, as Gino Bortelli.'

'Sorry, Gino. But I'm none the wiser.'

'My family are rather big in the construction business. I didn't want any special favours when I first came to Sydney. I'd not long finished an engineering degree at university in Rome, and I—'

'Excuse me?' she snapped. 'Are you telling me you're a qualified *engineer?* I thought you were a labourer.'

'That's what I was working as when I first met you.'

Jordan looked totally bewildered. 'But *why?* That would be like me still working as a waitress instead of a lawyer.'

Gino sighed, then reached for the other bathrobe

hanging on the back of the door. There seemed little point in staying naked. The erotic night he'd been planning was well and truly over.

'Could we go out into the other room?' he suggested, after he drew the robe on and tied the sash around his waist. 'I could do with a drink.'

He strode past her out into the hotel room proper, heading for the mini-bar.

'Do you want a glass of wine?' he asked, glancing over his shoulder at Jordan as she reluctantly followed him. 'There's a half-bottle of red here which isn't too bad.'

'No, thanks,' she returned crisply. 'What I want to know is why you lied to me about so many things.'

'Perhaps you should sit down?' he suggested, indicating the sofa opposite the television.

She didn't sit down, moving past the sofa to stand in front of the window, with her arms crossed and her eyes still sceptical.

Gino poured himself a full glass of wine, taking a decent swallow before turning to face her across the room.

'I was tired after studying for years. Tired of being pushed by my parents to be an over-achiever. It's a common enough phenomenon in Italian families. I demanded a year off, to just be myself and not my father's only son. I wanted to earn my own money. Be totally independent. Live a simpler, less stressful life. That was why I decided to work with my hands, and why I changed my name. Because I didn't want my employer recognising the Bortelli name and treating me differently.'

Jordan frowned. 'People would recognise the Bortelli name even out here in Australia?'

This was the moment Gino had been dreading. But the truth had to come out—especially if he wanted to continue seeing Jordan. And he did, very much.

'I think you might have misunderstood something about me all those years ago,' he began carefully. 'I didn't exactly come to Sydney straight from Rome. After I finished my degree I went home to my family first.'

'So where in Italy does your family live?'

'My family doesn't live in Italy, Jordan. They migrated to Melbourne not long after I was born. That's where they live. Melbourne.'

She stared at him with stunned blue eyes. 'You're saying you're Australian?'

'I hold dual citizenship. Both Italian and Australian.'

'Why didn't you tell me any of this ten years ago?'

'I wish now that I had. But back then I was also tired of being Italian. I needed a change. I needed to find myself. Then, after I met you, Jordan, I just needed you.'

She stared at him, her eyes going cold again. 'Only till your *family* needed you, Gino. Then you dropped me like a hot cake.'

Gino sighed. She didn't understand. She could never understand what it was like to be the only son in an Italian household.

'If anything happens to me, Gino,' his father used to say all the time, 'then it is your job to look after the family. Your mother and your sisters. And the business, of course.'

'And what about this weekend, Gino?' Jordan threw at him. 'Was it to be more of the same? You needed a change so you came to Sydney? Because Sydney is full of silly girls only too willing to give you sex?'

'I came to Sydney on business,' Gino pointed out, his sense of honour totally offended by her accusations. 'I was going to fly back to Melbourne tomorrow, remember?'

'Sorry,' she quipped sarcastically. 'I momentarily forgot under the pressure of all these amazing revelations. So you ran into me, and you thought, Wow, there's good old Jordan—the dumb bird who let me screw her every which way. I'll bet she's good for another go. I'll just give her a line of bull. She'd believe anything I tell her. And presto—you were right. I fell for it, hook, line and sinker.'

'Jordan, stop it!' Gino said, appalled at the way things were going.

'Stop what?' she snapped, her blue eyes blazing at him. 'Stop telling you how it really is? Don't the ladies do that to you down in Melbourne? No, of course they don't. You're a bigshot down there. They probably crawl to you on their hands and knees. Do you have a girl-friend, Gino? Do you make her go without panties? Do you do it to her all the time, the way you used to do it to me?'

Gino felt his own temper begin to rise. He'd tried to be patient with her. Tried to explain. But she seemed determined to twist everything in her mind, to make everything they'd once shared sound ugly and sordid.

'What in hell's wrong with you?' he snarled. 'Why are you trying to spoil everything? Look, I'm sorry I didn't tell you the truth back then. But I did have my reasons. And I'm sorry I left you the way I did. But I had my reasons for that as well. My father was dying, damn it. I *had* to go home.'

'Then why didn't you come back? After your father died? Tell me that. You obviously had the resources to. Yet you chose not to. What kind of love was that, Gino?'

'You really want to know?'

'Yes. I really want to know.'

Gino could see that all was lost. So what did it matter if he told her that last unpalatable truth?

'I didn't come back because you weren't Italian.'

Her mouth fell open. But no words came out.

'I promised my father on his deathbed that when I married I would marry an Italian girl.'

'You have to be kidding,' she blurted out.

'Unfortunately, no.' He knew only too well that he had been afraid that if he came back to Jordan he would forget his promise and marry her.

She shook her head at him, her eyes dropping limply to her sides. 'And have you?' she asked in a dull, flat voice. 'Married an Italian girl?'

'You think I would lie about something like that?'

'I have no idea what you would lie about, Gino. I don't know you. I never did. The man I lived with—and fell in love with—wasn't real. He was a pretend man. A fantasy lover. The real Gino is a stranger to me. So I'm asking you again. Are you married?'

'I told you. I'm not married.'

'But you do have a girlfriend, don't you?'

'Yes,' he bit out. 'I do.'

'So you're a cheat as well as a liar!'

Gino sucked in sharply. No one had spoken to him like this in his whole life.

His shock deepened when she suddenly unsashed her robe and pushed it back off her shoulders, letting it drop to the floor. For a long moment she stood there, totally naked, her chin tipped up as she watched him devour every beautiful inch of her.

When his flesh automatically responded, Gino's fingers tightened defensively around his wine glass. He didn't know what she was up to, but he suspected that if he made any move to touch her she would scream the place down.

'You like what you see, Gino?' she said at last, in a challenging fashion.

Gino's teeth clenched down hard in his jaw. The Jordan he'd known ten years ago had never been a bitch. The Jordan standing before him now was doing a very good imitation of one.

Perversely, it made him want her all the more.

'Take a good long look, because you're never going to see me like this again. Not that you'd overly care,' she went on savagely, as she moved over to snatch up her clothes. 'You'll fly home to your girlfriend and you won't give this little interlude a second thought. You won't even feel guilty.'

She couldn't have been more wrong. He'd never be able to put tonight—or her—out of his mind. And guilt was going to be his constant companion from now on.

As for Claudia… Gino could see that he would have

to break off their relationship. She was a very nice girl, but she wanted to get married.

After this, marriage was permanently off Gino's agenda. If he couldn't marry Jordan, then he wouldn't marry anyone.

In an amazingly short period of time Jordan was fully dressed, looking exactly as she had when he'd first seen her tonight. Except for her hair. As she hooked her bag over her shoulder she tossed her head at him, flicking her hair back from her face.

'I never forgot you, you know,' she threw at him. 'Never. A girlfriend of mine said it was because you were unfinished business. She said it was a pity I couldn't look you up, so that I could see you weren't as fantastic as I thought you were. And she was right. You're not. Oh, you're still great at sex—I'll give you that. You know exactly how to turn a girl on. But that's a small talent in the wider scheme of things. I want a man who knows what he wants and goes after it. Who doesn't let *anything* stand in his way. You're obviously not that kind of man.'

'How do you know?'

'I know,' she said, with a curl of her top lip. 'Actions speak a lot louder than words, Gino.'

'You're making a big mistake,' he said as she headed for the door.

She reached for the doorknob, then stopped to cast a cold glance over her shoulder. 'No, I'm *ending* a big mistake. You're finished business now,' she said, then wrenched open the door. '*Ciao.*'

CHAPTER SIX

JORDAN managed to make it home without shedding a tear. Pride prevented her from breaking down in the hotel, or during the taxi ride home. But the moment she was alone, with her door safely locked behind her, everything came crashing in around her.

Her legs suddenly buckled and she sank to the floor where she stood. Her knees hit the tiled foyer first, and her cry was not one of physical pain but of emotional distress.

'Oh, Gino,' she sobbed as her head tipped forward into her hands.

And there she stayed, as if she was in prayer.

But she wasn't praying, she was weeping. And despairing.

For there were no illusions left for her now.

All these years she'd thought that her memory of Gino had been spoiling her relationships with men. And maybe that was true. But it had been a bittersweet memory, because she'd always believed Gino had loved her.

But he hadn't loved her. He'd merely wanted her, the

way he'd wanted her tonight. Not for anything lasting, just for sex.

That discovery had been bad enough. Finding out that his whole persona had been an illusion was even worse. He wasn't some struggling Italian immigrant, trying to make a good life for himself through hard work. He was a silver-tail, slumming it for a while up here in Sydney. Roughing it—with her.

Tonight had just been a shorter version of what he'd done ten years ago.

Okay, so he probably *had* been going to change his flight till Sunday. But his motive had still been totally selfish. After all, why look a gift-horse in the mouth?

And, brother, what a gift-horse she was where he was concerned. Fifteen miserable minutes and she'd been up there in his room, ready and willing to take her clothes off. Ready for just about anything.

If she hadn't found that plane ticket he would have had his wicked way with her for the whole weekend, then flown off back to Melbourne, to his real life and his real girlfriend.

Thinking about that had Jordan sitting back on her heels and wiping the tears from the cheeks. What on earth was she doing, crying over such a man? He was a bastard through and through.

Scooping in a gathering breath, Jordan got to her feet and walked quickly to her bedroom. No more was she going to let Gino Betolli spoil things for her. No more. When Chad rang her in the morning she would accept his proposal of marriage, and she would do her level best not to think of Gino ever again.

But such resolves were easy to make, Jordan came to realise, once she'd stripped off and stepped into the shower. Living them was not so easy.

Her body—especially her naked body—kept reminding her of Gino, the after-effects of his torrid lovemaking conspiring to keep him in her mind. Just moving the soapy sponge lightly between her legs made her belly tighten and her breath catch.

This was what had happened to her when she'd lived with Gino. She'd been in a perpetual state of arousal. Her flesh had craved his constantly, craved release from the sexual tension he created in her.

It craved release now…

Jordan dropped the sponge, then slowly slid her back down the wet tiles till she was sitting on the shower floor. Her arms lifted to wrap around her drawn-up knees, her head dropping forward as she surrendered once more to tears.

'Oh, Gino,' she cried. 'Gino…'

The phone woke her, its persistent ringing getting through the blissful oblivion which had finally descended on Jordan last night, courtesy of the painkillers she'd taken—strong ones she used when she had a migraine. Unfortunately, they had to tendency to leave her a little groggy the next day.

Rolling over with a groan, she picked up the extension near her bed and shoved it between her ear and the pillow.

'Yes?' Not exactly a breezy hello.

'Jordan? Is that you?'

The sound of Chad's voice had her sitting up and

pushing her tangled hair out of her eyes. A glance at the bedside clock shocked her. It was nearly ten.

'Yes, it's me,' she said more brightly. 'Have you arrived yet?'

'Just. Thought I'd ring you before I got out in the New York traffic. You sounded sleepy just now. Did I wake you?'

'Sort of. I…um… I had a late night.'

'A late night doing what?'

A rush of guilt had Jordan being grateful Chad couldn't see her. Not that he was all that intuitive. Chad was the sort of man who only saw what he wanted to see. He honestly thought her turning down his proposal was just her playing hard to get. He clearly had no doubts that she would say yes, even leaving the engagement ring with her—a family heirloom which had belonged to his grandmother.

'Working,' she lied. 'I have to wrap up the Johnson case on Monday, remember?'

'You've become a bit obsessed by that case, don't you think?'

'No.' Her client was a young woman whose husband had been killed in a train derailment. Shock and grief had sent her into early labour, with their premature baby boy not making it. When the government had finally offered her compensation, several years later, they hadn't included anything for the pain and loss of her child. They'd called her son a foetus, not worthy of consideration as a human being. She'd come to Jordan wanting not a fortune, but justice.

Jordan aimed to get justice for her. Which she

would—if she could get her head into gear and prepare a killer of a closing argument this weekend.

'You work too hard, Jordan.'

'I enjoy my work, Chad.' More than enjoyed. She'd feel totally empty without it.

'Have you thought about what I asked you the other night?'

Jordan's chest tightened. She'd known he'd get round to this sooner or later.

'Yes,' she said.

'And?'

This was it: the moment of truth. Did she have the courage of her convictions? Or was she going to weaken and let Gino keep spoiling things for her?

She had a choice. She could pine over a relationship which had been doomed from the start. Or she could choose a new relationship which had everything going for it.

Okay, not quite everything. But everything that mattered. Great sex was not the be all and end all, she reasoned. Besides, it wasn't that Chad was a hopeless lover. He certainly wasn't. The problem—if there was one—lay in her own responses. Gino had somehow programmed her not to respond totally to any other man. He, and he alone, could make her lose her head and lose control. Last night had proved that.

But this phenomenon only occurred when he was around. He wasn't around now. He would never be around again.

The time had come to stop hiding behind her illogical passion for a man who, by his own admission, would never marry her. Next year she would be thirty. In ten years she'd be forty.

Time to make a decision.

'Yes, Chad,' she said firmly. 'I will marry you.'

CHAPTER SEVEN

GINO was on the top floor of his latest skyscraper con-struction-in-progress, making his way carefully along a not-too-wide girder, when his cellphone rang. He waited till he reached the relative safety of a corner before fishing it out of his pocket.

'Gino Bortelli,' he said, one arm wrapped securely around a post. The breeze was quite strong up that high.

'What is this I hear about you breaking up with Claudia?' came his mother's highly accented voice.

Gino smothered a sigh. The grapevine in the Italian community was very fast and usually accurate.

'It's no big deal, Mum. She wasn't right for me, and I wasn't right for her. We agreed to go our separate ways.'

'That is not the way I hear it, Gino. Claudia is very upset with you.'

Very upset that she wasn't marrying into the Bortelli money would be more like it.

Gino had been astounded at how vicious Claudia had become when he'd told her it was over between them.

Suddenly she'd shown her true colours, using quite obscene language which everyone in the restaurant had heard. There'd been no hint of a broken heart, just ambition thwarted. After she'd flounced out all the other patrons in the place had stared at him, making Gino wish he'd chosen to break up with her in a more discreet and private place.

That had been last Sunday—two days ago. In hindsight, he was surprised it had taken his mother this long to find out. Maybe he should have told her himself. But since returning to Melbourne on Saturday he hadn't wanted to have anything to do with his family.

It was because of them that he'd had to leave Jordan in the first place. And he'd not been able to go back for her. They'd sucked him emotionally dry till he no longer wanted get married and have children. The last ten years had been filled with nothing but unending responsibility and pressure, with him putting his mother's and sisters' needs first, never his own.

But enough was enough.

'Claudia was more in love with my money than she was with me, Mum,' he said firmly. 'Trust me on that. Look, I can't stay and chat. I'm working.'

His mother sighed. 'You work too hard, Gino. You should take some time off.'

'Maybe I will. But not today.'

'Before you go, did you decide what you were going to do with that derelict site in Sydney? The one Papa bought all those years ago?'

'Everything's underway. It's going to be a twenty-storey tower with apartments on the top ten floors, office space on the lower ten, shops on the ground floor, and parking underneath. I signed the contract with the architect last Friday.'

'That is good, Gino. Papa would be pleased.'

'How can he be pleased about anything, Mum, when he's dead?'

'Gino! How can you say such a wicked thing? Have you no faith? Your papa is watching over us from heaven. He would be very proud of you.'

Gino shook his head. There was no arguing with his mother's faith. So he didn't bother.

'He would be even prouder,' she added, 'if you married and carried on the Bortelli name.'

'I am still only thirty-six, Mum. I have plenty of time for that yet. Look, I have to go.'

'Will you be coming to dinner next Sunday?'

His mother held a big family get-together on the last Sunday of every month. Gino usually attended. He liked playing with his nieces and nephews. But he hated the thought of being bombarded by questions over why Claudia wasn't with him.

'I can't, Mum. Sorry. I have to go to Sydney to meet up with this architect. He wants to show me some preliminary plans.'

Not true. But his mother wasn't to know that. Still, he would have to go somewhere. Maybe to the snow? He liked skiing, and there was still some good snow in the ski-fields. He'd tire himself out every day and make sure he fell asleep each night the moment his head hit the pillow.

He hadn't slept well since returning from Sydney, his mind constantly tormented with what ifs.

What if he hadn't made that foolish promise to his father?

What if he'd been able to go back for Jordan without feeling lousy?

What if he'd told her the truth about himself *before* they'd gone up to his hotel room last Friday night?

This last *what if* was easily answered: he'd been too aroused to delay, or to risk Jordan rejecting him after his explanations.

His need for her had transcended common-sense.

Was he still in love with her? he wondered. Or did he just want to escape with her again, as he had all those years ago?

She'd claimed she'd never forgotten him.

Gino believed her.

How could either of them forget the fantasy life they'd lived together, such an erotically charged existence, full of passion and pleasure? But underneath all the sex had been true affection. He hadn't just used Jordan, he'd truly cared for her—and she for him.

But they were different people now. She was more cynical and less trusting. And he was…well, he was trapped by his previous deceptions.

And yet he would give anything, *do* anything, to be with her like that again.

'You should spend more time with your family, Gino,' his mother chided.

Gino's teeth clenched down hard in his jaw, the cords in his neck standing out.

'I have to go, Mum. *Ciao.*'

He grimaced as he hung up, the Italian word for goodbye reminding him of the last time he'd heard it. On Jordan's lips, as she swept out of the hotel room. And out of his life.

His life…

Gino glanced down at the city spread out below him. He was on top of the world so to speak. On top of the world financially as well as professionally. He had more money than he would ever need, a fancy penthouse and a fancy car: a Ferrari, no less.

As for Bortelli Constructions… Although it had already been a well-known building company when he'd taken it over, under his guiding hand the company had gone from strength to strength, gaining an enviable reputation for reliability and quality. His hard work and astute business decisions had made every member of the Bortelli family millionaires several times over, and he himself was close to becoming a billionaire.

But such successes counted for nothing if you weren't happy.

Jordan's various accusations and taunts still haunted him.

Perhaps because they were true. Technically, he had lied and cheated. But he wasn't the coward she thought he was.

He *did* know what he wanted.

Her.

But what was the point in pursuing her when she would not welcome his attentions?

Gino could see no way of her getting Jordan to spend

time with him—short of kidnapping her and imprisoning her in some secluded place with him.

That idea had some appeal as a male fantasy.

Unfortunately, he couldn't see the adult Jordan being one of those female hostages who would ever feel kindly towards her captor. When she'd stood naked in front of him and told him he'd never see her like that again he'd believed her.

Gino sighed, then headed for the steel cage which would carry him down to the ground again. It was knock-off time in the building trade. Not so for the boss, however, who had to go back to his office in the city and make sure the administrative wheels of Bortelli Constructions were kept turning.

Half an hour later his hard hat had been discarded and he was sitting behind his desk, a strong mug of coffee on his right and a load of correspondence in front of him. The clock on the wall was just ticking over to five when he picked up an envelope marked 'Personal', which his secretary hadn't opened.

Gino winced at the thought that it might be hate-mail from Claudia.

No, he decided as he ripped open the envelope. She wouldn't write. She'd e-mail or text message him. Girls like Claudia never put pen to paper these days.

Gino found himself staring down at a gold-embossed sheet of paper.

It was an invitation from Stedley & Parkinson.

Mr Frank Jones, the senior partner of the Sydney branch, was inviting Mr Gino Bortelli—and partner—to a new client dinner on the following Saturday evening in their boardroom. The arrival time was seven-thirty, the dress black tie. His RSVP was required by Friday; an e-mail address was provided for his reply.

Gino stared at the invitation for a good twenty seconds without drawing a breath. Then he gulped in some much needed air before letting it out with a long, slow sigh.

Fate, it seemed, had stepped in to give him one last chance with Jordan.

For surely the star of Stedley & Parkinson's litigation section would have recently gained a new client or two? If so, she would probably be obliged to attend this dinner.

Gino's heart raced with the thought of seeing Jordan again—especially in a situation where she could not think he was deliberately stalking her. Their running into each other again would appear to be sheer coincidence. Which, in a way, it would be.

He wouldn't be taking a partner, of course. He no longer had a partner. Not that he would have taken Claudia anywhere near Jordan.

Gino wondered if Adrian had received an invitation.

No, probably not. Adrian had told him he'd used Stedley and Parkinson's for legal work before. Which meant he wouldn't be a new client.

Still, it was likely that he'd been to such a dinner before, giving him first-hand knowledge of what kind of a do this was, and especially who attended from Stedley & Parkinson.

Reaching for his cellphone, Gino looked up the menu of numbers he kept in there, located Adrian's number and punched it in.

'Adrian Palmer,' Adrian answered straight away.

Although one of Australia's most up-and-coming young architects, Adrian didn't use a secretary, or a proper office. He worked out of his high-rise apartment, situated in the middle of Sydney's CBD.

'Hi, Adrian. Gino Bortelli here.'

'Gino! I was just working on the plans for your building. I think you're going to be seriously pleased.'

'That's great, Adrian. Look, I've received an invitation in the mail from Stedley & Parkinson.'

'For one of their new client dinners, I presume?'

'Yes. Have you ever been to one?'

'Yep—last month, actually. They have these dinners once a month. You should go, Gino. The food's always great, and so is the wine. Of course that means you'll have to fly up. But it's tax-deductible.'

'It says black tie. That's a bit formal for a dinner in a boardroom, isn't it?'

'That would have come down from Mr Stedley, the American owner. He's Ivy League and one of the country-club brigade over there in the States. He's a strong believer in social networking. Encourages his employees to socialise together, too.'

'You sound like you've met this guy. Don't tell me he flies over from the States to attend?'

'Nope. Met his son, though. Chad Stedley. He's doing a stint out here in the Sydney office. They sat me next to him at this dinner. Quite a talker. Got the story of his life between courses. Had a gorgeous-looking girlfriend. Another of their lawyers—Jordan something-or-other.'

Gino's heart screeched to a halt even whilst his head whirled. Jordan had said there was no special man in her life. Yet a month ago she'd been this Chad Stedley's girlfriend?

There seemed only two solutions to this conundrum. She'd either broken up with Stedley since then. A possibility, given the difficult nature of relationships these days. Or she'd lied last Friday night. Which didn't seem possible. Jordan had a real thing about lying.

'Jordan Gray?' Gino said.

'Yep. That was her name. You know her, do you?'

'I used to.'

'No kidding? An old girlfriend?'

'Something like that.'

'It's a small world, isn't it?'

'It seems so.'

'In that case you should think twice before bringing your current girlfriend along. You know what women are like. And that Jordan's a real looker.'

'Haven't got a current girlfriend,' Gino admitted. 'I was thinking of going alone.'

'I see. Well, I wouldn't count on your getting together again with this Jordan, if I were you,' Adrian advised drily. 'I gathered from the Stedley son and heir that an engagement was just around the corner.'

'An engagement!' Gino exclaimed, before he could think better of it.

'Yep. If that thought upsets you, then perhaps you shouldn't go at all.'

Upset him?

Already a tidal wave of fury was building up on his horizon. If Jordan had lied to him…

A boyfriend was bad enough. But if she'd willingly

had sex with him, then gone home to her fiancé, he wasn't sure how he'd handle it.

'No, no,' Gino said with pretend nonchalance. 'No sweat. It's been years since Jordan and I were an item. But I wouldn't mind seeing her again, having a chat about old times.'

Plus a chat about very recent times, Gino vowed darkly. Namely last Friday night.

'In that case be discreet. Chad Stedley came across as the controlling type. He might not like his girl's ex showing up in her life again.'

'He sounds delightful.'

'He's super-rich.'

'Meaning?'

'Women will put up with a lot to marry a super-rich guy.'

'Is that the voice of experience talking?'

'Hell, no. I'm rich, but not super-rich. Yet. Still, you must have come across a few gold-digging types. The Bortellis were listed as one the richest one hundred Australian families last year.'

'Ahh,' Gino said. 'You looked us up?'

'I always like to know who I'm doing business with, Gino. I steer well clear of the entrepreneurial type who has to borrow squillions, or relies on selling off the plan for his cashflow.'

'Very sensible.'

'If you do come to Sydney you could drop by and have a look at my preliminary plans.'

'I haven't decided whether I'll come yet. I might go to the snow instead.'

'That might be a wiser course of action.'

'Yes,' Gino said slowly 'It might.'

But Gino wasn't feeling wise.

If Jordan *had* lied to him…

There was only one way to find out in advance of Saturday night. He would put Confidential Investigations back on the job. That gave them three and a half days to find out if Jordan had broken up with this Chad Stedley or not.

More than enough time, he would imagine. He would also see if they could find out if Jordan would be attending this dinner.

At the same time he would send an e-mail to the RSVP address, accepting Mr Frank Jones's invitation to the dinner.

CHAPTER EIGHT

JORDAN reluctantly went through the motions of getting ready: same little black dress as last time, same shoes and jewellery.

Her hair she didn't have to do, thank goodness. She'd been to the hairdressers that morning, and had it shampooed and gently blowdried, giving her slightly wayward waves some control, but not straightening them too much. Her make-up took her less than ten minutes: just foundation, a touch of blusher, lipgloss and two coats of mascara.

Jordan rarely wore much make-up. Never had.

By half-past six she was ready—or as ready as she was ever going to be. Her taxi had been booked for seven, which left thirty minutes to do what? Watch half of an hour-long television show? Or have a glass of white wine and try to relax?

The second option won, hands down.

There was an already opened bottle of reisling in the door of her fridge—a fruity, slightly sweet wine, which Chad would have despised, but which Jordan liked.

She poured herself a small glass and carried it through her living room, heading for her front balcony.

Jordan slid back the glass door, giving a small shiver as she stepped into the cool evening air. Fortunately it wasn't too windy, the sea breeze quite gentle. Darkness had fallen some time back, the lights giving a magical quality to Sydney's two most famous icons, which were both visible from her seventh-floor apartment. The bridge on her right looked like a huge jewelled coat-hanger, whilst across the harbour the sailed roof of the Opera House resembled the set from a sci-fi movie.

Jordan sighed as she leant against the railing and sipped her wine, her mind swiftly distracted from the lovely view to the evening ahead.

She didn't want to go to this month's new client dinner.

But she simply couldn't get out of it. Not unless she had a very good reason.

When she'd told Chad during his early-morning call that she didn't want to go, not without him, he'd been flattered but insistent.

'You've taken on a new client this month, haven't you?'

'Yes,' she'd admitted. An angry young man who wanted to sue his employer for unfair dismissal after the boss had discovered he was a homosexual.

'Then you have to go, darling. Rules are rules. Just make sure you wear your engagement ring. Let all the men there know you're taken.'

Jordan had come away from that phone call just a tad unsure of her decision to marry Chad.

During his calls this week he'd become quite bossy

with her. And demanding. He really seemed to think she was going to give up working once they were married and living in the States.

As if she would!

She'd also been quite put out when he'd been less than effusive in his congratulations over her winning all that compensation money for Sharni Johnson. He hadn't sounded as if he cared about her success at all!

Yet she was expected to rave over how his 'wonderful' friends had thrown him all those welcome home parties. So far he'd gone out somewhere different every night.

Somehow Jordan doubted he'd told any of the females attending these dos that *he* was taken. Chad liked being the centre of attention.

Jordan wasn't jealous, but she resented double standards.

Guilt consumed her with this last thought. After all, she hadn't exactly been Little Miss Innocent since Chad had gone away, had she?

Over a week had gone by since she'd gone to Gino's hotel room, but the memory of her behaviour still haunted her.

She'd been putty in Gino's hands, quickly reverting to the naïve little fool she'd been ten years ago.

He'd said, 'Come with me'—and she had. He'd said, 'Don't come'—and she hadn't.

That was Gino's *modus operandi*. He commanded and she obeyed—and how she'd loved it!

Fortunately, fate had come to her rescue in the form of that plane ticket before she'd behaved even more foolishly.

Some damage had already been done, however. The damage which came when a woman experienced that level of sexual excitement, and the ecstasy which inevitably followed. Difficult to go back to the mundane after that. Difficult to forget.

That had always been her problem where Gino was concerned.

Forgetting...

Let's face it, Jordan, the voice of cold, hard reality piped up. You're never going to forget that man. You can marry Chad and go live in the States, put thousand of miles between you. But Gino's always going to be there, in your head.

Jordan groaned, tipped up her glass and swallowed the rest of her wine with one gulp. Then she whirled and headed back inside, to collect her evening bag and her keys.

At the last moment she remembered what Chad had asked her to do: wear the engagement ring which he'd left with her but which she hadn't as yet put on—even though she'd now accepted his proposal.

Did that omission say something?

It was not a ring she would have chosen, Jordan thought, as she hurried into the bedroom and retrieved it from a drawer. It was too fussy: a huge ruby, surrounded by two rows of diamonds, and on top of that the setting was yellow gold.

Jordan liked white gold. Or silver.

And she liked simplicity.

Of course Chad hadn't actually chosen this ring, she conceded. It was a family heirloom, having once belonged to his grandmother, who'd willed it to him when she died, to be given to his bride.

Jordan had been touched by the sentiment. But she suddenly wondered, as she slipped the ring on, if she'd be able to cope with Chad's high-powered and tradition-filled family—not to mention all his 'wonderful' friends. They sounded just a little overpowering.

It was one thing to live with him here, in Australia. Things were very easy-going here. But what would life be like in America? She'd never travelled there, her one and only overseas trip being to Europe, with most of her time spent in Italy.

No omission there. She'd stupidly thought she might find Gino. But she hadn't, of course. How could she have when she'd been looking for the wrong name?

Jordan gritted her teeth. Gino again.

Thinking of Gino reaffirmed her decision to marry Chad.

Okay, so Chad wasn't perfect. He was a touch arrogant. And obviously quite spoiled by his very wealthy, very indulgent parents.

No way was he as hard-working as she was.

But he wasn't a conniving, conning, cheating bastard. *And* he wanted to marry her.

Whereas Gino…

'Enough of Gino,' she muttered under her breath as she swept out of her apartment. 'I'm going to marry Chad and that's that!'

CHAPTER NINE

KERRY usually looked forward to the new client dinners. But tonight she would much rather have been out with Ben.

Running into him last Friday night—and finding out he was still single—had been a very pleasant surprise. He was her one ex that she truly regretted having broken up with. They hadn't argued or anything. Ben had simply had the urge to travel.

Now he was back in Australia, and obviously wanted to take up with her where they'd left off. They'd spent most of the weekend together, and a few evenings this week, with Ben eager to take her to a concert tonight.

But, as Frank's PA, Kerry was obliged not only to attend this dinner, but to help hostess the event. Frank was a widower, with no new partner, and he had no idea how to organise anything. It was always left to her to do the place settings, hire a caterer, buy the wine, choose the menu, and then make sure everything went off without a hiccup.

This month she'd chosen a new caterer, who was expensive but who came highly recommended. They'd also provided everything, right down to fresh flowers for the table. The chef was top drawer, having worked in several five-star hotels. The waiters were also experienced professionals, not fly-by-night casuals like some catering firms used.

Kerry still thought it would have been less trouble to go to a restaurant. But Stedley & Parkinson preferred the intimacy and the privacy of their boardroom.

Admittedly the boardroom was well equipped for such a function, having an excellent kitchen attached, plus two powder rooms just outside in the hallway. The boardroom itself was a very spacious and impressive room, with a huge mahogany table which comfortably seated twenty-four. The floors were polished wood and the walls white, a perfect backdrop for the colourful Australian artwork which decorated them. All originals, they were landscapes from famous artists such as Pro Hart and Albert Namatjira.

Kerry could understand why Frank chose to host these dinners here. She just resented the added workload, which was why she'd found this new catering firm, leaving her little to do except work out who would sit where.

Of course that wasn't always as easy as it looked. Certain tensions among the staff at Stedley & Parkinson had to be addressed, with rival lawyers kept well apart. And there was always a surfeit of men, too, even amongst the new clients. Kerry was relieved that Jordan was coming. She'd put her between Mr Bortelli—who wasn't bringing a partner—and Mr McKee, Jordan's client, who also wasn't bringing a partner.

All up, eighteen people would be at the dinner: six lawyers, their six most important new clients—four of whom had brought partners—and Frank and herself.

Of course not every new client the practice took on was invited. Only the ones who had serious money, or whose cases might provide the most publicity. Jordan's new clients were always invited, because she took on cases which the press—and the public—found interesting.

As Kerry walked around the boardroom, making sure all the place-names were right, she wondered if Jordan would wear something different this month. Last month she'd turned up in the same outfit she'd worn the month before—a classic, but boring little black dress, with a high scooped neckline, long sleeves and a straight, not-too-tight skirt which covered up far too much of her excellent legs. The double-strand pearl necklace she always wore with it was just as prim and proper, though her shoes were not too bad: black, strappy and high.

Nevertheless, now that Jordan was engaged to Prince Charming she would definitely have to upgrade her wardrobe from off-the-peg- working-girl clothes to designer gear.

Men like Chad Stedley expected their wives to outshine everyone else. Jordan might not realise it yet, but she was about to enter a totally new world, where fashion and appearances would be critical to her success as Mrs Chad Stedley.

No longer could she get away with dressing the way she did. Some serious shopping was called for before

Chad came back from the States. And Kerry was just the girl to go with her and give her advice.

'Oh, doesn't everything look lovely!'

Kerry glanced up with a smile already forming on her face.

'Speak of the devil,' she said, on seeing Jordan. 'I like your hair.' Too bad about the dress, Kerry thought ruefully.

'Everyone's still up in Frank's office, having pre-dinner drinks,' Jordan said.

'Yes—so why aren't you?'

'I walked by the door and simply couldn't bear to go in and make meaningless chit-chat. So I dropped my purse off in my office and came straight down here to talk to you.'

Kerry grinned. 'Coward. You just don't want to— Oh, my God! You're wearing the engagement ring. Here, give me a good look at it. Oh, my, it's fabulous! Chad must have picked it out. I know you, Jordan. You would have chosen a single diamond solitaire, half that size, set in a simple claw setting.'

Jordan shook her head wryly at her friend. 'And you'd be right. This is actually a family heirloom.'

'How did he get it to you? By international courier?'

'No. He left it with me before he went overseas.'

'Because he knew you'd eventually say yes.'

'How could he have known?'

Kerry rolled her eyes at her friend. 'Because multi-millionaires like him don't get turned down.'

'I'm not marrying him for his money, Kerry.'

'I know that. You're marrying him because you love

him, and because you've finally got over that Italian fellow. Speaking of Italians—I hope you don't have anything against Italian men in general, because I've seated you next to one tonight.'

'Oh?'

'He's Henry's new client. Contracts and mergers. I didn't expect him to accept the invitation, since he lives in Melbourne. But, lo and behold, he did.'

Jordan's heart skipped a beat. It couldn't possibly be Gino, could it? Would fate be that cruel?

'I hear he's quite a hunk,' Kerry added. 'And filthy rich. He's a builder. Of seriously big buildings.'

Jordan's chest tightened. Oh, no, she thought with a mixture of disbelief and despair. It had to be Gino.

Fortunately, Kerry was in the process of checking the name cards and wasn't looking at her. Jordan didn't want her friend putting two and two together. And she just might if she saw the near panic which was bubbling up inside Jordan.

'Does he have a name, this Italian?' she asked, using her extra-cool court voice—the one she could conjure up no matter how she felt inside.

'What? Oh—Bortelli. Gino Bortelli. Look, I'll have to love you and leave you, Jordan. I can hear voices coming down the hallway. I need to let the caterer know that everyone's arriving.'

She bustled off without giving Jordan a second glance, which was just as well.

For the life of her Jordan didn't know how she hadn't fainted. All the blood had definitely drained from her face when she'd heard that dreaded name, her head swirling alarmingly. She stumbled over and gripped the back of the nearest chair, afraid to turn around and face the main doorway. The voices were much closer, indicating that people were moving into the room.

'Ahh…so there you are, Jordan,' a male voice boomed.

Jordan winced. It was Frank—Kerry's boss. And *her* boss.

Impossible to do anything but turn round. Yet she knew as she did so that Frank wouldn't be alone. He would have their most valuable new client with him: the very wealthy Mr Gino Bortelli.

Despite being mentally prepared for the encounter, Jordan was still stunned by the sight of Gino, dressed to kill in a magnificent black dinner suit, complete with a white dress-shirt and a black bow-tie. Stunned, too, by what she saw in his black eyes.

Not surprise, as she would have imagined if this was a cruel twist of fate. But coldness. And contempt.

The realisation that he'd known she would be here tonight was instantaneous. The only question remaining was how come? Jordan hadn't told him where she worked.

Gino should have been as shocked as she was.

But he wasn't. Not at all.

Which meant what?

Somehow she managed a polite smile, but all the while her head was spinning with unanswered questions.

'Hello, Frank,' she said, reefing her eyes away from the man by his side.

'Mr McKee was looking for you,' Frank said, a touch irritably.

'Really? Where is he?'

'He had to go home. He said he could feel a migraine coming on.'

'What a shame,' Jordan said, thinking to herself that she wished she'd thought of that. Then she could have fled this extremely difficult scenario.

Running away from difficult scenarios, however, had never been Jordan's style. She liked to face things head-on.

Which was hardly what she was doing at this moment.

It took an effort of will, but she finally turned her eyes back to meet Gino's.

'And who's this, Frank?' she asked coolly, and watched with some satisfaction as Gino's shoulders stiffened.

But no way was she going to give him the opportunity to say anything embarrassing in front of her boss. And he might, if she admitted to already knowing him.

'An extremely valuable new client,' Frank replied pompously. 'Mr Gino Bortelli, CEO of Bortelli Constructions, one of Melbourne's finest building companies. Henry helped him out last week with a contract.'

Ahh, so that was how he came to be here. Jordan wondered if someone had mentioned her name whilst he'd been here, signing that contract.

No, that couldn't be right. Gino hadn't even known she was a lawyer last Friday night, let alone where she worked.

'Hopefully, Gino will do Stedley & Parkinson the honour of letting us represent him in all his future business dealings in Sydney,' Frank added.

Jordan was used to Frank sucking up to wealthy clients, but he seemed to be outdoing himself this time.

'Unfortunately Henry called in sick at the last moment,' he swept on, before Jordan—or Gino—could say a single word. 'So I've been introducing Mr Bortelli to everyone. Jordan's one of our finest young litigators, Gino. She's gained quite a reputation during the few short years she's been with us.'

'Don't flatter me, Frank. How do you do, Mr Bortelli?' Jordan said, but refrained from holding out her hand.

'Very well, thank you,' Gino replied with a cool nod.

'I'll leave you in Jordan's good hands. I seem to recall Kerry has seated you next to each other. But don't get any ideas, Gino. Our Jordan has recently become engaged. To Chad Stedley,' he threw over his shoulder as he turned away. 'Our senior partner's son and heir.'

'Congratulations,' Gino said, his tone polite but his coldly contemptuous eyes spearing into her very soul.

Jordan could not help the guilty colour stealing into her cheeks. Luckily, Frank had turned away, and was already showing other guests to their seats around the table.

'So, is this the way we're going to play it tonight, Jordan?' Gino went on caustically. 'Like we're total strangers?'

Jordan gave him a long, cold look of her own. 'Everyone is sitting down for dinner, Mr Bortelli. I suggest we do the same. This way…'

He followed her round to the far side of the table, where she indicated his seat, right next to hers.

Fortunately, nobody made any move to remove the place-settings on either side of them, meaning their conversation would not be easily overheard. Also fortunately, Kerry was seated to the left of Frank, on the same side of the table as Jordan, which meant she wouldn't witness any telling interplay between Jordan and Gino.

Once they'd settled in their chairs and the entrées had been served—tempura prawns on a salad base—Jordan decided to stop playing word games and cut to the chase.

'You're being here tonight is not a coincidence, is it?'

'My hiring Stedley & Parkinson as my legal representative was a coincidence.'

'But you knew I'd be here tonight?'

'Yes.'

Jordan's frustration level rose. 'Care to elaborate on that?'

'No.'

Jordan tried to think. Gino had always had difficulty taking no for an answer. She'd rejected him last Friday night. Had he had her investigated, perhaps? Found out where she worked? Found out about Chad?

She wouldn't put it past him.

'It must be difficult for you,' Gino said quietly, 'with your fiancé overseas. You must miss him.'

Jordan's heart lurched. 'How do you know that Chad's overseas?'

'Maybe Frank told me.'

'He didn't, though, did he? You've had me investigated.'

'My, my, what a suspicious mind you have. Must come from being a lawyer.'

'What is it that you want of me, Gino?'

He put down his entrée fork and slanted a smile her way.

It was a wickedly provocative smile—one which set her heart racing. And not from anger.

'What I've always wanted when I'm around you, Jordan,' he murmured, his sexy black eyes suddenly going from arctic cold to tropical heat.

When her hand began to tremble, she too put down her fork. Jerking her eyes away from his, she picked up her wine glass, gripping the stem tightly as she lifted it to her lips and swallowed a deep gulp.

The action allowed her to recover her composure a little. But her heart was still thudding loudly behind her ribs.

Finally, she turned her head to face him, her expression firm.

'I did not become engaged till after last Friday night,' she told him.

'And you think that exonerates you?' he muttered under his breath. 'You called me a liar and a cheat, Jordan. Yet all the while *you* were the liar and the cheat. I know exactly what happened last Friday night. You thought you could have your little bit of Italian rough whilst your wealthy lover was away. But when you found out I wasn't who you thought I was, you panicked and did a flit. But not before you dumped a whole lot of guilt on me. You even called me a coward. No one calls me a coward, Jordan, and gets away with it.'

Jordan's head spun with his vicious attack.

But Gino wasn't finished yet.

'What would happen, do you think, if I told your precious Chad what you were up to while he was away? I doubt you'd be wearing that ring for long. Or working here at good old Stedley & Parkinson's. They're a rather old-fashioned firm, aren't they?'

Once again all the blood drained from Jordan's face. It was as well she was sitting down. Shaken, she picked up her wine glass again and took another swallow, giving herself some more time to regroup. Finally, she put down the glass and picked up her fork.

'So this is what tonight's about, is it?' she bit out, spearing another prawn. 'Revenge. How typically Italian.'

'Indeed,' he agreed. 'You would have done well to remember that when you wounded my pride and my sense of honour.'

'You call it honourable to have me investigated?'

'A man has to do what a man has to do.'

'And what do you have to do, Gino?'

'I have to be with you again, Jordan,' he said, his voice vibrating with the most seductive passion. 'Tonight.'

Jordan only just stopped herself from gasping with shock. Instead, she lanced Gino with a dagger-like glare.

'Dream on, buster. Look, I told you last Friday night, and now I'm telling you again: it's over between us—has been for ten years. Last Friday was a big mistake on my part.'

Gino smiled a coolly confident smile. 'If you don't

do as I ask, I will inform your beloved fiancé of what happened last Friday night. Somehow I don't think it will rate with him that, technically, you weren't engaged at the time.'

'Why, you ba—'

'Hush,' he broke in swiftly. 'You wouldn't want dear old Frank hearing you swear at such a valuable new client, would you?'

Jordan shot him another savage glare before grabbing her wine glass again, and emptying it down her throat with a speed which had several pairs of eyes glancing her way across the table in surprise.

She never drank much at these company dinners. Never did anything which anyone could call remotely reckless, let alone wicked.

Jordan knew Gino's ultimatum was wicked. And without care for her future well-being. His wanting her was strictly sexual, his desire made stronger by his need to strip her not just of her clothes, but her pride.

But, despite all that, Jordan had the dreadful suspicion that in the end she would go along with what he wanted—not to keep him silent, but because, down deep, she *wanted* to spend the night with him.

That had to be wicked. *She* had to be wicked.

Either that, or she was still in love with Gino.

But how could she love a man who would do such an appalling thing as try to blackmail her into bed?

No, this wasn't love which was making her blood roar like red-hot lava around her veins. This was lust. A lust so exciting and so powerful she had no chance of resisting it.

Sexually, she was putty in his hands. Always had been. Always would be.

At the same time, she could not allow Gino to suspect her weakness. That would be setting herself up as a perfect victim for his voracious carnal appetite. Safety lay in letting him think that she despised him for doing to her.

Though she wasn't at all sure that she did. His daring excited her almost as much as his desire.

God, but she was hopeless where he was concerned.

Thank heavens she'd perfected the art of steely composure to cover any inner nerves.

'Blackmailers are notorious for never being satisfied,' she said curtly. 'If I do as you want, what's to stop you demanding more after tonight is over?'

'I give you my word that if you spend tonight with me I will go home to Melbourne in the morning and never bother you again.'

'Pardon me if I don't put much store in your word.'

'What alternative do you have?'

'I could tell Chad what happened last Friday. He might understand.'

'*I* wouldn't,' Gino growled.

And neither would Chad, Jordan conceded.

'It's not too much to ask, is it?' Gino went on. 'One night with me, in exchange for a lifetime as Mrs Chad Stedley.'

'What's to stop you causing trouble in my marriage at some future date?' she asked curtly.

'Nothing—other than my word. But I presume once you're married you will move to New York. As much as I'm going to enjoy having you at my beck and call tonight, I doubt I'd travel that far for a repeat performance.'

'Does your family know that you're a heartless, conscienceless bastard?'

His face darkened. 'Leave my family out of this.'

'Gladly.'

'So, what's your answer, Jordan?' he snapped. 'Do we have a deal or not?'

Jordan grimaced, then gritted her teeth. Why was it just him who could make her heart race like this? Who could make her forget her pride? Could make her crave the things he did to her?

It infuriated her that she was so weak with him when normally she was a strong person, with a mind of her own. If it was any other man she would tell him to go to hell. There again, if it had been any other man she would not have willingly had sex with him last Friday night.

'You do realise I will hate you for ever for doing this?' she grated out under her breath.

'It'll be worth it,' he returned coldly.

What would be worth it? she wondered, and worried.

An image popped into her mind, that of herself standing naked in front of him last Friday night and swearing that he would never see her like that again.

Bold, brave, foolish words. Words which Gino was obviously determined to make her regret.

The waiter taking away their empty entrée plates put paid to any conversation for a short while. The second of their crystal wine glasses was filled. Still white, but a Chardonnay this time, instead of the crisp

Chablis which had accompanied the seafood cocktail. Clearly the main course was going to be something light.

'I should tell you to go to hell,' Jordan bit out, once the waiters had moved away from them.

'You should, but you won't. You'll do what I want.'

'Don't be so sure.'

'But I am. Because I'm not the only one here who's heartless and conscienceless. Not to mention ambitious. Oh, yes, let's not forget ambitious.'

'You know nothing about the woman I am.'

'Neither do I want to. I might have once. But I now prefer to keep my knowledge of you to the biblical kind. So is it a deal, Mrs Stedley-to-be? Will you trade total surrender of your body tonight in exchange for my silence?'

'*Total* surrender?' she repeated, aghast and aroused at the same time.

'Didn't I mention that?'

'No,' she said, shaken by the level of her sexual excitement.

'I will not ask you to do anything you haven't done with me before,' he said.

Jordan suppressed a groan. That didn't leave much, if anything at all. Her sex-life with Chad had never been as adventurous as it had been with Gino. Not even remotely.

'You have ten seconds to seal this deal,' he said, with chilling finality, 'or I will do what I said I would. Immediately. I have your fiancé's personal phone number in the menu of my cellphone. A simple visit to the gents will give me the opportunity to call him right now.'

Jordan would have called his bluff if he'd been any other man.

But she knew Gino meant it.

'In that case,' she said, her stomach contracting as she tried to imagine the consequences of Gino's appalling ultimatum. 'It's a deal.'

CHAPTER TEN

WHEN she agreed, it confirmed to Gino what he'd suspected all week: the sweet, sensual, sincere girl he'd once known and loved had turned into a cold-blooded, gold-digging bitch.

She didn't love Chad Stedley. How could she when she'd gone to bed with *him* last Friday night?

But she was wearing Stedley's engagement ring.

Gino had been furious when he found out she was engaged.

No, furious didn't do his emotions justice; he'd been absolutely livid.

He'd come here tonight without any definite plan in mind. He'd just wanted to look her in the eye and let her know that he knew what kind of woman she was. But the moment he'd set eyes on her, standing there with her back to him, looking sexy in that prim little black dress, desire had consumed every pore in his body. By the time she turned round, he'd hated her for the way she could make him crave her, despite everything.

Blackmailing her into bed had not been on his agenda, however, till she'd added insult to injury by arrogantly pretending she didn't know him.

That had been the moment when he'd resolved to bring her down a peg or two. To use her own ruthless ambition against her, at the same time satisfying his own rapidly escalating desire.

Even so, he'd still been shocked when she'd agreed to his proposal. Shocked and stirred. Right now, he was so turned on it would have been embarrassing if he hadn't been sitting at a table.

'I hope you're happy now,' she muttered.

Happy? No, he wasn't happy. How could be happy when the only reason she was going to go to bed with him was so that she could marry someone else?

Or was that really the case?

A sidewards glance showed him that her face was flushed. Was that anger, or the same kind of excitement currently heating his own blood?

The sexual chemistry between them had once been electric. That chemistry had still been there last Friday night. There was no reason to believe that had changed just because she'd found out he wasn't who she thought he was.

Jordan might hate him, but underneath her hatred lay a desire as insidious and as irresistible as his own for her.

Gino could not wait to have her to himself—to have her stand naked for him the way she'd said she never would again—to have her do all the things he'd taught her ten years ago.

The main course arriving only slightly soothed the primitive passions which had begun boiling up within him.

The waiter announced that it was grilled Barramundi, served with a tomato and cucumber salsa, along with baked sweet potato and a fresh garden salad.

Gino fell to eating the meal with gusto. His appetite was always good when his testosterone was up and running.

Jordan, he noticed, just picked at her food. But she drank plenty of wine.

Good, he thought. She was even sexier when she was tipsy, and beautifully co-operative. Or she'd used to be.

'When?' she suddenly whispered.

He did not turn his head to speak.

'When, what?' he muttered, then forked some more of the mouthwatering fish between his lips.

'When does all this begin? And where?'

He let her wait for his answer till he'd savoured the fish, then swallowed.

'As soon as we can get away from here. I've booked a suite at the Regency. One of their themed honeymoon suites.'

He could feel her eyes burning into him.

'How could you?' she breathed.

'How could I what?'

'Book a honeymoon suite.'

In actual fact he hadn't booked the honeymoon suite with any ulterior motive. He certainly hadn't imagined Jordan would be sharing it with him when he had. But the Regency was having a huge convention there this weekend. The only rooms available had been a couple of the honeymoon suites. Gino hadn't thought to book in advance, and couldn't be bothered going to another hotel.

But he wasn't going to tell her that. Clearly his booking a suite had struck a nerve with her.

Good.

'It's called the French Bordello suite,' he told her with a devilish smile. 'I thought it rather appropriate.'

Jordan shook her head at him.

'You really are wicked.'

'And what are you, Jordan?' he countered coldly. 'An innocent?'

'No,' she agreed. 'If I was, I wouldn't have anything to do with you.'

I should have told him to go to hell, Jordan groaned silently as she dropped her eyes back to her plate.

Gino's blackmailing her into bed was bad enough. His booking a honeymoon suite was so insensitive that it bordered on sadism. Surely he must know she'd once have given anything to share a honeymoon suite with him? Becoming Mrs Gino Bortelli had been her ultimate dream.

Becoming Gino Bortelli's mistress for one night was more like a nightmare.

Yet the prospect excited her unbearably.

Her hands shook when she picked up her knife and fork, her stomach churning so much that she simply could not eat.

Gino could, she noticed bitterly. And so could everyone else. But it was no use. Her appetite was gone.

Putting her cutlery down, she picked up her wine glass and sipped it slowly.

'No wonder you're thin,' Gino said. 'You don't eat.'

Jordan ignored him and continued sipping her wine. But it wasn't long before she began to feel light-headed, so she put the glass down, picked up her fork and forced a few mouthfuls of the meal down past the lump in her throat.

'That's better,' Gino said, and she threw him a sour glare.

'It's a wonder I can eat at all, with what's ahead of me tonight.'

'Really? When I'm excited I eat all the more.'

'How can you possibly enjoy going to bed with a woman who hates you?'

'That's one thing you should learn about men, Jordan. They do not have to love or even like their sexual partner to enjoy themselves in bed.'

'You do realise that what you're going to do tonight is tantamount to coercion?'

'Oh, come now, Jordan. Coercion?' A dry laugh broke from his lips. 'I'll remind you that you said that when you beg me for more.'

Jordan sucked in sharply, both at his arrogance and at the hot wave of desire which suddenly flooded her body.

Still, after what he'd just said Jordan finally accepted that Gino had never loved her at all. She'd just been a sex object to him, a plaything.

What he'd loved about her was being able to take her virgin body and turn her into his ultimate fantasy female. Their affair had had nothing to do with love, it had just been sex.

Last Friday night had been more of the same. And so would tonight.

Jordan's thoughts hardened her heart to him, but it didn't dampen her desire. She still wanted to be with him, and the disgusting realisation was making her hate herself almost as much as him.

'You have no soul,' she muttered.

'Then we're well matched,' he countered.

'Why don't you stop talking and just let me eat?'

'Be my guest.'

Each mouthful felt like swill, but it was better to eat than to drink, or—heaven forbid—get into some destructive repartee with Gino.

By the time the waiter came round to remove her plate—everyone else had finished their meal by then—Jordan had managed to consume a reasonable amount, washed down with two full glasses of wine.

Frank standing up and toasting all their new clients was a welcome distraction. But she wasn't so keen when he also toasted her success with the Johnson case this week. It reminded her that there wouldn't be too many similar successes for her in the near future.

Not at Stedley & Parkinson.

Her allowing Gino to blackmail her into bed with him meant the death of her life here—because it meant the death of her engagement to Chad.

She could not in all conscience spend tonight at Gino's sexual beck and call, then go on to marry Chad; he deserved better than that.

Which meant she would have to call him tomorrow and break off their engagement, as well as resign from Stedley & Parkinson on Monday.

For how could she go on working here under those circumstances? Better that she get out now, with her reputation still intact. She would tell Frank that the pressure of the job and the distress of her broken engagement was too much, and that she needed a break from working. That way she could leave with proper references.

Maybe she'd treat herself to a holiday somewhere far far away.

Not Italy, though. China, perhaps. Somewhere different.

As she sat there, making plans, her mind reluctantly returned to Chad. He was going to be very annoyed with her. But he would survive. Jordan comforted herself with the thought that they hadn't shared a grand passion.

'Have you set a date for your wedding?' Gino suddenly asked, snapping her back to the reality of where she was and whom she was sitting next to.

She turned cold eyes his way. 'I thought I said I didn't want to talk.'

'Better than sitting here twiddling our thumbs.'

'I don't agree.'

'I hope it's not a shotgun wedding?'

'What? Don't be ridiculous.'

'Why is it ridiculous? Stedley's a very good catch. You wouldn't be the first girl to snare herself a wealthy husband with pregnancy.'

'I earn a very good salary. I don't need a wealthy husband.'

'You know the famous saying: you can never be too rich or too thin.'

'Can we terminate this conversation, please?'

'Fine. But I must ask one thing before we have sex tonight.'

Jordan winced at Gino's verbalising of what they would be doing later. Not for the first time tonight she thanked heaven no one could overhear their conversation. The empty seats on either side of them had been a godsend—as was the very convenient arrangement of flowers sitting between them and the people opposite.

'What is it?' she said with an irritable sigh.

'Does Chad wear a condom when he has sex with you?' Gino asked.

'Do *you* use a condom when you sleep with your girlfriend?' she shot back.

'Always. Now answer the question.'

Jordan didn't want to, but she could see no way out.

'Yes,' she admitted.

'I thought he might.'

Jordan blinked. 'Why do you say it like that?'

'Like what?'

'Like you think Chad's sleeping around on me.'

'Well, you're sleeping around on him.'

'Last Friday night was the one and only time.'

'What about tonight?'

'You can't possibly count tonight. You're forcing me.'

'Ahh, yes. So I am,' he said, but his tone was sarcastic, as though he knew full well she was more than willing.

Jordan closed her eyes against this most terrible

truth. What kind of person was she to do this? Okay, so she was going to break her engagement. That, at least, was the right thing to do. But she was still going to spend the night with a man who didn't care for her, and who had a girlfriend back in Melbourne.

Both of them were technically being unfaithful to their partners.

Gino was right. She was just as bad as he was.

When she opened her eyes again her dessert was sitting in front of her—some kind of chocolate concoction, with swirls of cream and berries decorating the plate. The waiter had also refilled her wine glass.

She reached for it first, hoping to drown her scruples with alcohol. Gino, she noted out of the corner of her eyes, was already eating his dessert. By the time she picked up her dessert fork he'd finished.

'Do you intend working after you've become Mrs Chad Stedley?'

Jordan sighed again. She wished she could tell Gino to shut up, in no uncertain terms, but she doubted he would comply.

'I will never give up working,' she told him, her tone curt.

'Not even when you have a baby?'

Jordan gritted her teeth. 'Not even then.'

'Do you want children?'

Jordan hated the way her heart lurched. 'What business is that of yours?' she snapped. *He* didn't want to marry her, or have children by her. All he wanted was to have sex with her.

'Just curious.'

'Don't be. We made a deal. And it only includes access to my body. Not my soul. Or my goals. Now, if you don't mind, I would like to leave this topic of conversation alone for the rest of this dinner. I've agreed to what you wanted. Be happy with that.'

'I won't be happy till you're in my arms again.'

Jordan smothered a groan. Why did he have to say things like that? And why did she have to respond so mindlessly?

She closed her eyes, thinking that happiness would never be hers again. Not if she did this. Being with Gino again would destroy her. She could feel it already—the disintegration of her will, the longing to surrender herself to him. It was insidious, this power he had over her. She could feel it, radiating out from him, drawing her into his spell.

Jordan put down her fork, knowing that this time she would not be able to force herself to eat a single bite.

'Men like you should be castrated,' she muttered.

Gino laughed softly. 'Then what would women like you do?'

'Have some peace in their lives.'

'How boring that sounds. At least you won't be bored tonight. You're going to feel more alive than you have in years.'

'And you, Gino? What will you feel?'

He smiled at her. 'You do like cross-examining people, don't you? My feelings will be my own. I don't share them with women who hate me.'

'Yet you expect me to share your bed? How perverse is that?'

'Extremely perverse,' he whispered as he leant towards her, his breath warmth against her ear. 'I will think about your hatred when you stand naked before me. And when you beg me to do it to you—as you will, Jordan my sweet. Because I know that part of you through and through. I know your secret needs and desires. You might hate me, but down deep, in that place reserved for the darkest of truths, you want me as much as I want you. No. Perhaps not *that* much. Here— give me your hand and see what you've already done to me.'

Jordan stiffened in the chair when he took her hand and pulled it into his lap, pressing it against him.

'Stop that,' she hissed as she snatched her hand away. 'I will not be humiliated by you, Gino. You will treat me with respect. If you cross the line of decency just once, the deal's off. I'll tell Chad myself I had a one-night stand with an old boyfriend and take my chances. Do I make myself clear?'

'Perfectly.'

'I have no intention of leaving this dinner with you, either. I will go to the Regency independently. Leave my name and a spare key card for me at Reception.'

'But they'll think you're a paid whore if I do that!' he protested.

'They wouldn't be far wrong, then, would they?'

Gino scowled. 'I'll tell them that my wife will be joining me after a late flight from Melbourne.'

'No,' Jordan snapped. 'I will not pretend to be your wife.'

'You've become very stubborn.'

'I'm an adult woman now, Gino, not a silly young girl.'

'I preferred the silly young girl,' he said, his expression still disgruntled.

'I'm sure you did. So the deal's off, is it? You don't want me any more now that you've discovered the stubborn new me?'

He stared into her eyes for a long moment. 'Stop trying to pick a fight with me, Jordan. You and I both know that neither of us wants that. Now eat your dessert; it's delicious.'

'I can't eat any more,' she said, and pushed the plate away.

'You need taking in hand, woman. Which I will take pleasure in doing as soon as this dinner is over.'

'In your dreams,' she snapped.

'No. In the French Bordello suite at the Regency. In a four-poster bed. All night long.'

CHAPTER ELEVEN

JORDAN was standing at the window behind her desk, staring blankly down at the city, when her office door opened.

'I thought I'd find you here,' Kerry said.

Jordan turned and smiled a small smile at her friend. 'Why's that?'

'Because you're in some kind of antisocial mood. You couldn't wait to get out of that dinner, could you?'

'I didn't have much of an appetite tonight,' Jordan said.

'The food was good, though, wasn't it?'

'Very good.' Jordan glanced at her watch. She would have to be leaving soon. Gino had warned her not to be late, and he'd already been gone ten minutes.

'How did you get on with Mr Bortelli?'

'What?' Jordan looked up. 'Oh, not too bad. He liked the food.'

'He didn't make a pass at you, did he?'

Jordan stiffened. 'Why on earth would you say that?'

'Just a feeling. You seem…agitated.'

For a split second Jordan was tempted to tell Kerry everything. But she just couldn't.

'I'm still strung up after last week. The Johnson case was rather draining. I…I might take a break from work shortly.'

'You know, I think that would be a good idea. Why don't you surprise Chad by flying over to the States?'

Jordan shook her head. 'No. I don't want to do that.'

'You're not having second thoughts about marrying him, are you?'

Jordan swallowed. 'Actually, I am.'

'Oh, Jordan,' Kerry said, her face falling.

'Yes, I know. I'm a fool. Probably a bigger fool than you realise.' Suddenly tears filled Jordan's eyes. She had to get out of here, and fast. Blinking madly, she wrenched open her desk drawer and retrieved her purse from where she'd left it earlier.

When she lifted her eyes back to Kerry's she had herself under control again. 'I need to go home and get a good night's sleep. See you on Monday.'

'Look after yourself,' Kerry called after her as she hurried from the office.

No one was in the lift on the ride down, giving Jordan the perfect opportunity to slip off her engagement ring and pop it into the zippered section of her purse.

No way could she wear Chad's ring whilst she was with Gino. He wouldn't allow it, anyway.

The security man in the foyer asked Jordan if she wanted him to call her a taxi. The Regency was a relatively short walk away—only a couple of blocks. But on a Saturday night any walk in the city could be dangerous—especially for a woman on her own.

Jordan would normally have taken a taxi, but not this time.

She welcomed the cool night air outside, welcomed the risk.

If someone mugged her or accosted her, then it was only what she deserved.

Of course no one did either, and she was pushing her way through the revolving glass doors of the hotel's entrance in less than ten minutes. By then her heart was pounding behind her ribs and her face felt flushed. Another glance at her watch showed that it was only just after ten-thirty.

Her stiletto heels clacked on the marble floor of the arcade as she hurried along it—past the bouncer who stood at the doorway to the Rendezvous bar, past the bistro and the boutiques. The arcade led into the hotel foyer proper, and the reception desk was on her left.

Jordan hated that she'd have to deal with a male desk clerk. She'd been hoping for a woman.

'Ahh, yes…Ms Gray,' he said, with a knowing little smirk on his fleshy lips as he handed her the key card. 'Mr Bortelli said you were to go right up. The French Bordello suite is on the twelfth floor.'

'Thank you,' she replied coolly, hoping her cheeks weren't as red as they felt.

The ride up to the twelfth floor felt surreal, with her conflicting emotions threatening to overwhelm her. Her brain kept telling her not to do this. She could still turn round and go home. But her body refused to obey.

Before she knew it she was standing in front of the

door which had *French Bordello Suite* marked on it in gold letters.

Should she knock, or let herself in?

Her right hand balled into a fist as she lifted it to knock.

A few short but agonising seconds passed before the door was wrenched open.

Gino stood there, his black eyes glowering impatience at her. He'd taken off his jacket, she noted, and the bow-tie. He'd also opened the top button of his white dress-shirt.

'You took your time,' he grumbled.

'I walked.'

'You what?' he snapped, then grabbed her hand and pulled her inside, kicking the door shut with his foot. 'What kind of risk-taker are you, woman?'

Jordan could have told him, in no uncertain terms, but decided not to say a word. Instead, she yanked her hand out of his, and was about to head further into the room when she ground to a halt.

'Good heavens!' she exclaimed.

Jordan just stood there, shaking her head at the over-the-top décor. Had the designer copied rooms in a real French Bordello? she wondered. Or simply come up with what a French Bordello might be like in his or her imagination?

The colours were too rich for Jordan's taste, the furniture way too ornate. At the same time there was no denying that whoever had designed this place had created a decadent, sensual atmosphere: dark red-coloured carpet on the floor, wood-panelled walls, two gold brocade-covered sofas, with elaborately carved legs. Marble-topped tables, gold velvet drapes at the window, subdued lighting from heavily fringed lamps whose bases were brass figurines of naked women.

The bedroom was separated from the sitting area by double doors, currently open, giving Jordan a glimpse of the bottom half of the four-poster bed Gino had mentioned. In there the colours were reversed—the carpet gold and the walls covered in a deep red wallpaper, the velvet drapes around the bed the same dark red colour.

'Does that mean you like it or not?' Gino said drily by her side.

'It's not exactly my cup of tea,' she replied.

'Wait till you see the bathroom.'

A stab of nervous tension suddenly set her bladder on edge. 'I think I need to go see it right now.'

'Be my guest,' Gino invited.

'Alone,' she added sharply.

No television, she noted as she hurried through the sitting room, nor a mini-bar. Though there was an antique cabinet in one corner which could have hidden anything. A bottle of French champagne—already opened—sat in a silver ice bucket on the marble-topped coffee table, along with some tasty little treats: strawberries…caviar… And—if she wasn't mistaken—chocolate truffles.

Was that Gino's doing? Or the hotel's?

The bedroom was as sumptuous as it looked from a distance. The bedspread was made of red and gold quilted satin, the pillows of gold satin, as were the sheets. The brass bases of the bedside lamps were more naked ladies in various poses. An elegant glass bottle stood next to one lamp, filled with what looked like a body lotion of some kind.

The bathroom lived up to Gino's warning: black marble dominated the room, covering the floors, walls and ceiling. The twin sink units were made of the same marble, the bowls as well. The toilet, bidet and corner spa bath were in a rich cream colour, the taps and other fittings gold-plated. The towels were scarlet, as were the floor mats. Several small alcoves had been carved high up in the marble walls. Tonight they held gold candles which were lit, looking like glow-worms in a dark cave—a dark, sexually charged cave.

Jordan could only imagine what Gino had in mind for that room later on. She shuddered anew as she washed her hands at the sink, grateful that the dim light wouldn't let her see the excitement in her eyes reflected in the mirror.

She combed her slightly breeze-blown hair, but didn't bother to refresh her lipstick. What was the point? It wouldn't be there for long.

Gathering herself, she exited the bathroom and returned to the sitting area, where Gino was standing at the window with his back to her. He turned at the sound of her entry. He was holding a near full glass of champagne, and he was frowning.

'I've been thinking,' he began.

'Yes?'

'I was wrong to blackmail you into this. It's not what I intended to do when I went to that dinner tonight. It's not what I want.'

Jordan had never been so astounded in all her life.

'What is it that you want, then?'

'I still want you, Jordan. That hasn't changed. But I want you to come to me willingly. I don't want to force you, or even to seduce you. I want what we once had together. You—eager to surrender yourself to me. I don't want you to hate me in the morning. And I don't want to hate myself.'

Jordan just stared at Gino, his amazing and highly unexpected turnaround bringing a fierce frustration which found its voice in anger.

'I don't think you know what you want, Gino,' she said sharply. 'Look, if it makes you feel any better, then I *have* come here willingly. It's not because you blackmailed me. You have some kind of hold over me. I admit it. You turn up out of the blue, crook your finger, and silly Jordan comes running. But don't delude yourself into thinking we can recapture what we once had. For one thing, I don't love you any more. How could I possibly love a man who has me investigated behind my back? But, yes, I still lust after you. You were right in what you said at that table tonight. You know what I like. You know all my dark little secrets.

'So here I am,' she added, reaching up behind her back and pulling the zipper down. 'Doing what I vowed I'd never do. But not because of your threat to tell Chad. I'm hoping that once I've had my fill of you tonight I'll be able to walk away in the morning and make a decent life for myself with a man who cares about me and wants to marry me.'

* * *

Gino watched, appalled but cripplingly aroused, as she peeled her dress off her shoulders and let it fall to the floor, leaving her standing there in her underwear.

Not prim and proper underwear, but sexy underwear. A black satin teddy, with suspenders attached to shiny flesh-coloured stockings.

Her glittering blue eyes held his boldly whilst she kicked off her shoes and then unflicked each suspender. With a haughty toss of her lovely blonde hair she moved over to the coffee table and put one foot up, rolling the stocking down to her toes before snapping it off.

Gino's gut crunched down hard at the thought that she might have performed like this for Stedley. Though if she had, then what was she doing here?

No, it's only with me that she's like this. She's virtually said as much.

The other stocking followed, then the pearls, which she tossed aside as carelessly as the nylons. When she hooked her fingers under the thin satin straps of the teddy Gino's stopped breathing altogether. His blood, however, was still roaring round his veins, engorging his flesh to titanic proportions.

She actually smiled as she peeled the garment down her body. A slow siren's smile.

'Don't look so gobsmacked,' she said, when she finally stood there in the nude. 'This is what you wanted, isn't it?'

Gino's hand gripped the stem of his glass with such force that it was a miracle it didn't snap.

'No,' he ground out. 'Not quite. Put the shoes back on.'

Now it was her turn to look gobsmacked.

'That's the way I pictured you when I was eating dinner tonight. That's what I want. For starters,' he added, all qualms gone over how he was going to treat her tonight. He'd tried to do the right thing, but she wanted none of it. *This* was what she wanted. To have her fill of him. And he was more than happy to oblige!

Jordan swallowed, her throat suddenly dry. She should never have started stripping in front of him, never have taken him on.

It had only been a matter of time before her reckless-ness backfired on her.

Gino no longer looked shocked. His expression was cold and implacable.

'Do it!' he ordered.

Jordan's feet found her shoes. The height of the heels changed the way she stood. The sharp angle of her feet made her straighten her shoulders and suck in her stomach, those actions thrusting her breasts forward and upwards.

Gino's black eyes narrowed as he looked her up and down, his heavily hooded gaze as hard as it was exciting.

Had he known she would feel different standing there in the nude with her high heels on? More exposed? More…aroused?

Yes, of course he knew. He knew she was standing there, trembling inside with anticipation of what would come next. Knew that she thrilled to his commands and his demands.

'That's better,' he said, a dark triumph in his eyes. 'Now come over here…'

CHAPTER TWELVE

JORDAN walked slowly towards him, each step bringing a heightened awareness of her female body.

By the time she stood before him her lips had fallen apart and her heartbeat had quickened, her chest rising and falling, her belly stretched tight with tension.

'Here,' he said, and held his glass to her lips. 'You look like you could do with a drink.'

He tipped up the glass and watched her drink it all down.

The champagne fizzed into her stomach, her head spinning—but not because of the alcohol.

Jordan could not recall ever being this excited. Or this mesmerised. This was different from ten years ago. Different from last Friday night.

Tonight, she accepted dazedly, was going to be an experience which would change her life for ever.

When he tossed the empty glass onto one of the sofas, then ran the back of his right hand across the hard tips of her breasts, a violent tremor rippled down her spine.

'Do you know how sexy you look?' he murmured, as he trailed his fingers down over her tautly held stomach. 'But you'd look even sexier if you moved your legs apart a little.'

When she just blinked, he smiled a rather cold smile. 'I thought we'd agreed on total surrender for tonight? Total surrender means doing as you're told when you're told. Of course if you've changed your mind about wanting your fill of me, that's your choice. Get dressed and leave. I won't stop you. But if you decide to stay, then we do things my way.'

The ruthlessness in his voice shocked her. But it turned her on at the same time.

'You seem to have lost your tongue,' he went on. 'But, since you're still here, I take it you agree with my conditions for tonight?'

Jordan swallowed, then licked her parched lips.

'That too,' he said, his coal-black eyes fixed on her mouth. 'But later—after we've had a relaxing bath. You stay right where you are till I run the water.'

'Gino—no,' she choked out, her excitement already at fever pitch.

'No, what?' he shot back.

'Don't leave me like this. I can't bear it.'

He glared at her with something akin to hatred. But then his eyes dissolved in a blaze of molten desire. With a tortured groan he caught her to him, his arms enfolding her into a rough embrace, his mouth brutal in its possession of hers.

She melted against him with a naked moan, glorying in the savagery of his kiss. If he'd been tender with her she might have started crying. This way she could lose herself in his wild passion, as well as her own.

The buttons on his shirt were pressing painfully into her chest. But she didn't care. She welcomed the pain…and the madness.

Soon his tongue in her mouth wasn't enough. She needed him inside her. Needed to be filled as only he had ever filled her.

Somehow she freed her mouth from his, her breathing like a marathon runner nearing the end of a race.

'Do it to me,' she cried.

His eyes glowered down at her, then glittered in a way which sent a shiver running down her spine. 'Here?'

'Yes,' she practically sobbed.

He grabbed her by the waist and lifted her off her feet, turning her round and carrying her over to the floor-length window. There, he stood her in the centre of it, her bottom and shoulders pressed up against the cool glass.

Jordan gasped when he lifted her arms upwards and outwards.

'Take hold of the curtains,' he ordered her. 'And don't let go.'

Her hands trembled as they clasped the edges of the velvet swags. What must she look like, standing there like some pagan sacrifice? Could she be seen from the windows of the building opposite? Were people watching them?

'Move your legs further apart,' Gino ordered, as he stripped off his shirt and tossed it aside.

Jordan closed her eyes, then did as she was told. Her hands clutched tighter at the velvet, so tight that it was a wonder she didn't bring the curtains down around her.

The sudden feel of Gino's breath on her face had her eyelids fluttering back open.

'I want you to watch, my love,' he murmured, leaning down to run his tongue-tip around her startled mouth. 'And to witness. Everything.'

'I…I am not your love,' she cried, shuddering when one his hands slipped between her legs.

'You are tonight.'

'No,' she denied, even as she trembled with desire.

'This tells me differently,' he murmured against her panting mouth. 'This tells me that tonight you *are* mine.'

His eyes held hers as his hand continued with its most devastatingly intimate exploration. Jordan tried to fight the feelings his skilful touch evoked, tried not to melt at his watching her like that. But it was a futile effort. Her whole body stiffened as it rushed towards a climax.

Gino's abandoning her barely a breath before her release brought a perverse cry of protest.

'Patience,' he growled, and went back to undressing in front of her.

Jordan's shoulders sagged, her upper arms beginning to ache. But the sight of Gino naked had her spine straightening again.

'You like what you see?' he taunted as he came back to her.

Jordan could no longer speak. She just wanted him

inside her. She didn't care who might be watching them—didn't care about anything but his flesh filling hers.

It did. Quite roughly. Surging up into her body with such force that she was momentarily lifted off the floor. His hands lifted to press against the glass on either side of her head, his mouth grazing her hair as he thrust into her, his chest rubbing against the tips of her breasts.

Jordan had never experienced a coupling so passionate or so primitive. Not even with Gino himself, all those years ago.

It spun her out of her head, out of her body. She was there, but not there. Gino had said he wanted her to watch and to witness everything. That was exactly what it felt as if she was doing: being both participant and observer.

Is that really me there, spread naked against the window, keeping myself a willing captive for this man?

I am doomed, she thought hysterically. Doomed!

'Gino,' she cried out as she came. 'Oh, Gino…'

Gino heard her call out his name. Felt her flesh start spasming around his.

What little was left of his control shattered, his mind exploding along with his body, his thoughts spinning out into the stratosphere.

She had to still love him to let him do such things to her, he reasoned wildly in the heat of the moment. Had to. The girl he'd known all those years could not have changed that much.

And if she loved him, then she didn't love Stedley.

She was just marrying him because she was getting older and wanted children. Women always wanted children.

He could give her children, if that was what she so desperately wanted. They could work something out—some arrangement: they could be lovers, or live together. He hadn't given any deathbed promise that he would not *live* with a girl who wasn't Italian.

Some common sense had returned, however, by the time she let go of the curtains and began to sag downwards.

She didn't necessarily have to love him to enjoy what he'd just done to her, he conceded, as he withdrew and scooped her up into his arms. She wasn't the same girl she'd been ten years ago. She'd changed.

He'd changed, hadn't he?

She'd told him how it was earlier: this was all about sex. A fatal-attraction kind of sex which had nothing to do with love, but with need: a dark, driving need which obsessed and possessed.

Gino gritted his teeth. He already felt obsessed and possessed.

Jordan had expressed the hope that one night with him would cure her of her need.

As Gino carried her into the bedroom he vowed to make sure that it did not.

CHAPTER THIRTEEN

JORDAN shivered when Gino lowered her onto the cool satin quilt, goosebumps breaking out all over her body.

'I'll go run us that bath now,' he said, as he slipped off her shoes and then wrapped the quilt tightly around her.

'Don't go to sleep,' he added, giving her a soft peck on her forehead before heading for the bathroom.

Jordan stared after him, her slightly fuzzy mind at a loss to understand his sudden change of attitude. Where had the ruthless lover of a few moments ago gone? Was his tenderness for real? Or just a ploy to seduce her into further compliance?

'Won't be too long,' he said jauntily as he walked back through the bedroom, returning with the ice bucket and two champagne glasses. A second trip out to the sitting room had him collecting the two plates of delicacies.

'Can't have you passing out from thirst and hunger, can I?' he remarked with a wicked smile as he headed back to the bathroom.

Any fuzziness in Jordan's head immediately cleared. Not true tenderness. A seductive ploy.

How silly of her to start hoping for anything different.

'All done!' he announced, on his third return to the bedroom. 'Just one more thing needed, my love. *You.*'

Jordan did her best not to swoon when he threw back the quilt, then scooped her up from the bed. But having her naked flesh held tight against Gino's was not conducive to calm.

The bathroom looked both romantic and decadent at the same time, what with the candles, the champagne and the spa filled to the brim with fragrant-smelling bubbles.

'You'd better put your hair up,' he suggested. 'Or it'll get wet.'

Jordan reached up to wrap her hair on top of her head in a knot, her eyes never leaving his.

'You are so beautiful,' he murmured, and kissed her lightly on the lips.

She blinked, then gasped when he went to step into the spa bath, still carrying her.

'Oh, do be careful.'

'I won't drop you,' he told her confidently. 'Don't worry.'

The water under the bubbles was deliciously warm, and Jordan sighed with relief when Gino finally sat down, angling her round so that she was sitting on his thighs, her back leaning against his.

'Comfy like that?' he asked.

Jordan swallowed. 'Are you?'

He laughed. 'I have a feeling I won't be soon. But I'll worry about that later. This is just like the old days, isn't it? We had plenty of baths together then.'

'I…I don't want to talk about the old days, Gino.'

'Fine. Here…have a sip of champagne,' he said, picking up one of the full glasses and holding it to her lips.

Jordan was about to blindly open her lips when a wave of rebellion struck. 'I'd rather have my own glass, thank you.'

'Okay. Take this one.'

He gave it to her, but didn't get the other glass for himself. Instead, he picked up the sea sponge which was lying on the bath's edge and rubbed it across her stomach.

When he moved it up to her breasts she gasped, spilling some champagne as she jerked away from Gino's chest.

'Relax,' he said, and used the sponge to press her back into her leaning position. 'You'll like it. I promise. Just lie back, sip your champagne, and keep your arms out of my way.'

It seemed silly to tell him to stop. Because of course she did like it—especially when the sponge grazed over her rock-hard nipples. Her pleasure was a double-edged sword, however, as her sexual tension increased with each passing moment. Soon every muscle she owned was twisted into a tight knot. She tried sipping more of the champagne, but nothing relaxed her for long.

'Tell me about that case you won,' Gino said.

Jordan turned her head and flicked startled eyes up at him.

'You…you can't be serious,' she choked out.

'Why not?' he returned.

'Because I can't think, let alone talk when you're doing that.'

'Yes, you can. Try it,' he said, moving the sponge down over her stomach again, then lower…

'Oh!' she cried as her hips bucked upwards.

'God, woman,' Gino growled.

When she felt his flesh suddenly slide up into her Jordan froze, gripping the champagne glass for dear life.

'Just relax now,' he advised again, as he eased her back down into a sitting position. 'Lie back and don't move. I want to hear about that case you won first.'

'How can I? I…I can't think.'

'You can, and you will.'

Jordan could not believe she was doing this. She was desperate to move, but he kept her still with his hands splayed across her stomach.

'What compensation did you get her in the end?' he asked, after she'd related the whole story to him.

'Three million.'

'A tidy sum.'

'Sharni still wasn't a happy woman. Because it wasn't about money, really. It was about justice. Money doesn't make people happy.'

'But it can help.'

'I suppose so.' She *so* wished he would stop talking.

'*You* wouldn't marry a poor man.'

Jordan sighed. 'I would have married you ten years ago, when I thought you were poor.'

'That was when you were young and naïve. When you were a romantic.'

'You think I'm not a romantic any more?'

'How can you be when you're going to marry Stedley? You don't love him, and I know it.'

Jordan didn't like the way this conversation was going. She could cope if they just stuck to sex.

'Could we have a change of subject, please?' she asked tautly. 'I didn't come here to talk about Chad. Whether I love him or not is immaterial. Chad loves me, and he wants to marry me—which is more than I can say for you. All you want is to have sex with me. And kinky sex at that.'

'You call this kinky?'

'Yes. And so was that episode against the window. You've always been kinky, Gino. Making me go without panties and…and doing it to me anywhere and everywhere.'

'You loved it all.'

Oh, why had she brought those things up? Just thinking about them turned her on even more.

Impossible to stay still. Impossible to be patient any longer.

'You're moving,' he chided, taking a firm grip of her hips and forcing her to be still.

'I *want* to move. I'm *going* to move. There! See? I'm moving. And you can't stop me.'

Stop her? He didn't want to stop her. Not any longer. He'd wanted to make her wait, to torment her. But he was the one in agony.

His blood pounded in his temples as his body rushed past that point of no return. But she still trembled violently, with undeniable pleasure, crying out in ecstasy.

Damn her, he thought wildly as his own flesh followed. Damn her to hell!

CHAPTER FOURTEEN

JORDAN came back to consciousness in the four-poster bed, her last recollection being Gino carrying her back there, wrapped in a huge bathtowel. Nothing more. She must have fallen asleep as soon as her head hit the pillow.

The room wasn't dark, Gino having left the bedside lamps on, but he wasn't in the bed. She was alone under the satin sheets. The lights were still on in the sitting room, and she thought she heard a noise coming from there.

'Gino?' she called out as she levered herself up onto one elbow. 'Gino, where are you?'

He materialised in the connecting doorway, a red towel slung low round his hips, the five o'clock shadow on his face giving him a slightly menacing air.

Feeling suddenly vulnerable, Jordan clutched the sheet up over her bare breasts, her actions making his eyes narrow.

'How…how long have I been asleep?' she asked.

'Not long.'

He walked over and sat on the edge of the bed, then reached up to undo the knot on top of her head. Her hair tumbled down over her shoulders. Gino brushed it back with his hands.

'I've been waiting patiently for you to wake up,' he murmured, then bent forward to kiss her on her lips. Lightly at first, and then more hungrily.

As usual, his kisses sent her heartbeat racing and any qualms flying. When he pushed her back onto the pillows and threw the sheet right back off the bottom of the bed she made no attempt to stop him.

But when he reached for the bottle of lotion near the lamp her whole body stiffened.

'What's that for?' she demanded to know.

'Nothing to be alarmed about,' he returned smoothly. 'It says here on the label that this is a love lotion, designed to enhance every sexual activity. It claims aphrodisiacal qualities, an exotic scent and a delicious taste. And, no, before you ask. I didn't buy it. It was here when I arrived, compliments of the management.'

Jordan swallowed when he started unscrewing the lid.

'Don't look so worried.'

'I…I'm not sure I want you to use that stuff on me, Gino.'

He frowned at her. 'Why not?'

'I don't know.' But Jordan *did* know. She was afraid that she might enjoy it too much. That it would make her even more mindless than usual. That she might let him do things she would later regret.

* * *

The sudden fear and vulnerability in her eyes touched Gino's conscience. At the same time he refused to back off entirely. This was what she'd come here for, wasn't it?

'Why don't you use it on me, then?'

His suggestion sent her eyes rounding. But not with fear this time. With surprise.

He recalled that he'd always been the boss in the bedroom.

Clearly the idea intrigued her. In actuality, the idea intrigued him, too. He'd never been the passive partner in lovemaking before. Not ever. Who knew? Maybe he'd enjoy it.

'Here—take it,' he said, shoving the bottle into her hands before whisking the towel from his hips.

A downward glance had his eyebrows lifting. He hadn't realised till that moment that he was well on the way to being aroused again.

'I am yours to do with as you will,' he said, and he lay down beside her, his arms bending upwards so that his hands rested behind his head.

Oh, yes, he thought as he felt his flesh swell even further. He *was* going to enjoy this. Very much so.

Jordan sat up and stared down at Gino's aroused body, not quite sure where she was supposed to start.

In the past she'd reacted only at his command, and never for her own pleasure. The thought of having his entire body at her disposal, however, was sparking an alien feeling of power which was more exciting than she could ever have imagined.

'You won't stop me?' she said, her voice sounding oddly husky.

'I will keep my hands exactly where they are,' he promised.

'You don't look like you need any aphrodisiac lotion,' she told him. 'But you did say that it tasted good, didn't you?'

Jordan's heart started thudding madly in her chest as she knelt up beside him, then tipped the bottle gently sidewards, letting the creamy lotion drip onto him.

He gasped.

'Cold?' she asked cheekily.

'Something like that.'

'I think that's enough,' she said.

'I agree,' he muttered under his breath.

'Now, now—you're not to complain, but to enjoy,' she chided as she put the bottle down on the bedside table. 'This was your idea, remember?'

'Maybe I made a mistake.'

'Not by the look of you.'

He groaned when she bent and licked him with her tongue-tip.

They were right, Jordan thought, somewhat dazedly. It did taste good—somewhere between olives and apples.

Definitely an aphrodisiac as well: it made her want to make love to him with her mouth. All the way.

A wave of heat flushed her skin as she bent her head to him again. First she swirled her tongue around, several times, then she began to slowly take him into her mouth, holding him firmly at the same time with her lotion-slicked hand.

He groaned, and twisted his hips from side to side. But he didn't try to stop her.

Jordan set up a relentless rhythm with her mouth, shocking herself by how much she enjoyed hearing the tortured sounds he began making.

It wasn't till he called out her name that she gave him some respite.

'Is there something wrong, lover?' she asked, as she sat up and pushed her hair back from her flushed face.

'You're treading a fine line there,' he warned her, his breathing ragged. 'I suggest you move on.'

Jordan's eyebrows lifted, his last words bringing a sudden stab of resentment.

That's what I've been trying to do ever since you left me, Gino. Move on. Yet here I am, in bed with you again. And it's all such an appalling waste of time.

Jordan's thoughts infuriated her—mostly because she knew she was incapable of walking away right now. She was way too excited.

But perhaps he was right: she wanted him inside her again.

At the same time, she liked the tension she saw in his face. It pleased her to know she could make him suffer, even if it was only physically. She vowed to take her time with him, to make him wait.

'Have to go to the bathroom, lover,' she said. 'Won't be too long. Just lie back and relax.'

Relax!

Gino grimaced when she climbed off the bed and padded her way across the gold carpet.

How could he possibly relax?

He tried some deep, even breathing, his eyes clinging to the bathroom door, willing it to open, desperate for her to come back. But when the door finally opened, and she re-entered the bedroom, she didn't rejoin him on the bed. Instead, she slipped into her high heels and went back into the bathroom.

A minute later she was back, a glass of champagne in her hand, her walk slow and sexy as she undulated towards the bed. As his gaze raked over her Gino's desire to touch was so acute that his hands instinctively began to move.

'Hands behind your head,' she snapped.

Her imperious attitude stunned him, as did the way it turned him on. But even as the blood roared around his veins he longed for that moment when he could take control again—when he could once again show her who was the master here.

'I'm beginning to see that there is more pleasure in taking than receiving,' she purred, a truly wicked smile pulling at her lips.

Any secret hope on Gino's part that she might have come here tonight for reasons other than sex evaporated in the face of that smile.

He swore quietly when she climbed up onto the bed and straddled him, her high heels still on, the glass of champagne still in her hands. As he stared up at her his level of arousal shot past pleasure, entering the world of near pain.

'Just you wait,' he warned her darkly.

'Now, now. Just be a good boy and keep those hands of yours right where they are.'

His pulse-rate went wild as she remained kneeling above him, holding his stricken gaze as she repeatedly put her finger into the champagne and then into his mouth.

Finally she put the glass down, took him into her hands and pushed him up inside her, not letting him go till he'd been totally enveloped by her body.

Gino moaned at the heat and the moistness of her.

He did not expect her to lean down and kiss him at that stage. That was not what she was here for. But was it the tenderness of her kiss which changed his mind on that score? Or the way she murmured his name against his lips? Whatever—his heart seemed to flower open in his chest, bursting with feelings he'd been trying to suppress.

When he moaned under her mouth, she abruptly terminated the kiss.

'I suppose this is what you want?' she said sharply, and she straightened, her eyes turning wild as she began to move.

He wanted to tell her that, no, it was not what he wanted. But his tortured body had a mind of its own. He struggled to stop himself from coming, not wanting her to see him lose control.

'Total surrender, Gino,' she grated out as she slowed to a more sensual pace. 'That's the name of this game. I know. Because I've been there…done that. You took me there. You don't want to give in…you're afraid that somehow you'll never be the same. And you could be right. I've never been the same. You ruined me for any other man.'

He heard her words, and understood what she was saying. But if he'd ruined her for any other man then she'd ruined *him*. She'd always been there in the back of his mind. Always.

Maybe they didn't love each other any more, but they could—if they gave themselves a chance.

What he had to do was tell her the total truth. How he'd never forgotten her either. How he hadn't run into her by chance. He'd deliberately sought her out.

But no words came from his mouth at that moment. Only raw, naked sounds of desire.

He lasted till she climaxed. After that there was no contest, his back arching from the bed as their bodies shuddered as one.

At some stage he took his aching arms from behind his head. But by then exhaustion had set in. He wanted to hold her, talk to her, but it was a typical case of the spirit being willing but the flesh very weak. When she climbed off him a fog had already begun to descend over his mind. Soon Gino didn't think or feel anything.

Jordan collapsed back on the bed, not moving or speaking till she heard the sound of deep, even breathing. Only then did she steal a glance over at Gino, relieved to see that he was fast asleep.

She still didn't move for a long while, her eyes glistening as she worked out what she was going to do. At last she rose, quietly collecting her clothes from the sitting room and dressing out there. Afterwards she went to the elegant reproduction French writing desk in the corner, and used the gold pen and perfumed paper to write Gino a note.

That done, she carried the note into the bedroom, where she propped it up against a lamp.

After one last tearful glance at his sleeping face she picked up her shoes and returned to the other room, where she slipped them on, retrieved her purse, and left.

CHAPTER FIFTEEN

GINO woke to an awareness of light, and of being alone in the bed.

His head and shoulders shot up from the pillow, his eyes darting around the room.

'Jordan?' he called out. 'Where are you?'

No answer.

He jumped out of bed and dashed into the *en suite* bathroom.

Not there.

Not in the sitting room either.

The realisation that she'd gone made him feel sick. Then angry.

She could have waited till the morning—not slunk off like some thief in the night.

He was striding through the bedroom on his way to the toilet when he spotted the folded piece of paper leaning against the lamp base.

Hurrying over, he snatched it up and opened it.

Dear Gino,
I decided to leave this way as I didn't want one

*of those morning-after scenes. Tonight was great,
but there is no future for us. We're just ships
passing in the night, just as we were ten years
ago. Please do not come after me. You will be
wasting your time. I have plans for my future and
they do not include you. Go home to Melbourne
and marry that Italian girlfriend of yours. She is
Italian, isn't she? Of course she is.*

Ciao. Jordan.

Gino slumped down on the side of the bed.

Shattered did not begin to describe his feelings.
Though it was a good start.

He'd made a big mistake not telling Jordan the truth
last night. Hell, he could have at least confessed that
he'd broken up with Claudia.

But of course his emotions had been very mixed up
last night. So had his intentions. From the moment he'd
arrived at that dinner he'd lurched from one train of
thought to another.

But his head was clear now. Jordan's leaving him
like this had cleared it in a hurry.

He scanned the note again, trying to read between
the lines, trying to find some shred of hope that he still
had a chance with her.

He couldn't really find any.

Her saying they had no future together reminded him
of his deathbed promise to his father. Clearly Jordan
wanted marriage, and he simply could not offer her that.

Nothing in that note made him feel good. Nothing

except for the bit about his Italian girlfriend. That part sounded somewhat jealous.

Why be jealous if she didn't care?

Gino's heat skipped a beat, but he did not dare to hope too much.

Still, it was all he needed to spark some action. He could not go to back to Melbourne until he'd explored every avenue. If there was the slightest chance Jordan still cared for him, he was going to grab it.

He didn't know the time, but it had to be quite late in the morning, judging by his extremely bristly chin.

Time to get himself showered, shaved, dressed, and on Jordan's front doorstep.

By mid-morning Jordan was totally sick of herself. She'd been crying on and off since arriving home at some ungodly hour in the morning.

She hadn't slept. Hadn't eaten.

Perhaps if she rang Chad and got that dreadful job over and done with she might feel better.

It was about lunchtime in New York—not the middle of the night or anything.

Feeling simply appalling, Jordan steeled herself for one of the worst phone calls of her life.

When Chad didn't answer straight away, her first emotion was relief. When a woman answered, any relief was swiftly replaced by irritation.

'Can I help you?' the woman said, in a sing-song fashion.

'Could I speak to Chad, please?' Jordan said through gritted teeth.

'Chad, darling. It's for you.'

Chad darling finally came on the line.

'Hi there,' he said.

'Chad. It's Jordan.'

'Jordan…'

'Yes, your fiancée,' she bit out. 'Remember me?'

'Ahh.'

'What does that mean?'

'I was going to call you,' he said, in the most guilt-laden voice Jordan had ever heard. And she'd heard quite a few during her lawyering years.

'Who was that woman?' she snapped.

'That was Caroline.'

'Am I supposed to know who Caroline is?'

'I was engaged to her once. Before I came to Australia. We…we had this fight, you see, and I thought… Well, I thought she didn't love me any more…'

'But she does?'

'Yes.'

'And you still love her?'

'Yes, I do. I'm sorry, Jordan.'

Jordan didn't know what to say.

'Look,' Chad went on, 'even before Caroline and I got together again I'd begun to suspect that my proposing to you was a mistake. I mean, men like me…basically, we want a woman who makes being a wife and mother their career. You're a great girl, Jordan. And I really enjoyed our time together. But the truth is you're not what I want in a wife.'

Not what he wanted in a wife.

'You want an American wife?' she said, her voice as deflated as her spirit.

'Yes. That's the bottom line. I want an American wife.'

Like Gino wanted an Italian wife.

'I'm sorry, Jordan,' he added.

Jordan didn't want his apologies. She wanted nothing further to do with him. Ever, ever again.

'About the ring…' he continued.

'What about it?'

'I…er…would you mind sending it to me via international courier as soon as possible? Caroline and I are having an engagement party next weekend.'

Jordan blinked, then shook her head. Why was it that the actions of men would never truly cease to amaze her? 'Sure thing. No trouble. I'll do it first thing tomorrow morning.'

'You're upset with me.'

Gee, how intuitive of you!

'Actually, I'm not, Chad. I'm relieved.'

'Relieved?'

'Yeah. When and if I marry, it will be to a man who really loves me. Bye, Chad.'

She hung up before he could say another single word. Then she sank down onto a nearby chair and wept inconsolably. Not for Chad. But for the fact that no man had ever really loved her or wanted her to be his wife.

All men wanted from her was sex.

By noon she was still curled up in that chair, weeping silent but wretched tears. She was also heartily sick of herself.

'Enough,' she muttered, and headed for the bathroom, and her second shower of the day. The first one had been to rid her of the smell of sex. This one was to wash away her never-ending tears.

She stayed in the shower for ages, tipping her face up into the stream of hot water and letting it cascade down her body. Afterwards she towel-dried her hair, then drew on the pink chenille dressing gown she kept hanging on the back of her bathroom door.

At last she thought she might manage some toast and coffee, and padded her way into her sparkling white kitchen. She'd just turned on the electric kettle and popped two slices of bread in the toaster when her front door buzzer rang.

Jordan froze.

Even before she recovered to walk over and answer her security intercom, she knew who it would be.

'Who is it?' she choked out.

'It's me. Gino.'

Dismay swept in, making her heart sink. 'How did you know where I live?' she demanded to know—before the penny dropped. 'Oh, yes. I forgot. You had me investigated.'

'Let me in, Jordan.'

'I might as well. Because you're not going away, are you?'

'No.'

She pressed the button which would release the lock in the door downstairs, sighing as she turned away and went back to where the kettle had boiled and her toast had popped up.

With a sense of weary resignation, she threw the toast away, then got another mug down from the cupboard.

She thought about brushing her hair, or putting on some other clothes, but decided not to bother. Let him see her at her worst, with puffy, red-rimmed eyes and not a scrap of make-up on. Then he might take one look and go away.

The knock on her apartment door was loud and firm.

Jordan resashed her robe, then went to answer it.

By the time her hand reached the doorknob, however, there were knots gathering in her stomach. What did he want of her now?

If he'd come for more sex then he was going to be disappointed. He couldn't force her into anything—not now that she and Chad were history.

She breathed deeply several times, then wrenched open the door, adopting a stony mask as her eyes swept over him.

He looked great, she conceded. His eyes clear, his grooming impeccable, his clothing designed to seduce. There again, he'd always looked sinfully sexy in biker gear. There was something about Gino in tight black jeans and a black leather jacket which would turn any girl's head.

But she was no longer a girl, she reminded herself sternly. She was an adult woman, with a mind of her own.

Time to use it.

'What is it that you want, Gino?' she said sharply. 'I thought my note said it all.'

His eyes searched hers. 'You've been crying,' he returned, with a disarming degree of concern in his face. 'Why?'

'Females cry a lot,' she snapped. 'For all sorts of reasons.'

'You never did when we lived together.'

'I was happy then.'

'And you aren't now?'

The door to a nearby apartment opening made Jordan wince.

'You'd better come inside,' she said quickly, not wanting any of her neighbours to overhear their conversation.

Gino didn't waste any time taking up her offer, she noted, pushing past her into the apartment with his usual confident stride.

Fighting off a sense of doom, Jordan closed the door, then followed him into the open-plan living area.

Gino was impressed with the size and quality of her apartment, but taken aback by the décor. It was so stark! Other than the polished wooden floors, everything was black and white. With no splashes of colour, no photos or pictures on the all-white walls. No knick-knacks on any of the black-lacquered side-tables.

The lounge furniture was black leather and hard-looking, with no big squashy cushions to provide any sense of warmth or comfort. The one rug on the floor was not fluffy and soft underfoot, but serviceable and hard, with a geometric pattern in black and white.

The place was soulless, and cold.

Was that how Jordan thought of herself these days? Was that why she was so unhappy?

Gino was determined to find out. Determined to tell her the truth at last as well.

'Would you like some coffee?' she asked, in a stiffly polite voice. 'I was just about to make some when you showed up.'

He turned round to see that she'd kept her distance, her hands clutching the lapels of her pink dressing gown in a vulnerable gesture which made him feel guilty. So did the evidence of her weeping.

He'd done that to her. Made her afraid. Made her sad.

'Yes, please,' he replied. 'I take it—'

'Black and strong with three sugars,' she finished for him.

His heart turned over. 'You remembered.'

Her eyes suddenly shimmered. 'How could I forget?' she retorted. 'You practically lived on the damned stuff.'

'I'm Italian. We love our coffee.'

'Don't remind me.'

Gino frowned. 'That I love coffee?'

'That you're Italian!' she snapped, then stormed off into the kitchen, which was visible from the living room. Gino wandered over to sit up at the white break-fast bar, shaking his head when he saw that absolutely everything in the kitchen was white, and very shiny.

'And what does *that* mean?' she said sharply, without turning round from her coffee-making.

'What does what mean?'

'The way you're shaking your head. I can see your reflection in the mirrored splashback.'

Gino didn't doubt it. 'I was wondering why the obsession with white?'

She spun round. Not a good idea when one was holding two full mugs of steaming hot black coffee. But she managed not to spill any.

'White's a very practical colour. Everything goes with it.'

'Everything so long as it's black?'

'Chad loved my place.'

'That says a lot for the man,' Gino shot back, before he suddenly realised something. 'You just said *loved*. Not loves. Would you like to tell me what *that* means?'

Jordan smothered a groan. Trust him to pick up on that. She hadn't meant to tell Gino about Chad. Not unless he'd tried to blackmail her again. But the cat was out of the bag now, so there was no point in trying to lie.

She'd never been a good liar, anyway.

'I rang to break it off with Chad this morning,' she confessed with creditable calm. 'But he got in first.'

'He broke off your engagement?'

'Yes. He discovered that he wanted an American wife after all. Name of Caroline. I gather he spent last night with her.'

'And that's why you've been crying?'

'What do *you* think?'

'I think you're better off not marrying someone who doesn't love you.'

She slanted Gino a reproachful glance as she made her way from the kitchen with the coffee. 'Spoken by an expert on the subject.' She put the mugs down onto the coffee table, then returned to the kitchen for some chocolate biscuits.

'If you were *my* fiancée,' he said, 'I would never look at another woman, let alone sleep with one.'

His words evoked instant fury in Jordan. 'Well, that's not ever likely to happen, is it? My being your fiancée. Look, you had your chance to marry me ten years ago, Gino, and you didn't. You left me and never gave me a second thought till you just happened to run into me again.'

'That's not true,' he denied heatedly. 'Not a day went by when I didn't think of you. Why do you think I never got married? I'll tell you why. Because if I couldn't have you as my wife, I didn't want anyone. That's the bitter truth of it. As for my not coming back for you—I stayed away for ten years because I knew I could never offer you what you deserved. And you're wrong about my running into you by accident last Friday night. That was no bloody accident.'

Jordan just stared at him, her mind spinning at his impassioned declarations. His eyes blazed as they held hers, his hands balled into fists on the counter-top.

'I'd avoided coming to Sydney on business all this time—always delegating and sending someone else when necessary. I knew to keep away from the place. Knew I wouldn't be able to handle being near you. But ten years had gone by. I'd been dating this girl for a while, and my family were pressuring me to marry her. I was getting older, and it seemed ridiculously romantic to let the memory of an affair stop me from marrying and having children of my own. I knew I didn't love

Claudia, but I told myself that Italian marriages weren't always a matter of love, but of caring and compatibility. I convinced myself that it would work.'

Jordan was amazed at how much his thoughts and feelings had echoed her own. It had killed her, that trip she'd made to Italy, thinking he was somewhere close but still out of reach.

His eyes begged for understanding as he went on. 'I knew I couldn't do it till I'd made one last trip to Sydney. To see how being in your city would affect me. There's this derelict building site in the middle of Sydney's CBD that Dad bought just before he died, and I hadn't done anything with it. I told my mother that now the time was right to build on it. But really it was just an excuse to come up here and see how I felt. The moment I flew into Mascot that Friday the memories just swamped me, and I knew I couldn't leave without at least finding out what had happened to you. I thought you'd probably be married, a beautiful girl like you. So I was astounded when the PI I hired reported you were a lawyer, and single. More than astounded when I was told where you worked. Hell, I'd been there that very afternoon!

'That near-miss almost sent me crazy. I knew then that I had to see you for myself. So I had you followed when you left work that night. Which was how I came to be down in that bar. It wasn't a coincidence, Jordan. It was all my doing.'

Jordan didn't know what to think. Or feel. He had to be telling her the truth. And yet…

'Why didn't you tell me any of this last Friday night?'

'I wish I had. But I wasn't sure how you felt about me. Or where you were at in your life. I told myself I just wanted to see you again and make sure you were happy. But then we danced and I...I lost my head over you—as usual. Of course there was that little added problem of my having deceived you ten years ago. I suspected—rightly so—that you weren't going to be too thrilled with that. And once you were in my arms I didn't want to take the risk of your rejecting me. Which you did, Jordan. As soon as you found out. You rejected me, then stormed off and accepted another man's proposal of marriage.'

'You could have told me all this at dinner last night!' she pointed out, determined not to take everything he said at face value. She'd learned from her years of being a lawyer that people twisted the truth to their own selfish ends all the time.

'After I found out you were engaged to another man?' he countered. 'Come on, Jordan, be reasonable! I have my pride.'

'And I have mine!'

'For pity's sake, can't we get beyond this ridiculous repartee? I've come here to talk to you. To make you see the truth.'

'The truth is not necessarily the same for different people.'

'Spoken like a lawyer.'

'A lawyer who's sick and tired of being taken for a ride. Your actions speak louder than your words, Gino.'

'My actions brought me here today. I could have flown back to Melbourne this morning and not given you a second thought—as you've just said. But I didn't. I came here to talk to you. The least you can do is give me a hearing.'

'If I must.'

'I'm not leaving till I've said everything that has to be said.'

'In that case, come and have your blasted coffee whilst it's still hot.'

Gino's mouth thinned with frustration as he slid off the stool and walked over to scoop up the mugs from the coffee table.

'What on earth are you doing?' she asked, as she followed him with the plate of biscuits.

'Taking these out onto your balcony. This place gives me the shivers.'

'Huh. You have no sense of style. This is the latest thing in minimalism.'

'How New York! But you're Australian, Jordan. You live in a land of colour and contrasts—of blues, greens, reds and browns. How can you bear to live in this colourless place? At least from your balcony we can see the sparkling blue water and feel the warmth of the sun.'

'How dare you come here and criticise my home!'

'I dare because I care.'

'Since when?' she snapped.

'Since the first moment I saw you. Now, stop arguing with me, woman, and make yourself useful. I can't open that sliding glass door with both my hands full, you know.'

She obeyed blankly, he noted, her face in shock.

For Gino's part, he felt more hopeful than he had since he'd awoken that morning and read that ghastly note. A smile pulled at his mouth as he stepped out through the open doorway.

The balcony was a distinct improvement on the inside, facing east and having privacy walls at each end. Her outdoor furniture wasn't too bad, either, made of a rich red wood. She even had a couple of potted palms in the corners.

The day was pleasantly warm and not too windy, despite it being August. Lots of boats were out on the harbour. Water-lovers always came out in their droves on days like this.

'This is much better,' Gino said, as he put the mugs down on the table and then settled in one of the seats.

His comment seemed to snap her out of her bemused state, and her blue eyes turned cold on him again.

'We'll have to talk quietly,' she said waspishly as she sat down. 'I don't want the neighbours hearing us argue.'

'I have no intention of arguing any more. Have you?'

'Absolutely not!'

'Good. But perhaps we should enjoy our coffee first. Then, if things get a bit heated, we can go back inside.'

Jordan sipped her coffee in silence, whilst Gino gulped his down, then wolfed several of the biscuits. Her appetite had once again disappeared, her emotions in total disarray.

But she was determined not to fall victim to Gino's empty charms. Or to his sudden declaration of caring.

If he cared, then let him show it. And not just in the bedroom.

'I have a proposition to put to you,' he said at last.

'I'm sure you have.'

'No, not that kind of proposition.'

'Then what kind?'

'I want you to come to Melbourne with me when I go back. I want you to stay with me, at my place.'

Jordan just gaped at him.

'I know you don't believe I really care for you. You've said more than once that all I want from you is sex. I want to prove to you that that's not so. You'll have your own bedroom during your visit. There will be no sex. Just a getting-to-know-each-other-again process. Then we'll find out if what we feel for each other is love, or just lust.'

'And if it is love?' Jordan choked out. 'What then? You still won't marry me.'

Gino pulled a face. 'We'll cross that bridge when we come to it.'

'I…I don't know, Gino.' She'd promised herself not to give in to what he wanted this time. Promised herself to stay strong.

But what if he did love her as she loved him?

Jordan swallowed, a lump coming into her throat with her finally admitting what she'd been trying to ignore all her life. She did still love Gino. She always had and always would.

Impossible now to walk away. She wasn't that strong.

'All right,' she said quietly, despite being gripped

by the fear of having her heart broken even worse this time.

The delight in his face soothed that fear somewhat. 'You mean it? You'll come home with me today?'

'Not today, Gino. I have to go to work tomorrow and sort things out. I have clients, and cases.' And a ring which had to be sent back to Chad.

'Why don't you resign? Good lawyers like you are needed everywhere. You could get a job in Melbourne as easily as Sydney.'

'But I might not be staying in Melbourne,' she pointed out. 'Things might not work out between us.'

'They will.'

She shook her head, not having his confidence. 'Look, I was going to resign anyway,' she admitted. 'Then go overseas for a while. I feel tired, Gino, very tired.'

'Yes, I can see that,' he said.

His gentle tone touched her. As did his soft eyes. 'I…I'm not going to promise anything.'

'You don't have to.'

'If you try to seduce me I'll leave immediately.'

'I won't.'

'A week,' she said at last. 'I'll give you a week.'

'That's not very long.'

'Take it or leave it.'

'I'll take it.'

CHAPTER SIXTEEN

'So what's up?' Kerry said, as soon as Jordan came out of Frank's office on Monday morning. 'You don't look too happy.'

Jordan had mulled over what she would tell Kerry all night, finally deciding that her friend deserved the truth—or at least an edited version of it.

'Could you get away for a cup of coffee?' she asked her.

Kerry frowned. 'That bad, is it?'

'Not bad. Life-changing.'

Kerry's finely plucked eyebrows arched upwards. 'Life-changing? In what way?'

Jordan scooped in a deep breath, then let it out slowly. 'I've just handed in my resignation.'

'What?' Kerry leapt out of her chair. 'Oh, my goodness, Jordan, *why?*'

'I can't tell you the full reason here.'

'What reason did you give Frank?'

'That Chad had broken our engagement over the weekend and I needed to get away for a while.'

'He didn't!'

'Yes, actually, he did. But if he hadn't I would have. I finally realised that I just didn't love him enough to marry him.'

Kerry grimaced. 'It isn't because of that Italian guy again, is it?'

Jordan didn't know whether to laugh or cry.

Overnight, she'd done her best to feel positive about the possibility of a future with Gino, but deep in her heart she knew things wouldn't work out. He was never going to marry her, and she'd never just live with a man; she was old-fashioned that way.

At the same time, she couldn't see herself marrying any other man—so why not grab what happiness she could whilst it lasted?

'I don't want to say any more till we're away from prying ears and eyes.'

'Okay. I'll just go tell Frank that I'll be away from my desk for a while. I'll say you're upset and I'm taking you downstairs for a cuppa.'

'Good idea,' Jordan said, thinking that wasn't too far from the truth. Handing in her resignation had been one of the hardest things she'd ever done.

Still, Frank had been very understanding, promising to arrange for another lawyer to take over her case-load, which thankfully was minimal at the moment. She'd spent the last few weeks on the Johnson case.

Several minutes later she was sitting over a cappuccino in the café downstairs, with Kerry impatiently waiting for her to elaborate.

'Before you jump to conclusions,' Jordan began. 'I

didn't decide not to marry Chad because of a memory. I ran into my Italian again.'

'You ran into him? Where?'

Jordan had already decided not to mention anything about their original meeting in the Rendezvous Bar.

'At the new client dinner last Saturday night. You seated me right next to him.'

Kerry gaped at her. 'Are you saying Gino Bortelli is your Italian?'

'Yes.'

'Oh, my goodness… But…but he's not a labourer. He's rich and successful! From what I've heard his family's loaded.'

Jordan sighed, then explained what had happened all those years ago.

'I see,' Kerry bit out, not looking too impressed. 'Now I know why you acted so oddly last Saturday night.' Her eyes suddenly widened, as they did when realisation struck. 'You spent the night with him, didn't you?'

'Yes,' Jordan admitted.

'Sunday too, I'll warrant.'

'No. We just talked on Sunday. That's when he asked me to go to Melbourne, and I said I would.'

'Oh, Jordan, don't be such a fool. He used you all those years ago and he'll use you again. Men like him, they change their girlfriends as often as their cars.'

'You're not telling me anything I don't already know, Kerry. But I *have* to do this. I don't have a choice.'

'You love him that much?'

She nodded, tears pricking at her eyes.

Kerry sighed. 'If you ever want to come back, Frank would rehire you in a flash. You know that, don't you? He thinks you're great. We all do.'

'Thank you for saying that. But I won't be back. If things don't work out with Gino I'm going overseas for a while. I might get a job in London. My dad was born in England, so I'm allowed.'

'This is goodbye, then?

Jordan hesitated. She'd never been the kind of girl who kept in touch with old friends. When she moved on, she moved on.

After her original affair with Gino, and then her mother's death, she'd become a loner, through and through.

'I'll keep in touch,' she heard herself say. 'I promise.'

CHAPTER SEVENTEEN

THE moment he saw her walking through the arrivals gate Gino wanted to rush over and throw his arms around her.

Instead, he just waved, smiled, and walked slowly towards her.

She didn't smile back, her eyes coolish as they flicked over him.

'Hi, there,' he said, whilst privately wondering if she was having second thoughts.

'Hi,' she returned.

'Had a good flight?'

'So-so.'

Gino did his best to ignore her less than joyous attitude. But it wasn't easy.

'I have a car waiting outside,' he said. 'Let's go get your luggage. Do you have much?'

'Just one case. I hope I've brought enough warm things. I nearly died when the pilot said the outside temperature here was twelve degrees.'

His eyes travelled over her black trouser suit,

which looked a bit on the thin side. Okay for an office, but not up to Melbourne on a rainy winter's day. 'It is still pretty cold down here, and wet. But my place is temperature-controlled.'

He made small talk with her whilst they waited next to the carousel, asking how her resignation had gone and if there'd been any trouble.

None, apparently.

But her body language remained tense, and negative.

Hopefully, she'd relax once she saw that he'd meant what he'd said about there being no sex this week, just companionship.

Gino had worried that it would be almost impossible for him to keep his hands off her. But nothing was too great a sacrifice, he realised as he stood beside her, if it meant convincing Jordan he was sincere.

'That's mine,' she said, pointing to a medium-sized black bag.

He swept it up with ease, smiling at her as they began to walk towards the exit. 'You do travel light.'

Still she didn't smile, her lovely face taut, her eyes not happy. 'I don't own a lot of clothes.'

'We'll go buy you some nice new things tomorrow. Melbourne is, after all, the fashion capital of Australia.'

'First you criticise my apartment,' she snapped. 'Now my clothes.'

'There's nothing wrong with your clothes,' he lied. 'But black is definitely not your colour.'

'I don't want you to buy me any clothes,' she said firmly.

'Fine. I just thought you might enjoy it. Most women

enjoy clothes-shopping—especially when someone else is paying.'

Jordan ground to a halt, her blue eyes flashing at him. 'I am not most women. And I am not your mistress. *Yet.* If and when I agree to such a role in your life, *then* you can tart me up for your pleasure. Till then, you will take me as I am.'

His black eyes flashed back at her. 'I thought I wasn't supposed to take you at all.'

Colour zoomed into her cheeks. 'You know what I mean.'

'I can't say that I do. When I offered to take you clothes-shopping my intention was not to dress you up for my pleasure but to remind you that you are a beautiful woman who looks her best in feminine clothes. You seem to have forgotten that somewhere along the way.'

'I did tell you that I'd changed.'

'Not for the better, it seems.'

'I didn't come all this way to argue with you.'

'No kidding. You were ready for a fight the moment you got off that plane.'

His accusation took Jordan aback. But she quickly realised he was right. Her mental boxing gloves had come up the moment she set eyes on him, looking superb in a sleek grey business suit, with matching overcoat and a scarf slung elegantly around his neck. Suddenly she'd felt dowdy and out of her depth. She'd been more comfortable with the Gino of ten years ago, the one who'd worn jeans and T-shirts and spoken with an Italian accent.

The Gino of today was too slick for her, and too clever by half. He could even out-argue her, which was not an easy thing to do.

'I should not have come,' she said wretchedly.

'Don't be ridiculous. You'll be fine once I get you home and get a couple of glasses of wine into you. I'll even cook you dinner like I used to. Would you like that?'

She blinked, then stared at him. 'You still cook?'

'Not all that often these days. But I will, for you.'

Gino wanted to whoop for joy when she finally smiled.

'Could I pick the meal?'

'Only if you promise to let me take you clothes-shopping tomorrow.'

Her head tipped charmingly to one side, her blue eyes dancing at him. 'The Gino of ten years ago was not as good a negotiator as you.'

'I didn't need to be. Though you took a good bit of persuading at times. You've always had a stubborn streak, Jordan.'

'And you've always had an inflated ego.'

'Good God—she's doing it again. I refuse to talk to you any more, woman,' he said, picking up the suitcase with his right hand and clasping her arm with his left. 'There will be total silence from this moment, till I get you safely in my car and on the way home.'

'You don't need to impress me, Gino,' were her first words after that. He'd just helped into the back of a white limousine.

'There's every need,' he replied. 'I want you to know that you won't lose financially by not marrying Stedley.'

Jordan gave him a startled glance. 'It might have escaped your attention, but I make a very good living as a lawyer. There is no mortgage on my apartment. And I have a very nice car in my garage.'

'But a pathetic wardrobe.'

'Now who's trying to pick a fight?'

Gino grinned. 'I just had to get that in again.'

'What makes you such an expert in female fashion, anyway?'

'I have six sisters.'

'Six!'

'Yep: two older and four younger. They're all clothes-mad. So is my mother. Mum always dragged me along on when she went shopping. Dad refused to go, and she wanted a male opinion she could trust.'

'Why didn't you tell me about your big family all those years ago?' Jordan asked him. 'Why did you let me think your were an only child?'

Gino knew he had to make her understand why he'd lied to her. But it wasn't going to be easy.

'Do you have any idea what it's like being the only son in an Italian household?'

'Not really.'

'I was my father's son and heir—the one who would take over the business when he retired or died. As far back as I remember, my father lectured me on my duty and my responsibility towards the family. If anything happened to him, I was to be the provider and the protector. There was no question about my doing anything else with my life except becoming an engineer, like him. At the same time I was encouraged to hold strong to my Italian roots and culture. That was why I was sent back to the university in Rome. I stayed with an aunt and uncle there till I graduated, living and breathing the Italian way of life. My aunt continually introduced me to Italian girls of suitable marriage age. I'm sure she thought they were all sweet little virgins. But they weren't. Not a single one.'

'I see,' Jordan said, looking thoughtful.

'Don't get me wrong. They were all very nice, very attractive girls. But I didn't fall in love with any of them. I certainly didn't want to marry any of them, although I could have had my pick. By the time I finished my four-year stint over there I was very homesick for Australia, and totally fed up with all things Italian. I might have been born in Rome, but I'd moved to Australia when I was one. Australia was my country and my home. I was also sick of always being introduced as Giovanni Bortelli's son. I never knew if people liked me for myself, or because of my father. When I finally came home, and my father wanted me to go straight into the business with him, I rebelled. I'd had enough, I told him. I needed some space—needed to be free for a while from the pressure of being his son. He reluctantly agreed to give me a year to do just that. Probably because he could see if he didn't I would just take off and never come back. I refused to tell him where I was going, but I did finally tell my mother. Not where I was living, but where I was working. That's how she knew where to contact me when Dad became ill.'

Gino picked up Jordan's hand within both of his. 'I

didn't *mean* to hurt you,' he said sincerely. 'But I know I did. I was just an overgrown boy, Jordan, masquerading as a man. I was selfish and totally self-centred. I like to think I'm a real man now, capable of compassion and caring for others. I won't hurt you again. I promise.'

Jordan wanted to believe him. She *did* believe him, actually. Or she believed his good intentions. But he would hurt her again. History was bound to repeat itself, as it always did.

His Italian family was still a huge obstacle to their finding happiness together, as was that deathbed promise to his father. Gino was never going to go against that promise and marry her.

But none of that seemed to matter when Gino was holding her hand and looking deep into her eyes, the way he was doing right at that moment.

'It's all right, Gino,' she said softly. 'I understand what happened ten years ago. And I forgive you.'

'You've no idea what it means to me to hear you say that.'

'Does your mother know about me?'

'No.'

'Are you going to tell her?'

'Yes.'

'When?'

'Today, if you want me to.'

'No. No, I don't want you to do that. Not yet.'

She turned her head to gaze through the passenger window.

It had begun to rain outside—a soft, gentle drizzle.

'I've never been to Melbourne before,' she said at last.

'You'll like it.'

She turned back to face him. 'How can you be sure?'

He smiled. 'Because I live here.'

She had to laugh. 'You're an arrogant devil.'

'Confident. Not arrogant.'

'What's in a word?'

'You're a lawyer. You should know there's a lot of difference between confident and arrogant.'

'How would you describe me?'

'How many words can I use?'

'As many as you need. What did you think of me the first night we met.'

'Mmm. My first impression was that you were beautiful.'

'Gee, don't get too deep on me.'

Gino grinned. 'The male perspective on first meeting a female is inevitably shallow. It's a hormonal thing. But by the end of the night I knew you were also intelligent, hard-working and kind.'

'Flatterer.'

'I haven't finished. After I moved in with you I swiftly discovered you possessed a unique combination of qualities. Sweetly innocent, yet capable of great sensuality. Strong-willed and stubborn on occasion, but mostly soft and giving. What impressed me the most, however, was your loyalty. I always knew that your love was mine. I never worried that you would ever look at any other man. Not while you were with me.'

His last compliment choked her up. In truth there'd never been another man for her, even after he'd left her.

Which was why she was here, sacrificing everything just to be with him.

'And now, Gino? What am I now?'

'You're still you, Jordan,' he said gently. 'Underneath.'

'Underneath what?'

'Underneath the rather formidable façade you've developed over the years. You're still a compassionate, caring woman, Jordan. I could hear that in your voice when you told me about the Johnson case. But being a lawyer has also made you cynical.'

'It's impossible not to become a cynical. The things I've seen, Gino, and heard. People are rotten.'

'No. *Some* people are rotten, Jordan. Lots of people are good. Don't let the minority colour your view of life. I know that that insurance company did the wrong thing by your father. But revenge, whilst temporarily satisfying, can prove to be self-destructive in the long run. Frankly, I think it's high time for you to give the law a break.'

'That's what I'm doing, isn't it?'

'I meant for longer than a week.'

Jordan knew what he meant. He wanted her to stay with him, live with him. Become his *de facto* wife.

But Jordan wanted to be his *real* wife.

'Let's just take one day at a time, Gino.'

'Fine,' he said equably. 'I can do that.'

CHAPTER EIGHTEEN

'I love your place, Gino.'

Gino glanced up from his cooking with a wry smile on his face.

'You're just saying that.'

'No, no. I mean it.'

'You don't think it's too eclectic? And cluttered?'

'Not at all.'

Jordan could see now why he'd hated her apartment so much.

Gino's penthouse was as far removed from minimalist as one could get. Everywhere there was colour and warmth.

The walls were all painted a soft, creamy yellow, most of the floors were covered in a deep jade-green carpet, and the furniture was a mad mixture of modern and antique—which probably shouldn't have gone together but somehow did. There were cushions of every hue and fabric dotted about the living rooms, plus lots of ornaments, and more photos in frames than she'd ever seen.

The kitchen was huge, and mostly wooden, even the

benchtops. A rich wood—probably cedar. The splash-backs were beaten copper, the appliances stainless steel, the floor covered in multicoloured slate. Every imaginable kitchen utensil hung from copper pipes running overhead, put there because Gino said he hated hunting through drawers for things. There was a central island with a sink and a stove, on which Gino was currently cooking the most delicious Bolognese sauce Jordan had ever tasted. He'd cooked it for her every Saturday night during the time they'd lived together.

A secret recipe, he'd once claimed.

Its smell was enough to make anyone's tastebuds water.

'More wine?' Gino asked, putting down his wooden spoon and lifting the bottle of red which he'd opened earlier.

'I shouldn't,' she said, even as she held out her near empty glass.

'Why shouldn't you?'

'You know what I'm like when I drink.'

'That's all right,' he said as he refilled her glass. 'I won't let you have your wicked way with me.'

'You won't?'

'Absolutely not. I meant what I said, Jordan. I need to prove to you that there's more than just sex between us. Hopefully, by Friday, you'll be convinced.'

'Friday? That's not a week. That's only four days.'

He shrugged, then grinned. 'I figured four days was about my limit with you under my roof.'

By Thursday evening, Gino was definitely at his limit.

Not that they hadn't spent a wonderful few days

together. Gino had taken the week off work and spent every waking moment with Jordan. They'd gone shopping together, with Jordan giving in and letting him buy her some lovely feminine clothes. They'd lunched out, but had stayed in each evening, with Jordan very happy for him to cook for her. Afterwards, they'd watched television together, or just sat and talked.

Gino had talked more in the last few days than he had in years, holding back nothing in telling Jordan all about his life and his family.

What he hadn't done was make love to her.

Sleeping had become increasingly difficult each night. Not just because of sexual frustration, but because of the frustration associated with their future together. He wanted to ask Jordan to marry him. But how could he without being tormented? He wished to goodness he'd never made such a stupid promise to his father. But of course he hadn't been thinking clearly at the time.

Now he was trapped in a situation which seemed to have no solution. Not one which Jordan would feel happy with. She was at an age where she wanted marriage and motherhood.

To offer her a *de facto* relationship was a second-rate compromise.

At the same time there was no question of letting her go. Gino had done that once. He was not about to do it again.

He loved this woman. And he wanted her like crazy.

Maybe it was time to stop talking and show her how much.

* * *

'I hope this tastes as good as it smells,' Jordan said, as she carried a steaming dish into the dining room.

By Thursday, she'd decided it was her turn to cook.

Cooking was not her forte, but she'd become competent enough over the years, though her repertoire of recipes was limited. She'd sensibly stuck to a tried and true favourite of hers, a Thai-style stir-fry with *hokkien* noodles, and chosen a Margaret River white wine to go with it. She'd even set the dining table, though their other evening meals had been consumed very casually, either at the breakfast bar or in front of the television.

A search of the many kitchen cupboards had uncovered a wide array of place-mats, serviettes, glassware and crockery. She'd chosen yellow placemats and serviettes, plain crystal goblets, and white crockery with yellow flowers on it.

Gino didn't say a word as she put the serving dish onto the mat in the middle of the table—which was not like him at all. Come to think of it, he hadn't sat at the breakfast bar whilst she'd cooked, either, making the excuse that he'd wanted to watch the news on television.

Something wasn't right, Jordan realised with a rush of foreboding. Yet she couldn't think what: they'd been so happy together this week.

'You're very quiet tonight,' she said, as she sat down opposite him and flicked out her serviette.

'Mmm,' came his very uninformative reply, his face remaining pensive as he silently served himself some of the food.

Jordan took a sip of her wine before serving herself a smallish portion, her appetite having suddenly declined.

'What are you thinking about?' she asked, after she'd forced a few mouthfuls down.

Her question seemed to startle him. He frowned as he put his fork down and looked up.

'Us.'

'What about us?'

'I think we should leave this conversation till after we've eaten.'

'I don't agree.'

Gino's eyes hardened a little at her sharp tone. 'Very well. I was thinking how much I love you.'

Jordan's mouth dropped open. As a declaration of love went, this one had been delivered in a less than romantic fashion.

'It's not just lust,' he went on firmly. 'It's love. It's always been love.'

Jordan didn't know what to say. He'd simply dumb-founded her.

'What about you?' he demanded to know. 'How do you feel about me?'

She blinked, then licked her lips. 'I think you know how I feel about you, Gino.'

'I want to hear you say the words.'

'I love you,' she said, her heart turning over at finally giving voice to her feelings. 'I never stopped loving you.'

He groaned, then leapt to his feet, his black eyes instantly ablaze with desire. 'You can't possibly expect me to sit here calmly eating after you've just said that, can you?'

'No,' she choked out, the desire she'd been trying to control all week suddenly breaking free.

He strode round the table, yanked her chair back from the table and scooped her up into his arms.

'There's more I want to say,' he growled as he carried her towards the bedroom. 'More for us to decide. But not right at this moment. I need to make love to you, Jordan. Make love, not have sex. You want that too, don't you?'

'Yes,' she said, emotion flooding her heart. 'Oh, yes.'

Gino cuddled her close to him afterwards, stunned by the passion and the power of their mating. There'd been no foreplay. Nothing but a rapid stripping of their clothes and an immediate fusion of their impatient bodies. It had been all over in seconds, both of them crying out in release together.

'You must know that I *want* to marry you,' he said thickly, his lips buried in her hair. 'But I can't.'

'I know,' she said sadly.

'It isn't right,' he said with a groan. 'I want you to be my wife.'

Jordan heard the pain in his voice, and knew she had to do something.

She cupped his cheeks with her hands and lifted his head so that their eyes could meet.

'I will *be* your wife,' she said. 'In every way that counts. I will love you and look after you and have your children, if that's what you want.'

His eyes widened. 'You'd have my children? Even though I can't give them my name?'

'There's no reason why I can't take your name, Gino. That's a simple matter of changing it by deed poll. All we'll be missing is a piece of paper. Our love is stronger than that, surely?'

Jordan was shocked when his eyes started glistening. 'You are a truly wonderful woman.'

'An ordinary woman, in love with a truly wonderful man. We can make things work if we love each other enough, Gino.'

'Yes. Yes, you're right.'

Still he didn't look totally happy.

'I suppose you're worried about your mother,' Jordan said. 'And your six sisters. You're worried what they'll think.'

'They'll get used to the idea.'

Jordan suspected that Gino's family would look askance at their relationship for ever. It was not the Italian way to live together without the blessing of the church.

But that was just too bad.

'When are you going to tell them?' she asked.

'Tomorrow. After we've gone ring-shopping.'

'Ring-shopping?'

'Just because we won't have that piece of paper it doesn't mean we can't have proper rings.'

'Rings, as in plural?'

'Of course. An engagement ring and a wedding ring for you. And a wedding ring for me. I want everyone to know that I'm taken.'

Jordan struggled to hold back her tears. 'I'd like that.'

He smiled. 'I thought you might.'

CHAPTER NINETEEN

'HAPPY with those?' Gino asked as they emerged from the jeweller's into Collins Street.

'They're lovely,' Jordan replied, not able to take her eyes off her engagement ring. It was absolutely stunning, yet very simple. A single brilliant-cut diamond set in white gold, with two smaller baguette diamonds on the shoulder settings. The wedding band next to it was even simpler. Just a narrow white gold band.

Gino's ring, by contrast, was wider, and made in yellow gold, with small diamonds set at regular intervals around the whole circumference. It suited his more flamboyant style, she thought.

They were walking slowly back to where Gino had parked his car when his cellphone rang.

Jordan stood there in the watery sunshine, admiring her rings whilst Gino answered it.

'I did tell you I didn't like their scaffolding,' Gino muttered irritably at one stage. 'No. No, I need to see this for myself. I'll be there in about twenty minutes.

Problems at work,' he said to Jordan as he put the phone back into his trouser pocket. 'No point in trying to explain it. Look, I could be there for a couple of hours. I'll drop you off home first. What time is it now? Half-past twelve. I shouldn't be any later than three in getting back. Possibly four. You can catch up on your beauty sleep. You didn't get much last night,' he added, with a wicked gleam in his eye.

'You didn't, either.'

'I got more than I did the last few nights, I can tell you.'

'Are we still going to visit your mother tonight?'

'Absolutely. I'll ring her from work and line up something.'

Jordan felt her stomach tighten. 'Maybe she won't want to see me.'

'Don't cross your bridges till you come to them, Jordan.'

By three p.m., Jordan found herself clock-watching. Nerves over the evening ahead had meant she'd been incapable of settling to anything. And sleeping had been out of the question.

By four, her agitation was beyond bearing.

She didn't like to call Gino on his cellphone. He'd promised to be home as soon as he could. But he'd left the number with her, and it seemed silly to stew when a simple call would soothe her mind.

Picking up Gino's home phone, she punched in his number and waited for him to answer.

His phone rang a few times, then switched to his voicemail, which said that he couldn't come to the phone right now, but to leave a message and he'd get back as soon as he could.

Jordan hesitated, then hung up, thinking that he was probably driving home at this very moment.

Ten minutes later she wished she'd left a message. Gino still wasn't home. She was just about to call his number again when the phone rang. With a rush of relief, she hurried over and swept up the receiver.

'Gino?' she said.

'Is that Jordan?' a female voice asked—a voice with a distinct Italian accent.

'Er…yes.'

'This is Maria Bortelli. Gino's mother.'

'Oh…' Jordan didn't know what to say. Had Gino dropped in to see his mother before coming home? If so, then why wasn't it Gino on the phone?

She didn't like the sound of this.

'I knew Gino would want me to ring you. He called me and told me about you.'

'I see,' Jordan said. 'You're…not upset with me, are you?' Certainly she sounded upset.

'Upset with you? No, no. Not with you. Or Gino. That is not why I am calling. There has been an accident, Jordan. At one of Gino's building sites.'

Jordan's heart jumped into her mouth.

'What kind of accident? Dear God, please tell me Gino's alive. Tell me he's all right.'

'He has had a nasty fall. Some scaffolding gave way under him. The doctors are doing tests on him right now. His hard hat was knocked off in the fall.'

'Is he conscious?'

'No.'

A tortured cry escaped Jordan's lips. If Gino died, what would she do? He was her life now, her reason for living.

'You should come,' Mrs Bortelli said. 'Gino would want you to be here. With him.'

'Yes, yes,' Jordan said, her heart thudding wildly in her chest. 'I'll catch a taxi. Just tell me where to go.'

The ride to the hospital felt endless, the roads choked with Friday afternoon traffic. The taxi dropped her off at the entrance, and Jordan rushed through the glass doors, her eyes already searching for the lifts. Mrs Bortelli had told her what floor to go to, and what ward.

Finally she spotted the lifts, over in a far corner of the foyer.

As she hurried over, Jordan could not help noticing a woman standing by the lift doors, staring at her. She was in her late fifties, perhaps, an elegantly dressed lady, with wavy dark brown hair and even darker eyes.

'Jordan?' she said.

'Yes?'

'I am Maria Bortelli.' Her dark eyes swept over her, her warm smile coming as a surprise. 'You are as beautiful as Gino said.'

Jordan was so taken aback she didn't know what to say.

'Come,' Mrs Bortelli went on, and took Jordan's arm. 'They have taken Gino up for surgery, so he is now on a different floor to the one I told you.'

'Surgery! What kind of surgery?'

'Brain surgery. There is some bleeding which has to be stopped.'

When Jordan swayed, Mrs Bortelli held her steady.

'*Si, si*—I know how you feel,' she said gently. 'I felt the same way when they first told me. But I keep telling myself not to worry. My Gino is strong, and he is in good hands. I have been down here in the hospital chapel, praying for him.'

Jordan had never been a big one for prayer. She'd always believed that God helped those who helped themselves. But she suspected she was about to get acquainted with the practice.

'Did my son buy you those rings?' Mrs Bortelli asked during the ride up in the lift.

Jordan lifted her hand to stare blankly down at her engagement and wedding rings.

'Yes,' she choked out. 'This morning.'

How happy they had been! And now...

'Gino told me about the promise he made to his papa.'

'He did?'

'It was foolish of him.'

'He knows that now. But he won't dishonour it.'

Mrs Bortelli shook her head. 'He is a good son. But it is not right to expect you not to have a real marriage. Still, we will just have to make the best of it. He loves you, and refuses to marry any other girl.'

The lift doors opened and the two women stepped out into the wide corridor, with its familiar hospital smell of polish and disinfectant.

'You don't mind that I'm not an Italian girl?' Jordan said.

'Why should I mind?'

'Gino's father obviously minded.'

'Giovanni was much older than me, and old-fashioned. Ours was an arranged marriage, not a love-match. I promised myself that my children would only ever marry for love. That is one promise *I* will never dishonour. Love is far more important than a piece of paper.'

'I'm so glad you feel that way.'

When his mother smiled, Jordan could see where Gino got his looks and his charm.

'You and Gino will make beautiful children together.'

'If we get the chance,' Jordan said, her emotions suddenly catching up with her again. 'Oh, Mrs Bortelli,' she cried, tears flooding her eyes, then spilling over down her cheeks. 'I love him so much.'

'I can see that, my dear. Come,' she said, and linked arms with Jordan. 'He won't be out of surgery for some time. We will go back down to the hospital chapel and pray some more.'

Gino knew he was dreaming. It had to be a dream. Because he and Jordan had just been married, in an old church he did not recognise. Jordan looked like an angel dressed in white, a beautiful Botticelli angel. She beamed up at him as they walked arm in arm back down the aisle out into bright sunshine.

Not Melbourne, he realised as his eyes looked down the ancient stone steps upon a city which he recognised.

They were in Rome.

That was it, Gino realised in his dream. That was the way. Why hadn't he thought of it before?

He struggled to wake up. But he couldn't seem to shrug off the blanket of sleep which was imprisoning his body. Why couldn't he wake up? he thought frustratedly. What was wrong with him?

The nurse in Recovery assigned to Gino was watching him carefully.

'You shouldn't be waking up yet,' she said, when his eyelids started fluttering wildly.

When he began muttering, and trying to lift his head, she put gentle but firm hands on his shoulders.

'Lie still,' she whispered. 'Everything went fine in the operation. But you must rest some more.'

His eyelids shot open, frightening the life out of her.

'Jordan,' he choked out.

'You want me to tell Jordan you are all right?'

He shook his head from side to side.

'Tell her. Tell her there is a way,' he said, then promptly fell back to sleep again.

And rightly so. He shouldn't be coming round for quite a while yet.

Just then Dr Shelton strode in, and the nurse was relieved that his patient was no longer thrashing about. As the doctor checked his patient's vital signs, the nurse explained what had happened.

Dr Shelton frowned.

'Amazing,' he said. 'He shouldn't be coming round for at least another half-hour or so. Jordan, did you say?'

'Yes.'

'Man or woman?'

'He didn't say. But my guess is a woman.'

The doctor's smile was wry. 'That would be my guess, too.'

Jordan sat in the waiting room, surrounded by the other women in Gino's life. His six sisters had descended at various intervals during the last couple of hours, all very anxious about their beloved brother.

Jordan had been touched by their love and concern, and totally overwhelmed by their warm acceptance of her. None of Gino's sisters made her feel like an interloper, or resented her not being of Italian heritage. They'd been a little surprised, but also fascinated, when she'd told them about her affair with Gino all those years ago. His youngest sister, Sophia, had thought it the most romantic story she'd ever heard. They'd all echoed their mother's opinion that it had been very foolish of Gino to make that promise to his father.

But they all knew that their brother would not break his promise.

Telling them her story had distracted everyone from the seriousness of the moment. But now the story had been told, and they'd all suddenly fallen silent.

As if on cue, a doctor dressed in surgical greens entered the room. He was a tall, slim man, in his late forties, perhaps, with a long face, a receding hairline and intelligent blue eyes.

Mrs Bortelli immediately jumped up and rushed over him.

'Is my son going to be all right, Doctor?' she asked.

He took both her hands in his, smiling as he patted them.

'He's going to be fine,' he said, to a collective sigh of relief from the sisters.

Jordan, however, just closed her eyes and thanked God for answering her prayers.

'We stopped the bleeding and flushed out the old blood. The scan shows his brain is looking totally un-damaged. He's still out of it, but should be awake and back in his bed within an hour. Now, is there a lady here called Jordan?'

Jordan bolted to her feet. 'That's me.'

'I have a message for you from my patient.'

'A message? But…but…how?'

'He came round for a few seconds and asked the nurse to tell you there is a way. Does that make any sense to you?'

'Yes,' she choked out, nodding and crying at the same time. 'Yes, it makes perfect sense.'

CHAPTER TWENTY

JORDAN emerged into the late-afternoon sunshine, Gino's arm hooked through hers.

"I never thought I would see this day," she said to him. 'Oh, Gino, I'm so happy I could burst.'

'Happiness becomes you.' He leant over to kiss her glowing cheek. 'So does white.'

She turned her smiling face and kissed him back on the mouth.

After a full thirty seconds, the photographer cleared his throat very noisily. The happy couple broke apart, the bride blushing, the groom beaming.

'I need the entire wedding party, please?' the photographer commanded, as he waved his arms about with theatrical panache. He was Italian, but spoke English very well, having spent some years in England.

'That's the only drawback with Italian weddings,' Gino muttered under his breath as everyone tried to assemble on the old church steps. 'Sometimes they make *Ben Hur* look like a small production.'

'I know what you mean,' Jordan returned, with a little laugh.

Aside from the bride and groom, the wedding party had six bridesmaids, six groomsmen, five small pageboys and seven little flower-girls. And that didn't count the mother of the groom and Gino's uncle Stefano, who'd kindly given Jordan away.

'If we'd had this wedding in Melbourne it would have been even bigger,' Gino told her. 'Probably two or three hundred guests. Today we only have a hundred.'

'Speaking of guests, thank you so much for flying Kerry and Ben over,' Jordan said, waving to her friend and her fiancé. 'It was very generous of you.'

'Couldn't have everyone sitting on my side of the church now, could I?'

'No more talking, please,' ordered the photographer. 'Just smile!'

They all smiled whilst he clicked away for ages. Finally he stopped, after which Jordan was besieged by every single male guest, wanting a kiss from the bride.

'Enough!' Gino said at long last, and shepherded Jordan down the steep steps to the waiting limousine which would whisk them off to the reception venue— a lovely villa overlooking the River Tiber. More photographs were scheduled to be taken in the lush gardens, which featured some simply amazing fountains.

'It's so good to have my beautiful bride to myself,' Gino said with a possessive clinch once they were alone in the back of the limousine. 'My beautiful *Italian* bride.'

'Not quite yet,' she returned. 'We have to wait six months to apply for spousal citizenship.'

'That's just another piece of paper,' Gino said. 'You are already Italian in spirit. Everyone says so.'

Jordan smiled. 'I simply adore Italy. And Italians. All your family make me feel so loved.'

'You are a very lovable woman,' Gino said, and kissed her softly on the cheek.

Jordan's heart turned over. 'You haven't told me where you're taking me on our honeymoon,' she whispered.

'We will stay tonight in Rome, then tomorrow we are going to set sail on a cruise through the Mediterranean on a luxury yacht. I hope that is to your liking?'

'Anywhere with you is to my liking, Gino.'

Gino smiled at the woman he loved more than life itself. 'You are going to make the most beautiful mother.'

'Yes,' she returned, her lovely blue eyes twinkling with sudden mischief. 'In about eight months' time.'

Gino's breath caught. 'You're pregnant already?' She'd only stopped taking the pill last month.

'It's not really a surprise, is it? You never leave me alone.'

'You don't mind become a mother this soon?'

'Are you kidding me? I'm nearly thirty years old. It's way past time, don't you think?'

"It is the right time,' he said. 'Ten years ago would not have been the right time, Jordan. I would not have made a good father then. I will be a good father to our children now: more patient, and less selfish.'

'I needed to grow up too,' she conceded. 'And to do what I had to do. But I think I've had my fill of being a legal crusader now. I want to live a more peaceful life as a wife and mother.'

Gino's laugh took her aback.

'What does that laugh mean?'

'Who are you kidding, Jordan? You were born to be a lawyer—just as I was born to be an engineer. I bucked my destiny for a while, but I actually love building things—just like you love getting justice for your clients. You'll soon become bored with being just a wife and mother.'

'You think so?' Admittedly, there had been times in the last few months when she'd missed the cut and thrust of the court room, the adrenaline rush she got when she heard that the jury had reached its verdict, and she missed the kind of satisfaction she got from winning cases like Sharni Johnson's.

'I *know* so,' Gino said. 'Look, when we finally return to Melbourne, why not open your own practice? Then you can work your own hours and pick only the clients you really care about.'

Jordan smiled. 'You know me too well.'

'Indeed I do,' he said, with that knowing gleam in his eyes. 'So, my love, what are you wearing underneath that gorgeous wedding dress of yours?'

'That's for me to know and you *not* to find out,' she retorted saucily. 'Not till tonight.'

He peered deep into her eyes till she blushed.

'I think I know already.'

'You're a wicked man,' came her shaky admission. 'You make me do wicked things.'

'You love it.'

'I love *you*.'

Gino sighed a triumphant sigh. 'I will never tire of hearing you say that.'

'I love you,' she repeated, her eyes sparkling as she lifted her mouth to his.

CONTRACT WITH CONSEQUENCES

MIRANDA LEE

CHAPTER ONE

'DON'T you think you should start getting dressed?'

Scarlet glanced up from the Sunday paper which she'd been pretending to read for the last hour or so. She hadn't felt like talking, especially since the conversation always came round to the radical choice which Scarlet had made this year. Her mother had initially supported her decision to have a child on her own by artificial insemination, but lately she'd been expressing the opinion that it might not be such a good idea.

Scarlet needed negativity at the moment like a hole in the head!

Okay, so the procedure hadn't worked the first two times. That was not uncommon, she'd been told by the clinic. She just had to keep on trying and sooner or later she would conceive. It wasn't as though there was any-thing physically wrong with her, except perhaps that she was getting older. Which was why she'd decided to do this in the first place.

'What time is it?' she asked.

'Nearly noon,' her mother replied. 'We really should make an appearance at the Mitchells' no later than quar-ter-to-one. I know Carolyn's planning on serving lunch around one-thirty.'

Carolyn and Martin Mitchell had been their friends and

neighbours for almost thirty years. They had two children: a boy, John, the same age as herself, and a girl, Melissa, who was four years younger. Over the years Scarlet had got to know the family well, though she liked some members more than others. Mr Mitchell had not long retired and today was their fortieth wedding anniversary, a milestone which Scarlet knew would sadly never figure in her own life.

Janet King's heart squeezed tight when she heard her daughter sigh. Poor love. She'd been so disappointed when her period had arrived this week. It was no wonder she didn't feel like going to a party.

'You don't have to go,' she said gently. 'I could make some excuse—say you're not feeling well.'

'No, no, Mum,' Scarlet said quite firmly, and stood up. 'I'm fine to go. Truly. Do me good.' And she hurried to her bedroom, thinking that it *would* do her good. She could have a few glasses of wine—now that she wasn't expecting. She also wouldn't have to spend the rest of the day defending her decision to have a baby on her own. Because no one—other than her mother—knew about her baby project. Frankly, she was sick and tired of her mum telling her how hard it was, bringing up a child on her own.

Admittedly, Janet King had first-hand knowledge of the subject, Scarlet's father having been killed in a car accident when Scarlet had been only nine. Scarlet knew full well how difficult life had been for her mother at that time, both emotionally and financially. Difficult for herself, as well. She'd adored her father and missed him terribly.

So, yes, she appreciated that raising a child without the support of a partner *would* be hard at times.

But not as hard as never having a child at all!

Just *thinking* about such a prospect made Scarlet feel physically ill.

She'd always wanted to be a mother, ever since she'd
been a little girl. She'd grown up dreaming of one day falling in love with a wonderful man—someone like her darling dad—getting married and having a family of her own.

Scarlet had honestly believed it was only a matter of
time after leaving school before that happened. Her plan
had been to marry young so that she could enjoy her children. Never in her wildest dreams had she envisaged reaching the age of thirty-four still single and without her Mr
Wonderful anywhere in sight.

But that was how her life had panned out. Sometimes,
Scarlet simply couldn't believe it.

Shaking her head, she stripped off her dressing gown
then turned her attention to the outfit which she'd already
laid out on the bed earlier that morning—a purple woollen
tunic dress, black silk polo underneath, black tights and
black ankle boots. It didn't take her long to dress—she'd
already showered and blow-dried her hair—after which
she made her way along to the main bathroom to put her
hair up and do her make-up.

Neither job took Scarlet all that long. At thirty-four, she
had her grooming routine down pat.

The sight of the finished product in the large vanity
mirror brought a puzzled frown to her forehead. Why,
she wondered for the umpteenth time, had it come to this?

It wasn't as though she was an ugly girl. She was very
attractive with a pretty face: cute nose, full lips, blonde
hair and a good figure. Okay, so her breasts *were* on the
smaller side, but she looked great in clothes, being tall and
slender. On top of that she had a bright, outgoing personality. People liked her. *Men* liked her.

Despite that, she'd had a lot of trouble finding herself a
steady boyfriend over the years. In hindsight, Scarlet now
realised that her choice of career hadn't helped, but that

hadn't occurred to her at the time. Not wanting to leave home and the Central Coast, she'd taken a hairdressing apprenticeship in the salon where her mother had worked, a move which had confounded a lot of people. She had, after all, achieved very high marks in her exams and could have pursued some high-flying profession such as communications or law, if she'd wanted to.

But becoming a journalist or a lawyer was not what Scarlet wanted out of life. She had other priorities which didn't include more years of studying and even more years clawing her way up the ladder to what some people thought of as success in life. At the same time, she did want an interesting job which she enjoyed.

Despite her teachers' warnings to the contrary, Scarlet had loved being a hairdresser, had loved the camaraderie with her co-workers and clients. Loved the feel-good feeling which came with completing a colour or a cut not just adequately but brilliantly. She soon gained a great reputation as a stylist and by twenty-five she and her mother had opened their own salon in a small shopping centre not far from Erina Fair. They would have preferred to locate their salon in Erina Fair—the shopping hub of the Central Coast—but the rents there were way too high. Because of their loyal clientele, their business had still been a huge success.

But only on the financial front. Scarlet eventually had begun to see that being a hairdresser with mainly female clients was not conducive to meeting members of the opposite sex. Being an only child with no siblings wasn't an asset, either. Maybe if she'd had an older brother...

Not that she didn't try to meet men in other ways. For years she'd maintained a group of girlfriends from her school days and they went out regularly together to parties, clubs and pubs where, for some perverse reason, she would always be hit upon by the type of good-looking sleazebag who was only interested in one thing—though she didn't work this out till she'd been burned a few times.

One by one, she watched as her girlfriends found nice guys to marry—mostly through their more diverse careers or family connections. Scarlet had been a bridesmaid so many times, she began to dread weddings, not to mention the after-wedding parties where her married 'friends' always tried to hook her up with some guy who was usually drunk and was only there to have sex with at least one of the bridesmaids.

When the last of her unmarried girlfriends had found her future husband on an Internet dating site, Scarlet had tried that method, but it had been an unmitigated disaster. For some reason, she still seemed to attract the wrong type who only wanted the one thing.

Scarlet had never been a girl who liked sex for sex's sake. Not that she hadn't tried it a few times in her younger days; she had. But she had found the experiences so lacking in pleasure that by her twenty-first birthday she vowed to reserve giving her body till she really liked the guy she was with. Unfortunately, she'd really liked some of the good-looking sleazebags who'd successfully picked her up during her twenties. Even then, there'd been no bells and whistles going off for her in bed, leading Scarlet to the conclusion that maybe she needed to be deeply in love to enjoy sex. Either that, or she was seriously undersexed.

By the time she turned thirty, Scarlet had been so desperate to find someone to love—and who would love her in return—that she'd made the mammoth decision to change careers. She went to college at night, gained her real-estate licence then applied for a job at one of the Central Coast's largest and most successful agencies.

It had seemed a good move at the time. Suddenly, she

was surrounded by lots of eligible young men who thought she was the best thing since they had built the freeway connecting the central coast to Sydney. She had admirers galore, one of whom stood out from all the rest. Jason was an estate agent at a rival agency and a coastie—like herself. A charming, extremely handsome guy who came from a local family and didn't try to get her into bed on their first date. Hallelujah! When they did finally go to bed, the sex, whilst not quite of the earth-moving variety, had been pleasurable enough for Scarlet to conclude she'd finally fallen in love, feelings which she assumed were mutual when Jason proposed to her on her thirty-second birthday.

Plans for their wedding were well underway when disaster struck.

It had been eighteen months ago, at their street Christmas party. Jason was unable to go with her, saying he had a work-related dinner at the Terrigal hotel which he was obliged to attend. She was showing everyone her engagement ring and having a wonderful time when John Mitchell—the party was at the Mitchells' house that year—took her aside and very quietly told her the most devastating piece of information.

Her first instinct was disbelief and denial. It couldn't possibly be true: her fiancé was not gay. He couldn't be!

It was the gentleness in John's voice—and the compassion in his eyes—which finally convinced her he was speaking the truth. For it wasn't like John Mitchell to be that nice to her. Deeply distressed, she left the party straight away, sending Jason a text that she had to see him. She arranged to meet him at the park opposite the Terrigal hotel where she confronted him with John's allegation. He initially denied being gay, but she wouldn't let him lie to her any more, and he finally admitted the truth. He begged her not to tell anyone else, as he hadn't fully accepted it himself, and she hadn't, but she broke her engagement.

Christmas that year, therefore, was not very happy. Neither was the New Year. Totally shattered, Scarlet resigned her real-estate job—she couldn't bear to run into Jason all the time—and went back to hairdressing where she hid herself away for the whole year, her spirits very low. She never told anyone the truth about Jason—not even her mother—saying instead that she'd found out he was cheating on her. Her girlfriends were very sympathetic whilst encouraging her to keep on dating. But she simply hadn't had the courage to put herself out there again. She'd felt like a fool, and a failure.

Scarlet had been quite relieved when John Mitchell hadn't come home last Christmas. She hated the thought of his looking at her with pity again, or saying something crass like 'I told you so'. Apparently, he'd broken a leg climbing up some stupid mountain in South America and was unable to travel. She was relieved, too, that he wouldn't be at the party today. He'd planned to come, but his flight from Rio had been indefinitely delayed because of volcanic ash in the air. Fate was being kind to her for once.

Scarlet knew it was silly of her to feel awkward about seeing John Mitchell again. But she did.

To be fair, he was not an easy guy to be around at the best of times. Despite being a very good-looking man, John's social graces left a lot to be desired. Had a brilliant brain, though; this Scarlet knew first-hand, since they'd always been in the same classes at school, right from kindergarten through to their final exams. But being classmates and neighbours had not made them friends. John had never played with the other kids in the street, despite Scarlet asking him more than once. All he'd cared about was studying and surfing—the beach was a relatively short walk away.

Scarlet recalled how John had bitterly resented being asked by her mother to mind her on the school bus when bullying had become rife. Admittedly, he'd done it, even to the extent of fighting with another boy who had called her a foul name. He'd got suspended for a day over that, and a bloody nose as well, which hadn't exactly endeared her to him. Not that he had said anything directly to her. But when she'd thanked him, he'd scowled. Scowling at her was something he'd done quite often back then. She remembered once going to him for help with a maths problem in high school—he really had been terrific at maths—only to be told bluntly to stop being so bloody lazy and work it out for herself. Naturally, she hit back—Scarlet was not a girl to accept such rudeness meekly—screaming at him that she thought he was the meanest, most horrible boy she'd ever met and she would never ever ask him for help again, even if she were dying. A rather over-dramatic declaration, but she'd meant it at the time.

After graduating, John had gone on to Sydney university to become a geologist. She'd hardly ever seen him after that. He'd gone overseas to work once he had his degree, and only darkened his family's doorstep around Christmas, when he would stay for a week or two at most. Even then, he spent most of his time surfing by himself.

He did deign to attend the Christmas street-party which they held every year, and where their paths inevitably crossed. And, whilst John wasn't openly rude to her any more, their conversations were hardly warm or communicative. What she knew about his life was gleaned via his mother who belonged to the same quilting group as Scarlet's mother. According to Carolyn Mitchell, her son had become extremely wealthy in recent years after finding oil in Argentina and natural gas in some other South American country. He'd also bought a house in Rio, so it seemed likely that he wasn't coming home to Australia to live any time soon.

And wasn't getting married any time soon, either, Scarlet warranted. Loners like John didn't get married.

However, Scarlet had no doubt there was a woman—or women—in his life. Good-looking guys with money to burn didn't do without sex, even if they were antisocial bastards with about as much personal charm as a rattlesnake!

The bitchiness of this last thought startled Scarlet. It wasn't like her to be bitchy.

John Mitchell brought out the worst in her. But she really hated the way he didn't need anybody; hated his self-containment. She couldn't imagine John Mitchell ever having his heart broken. His heart was as hard as one of his precious rocks.

'Better get a move on, Scarlet,' her mother called through the bathroom door. 'It's twelve-twenty-five.'

After giving herself a vigorous mental shake, Scarlet hurried back to her bedroom, where she quickly hooked a pair of silver and crystal drops through her earlobes, then bolted back to the living room where her mother was waiting for her, dressed in a tailored cream trouser suit with a caramel-coloured blouse underneath.

'You know, Mum,' she said, looking her mother up and down. 'You don't look a day over fifty.' Yet she'd turned sixty-two last birthday.

'Thank you, darling. And you don't look a day over twenty.'

'That's because I have great genes,' Scarlet replied.

'True,' Janet agreed, though the thought did occur to her that maybe her daughter had inherited one particular gene which wasn't as desirable as a youthful face, good skin and a slender figure—she herself had found it very difficult to get pregnant, which was why she'd only had the one child. It surprised her that a girl as intelligent as

Scarlet hadn't asked her about that. But she hadn't, and Janet wasn't about to mention it. Not today.

'Come on, let's go,' Janet said instead, and picked up the present from the kitchen counter. Inside the rather exquisite red box was a ruby-coloured water jug and matching glasses which she'd found in a local antique shop and which she knew Carolyn would love. Martin probably wouldn't, but then Martin was one of those men who didn't enthuse over anything much. Except his grandson. There was no doubting that Melissa's little boy, Oliver, was the apple of his grandfather's eye. 'I won't need a jacket, will I?' Scarlet asked her.

'I shouldn't think so. Besides, it's not as though you have far to walk if you do get cold.'

'You're right. In that case, I won't take a handbag, either. Here, let me hold the present whilst you lock up.'

They went out the front way, Scarlet glad to see that the early cloud had lifted, letting the June sun do a decent job of warming up the air. Winter had not long arrived down under, but it had already been one of the coldest in a decade. And the wettest. Fortunately, the rain had stayed away today, which meant they wouldn't be confined indoors at the party. By the look of the number of cars already parked up and down the street, this was going to be a well-attended affair. There was nothing worse, in Scarlet's opinion, than having lots of people jammed into a couple of rooms. Admittedly, the Mitchells' two-storeyed home was very spacious, with large open-planned living areas. But even so…

'They've been lucky with the weather,' she remarked to her mother as they walked together across the road.

'Indeed. I…'

Whatever her mother was going to say was cut off by

the Mitchells' house. The front door was reefed open and Carolyn ran out, looking flushed but happy.

'You'll never guess what's happened,' she said excitedly. 'I've just received a call from John. His plane was able to take off last night after all. Admittedly, a few hours late, but because of favourable winds they made good time and landed at Mascot a couple of hours ago. He tried to ring me earlier but I was on the phone so he hopped on a train. Anyway, he's going to be arriving at Gosford station in about twenty minutes. The train's just pulled into Woy Woy station. He said he'd catch a taxi, but you know how scarce they can be on a Sunday. So I told him to wait outside the station on the Mann Street side and I'd get someone to pick him up.

'Of course, he said that I shouldn't bother, but I said what tommyrot, that if he could fly here all the way from Brazil we could at least pick him up from the station. But once I hung up, I began thinking who I could ask. I couldn't very well leave my guests and I didn't like to ask Martin. Then I saw you two through the front window, and I thought who better than Scarlet? You don't mind, do you, dear?'

What could Scarlet possibly say?

Scarlet forced a smile and said, 'It would be my pleasure.'

CHAPTER TWO

THE train trip from Sydney to Gosford was a very pleasant one, once you left the city, especially if the train was half-empty and you were able to get an upstairs window seat on the right side, which John had. After crossing the Hawkesbury River, the track followed the water in long leisurely curves, giving even the weariest traveller a panoramic and relaxing ride.

Not that John was weary. That was the advantage of flying first class; you could sleep on board and arrive at your destination, refreshed and ready for anything.

Which was just as well, given what he would have to endure today.

Parties were not John's favourite pastime. He wasn't much of a drinker and didn't care for empty chit-chat. But it had been impossible not to come to his parents' fortieth wedding anniversary. He loved his mother dearly and would not hurt her for the world.

His father, however, was another matter entirely. It was difficult to love a parent who'd rejected you when you were only a child.

Nevertheless, John *did* still love his father, a discovery he'd made when his mother had rung him recently to tell him that his father had had a heart scare. John had actually been relieved that his old man hadn't died. He'd actually *cared*.

There was no getting over the fact, however, that what his father had done all those years ago had hurt him terribly. Thank God he'd had Grandpa. If it hadn't been for his grandfather stepping in, then Lord knew where he would have ended up. He'd probably have run away from home and been living on the streets. Maybe even ended up in jail. That was how wretched he'd felt after his brother had died. Wretched, confused and angry.

Yes, he'd become very angry. Sometimes, when he looked back over his teenage years, he felt guilty over the mean way he'd acted, especially how he'd been to Scarlet.

He'd been extra-mean to her.

But that was because he'd liked her so much. It had been perverse of him; he could see that now. But back then feeling anything for anyone scared the hell out of him. He didn't want to like her, or need her. So he'd pushed her away right from the first time she'd rocked up at his front door and asked him to come out and play. Not that she took no for an answer easily. Scarlet had always been a stubborn child with a will of iron. But she'd got the message in the end and had stopped asking him to come out and play. Perversely again, he'd been deeply hurt by her perfectly understandable rejection, deciding childishly that if she was going to ignore him, then he would ignore her.

Anything she could do he could do better!

Unfortunately, they had always been put into the same class—the 'gifted' class—so ignoring her totally had been a bit difficult. But he did his best. He hadn't been able to believe his bad luck when they'd been put in the same classes in high school. But worse had been yet to come. During that first year, puberty had struck both of them. Overnight, Scarlet had gone from a pretty but skinny little thing to a seriously hot-looking babe, whereas he had gone from an okay-looking boy into a too-thin, too-tall streak of hormone-muddled misery. Once the testosterone had started charging through his veins, however, he had begun fancying Scarlet like mad, which naturally had made him act even worse around her. But, privately, he had fantasised about being her boyfriend.

No no, let's not sugar-coat this, John. You didn't fantasise about that. You never wanted to be Scarlet's boyfriend. Being her boyfriend would have required a degree of emotional intimacy, something you were incapable of. Still are, if truth be told. You just wanted to have sex with her.

John smiled wryly to himself at the thought of how Scarlet would react if he ever confessed to lusting after her when they'd been at school together. Not that he ever intended telling her. What would be the point? She'd made it patently clear to him over the years that she couldn't stand him. Not that he blamed her. He'd started the hostility between them.

It was one of the many things he regretted now. She really was a lovely—if somewhat spoiled—girl, and hadn't deserved the way he treated her. Hadn't deserved getting conned by Jason Heath, either. Telling her the truth about that bastard was one thing he didn't regret. Scarlet might have ended up feeling miserable in the short term, but she'd have been even unhappier in the long term if he'd let her remain ignorant. He hadn't really loved Scarlet, he'd just been using her to hide behind.

John wondered if Scarlet would be at the party today. He wouldn't mind catching up with her and seeing how she was. His mother had told him during one of her phone calls that Scarlet had been inconsolable after finding out that Jason had been cheating on her—apparently, that was the story she'd put around to explain her broken engagement. Scarlet's teachers hadn't been the only ones to be shocked when she hadn't gone on to university. He'd been appalled, and had told her so on one occasion. After all, she was as smart as he was!

John chuckled wryly at himself, recognising his arrogance. At least he didn't strut around like some men, bragging about his successes. Bianca used to say that he was the strong, silent type.

John's heart contracted fiercely as it always did when he thought of Bianca. One day, perhaps, he would get over her death. But not yet. The memory was still too raw, too painful. One thing was sure, though—he would never go back to Brazil. That part of his life was over. For the next couple of years at least, he would live and work in Australia. Not here on the Central Coast, however. Aside from the fact it was hardly the mining capital of the world, he was never comfortable spending time at home. Too much bad karma.

No, he would base himself in Darwin, where he already owned an apartment and where he stayed for a few weeks each year. Not that his family knew about any of that. If he'd told them he holidayed here in Australia every winter, they would have been offended that he hadn't visited, or asked them to join him—his mother especially—so he'd simply never told them.

But he'd have to tell them something soon, he supposed. Though not the total truth, of course.

Over the past couple of weeks, John had tidied up all his loose ends in Rio. He'd given away his house to Bianca's family, as well as everything in it. He wanted no memories of his life there. All he'd taken with him to the airport was his wallet, his passport and his phones, plus the clothes on his back. During his long wait to board his flight—which had turned out to be even longer than he'd anticipated— he'd bought a small winter wardrobe at one of the many boutiques. He'd also used the opportunity to have his thick dark hair clippered again in the close-cropped style he'd become used to since being in hospital last year. One of the nurses had become frustrated with his increasingly shaggy mane and shaved it off to less than a centimetre all over his head. Despite having worn his hair longish all his life, John found he rather liked the buzz-cut look. It suited him and was easy to look after. He didn't even have to own a comb. John always liked to travel light.

The train pulling into Point Clare station brought his mind back to the present. In a few minutes they'd be at Gosford station. He wondered idly who would be picking him up. Not his father, that was for sure. Maybe Melissa. Or Leo, Melissa's husband. Yes, probably Leo.

He liked Leo. He was one of the good guys. Anyone who'd married his little sister had to be. Melissa was, without doubt, the most spoiled girl he'd ever known. Even more spoiled than Scarlet.

Scarlet again…

It would be good if she was at the party. Good to know if she'd finally forgiven him for telling her about Jason. But he rather doubted it. When news was bad, people liked to blame the messenger. Scarlet had been furious with him that night, calling him a liar at first. She'd finally calmed down enough to listen to what he was saying, but he suspected he was still not her favourite person. But then, he never had been, had he?

The announcement that they were approaching Gosford station had several people in the carriage standing up and making their way down to the doors at the lower level. John knew there was no need to hurry so he stayed where he was, gazing out at the expanse of almost-still water on his right, and the many boats moored there, bobbing gently up and down. Spread out around this expanse of water lay Gosford, the gateway to the Central Coast beaches, but not a beach town in itself, the sea being a few kilometres away. The train rumbled over a bridge then went past Blue-Tongue Stadium which had been a park in the old days but now hosted football matches and the occasional rock concert. Soon, they were pulling into the station where John took his time alighting.

It was a habit he'd got into when coming home, being slow to get off the train, doing everything he could to shorten the time of his visits. He still wasn't looking forward to today, but he no longer felt the gut-wrenching tension he used to feel at the prospect of being around his father. Which was a good thing. Not that he intended to stay too long. Masochism was not his style!

No one was there, waiting for him at the spot where his mother had instructed him to go, so he dropped his bag by his feet and waited. Less than thirty seconds later, a shiny blue Hyundai hatchback zoomed up the ramp and braked to a halt beside him.

He didn't recognise the car. But he recognised the beautiful blonde behind the wheel.

It was Scarlet.

CHAPTER THREE

YOU could have knocked Scarlet over with a feather once she realised that the gorgeous man standing at the five-minute pick-up spot, dressed in snug-fitting black jeans, black T-shirt and a black leather bomber jacket, was actually John Mitchell. It was a realisation that didn't come instantly, not even when he stepped forward and tapped on her passenger window. She'd thought he was some stranger wanting directions.

But as soon she wound down the window and he took off his wrap-around sunglasses, the penny dropped.

'My God, *John*!' she gasped as she stared into his familiar blue eyes.

'Yup,' he agreed. 'It's me.'

Scarlet could not believe how different he looked without long hair. Not better looking—he'd always been good-looking—but way more masculine. Without the softening effect of his hair, his facial features came into sharper focus: his high cheekbones. His long strong nose. His square jawline. Of course the clothes he was wearing added to the macho image. Scarlet wasn't used to seeing John dressed in anything other than board shorts and T-shirts, his visits home long having been confined to summer. And, whilst she already knew he had a good body, there was something about a man dressed all in black that was very, very sexy.

Once she realised her staring was tipping into ogling, an embarrassed Scarlet swiftly pulled herself together.

'I didn't recognise you there for a moment,' she said brusquely. 'What happened to all your hair?'

He shrugged, then ran a slow hand over his near-smooth head, the action sending an erotically charged frisson running down Scarlet's spine.

'It was easier to look after,' he said. 'Where do you want me to put my bag? On the back seat, or right in the back?'

'Whatever,' she said, her offhand attitude a defensive reaction to her underlying shock at the situation. She wasn't used to finding John sexually attractive. It was highly irritating. There she'd been on the way in, thinking how awkward driving him home would be, only to find that it was going to be extra-awkward now. She hoped he hadn't noticed anything untoward. She would have to make sure she didn't act any differently with him from usual. No way was she going to compliment him on either his haircut, or his clothes, reminding herself forcibly that, underneath his sexy new facade, he was still the same selfish, rude, anti-social bastard who'd given her hell over the years.

'Mum shouldn't have asked you to do this,' he said as he climbed into the passenger seat and shut the door after him. 'I could easily have caught a taxi.' And he nodded towards the taxi rank ahead where several taxis stood, waiting for fares.

'No pointing in worrying about it now,' Scarlet said as she drove past them.

'I guess not,' he agreed. 'This is more pleasant than a taxi, anyway. Thank you, Scarlet.'

She could not have been more taken aback. Not only did John look different, he was acting different too. She almost asked what had happened to him in the eighteen months since he'd last graced home, but decided not to go down such a personal road. He might start asking her what had been happening to her. No way was she going to tell John Mitchell anything! Best keep any chit-chat in the car strictly superficial.

'Your parents have been lucky with the weather,' she said as she drove down the almost deserted main street of Gosford. 'This is the first decent day we've had so far this winter.'

He said nothing in return, for which she was grateful. But his silence didn't last for long.

'Mum tells me you haven't met anyone else,' he said when they stopped at a set of lights at East Gosford.

'No,' came her rather terse reply.

'I'm sorry, Scarlet. I know how much you've always wanted to get married and have a family.'

Her head whipped around, her face flushing with a sudden spurt of anger. 'Well, if you know that, then you shouldn't have said anything to me about Jason. If you hadn't, I would have been none the wiser, and I would have been married by now. Instead, I...'

Scarlet broke off when she felt tears sting her eyes, her knuckles showing white as she gripped the steering wheel tight and battled for composure.

John was appalled at the level of Scarlet's distress. Appalled and sympathetic, but not guilty.

'I am truly sorry, Scarlet,' he repeated. 'But I had no choice in the matter. I couldn't let you marry a man who was just using you.'

'There are worse things to happen to a woman than having a gay husband,' she threw at him.

'He didn't love you, Scarlet.'

'How on earth could you know a thing like that?'

'Because he told me.'

'You!'

'Yes. I felt sorry for him—he was too scared to publicly accept who he was. Even I wasn't as lonely or lost as that.'

Scarlet was moved by the grim bleakness in John's voice and the stark reality of what he'd just revealed.

'The lights are green, Scarlet.'

'What? Oh yes, so they are.'

She drove on, her thoughts muddled by the sudden sympathy she felt for the man sitting next to her. Who would have believed it? First, she'd started finding John incredibly sexy. Now she was feeling sorry for him as well. Life could be very perverse, she decided.

'So why *haven't* you found anyone else?' John persisted.

Scarlet sighed a sigh of sheer frustration. The one thing she could have depended on with John in the past was his brooding silences. Now, suddenly, he was turning into a conversationalist! And there she'd been, thinking she wouldn't have to answer any awkward questions today.

'I've stopped looking, okay?' she replied somewhat aggressively. 'I could ask you the same question, you know,' she swept on, always having been skilled at the art of verbal counter-attack. She hadn't been captain of the debating team at school for nothing! 'Why is it that *you've* never found anyone? No one you dared to bring home, that is.'

He laughed. John Mitchell actually laughed. Things were getting seriously weird here.

'Come now, Scarlet, you know my mother. If I brought a girl home, she would immediately start wanting to know when the wedding was.'

'I could tell her that. It would be never!'

'You know me too well, Scarlet.'

'I know you well enough to know you're not interested

in marriage. If you were, you'd be married by now. You'd have no trouble finding a wife.'

'Thank you for the compliment,' he said. 'But you're right. Marriage is not for me.'

'That's still no reason not to bring a girl home occasionally.'

'I can't agree with you on that score. There's enough tension whenever I come home as it is.'

This was true, Scarlet conceded. John and his father didn't get along. She'd always blamed John for this; he'd been such a difficult boy. But she now wondered if there'd been some secret reason for John's antisocial attitude, something which might have happened before they'd come to live in her street. He certainly wasn't being his usual gruff self with her right at this moment. Frankly, he'd spoken more words to her since getting into her car five minutes ago than he had over their whole lifetime together! Curiosity demanded she use this uncharacteristic chattiness to find out some more about his personal life.

'Do you have anyone back in Brazil at the moment?' she asked, glancing his way.

His face, which had been open and smiling, suddenly closed up again.

'I did have,' he answered. 'Till recently.'

'I'm sorry,' she said quite sincerely, and wondered what had happened.

'So am I,' he said. 'Now, that's enough personal information for one day.'

Scarlet's teeth clenched hard in her jaw. She should have known that his being nice and normal wouldn't last.

'Why didn't you keep going straight along the main road?' he asked when she swung right onto Terrigal Drive. 'It's quicker.'

'Not any more, it isn't. It's suffering from terminal roadworks. If you came home a little more often, you would know that,' she pointed out somewhat waspishly. 'Apart from that, I'm the driver here. You're the passenger. The passenger does not tell the driver where and how to drive. That's bad manners.'

He laughed again, though this time it had a harsher sound. 'Glad to see you haven't changed, Scarlet.'

'I was just thinking the same about you. You might look different, John Mitchell—you're certainly dressing a damned sight better—but deep down, you're still the same obnoxious boy who thinks he's smarter than everyone else.'

This time he made no come-back, leaving Scarlet to feel totally ashamed of herself. She'd overreacted, as usual. She'd always had a quick temper, especially around John.

'I'm sorry,' she said swiftly into the uncomfortable silence. 'That was very rude of me.'

'Oh, I don't know,' he said, surprising her with a wry little smile. 'It wasn't far off the truth. I can be quite arrogant.'

She couldn't help it. She smiled back at him.

Their eyes met for a long moment, Scarlet being the first to look away, John's eyes still on her as she struggled to put her mind back on her driving. It kept rattling her, this sudden attraction between them.

'Will you stop staring at me?' she snapped at last, but without looking his way.

'I wasn't staring,' he denied. 'I was just looking and thinking.'

'About what?'

'Don't forget there's a speed camera just along here.'

Scarlet rolled her eyes. 'For pity's sake, John, I *live* here twenty-four-seven. I know about the speed camera.'

'Then why are you doing nearly fifty?'

'I can do fifty. It's not a school day.'

'The sign said forty. Roadworks ahead.'

Scarlet jammed on her brakes. Just in time, too.

'If they dig up one more road around here,' she muttered, 'I'm going to scream.'

'No screaming,' John said in droll tones. 'Can't abide screaming women.'

When she glared over at him, Scarlet was astounded to find him smiling at her.

'John Mitchell,' she said, her mouth twitching. 'You've actually found a sense of humour.'

'I have today, it seems. Which is just as well. I'm almost home.'

Which they were.

The street where Scarlet lived was no different from most streets on the Central Coast, full of a motley collection of houses of all different shapes and sizes. It was a family-friendly street where the inhabitants actually stayed put, rather than moving every seven years or so, as seemed to be ingrained in the Australian psyche. Of course, it *was* in Terrigal, which had been voted recently one of the ten most desirable places in the world to live.

It would be difficult to find anywhere better to bring up a family. Admittedly, they didn't have ocean or lagoon views in their street, but that made the houses more reasonably priced. They still enjoyed the wonderfully mild climate which came from living near the sea. On top of that they were so close to everything, not just the beach. Erina Fair shopping centre was only a ten minute drive away and Sydney a little over an hour.

Scarlet could never understand why John didn't come home more often.

'Looks like a big turn-out,' John said once Scarlet turned the corner into their street.

'You have your mother to blame for that. If she didn't put on such a good spread, she wouldn't get so many people accepting her invitations. It's always like this when it's your family's turn for the Christmas party. Look, there's your mum and sister on the front porch, waiting for you.' No father, though, she noted. 'I'll just stop in our driveway and you can get out. I want to put the car in the garage.'

'Fine,' he agreed, hopping out and taking his bag from the back seat before slapping the car on the roof and shouting thanks to her.

She pressed the remote for the garage door, watching John in the rear-vision mirror whilst she waited for the door to roll its way slowly upwards. He really did look amazing today. Great buns in those jeans. Great body all round. If he'd been anybody else, she might have been tempted to flirt with him.

Just the thought made her laugh. *Flirt* with John Mitchell? What would be the point in that?

Scarlet laughed again. She was still amused over the idea when she returned to the party.

CHAPTER FOUR

SCARLET looked for John straight away. When she couldn't spot him anywhere amongst the crowd of partygoers who'd all gathered under the outdoor entertaining area, she wandered back inside the house. But the only person she found there was his mother, getting a couple of bottles of wine out of the fridge. The large open-plan living room was empty of people, with no sign of John anywhere.

'Ah, Scarlet,' his mother said. 'Thank you so much for getting John. It was very good of you.'

'No trouble, Mrs Mitchell. Where is he, by the way?'

'Upstairs in his bedroom,' Carolyn retorted, sounding a bit annoyed. 'Said he had to go get my anniversary present but I think he's just avoiding talking to people. Look, could I bother you to go up there and bring him down? All the food is ready. You look lovely today, by the way, dear,' Carolyn rattled on before Scarlet could accept or reject the request.

Strangely, she didn't mind the mission. It would give her the chance to see if he still had all those girlie posters over his walls.

He didn't. The room was stripped bare of all boyish paraphernalia. John was standing by the window, staring down at the street, his bedroom being at the front of the house. His bag had been slung on top of the bed, unopened. Scarlet glanced around but couldn't see any present anywhere.

'I've been sent to bring you downstairs,' she called from the open doorway.

He turned from the window and smiled a rueful smile. 'Poor Scarlet,' came his ironic remark. 'You've been given all the awful jobs today.'

She didn't deny it. The strange truth, however, was that she hadn't minded driving him home as much as she'd thought she would. And she didn't really mind coming up here to collect him. But she wasn't about to tell him that.

'Did you find your mother's present?'

'I did,' he said, and patted the right hip pocket of his leather jacket.

'Something small and sinfully expensive?'

'Could be.'

'Let me guess—a real ruby.' What else would a geologist son give to his mother on her ruby wedding anniversary?

'You always were a clever little minx.'

'And you always were a sarcastic bastard.'

He scowled at her for a second, then smiled. 'I tell you what. I promise to go down and face the small talk if you promise not to leave my side.'

'And what, pray tell, do *I* get out of that deal?'

His smile broadened. 'My suddenly sparkling company?'

'Not good enough, I'm afraid. I have no faith in your company becoming suddenly sparkling. I will need more of a bribe than that.'

'Would a real diamond do the trick?'

Scarlet wasn't sure if he was serious, or just teasing her. Whatever, she was tempted to do some teasing of her own.

'I have no use for a diamond,' she replied haughtily.

'Unless it's sitting atop a band of gold and comes with a proposal of marriage.'

The look on his face was priceless.

'No?' she went on saucily. 'Pity. You're not bad looking, after all. And you're filthy rich. Not to mention not gay. What more could a girl possibly want?'

'Nice try, Scarlet. You had me going there for a while.'

She grinned. 'I did, didn't I? Revenge *is* sweet.'

'Revenge for what?'

'For all the times you made me want to kill you.'

'Mea culpa,' he said, his tone droll.

'You're right there. But today is meant to be a happy day, so I'll put aside my petty grievances and do what you ask, without payment of any kind. Not that I thought you meant to give me a diamond for real.'

'If I did, you've missed out now. Still, be a nice, sweet, agreeable companion for the rest of the day and I might give you one.'

'In your dreams, lover.'

He laughed. 'You're right there, Scarlet.'

John knew full well that that was one thing he would never be—Scarlet's lover. Which was a pity. She looked utterly gorgeous today in that purple and black outfit. Shame she wasn't one of those girls who could enjoy a fling without always looking for a ring on their finger in return.

But that was the way she was and nothing would ever change that. Which was also a pity. John suspected one of the reasons Scarlet hadn't found her Mr Right was because she had 'desperately seeking marriage' written all over her. What she needed to do, in his opinion, was lighten up.

Perhaps he would tell her that later today if he found the right opportunity.

'Come on,' he said, flashing Scarlet a warm smile as he hooked her arm through his. 'Time to get ourselves downstairs before they send out a search party.'

CHAPTER FIVE

SCARLET could not believe how much she enjoyed the party, and John's company, though she would not go so far as to say he'd 'sparkled'. After giving his delighted mother her ruby—which was uncut but simply enormous—he'd actually deigned to make a small speech, praising his parents' fortitude in staying married for so long and wishing them all the best for the future. Then, even more surprising, after the buffet luncheon was over he'd made the effort to talk to his father. It had been a slightly awkward conversation—Scarlet had been hovering nearby at the time—but it was Martin Mitchell who'd sounded the more awkward, she thought, after which the fool had spent the rest of the afternoon playing with Melissa's little boy. Admittedly, Oliver was a delightful child, with a highly engaging personality. But still, one would have thought Martin could have afforded to spend some more time with a son who'd flown all the way from South America to be with his parents on their special day.

Scarlet had felt seriously annoyed with the man, which made her even more solicitous towards John. She also downed a good few glasses of wine, which she had a tendency to do when she was upset. Being tipsy brought out the flirtatious side in her, which was helped by the fact that he invariably sought her out if she left his side for too long, whispering to her each time that she wouldn't get a diamond if she kept deserting her post.

By five-thirty, the party was winding down, with people gradually leaving. By six, the Mitchell place was almost empty of guests, and Scarlet and her mother stayed back to help Carolyn and Melissa clean up. Oliver had been put down for a nap, whilst the men—Martin, John and Leo—had retired to the living room to watch the evening news on TV.

'I had my four-month ultrasound on Friday,' Melissa said out of the blue as she and Scarlet were restacking the dishwasher together. Their mothers were outside at the time, piling up more dirty plates to carry in.

Scarlet stiffened as she always did these days when girls she knew started talking about their pregnancies. She'd known Melissa was pregnant again, but the subject hadn't come up that day as yet.

'Oh?' she managed to reply as casually as she could manage. 'Everything well, I hope?'

'Marvellous. Leo was there with me, of course. He actually cried when they told him it was a little girl. So did I. Oliver's a darling boy, but there's something about little girls, isn't there?'

Scarlet was on the verge of tears herself. She didn't give a damn if she had a girl or a boy. She just wanted a baby.

'Would you like to see the pictures of the ultrasound?' Melissa asked her. 'I brought them with me to show Mum. They're just upstairs. I'll go get them,' she added before Scarlet could say yes or no.

John saw the stricken look on Scarlet's face the moment he walked into the kitchen.

'What is it?' he asked straight away. 'What's happened?'

'I have to get out of here,' she muttered.

Too late. Melissa was back in a flash with the dreaded

pictures. Scarlet had no choice but to look at them and make all the right noises, for how could she do anything else without making a complete fool of herself? Melissa insisted John look at them too, which he did, though he didn't gush, for which Scarlet was grateful. At some stage, their respective mothers re-entered the kitchen. Scarlet now had to endure Carolyn Mitchell raving on about how lucky Melissa was to be having a little girl and how lucky they were as grandparents to have their daughter living so close. She then added that it was obvious they were never going to get any grandchildren from John and, even if by some miracle they did, they'd probably never see them, since he preferred to live in South America than Australia.

John had no idea what had distressed Scarlet earlier, but he suspected—by the look on her face—that she still wanted out. He did, too. Hell, yes. And the sooner the better.

'Sorry to love you and leave you, folks,' he said once his mother stopped to draw breath. 'But I asked Scarlet out tonight and she said yes. So if you don't mind, we'll be off.' So, saying, he took hold of a startled Scarlet and steered her firmly towards the front door. 'Don't wait up,' he called over his shoulder, then whispered in her ear. 'We'll have to take your car, as I don't have one here, but don't worry; I can drive. I've only had two light beers all afternoon.'

Scarlet would have agreed to anything he said at that moment, she was so grateful to be away from Melissa and the pictures of her baby.

Five minutes later, John was reversing her car out of their garage, Scarlet only then realising she'd have a lot of questions to answer when she finally got home that night.

'Nice wheels, Scarlet,' John said once they were underway. 'The last time I was home you were driving an old white rust bucket.'

'I decided to spoil myself this year,' she replied. New car and a baby. At least that *had* been the plan.

Suddenly, the tears which had been threatening ever since Melissa brought up the subject of her pregnancy came back with a vengeance. Scarlet tried to choke them back but it was way too late. Maybe if she'd cried earlier in the week when she'd realised she hadn't conceived, she might have stood a chance of controlling her emotion. Instead, it had been building up in her for days, this feeling of help-lessness and hopelessness. She'd tried so hard to stay posi-tive. So very hard.

Her head dropped into her hands as her shoulders started to shake, noisy sobs bursting from her lungs.

John didn't know what to do for a split second. He'd known Scarlet was upset over something but he hadn't expected this level of grief. It wasn't like Scarlet at all!

To keep on driving seemed heartless so he pulled over to the side of the road and switched off the engine.

He didn't try to comfort her physically. It was too darned awkward in a small car with the gear stick and hand brake between the front seats. So he just sat there and let her weep. Bianca had once told him that women needed a good cry occasionally. Most times, they didn't require the men in their lives to solve their problems, just to be supportive and to listen. John wished he had a handkerchief to give her. But he wasn't the handkerchief-carrying kind of man.

Finally, when the weeping subsided, Scarlet snapped open the glove box and extracted a small box of tissues. She blew her dripping nose at length, then threw him a pained look.

'Thank you,' she sniffed.

'For what?'

'For getting me out of there.'

'Am I allowed to ask what upset you so much?'

'No,' she grumped, crumpling up the tissues into her hand and turning her face away from him.

'*No?*' John was never at his best when his will was thwarted. 'Scarlet King, we are not moving from this spot till you tell me what's going on.' As he made his stand, John's mind started running over what had happened after he'd walked into the kitchen. Melissa had come downstairs with the photographs of her ultrasound, insisting that they both look at them. Then his mother walked in and made some crack about his never giving her grandchildren. Which was probably true.

But, John realised in what could only be described as a light-bulb moment, Scarlet wanted to give *her* mother grandchildren.

'It was because of Melissa's pregnancy,' he said with typical male satisfaction at having worked something out for himself.

The lack of sensitivity in John's tone—not to mention the underlying arrogance—brought Scarlet back to herself. Her head whipped round, her blue eyes glaring daggers at him.

'Yes, of course it was your precious sister's pregnancy which upset me,' she snapped. 'Plus the way she shoved those damned photographs in my face. How do you think I felt when she told me she was going to have a lovely little girl to go with her lovely little boy when I would give my right arm to have just one baby of any sex?'

'But you will, Scarlet. One day,' he added.

'Oh really? You can guarantee that, can you, John? I'm thirty-four years old. My biological clock is ticking away like a time bomb. Already the odds of my conceiving a child are going downhill. If I don't have a baby soon, I might never have one.'

'Don't be ridiculous, Scarlet. Women of forty and older are having babies all the time.'

'I'm not being ridiculous, and women over forty are *not* having babies all the time. Most of the older mothers you read about these days are celebrities and actresses who have access to the best fertility clinics in the world. Have you noticed how many of them are having twins? You don't honestly think they're being conceived naturally, do you?'

John hadn't really thought about it at all. 'I will bow to your better knowledge on the subject. But you're not over forty yet, Scarlet. Not by a long shot. There's no reason to panic.'

'I have *every* reason to panic.'

'Look, if you're so damned desperate to have children, then why don't you just go out and get yourself pregnant? You're gorgeous—you'll have all the offers you could want.'

Scarlet gave him a totally scandalised look, determinedly ignoring the fact that he thought she was gorgeous. 'You think I would risk falling pregnant to just anyone, potentially also risking my sexual health? No, thank you very much. I have no intention of doing that.'

'So you're just going to wait till Mr Right comes along?'

'Actually, John, I have no intention of doing that either.'

'Oh? And what, pray tell, *are* you going to do?'

'If you must know, I'm already doing it.'

'Already doing what?'

Scarlet knew she'd just backed herself into a corner. Her and her big mouth! John always did have this bad habit of making her want to bring him down in flames, which was very immature of her. They weren't bickering children or rival classmates any more. They were grown up people.

Suddenly, it didn't seem such a bad idea to tell him what she was up to. John wouldn't tell anyone else, not if she asked him not to. Frankly, it would be good to talk to someone other than her mother, someone more objective. John was an intelligent guy; he would see the sense in her plan. Scarlet needed reassurance at that moment that she was doing the right thing.

'The thing is, John,' she said, still slightly hesitant. 'I… Um… I've decided to have a baby by artificial insemination.'

When he said nothing, she turned her face to look at him. He was frowning, like he didn't understand the concept at all.

'I investigated it thoroughly on the Internet first,' she rattled on, feeling compelled to explain it more fully. 'Trust me when I say I've given this a lot of thought and research. Anyway, I found a local clinic where they had a whole catalogue of sperm donors to choose from. All their background information was listed: their physical characteristics, health records, intelligence levels. I picked one out which I liked the sound of. He's American, tall, good-looking, with dark hair, blue eyes and an IQ of a hundred and thirty. Some of them had higher IQs—most of the donors are university students—but I didn't want a child who was a genius, just one smart enough to do well in life without having to struggle.'

'If you've already decided on this course of action, Scarlet,' John said when she finally stopped talking, 'then why were you so upset over Melissa's pregnancy?'

Scarlet sighed. 'I guess you might as well know the rest. The thing is it hasn't worked so far. I've failed to fall pregnant twice now and I… I… Well, when Melissa showed me her ultrasound pictures, I began to worry that something was wrong with me and I would never be a mother, and I… I…' Scarlet broke off when she choked up again.

'For what it's worth, Scarlet,' John said quietly into the sudden silence, 'I admire that you've taken positive action to get what you want in life. You have courage. At the same time,' John couldn't help himself from telling her, 'I think you're being quite selfish in deliberately having a child who will be denied a father figure in his life.'

Scarlet was both astonished and angered by this unexpected criticism. 'I wouldn't say that having a father figure in life is the be-all and end-all. I would have thought that you, of all people, would appreciate that.'

'*Touché*. But I did have a grandfather. Your baby won't even have that.'

'Maybe not, but it will have a wonderful grandmother.' Only one, though, she realised. Her paternal grandparents had both died some years ago.

'True,' John agreed. 'But what about when she's gone? What then?'

'I can't think about then,' Scarlet snapped.

'Just like your fictional name-sake.'

She glared at him. 'I thought you would understand.'

John shrugged. He wasn't sure why he found the idea of Scarlet having a baby with Mr IQ-of-a-hundred-and-thirty so uncomfortable, but his whole body objected.

'Wanting a baby is not exactly complicated. It's a basic drive in most women. And quite a lot of men too, I'm told,' she added caustically.

'I dare say you're right. Look, it's obvious that you're determined on this course of action, so I have a suggestion to make which I think would be infinitely preferable to your being impregnated by some stranger who will impart nothing to your child's life but a set of genes, which may not be as desirable as they read on paper. After all, what do you really know about this sperm donor? Nothing of any depth, that's for sure. You don't know his background or his family or his mental health. Perhaps it is a blessing that you haven't conceived his child so far.'

Scarlet could not believe that John was being so negative. All life had some risk, didn't it? There was no such a thing as a perfect plan, or a perfect partner, or a perfect anything! She had no idea what his counter-suggestion was going to be, but if he thought she was going to change her mind about trying for a baby then he was delusional.

John knew that what he was about to propose would shock her. He was pretty shocked at it himself. But something deep inside him was driving him on—the thought of Scarlet having a baby to some anonymous stranger was repulsive. She deserved better than that. She deserved…

'So, Scarlet, in the interest of the future happiness and security of your offspring, I propose that you ditch your present sperm donor in favour of…me.'

Scarlet could not have been more shocked if he'd suggested immaculate conception. She just stared at him with rounded eyes, looking for the catch. Or the joke.

'You *have* to be kidding me!' she exclaimed at last.

'Actually, no,' he said, feel perversely pleased with his offer now that he'd made it. 'I'm not.'

'But… But… *Why*?'

'Why not? I qualify, don't I? I'm tall, reasonably good-looking, with dark hair and blue eyes. Unfortunately my IQ is a good bit over a hundred and thirty but that's a moot point. I promise I won't interfere with the way you bring up the child, so it won't be so different to what you had planned. Though I would like to see the child occasionally. On top of that, he or she'll have a second pair of grandparents living just across the road. And, whilst my father wasn't a great father, I saw today that he has the makings of a great grandfather. That can happen sometimes, you know. His father—my grandfather—admitted to being a pathetic parent but he came into his own as a grandparent.'

Scarlet shook her head from side to side. 'I'm having serious trouble taking this all in.'

'Take your time.'

Scarlet blinked, then frowned. 'I still can't see why you would offer to do this.'

'I am capable of kindness, you know.' Or so Bianca had believed.

'This is more than just being kind,' Scarlet said, trying to get her head around John's offer. Who would have believed he would do such a thing? She shook her head from side to side. 'I have to confess that I'm tempted. Mum would certainly be more comfortable with you being the father than some stranger.'

'I would imagine so. She quite likes me, you know. Has done ever since I promised to look after you on the school bus.'

Scarlet rolled her eyes at him. 'I seem to recall you weren't thrilled at the time.'

'I didn't mind.'

'Rubbish! Come now, John, you've never been the Good Samaritan type. Which makes your offering to be my sperm donor all the more puzzling. Heavens, I don't know what to think or what to say.'

'Just say yes, Scarlet.'

'But it's such a difficult decision. I mean…it's a big thing to have a child together. Different if we were in love.'

John snorted. 'As we both know, being in love is no guarantee of future happiness. People fall out of love all the time.'

'It's still important for parents to like and respect each other.'

'You think I don't like and respect you?'

'We haven't exactly been the best of friends over the years.'

'But that's all in the past, when we were just stupid kids. We got along very well today, didn't we?'

'Yes,' she agreed reluctantly. 'Yes, we did. Oh Lord, I still don't know. If we go ahead and do this, what on earth are we going to tell everyone?'

'We'll cross that bridge when we come to it. Your priority at this point is becoming pregnant. Your body obviously isn't clicking with the sperm donor you chose,' he went on with cool, corrupting logic. 'You need to try someone different.'

Scarlet knew that, if she failed to get pregnant again with her chosen sperm donor, she'd regret not accepting John's offer. It was a case of do now, or possibly die childless!

'Okay. Okay. I'm going to throw caution to the winds and just say yes.'

'Great,' John said, feeling more excited than when he'd found oil. 'So what's the plan?'

'I'll contact the clinic first thing tomorrow morning and arrange for a time for you to go in and give them a sperm sample. Then, when—'

'Hang on!' John interrupted immediately. 'That's not how it's going to be done at all!'

'What do you mean?'

'I mean I have no intention of becoming a father via a turkey baster. Or a syringe. Or whatever they use these days. If we're doing this, let's do it right.'

'You mean you…you want to have sex with me?'

CHAPTER SIX

JOHN smiled wryly. 'Don't sound so shocked, Scarlet. I've wanted you since the first moment I saw you today, not to mention for years while we were growing up.'

Scarlet blushed furiously, shocked, yet secretly elated to discover that the feelings which had so blindsided her today had been returned for so long.

'But don't start thinking that I'm doing this just because of that—because I'm not.' Even as the denial left his mouth, John suspected he was morally skating on thin ice here. If what he was saying was strictly true, then why not just do what she suggested—go to this clinic and give them a sperm sample?

The truth was he *did* want to have sex with her. At the same time, he *did* also believe that normal intercourse was the best chance Scarlet had for falling pregnant. Clearly, the coldly clinical method hadn't worked. She needed to relax, to enjoy herself.

John decided to be bluntly honest with her. 'Not that I won't enjoy having sex with you,' he admitted. 'But that's not the only reason I'm suggesting we actually sleep with each other. It's because I think you're more likely to fall pregnant that way. Which is what you want, isn't it? To have a baby?'

John's saying the word 'baby' dragged Scarlet back to the present. She'd been off in another world ever since he'd confessed to wanting to have sex with her since they were teenagers. 'What? Oh yes, yes, that's what I want,' she said. 'A baby.'

'So what do you say, Scarlet?'

'I don't know…' The idea of actually sleeping with John made her head spin.

He sighed. 'What don't you know?'

'I don't know what I don't know!' she blurted out, feeling totally confused and conflicted.

'Look, I can understand that my suggestion has come as a bit of a shock to you, so why don't we go somewhere for coffee and talk about it rationally?'

'I don't think I'm capable of being rational about this. You've totally blown me away. I have to think about this on my own.'

John nodded. He wanted her to say yes with a depth of desire which shocked him; something in him was demanding that he—and only he—should give Scarlet the baby she so desperately wanted. However, much as he hated it, she needed time.

'I'll take you home.'

Scarlet sighed. The idea of going home and facing her mother while she was trying to decide something so huge didn't appeal either.

'How about we drive to Erina Fair and see a movie? You can pick something you'll like, some macho action flick with lots of car chases and killings. You can get all involved in that whilst I sit in the dark and think.'

He laughed. 'You are such a sexist, Scarlet. I happen to like a wide range of movies, not just macho action flicks, as you put it.'

'Oh sure,' she said in droll tones.

'I'll prove it to you.'

He surprised her by choosing a romantic comedy, one of those friends-into-lovers plots which had become popular lately. Scarlet might have enjoyed it if there hadn't been so many sex scenes, all of which were extremely raunchy. Clothes were stripped off at regular intervals as the two friends had wildly uninhibited sex in every conceivable place and position: on the floor. On the sofa. In a lift. Even in a meadow.

Of course, each of them had perfectly toned and buffed bodies which photographed beautifully from every angle; no doubt they were faking their orgasms. But still...it was obvious they knew what seriously fantastic ones felt like, and sounded like. Did people *really* make loud noises like that? Scarlet never had. Before long she began worrying that, if she agreed to John's proposal, he might expect her to be like that girl on the screen. And she wasn't, not even remotely. Her breasts were a lot smaller, for starters; her body wasn't as gym-bunny perfect and she certainly didn't come every single time. Actually, she didn't come very often at all, and never during actual sex. The ending annoyed her as well: it was pure Hollywood fiction where the protagonists fell in love and lived happily ever after. As if that ever happened!

'Is that what you're afraid of?' John said as they left the theatre. 'That if we have sex you might fall in love with me?'

Laughter spluttered from Scarlet's lips before she could smother it.

'Right,' he said drily. 'Obviously, that's not what you're afraid of.'

'No,' she said. Her fears had nothing to do with love. She stopped walking to turn and look up at him with thoughtful eyes. 'You have to admit that I don't really know the adult you, John. You're somewhat of a mystery man these days.'

'Not as much of a mystery man as your university student.'

'True. But I would still want to know more about your life in South America before I agreed to your being the father of my child. After all, your proposal is not the same kind of a deal as I would have had with my student donor. He doesn't want to be a part of my child's life. But you do, even if it is only in a limited way.'

'Okay, let's find a place to have some coffee and I'll tell you all about myself.' Even as he said this, John knew damned well he was not going to tell her the absolute truth. She could know about his work; nothing but good news there. Scarlet certainly didn't need to worry that he couldn't support a child financially. But no way was he going to tell her about Bianca. He could hardly bear to think about what had happened to that poor woman. Talking about it was out of the question.

Still, Scarlet would probably want some idea of his past love life. So he'd confess to a succession of girlfriends over the years, none of whom he'd fallen in love with, most of whom had broken up with him because of his inability to commit. That should do the trick of explaining his present partnerless existence, and did have a great deal of truth in it—though one could hardly call the sexual partners he'd had in the last decade 'girlfriends'.

'That pizza place over there looks open,' he said and took her arm.

Scarlet stiffened inside at his touch. Her whole body flared to life at the thought of how much more of her he would be touching if she agreed to his proposal. Just the thought of getting naked with him made butterflies erupt in her stomach.

Suddenly, she couldn't do it.

'No, John,' she said, and pulled her arm away from him.

'No what?'

'No, I've decided not to accept your offer. Thank you for making it; it was amazingly generous of you. But it's just not going to work for me. Please don't argue with me about this or tell me I'm being irrational. Because if you do I know I'm going to burst into tears again.' Which was true. Her emotions, already fragile, were in danger of embarrassing her once more.

She couldn't tell what John was thinking. His face had always been hard to read.

'I see,' was all he said. 'Well, it's your life, Scarlet. You do what you think best.'

'Thank you,' she said, struggling to keep the tears in check.

'No point in going for coffee then, is there?' he said brusquely. 'I'll take you home.'

CHAPTER SEVEN

SCARLET'S mother was still up watching television when she let herself into the house. Which perhaps was just as well. It stopped her breaking down, which was what stupidly she wanted to do again.

Her mother looked up at her from the sofa. 'You're home earlier than I expected.'

Scarlet glanced at the clock on the wall. It was only just after nine.

'Yes, well, there's not all that much to do around here on a Sunday night,' she said as she walked behind the kitchen counter and reached for the kettle. 'We didn't feel like eating or drinking any more so we went to a movie.'

'Any good?'

'So so,' she said, filling the kettle with water then turning it on. 'What movie are *you* watching?' Her mother always watched a movie at eight-thirty on a Sunday night.

'A very boring slice-of-life story which I'm just about to turn off.' Which she did. 'If you're making tea, make one for me too, please.'

'Okay,' Scarlet said, thinking she really had to get herself to bed before the third degree began in earnest.

Janet twisted round on the sofa so that she could watch her daughter's face. 'I was surprised to see you getting on so well with John today.'

'So was I,' Scarlet agreed, quite truthfully.

'He hardly left your side all afternoon.' *And hardly took his eyes off you as well.* Though that wasn't entirely new. Janet had always thought John had a secret crush on Scarlet when they were at school. He just hadn't had the confidence back then to do anything about it. The man who'd asked Scarlet out tonight had been a different kettle of fish entirely. Janet had been taken aback at how good he'd looked when he'd arrived. Not all men suited having their hair cut so short but John did. He had a well-shaped head, flat ears and a handsome face. A nice body, too. All in all, a fine looking man. Unattached too, according to Carolyn.

'You don't think that…?'

'No, Mum,' Scarlet cut in forcefully. 'That's never going to happen between John and me, so please don't go there.'

Janet was not about to give up *that* easily. 'If you say so, dear. But what does John say? Did he want to see you some more whilst he was home?'

'Mum, he only asked me out tonight because he can't stand being around his father for too long. I dare say he'll be flying back to where he came from immediately. My guess would be tomorrow.'

'Surely he'll stay a little longer than that after coming all the way from Brazil?'

Scarlet shrugged. 'I doubt it. Here's your tea, Mum. I'm taking mine to my room. I'm tired.'

Janet frowned as Scarlet went upstairs after coming out of the kitchen a few minutes later. She knew her daughter better than anyone else in this world. She could sense her state of mind, especially when she tried to hide it. Which she was doing right now.

Something had happened between her and John tonight, something which she didn't want to talk about, something which had made her very tense. Had he made a pass? Janet wondered. She wouldn't have been surprised if he had. Scarlet was lovely looking, but she had impossibly high standards when it came to men. They only had to put a single foot wrong and they were out the door. If Scarlet hadn't been searching for perfection in a partner, she would long have been married by now. Of course, Janet didn't condone men who were unfaithful the way Jason had been. But a girl sometimes had to turn a blind eye to minor failings if she wanted to become a wife and mother as much as Scarlet did.

Not that it mattered now, Janet thought with a resigned sigh. She'd obviously given up on the idea of marriage. Even if John *were* interested, he'd be fighting a losing battle with Scarlet. All she wanted was a baby.

Janet stood up from the sofa and walked over to pick up her tea. She hoped and prayed Scarlet would fall pregnant next month.

The same thought kept Scarlet awake long after she climbed into bed. She tossed and turned, her mind torturing herself with that most horrible 'what if?' What if she *didn't* fall pregnant next month? What then? Would she keep on trying or resort to more complicated and expensive procedures like IVF? How long could she keep doing this before she went stark, raving mad?

Already she could feel herself unravelling.

Maybe she should have accepted John's offer. Why *hadn't* she? Was it just because the idea of having sex with him terrified her? Was she so frightened of not living up to his expectations? That seemed a truly pathetic reason to knock back what was in many ways an excellent proposal. Then why, Scarlet? What are you so afraid of where John is concerned?

Her whirling mind eventually went back to that movie

they'd seen tonight, with its truly cheesy ending. Surely she couldn't be afraid of something similar happening to her? It seemed ludicrous in the extreme to think she would fall for John just because she went to bed with him.

For the umpteenth time, Scarlet sat up and punched her pillow before turning it over and slumping back down again.

'I'm getting sick of this,' she muttered as she stared blankly up at the darkened ceiling. 'I have to go to work in the morning. It's all your fault, John Mitchell. You should have minded your own business. You don't really want to be the father of my baby. You don't really want to be the father of *any* baby. So why on earth did you make such a ridiculous offer in the first place? It just doesn't make sense!'

The man himself was thinking along those same lines as he stood at his bedroom window, staring down at Scarlet's house as he'd done so many times when he'd been a boy, wanting to join in as she played with the other kids.

A wry smile pulled at his face. Here he was, years later, still wanting Scarlet, though admittedly in quite a different way!

Okay, so his offering to be her sperm donor had begun as a gesture of kindness, but it had quickly changed to one driven by his male hormones. He wanted her, naked and willing, in his arms, a prospect which he now realised had always been in the realms of fantasy. John only had to recall the way she'd reacted to his taking her arm tonight to know he wasn't on her 'ten most desirable men in the world' list. Perhaps that was why she'd rejected his offer. That and the fact she didn't want a selfish, self-centred commitment-phobe as the father of her baby. Much better to have some anonymous stranger.

Good one, John.

A light suddenly came on in the King house. John had no idea if it was Scarlet's bedroom or not. But he suspected it was. She was sleepless, just like him.

Another memory suddenly popped into his head—that of his taking her arm when they'd left his parents' party together. Scarlet hadn't pulled away from him then. Hadn't found his touch in any way repulsive. Then there'd been the way she'd looked at him when she'd first driven up to Gosford station earlier that day. That hadn't been the look of a woman who found him unattractive.

Maybe he was reading this situation all wrong. Maybe there was something else bothering Scarlet. Maybe she had been tossing and turning in her bed over there, wishing now that she hadn't rejected his offer. Because in truth it had been a good offer, far better than her having some stranger's child. He still didn't fancy that idea one little bit.

It suddenly occurred to John that Scarlet might eventually reconsider his offer. He suspected, however, that she would not come to such a decision lightly, or in the immediate future. To hang around home, hoping for her to change her mind, was not a bearable thought. Despite his recent discovery that he still loved his father, John still found being around him difficult. He couldn't even escape by going surfing; the doctors said such activities were out of the question till his leg was stronger. He'd already told his mother when he arrived home that he was booked on a flight tomorrow evening, letting her think he was returning to Brazil, whereas in fact he was going to Darwin. She'd been disappointed by his early departure, but resigned.

Would Scarlet be disappointed by his early departure? he wondered. Or relieved.

He could hardly ask her now.

Another thought came to him. What if she *did* change

her mind about his offer? She would need to know how to contact him, without having to ask his mother. No way would Scarlet do that. He knew her. She was like him in some ways—overly proud. And too independent for her own good.

Turning from the window, he made his way downstairs where everything was quiet; his parents had gone to bed some time ago. Switching on the kitchen light, he went to the drawer where his mother kept an assortment of biros, writing pads and different-sized envelopes. Selecting what he wanted, he returned to his room, switched on his bedside lamp and sat down to write. It took him several attempts before he got the wording just right but eventually he was satisfied.

Dear Scarlet.

By the time you read this I will have left. Not Australia, as my family believe. I have an apartment in Darwin where I go every winter for a few weeks' rest and recreation. This time, however, I intend to stay longer, though please keep this information confidential. Scarlet, I presume you are determined to keep trying for a baby by your anonymous donor. And that is your right. But if it is not successful, I wish you to know that my offer is still open. I can't promise you romance but I do promise you what I think you need very badly. Here are my mobile and satellite phone numbers so that you can contact me no matter where I am.

Your friend always, John.

He added the numbers then slipped the note into an envelope and wrote Scarlet's name on the front, having already decided to drop the letter into her mailbox tomorrow whilst she was at work.

By the time she got home he would be long gone.

Then it would be up to her.

CHAPTER EIGHT

Exactly one month and one day later

IT HADN'T worked. Again.

Despair clutched at Scarlet's already cramping stomach as she hunched over the toilet seat. There had to be something wrong with her. Because it didn't make sense. The clinic had tried a different procedure this time, putting the sperm right into her womb instead of just on the cervix. It was a more expensive procedure but was supposed to give her a better chance of conceiving.

A total waste of money as it turned out.

She dreaded telling her mother. Yet, she would have to. Scarlet wished now that she hadn't confided her plan in the first place. She should have just gone to the clinic on her own, in secret. That way, she could have handled her disappointment in private, without the added pain of watching her mother's disappointment. Her mum sometimes pretended that she didn't mind not having grandchildren but Scarlet knew that wasn't the case. She'd often said how she'd wanted to have a bigger family herself.

Scarlet frowned at this last thought. If her mother had wanted more than one child, then why hadn't she had some more? Scarlet's Dad hadn't died till she was nine. Scarlet sucked in sharply at the possibility that her mother had been unable to conceive more babies. But if that were so, then why hadn't she mentioned it to her? It might be an important clue over why she was having such trouble conceiving herself.

Not that she could go out and ask her right now. They were both at the salon, working. Wednesday was always a busy day. It would be impossible to question her till they were on the way home late this afternoon.

Janet knew, the moment she saw Scarlet's pasty face and dull eyes, that her period had arrived. The poor darling, she thought sadly as she watched her daughter put on a smiling face for a client.

'You know, don't you, Mum?' Scarlet said the moment they were alone in the car on the way home. She'd seen the sympathy in her mother's eyes when she'd come out of the powder room a couple of hours earlier. The sympathy and the sadness.

'Yes,' was all Janet could bring herself to say. She was close to tears. Not for herself but for her daughter.

'Mum, I've been thinking, was there any physical reason why you didn't have more children?'

Janet swallowed. She'd been expecting this question for ages.

'Not that I know of,' she answered truthfully. 'I was thoroughly checked out, the same way you've been. One doctor said I wanted to fall pregnant too much. He said stress and tension can sometimes be the problem.'

'Yes, I've read about that,' Scarlet said. 'That's why couples sometimes fall pregnant after they've adopted a child.'

'Your father and I were going to adopt a child,' Janet confessed. 'But then he was…' She broke off, unable to continue.

'Oh, Mum. I'm so sorry. I know how much you loved

Dad.' After the funeral, she'd listened to her mother cry at night for months and months. It never surprised Scarlet that her mother hadn't ever dated again, or remarried. She'd been a one-man woman.

Scarlet knew she'd never find that one true love like her mother had. But she was going to become a mother, come hell or high water. All afternoon, she'd been thinking about the letter John had left for her a month ago. When she'd first read it, she'd been incredibly touched, especially with his intuitive observations about her fragile nervous state. She'd almost changed her mind about going back to the clinic and rung him straight away. But, in the end, she simply hadn't had the courage to take what would have been a really big step for her. It seemed so much simpler not to involve other people, and to not face the problem of actually having sex with John. Scarlet understood that sex for men was not the big deal it could be for women. For her, anyway. She'd become more edgy about it as she'd got older. Less confident. More…nervous.

But the time for being Nervous Nelly was long gone. If she didn't take John up on his offer she would always regret it.

Of course, *he* might have changed his mind by now. God, she hoped not!

Well, if he had, she'd just have to persuade him otherwise, Scarlet vowed with renewed resolve. If he waffled, she'd remind him how much he'd always wanted to have sex with her!

Scarlet might have been shocked at herself if she hadn't been so fired up.

'Mum, I think that I might go away for a while. On a holiday.'

'Oh? Where to?'

'Somewhere warm. In Australia, of course. I don't want to go overseas.'

'Cairns is nice at this time of year,' her mother suggested.

'I was thinking of Darwin. I've never been there. And I've always wanted to see Kakadu.' A total untruth. Scarlet had seen one or two documentaries about the Northern Territory and was not at all interested in vast wetlands filled with biting insects, wild buffalo and crocodiles.

'Really?' her mother said, sounding surprised.

'I could go on some organised tours. That way I'd have company. You could manage without me, couldn't you, Mum? Lisa would be happy to do more hours. Joanne, too.'

'Of course I could manage. I managed when you left to be an estate agent, didn't I? When were you thinking of going?'

'Not sure yet. Possibly the end of next week.' Scarlet knew exactly when she would ovulate. She'd been charting her cycle for months. Two weeks after her period started was the beginning of her peak days for conceiving. No point in going to Darwin much before then. At the same time, she had to make it seem like she was going on a real holiday. She could hardly just go for a few days.

'For how long?'

'Um. A week or so. Maybe ten days,' she added for good measure.

'So you won't be going to the clinic for another procedure next month?'

'No, Mum. I've decided to have a break from that for a while.'

Her mother actually looked relieved. 'I think that's a good idea, love. And so's this holiday. Who knows? You might meet a nice man.'

'You never know, Mum,' Scarlet said, then deftly changed

the subject onto the traffic and the never-ending roadworks. She'd always been good at making conversation, but underneath her breezy chit-chat Scarlet was beginning to feel anxious about what John would say when she rang him. Which she fully intended to, at the first available moment. For if she procrastinated, her courage might falter.

As soon as they arrived home, Scarlet made the excuse that she needed to lie down for a while. When her mother offered to make her a cup of tea, she declined, saying she was going to take some pain killers and have a short nap before dinner. Fortunately, it was her mother's turn to cook. Also fortunately, Scarlet's bedroom was at the back of the house, some way from the kitchen. Once her mother turned on the television, she would not hear Scarlet talking on the phone.

Scarlet's hands were literally shaking as she drew John's letter out of the bedside drawer where she'd put it over a month ago. He'd given her two numbers, one for a regular mobile, one for a satellite phone. She sat on the side of her bed and tried the mobile number first. It rang, thank heavens. She would have hated for it to be engaged. As it was, she'd already worked herself up into a right state.

'For pity's sake, John, answer the damned thing,' she muttered under her breath after it had rung several times.

But he didn't, and the phone eventually switched to his message bank. A despairing Scarlet didn't leave any message, choosing instead to try the satellite phone first. She actually prayed as she punched in the numbers.

CHAPTER NINE

JOHN was putting a few more pieces of wood on the camp fire when he heard the distinctive ring of his satellite phone. Frowning, he crawled into his one-man tent, picked up the phone and carried it back out into the moonlight, where he stared at it briefly before sweeping the phone up to his ear.

'Hello, Scarlet,' he answered, trying to sound cool when inside he was anything but.

John had been relieved at first when she hadn't contacted him. Once he'd cleared his head, he'd told himself that it had been a crazy idea anyway. But as the days had crawled by, John's every waking moment had been haunted by the thought of going home at Christmas and seeing Scarlet with a stranger's child growing in her belly. Once again, he'd been repulsed by the idea.

After several particularly restless nights, he'd been tempted to ring her. But what could he say that he hadn't already said? It was obvious she didn't want him to father her child. To have pursued the matter would have made him look foolish.

So in the end, he'd done nothing. Literally. He hadn't tried to find work with any of the mining companies. He hadn't gone fishing, either, the way he usually did when he was holidaying in Darwin. Hadn't done a damned thing. He had just moped around the place, watching endless movies on TV and doing way too much thinking. And way too much drinking. Bianca would have said he was running away from real life. Again.

In the end, he'd had his heli-fishing mate drop him into this isolated spot for a few days and had been camping out alone. Nothing cleared the head better than communing with nature, he'd found.

And it had worked, to a degree. He'd finally begun to see the sense of Scarlet's decision not to accept his offer. Finally found some peace of mind over the situation. Or so he'd believed.

It had only taken one little phone call to shatter that illusion.

'How did you know it was me?' she asked, clearly taken aback.

'The caller ID said you were from New South Wales,' he explained. 'You're the only person in that state who has my satellite number.'

'Oh. I see.'

John suddenly had the most appalling thought. What if she was ringing to tell him she was finally pregnant? It was possible, he supposed. She might think he would like to know.

'Why are you ringing, Scarlet?' he asked abruptly.

Scarlet's heart sank at his brusque tone.

'You've changed your mind about your offer, haven't you?' she said.

The tension in John's gut immediately melted away.

'Not at all,' he replied.

'Really?' she gasped, renewed hope flooding her heart.

'Yes, really. So what happened, Scarlet? Given the time lapse since we last spoke, I presume you went back to the clinic for another go and it didn't work.'

'I got my period today,' she confessed with a sigh.

'Like I said in my letter, my offer is open.'

Scarlet had reached the stage where she would have given anything a try. But she wasn't so desperate that she still wasn't slightly bothered by one thing. 'I know I shouldn't look a gift horse in the mouth, John, but I still can't work out why you're doing this for me. Aside from the sex angle, that is. Which I also still can't fathom. I mean, if you always fancied me, then why didn't you do something about it before this?'

They were logical questions, John accepted. He wished he had some logical answers for her. He had to tell her something, he supposed, something which would satisfy her intelligence. Scarlet was no dummy.

'Can I be blunt with you?' he said.

'Please do.'

'I didn't do anything before this because I thought you would just knock me back,' he said, not untruthfully. 'Until we met again last month and I realised that the attraction was mutual. However, contrary to your belief, I also like you a lot, Scarlet, and I want to help you get what you obviously want very much—which is a baby. And, as strange as it seems, I also quite like the idea of having a child of my own. But if I'm to be brutally honest, what I want most is you, in my bed, for a good deal longer than you spend at that wretched clinic each month.'

Scarlet's silence at the other end of the line indicated a degree of shock. Or deep thoughtfulness. John suspected the former. He had gone overboard a bit in his attempt to focus on the sex angle. But he didn't want her questioning him further over his motives. He didn't understand them fully himself! All he knew was that his blood was racing through his body with a surge of entirely male, powerful satisfaction at her agreement. For a short time, Scarlet was going to be his.

Scarlet had been rendered speechless by the decidedly R-rated images which had sprung into her mind. She was seriously glad that John couldn't see the burst of heat which flamed into her cheeks.

'Come now, Scarlet, you must know how very desirable you are.'

Now Scarlet felt hot all over. A shiver ran down her spine at the realisation she might shortly find out just how desirable he thought she was.

'I hope your silence doesn't mean you've changed your mind about this?' he said, his voice sounding curiously expressionless.

'No,' she choked out, still blushing at her earlier train of thought. Thank heavens they weren't face to face!

'Good.' His voice relaxed again. 'When can you get yourself up here?'

Scarlet swallowed, then sat up straighter. She'd always been more comfortable following a plan.

'I thought as soon as possible,' she said briskly.

'How about the beginning of next week?'

'Well, I'll have to get stuff organised at work…'

He rode over her objections. 'I'm sure you can sort it. Once you've booked your flight next week, text me your time of arrival and I'll be at the airport waiting for you.' He sounded equally brisk, and it was as difficult as ever to guess what he was feeling. 'Don't send the text to this number. Send it to my mobile. I'll be back in Darwin by then.'

Scarlet rolled her eyes in exasperation. Why was it then men wouldn't *listen*? 'Where are you, anyway?' she asked.

'Camping out in one of the national parks.'

Scarlet had been doing some mental calculations.

'Wait—next week is way too early. I can't possibly fall pregnant till a week after that. I never ovulate before day fourteen on my cycle. I know this for a fact because I've been taking my temperature every day for the last year and—'

'Scarlet,' he interrupted. 'If you want to get pregnant, then let's try this *my* way.'

Truly, he could be as irritating a man as he'd been an irritating boy! 'Which is?' she snapped.

'Not taking your temperature every day, for starters. Not caring about when you bloody ovulate either. Because, let's face it, that method hasn't been working too well for you up till now, has it?'

'I guess not,' she admitted grudgingly.

'I suggest you leave this whole operation up to me. Put yourself entirely in my hands. No arguments, no more buts.'

'Yes,' she bit out.

'Good,' he said, smiling wryly to himself at the thought that 'yes' wasn't a word Scarlet was used to saying. But she was going to say it a lot during their time together. He would *make* her say it. No, he would make her *want* to say it. For that was what he craved all of a sudden. Not just Scarlet's compliance but her complete surrender.

The thought excited him unbearably. Was this what had been lurking at the back of his mind? Not just desire for sex, but a desire to seduce? To possess? To control?

The idea perturbed him. He'd never been into that kind of thing. Sex for him was usually just a physical release with no strings attached. He'd always steered well clear of becoming emotionally involved with the women he slept with. John could see, however, that this was a different situation entirely. If truth be told, his emotions were already involved. The problem was which ones?

He almost told her to forget it then; that *he'd* changed his mind. But it was too late. The roller coaster of destiny was already moving and he was solidly strapped in. There would be no escape till it came to rest at the end of the ride.

CHAPTER TEN

BECAUSE she had a window seat and her head was too fuzzy to read, Scarlet spent most of the four-and-a-half-hour flight to Darwin staring down at the landscape below. With no clouds in the sky, there was nothing to hinder her view of what was really an incredible sight. What a big country Australia was, big and rugged and mostly uninhabited. The last frontier, some people called it.

Scarlet had never flown over the outback of Australia before. Or *been* in the outback, for that matter. Holidays before her dad had died had been confined to trips to Sydney, or the Gold Coast. Once, they'd gone to the Blue Mountains where they'd visited the Three Sisters and the Jenolan Caves. After her dad had died, she and her mother hadn't gone on holidays for years. Eventually, they had started going to Fiji each year, because it was reasonably close to Australia and good value for money.

She'd never been to Darwin. But she knew quite a bit about the place. Or she did now, having looked it up on the Internet this past week. Scarlet was not a girl who ever liked to appear ignorant. Up till now her knowledge of the capital city of the Northern Territory had been rather superficial and sketchy. Although she already knew that Darwin had been struck by a cyclone in the seventies, she hadn't realised it had happened on Christmas Day, of all

days, which she found very sad. She also hadn't appreciated the devastation it had caused. The photographs of the
aftermath had been horrendous. Understandably, it had
taken decades to rebuild the city but it was now a thriving
mining town and tourist Mecca, the gateway to Kakadu
National Park and lots of other famous Aboriginal sites.
Its harbourside position in the extreme north of Australia
meant its climate was very hot and humid in the summer,
but wonderfully mild in the winter.

She'd dithered considerably over what to bring, in the
end packing probably more than she would need. But it
had been so hard to choose. Scarlet had always loved nice
clothes, and had a wardrobe full of outfits for every occasion. Her mother had thought she was crazy putting in
a couple of pretty dresses, but that was because she believed Scarlet was going to spend her 'holiday' either laz-
ing around the pool of the hotel she'd supposedly booked,
or going on day bus-tours, all of which required nothing
more than Bermuda shorts, solid shoes, a hat and insect
repellent. Her mother had stopped criticising her choice of
wardrobe when Scarlet reminded her about that nice man
she might meet.

'Who knows?' she'd added for good measure. 'He might
ask me out to dinner!'

Which she'd assumed John would at some stage.

But what if he didn't? Scarlet now wondered.

During the past week, Scarlet had tried not to think
about what John's plans were for the next ten days. For
what was the point? She'd already agreed to his terms,
whatever they were.

But, now that the moment was at hand, it was almost
impossible not to wonder, and worry. Maybe she should
have warned him that she was a bit of a lemon in the bedroom. It was one thing to have private fantasies where she

stripped off without a qualm and had multiple orgasms every single time she had sex. The reality was totally different. She was rather shy at being naked in front of a man.

Her stomach tightened as she tried to imagine what it was going to be like, having sex with John. For some crazy reason she was terrified of disappointing him. She wanted him to find pleasure in her body.

The announcement that they'd begun their descent into Darwin tightened her stomach further. If Scarlet hadn't been so besieged by nervous tension, she might have noticed that she'd stopped thinking about what she'd come to Darwin to achieve. All her thoughts were on one subject and one subject only: John.

Seeking distraction, she stared once more at the ground below, surprised to see that the red and brown of the outback had given way to a greener landscape, one with lots of trees and, yes, water out to the left of the plane. It looked like a harbour but obviously not Darwin harbour. There were no houses along the foreshore and not many boats on the water. Of course, it always took a good while for a commercial jet to descend into an airport, so they weren't over Darwin yet.

When the plane banked sharply, the setting sun shone straight into Scarlet's eyes. She automatically shut them, then kept them shut, always having found landing stressful, though this time her stresses were many and varied.

The landing seemed to take for ever, but exiting the plane was relatively quick, thank goodness, as her seat was right down the back, not far from the exit. She walked across the tarmac towards the terminal building, her only thought at that moment being that every step brought her closer to John.

John stood at a window in the arrivals area, scanning the passengers as they left the plane. He spotted Scarlet immediately, the rays of the setting sun bouncing gold off her blonde hair which was down and blowing in the breeze. She was wearing jeans and a white jacket, with a white-and-blue top underneath. She looked utterly gorgeous, sexy and…very tense. Her forehead was scrunched into a frown and her walk was fast and anxious, passing several other passengers before entering the terminal building.

Clearly, she didn't see him standing nearby, although her eyes were darting around the place. When he stepped forward to make his presence known, she gave him a tight smile, obviously very nervous indeed. At her request, he led her to the nearest ladies' room, waiting patiently outside for her return, using the time to gather his thoughts and assess his reaction to her arrival.

There was only one word to describe the way he was feeling.

Excited. More excited than he'd been in years. Not just sexual excitement, though that was there as well. Hell, yes! He'd had a hard-on for days. But there was another excitement firing him up: the excitement which came from rising to meet a challenge.

During the last week or so John had given a lot of thought to why he was doing this. He'd finally come to the conclusion that it was his male ego that had directed his offer to Scarlet. There wasn't anything mysterious or confusing about it. It was his competitive spirit coming to the fore. He, John Mitchell, was going to do what no other man could do. His intense desire to give Scarlet a baby wasn't just sexual, it was *primal*. Man doing what he was put on earth to do: propagate.

Scarlet had been spot on when she'd said having a child was a basic drive for men as well as for women. It was.

All these realisations had led John to approach his time with Scarlet as much more than an opportunistic affair. It was an important project, to be researched and carried out with meticulous attention to detail. When he'd been looking for oil in Argentina he hadn't just lucked upon the discovery. It had taken months of painstaking work, both physical and intellectual. So he'd set about researching the reasons for an otherwise healthy woman not conceiving with the same dogged determination. After reading every article on the Internet on the subject, he'd come to the conclusion that Scarlet's most likely problem was stress, something he'd already suspected. She needed to relax more and stop obsessing about having a baby.

Which was where he came in. His job was to relax her, and the best way to relax her was through sex. Not just ordinary old sex—great sex. The kind which would eventually make the woman forget everything but having her partner deep inside her. John had concluded that Mother Nature had created orgasms for a reason, so making sure that Scarlet had fun was his number one priority.

Luckily, John knew his way around a woman's body very well indeed. Knew what pleasured them. Knew what was likely to satisfy them. Scarlet had obviously had some negative experiences where the opposite sex was concerned. It made sense that she'd been turned off men to a degree.

She'd probably expect him to make a pass tonight. All the more reason why he wouldn't. Let her be impressed with his gentlemanly manners and his apartment. It was a very nice apartment. He'd give her one of the two guest rooms, the one which opened out onto the balcony with a view of the harbour, the same balcony his bedroom opened onto. Tomorrow, he would take her sightseeing during the day, wine and dine her in the evening, then make love to her afterwards. Romantic sex, the kind with silk sheets and candles.

John's mouth quirked. Unfortunately, he didn't have silk sheets or candles. He wasn't that kind of guy. Damn. Still, perhaps it was for the best not to get too romantic—it might…confuse the issue.

Such thinking brought a rueful laugh to his lips. Scarlet King, fall in love with *him*? Not bloody likely!

Scarlet felt marginally better by the time she emerged from the ladies' room. Besides a much-needed trip to the loo, she'd taken off her jacket and brushed her hair. But the sight of John standing there brought a swarm of butterflies to her stomach. She still couldn't get used to how sexy she found him. He looked very attractive, dressed in fawn cargo shorts and a white polo shirt which highlighted his tan, as well as his broad-shouldered, very fit body.

She also couldn't get used to the way he kept looking at her, like she was a freshly cooked pizza and he a starving Italian. His obvious desire was both flattering and nerve-wracking at the same time. Her pulse-rate definitely moved up several notches.

Scooping in a deep breath, she hooked her bag over her right shoulder, draped her jacket over her left arm and moved towards him, fiercely aware of the movements slow walking and fast breathing were creating in her female body. The soft rise and fall of her breasts. The sway of her hips. Lord, but she was blushing now!

Thankfully, his eyes had by then moved in the direction of the nearby carousel where the luggage was coming out.

'What does your bag look like?' he asked, glancing back over his shoulder at her.

'It's black with a big pink ribbon tied to the handle. There it is now,' she said, pointing.

John strode over and scooped her bag off the carousel, his eyebrows lifting when he felt the weight of it. 'I only asked you to come for ten days, Scarlet,' he said with dry amusement as he steered her towards the exit, dragging the bag behind them. 'Not for life.'

'I hate going away anywhere and getting caught with either not enough clothes or all the wrong ones.'

'Can't say it's a problem I have often.'

'You're not a female.'

'Which is rather a good thing,' he said with a wry little smile.

Scarlet ground to a halt and stared up at him.

'What?' he said.

'Do I know you at all, John Mitchell? I thought I did. I thought I had you pegged as that introverted, antisocial pain-in-the-neck kid from across the street who'd grown up into an irritatingly gorgeous but pain-in-the-neck adult. Instead, suddenly, I find out you're nothing like that at all. You're actually quite witty and charming and…and…'

'Maybe you never knew the real John Mitchell,' he countered.

'Obviously I didn't. What other surprises do you have in store for me?'

'Shall we go and find out?' he said, taking her elbow again and leading her out to the visitors' car-park.

His SUV didn't surprise her, despite being relatively new and relatively unused. But the sheet of paper waiting on the passenger seat did. It was the printout of a medical bill of health.

She shook her head from side to side as she read it. 'It was very thoughtful of you to do this, John,' she said.

'I just didn't want to you to worry about anything at any stage. I wasn't going to offer you less than what you were getting at that clinic. I'm quite sure your anonymous donor had a similar clearance.'

'Yes. Yes, he did,' she said, frowning. 'I should have thought to ask you, but I didn't. It was silly of me.'

'Not silly. Just human. You've been upset lately. And very busy. But you would have thought of it eventually, and you would have worried. Now, you don't have to.'

'No,' she said, and smiled over at him. 'I don't. Thank you again, John. For everything.'

'Don't start canonising me yet, Scarlet.'

'I see,' she said, and gave him a much more typical Scarlet look. Very droll. 'I'll try not to jump to saintly conclusions about you in future.'

'That would be wise.'

By the time they left the airport, the sun had set and night was only a few minutes away. Despite the roads into the city being well lit, it wasn't easy for a newcomer to Darwin to see much during the short drive to the city, so John didn't bother doing the tourist-guide bit of pointing things out to her. Scarlet did remark on how good the road was. John explained that most of the infrastructure was fairly new and well planned, one positive legacy of the cyclone. In just over ten minutes, they were entering the Central Business District which naturally, was a lot smaller than Sydney's.

'It all looks very neat and tidy,' Scarlet commented as he drove up Stuart Street then turned left into the Esplanade which was one of the best streets in Darwin to live in, in John's opinion. As well as being right on top of the CBD, it was facing the water in a south-westerly direction which meant you could still see the magnificent sunsets as well as get the advantage of the sea breezes.

His apartment was towards the southerly end of the street in a multi-storeyed building whose walls were cement rendered in an attractive grey-blue colour. There were lots of balconies facing the water, all of them enclosed with glass panels and black railings. The gutterings, trim and window frames were all black which looked extremely smart indeed. The garages were in the basement, with John having two allotted spaces for himself and guests. He parked in one, then helped Scarlet out before removing her bag from the back. She didn't say a word as he led her over to the lift. Maybe she was worrying that he would pounce the moment they were alone.

Her head whipped round to stare at him when he pressed the top floor button.

'You live in a penthouse?' she asked, taken aback.

'Not exactly. Penthouses usually occupy the whole top floor. There are two top-floor apartments of equal size, one of which is mine.'

She fell silent once more till John showed her into the apartment, at which point she stared at him again, shaking her head at the same time. 'You really are very rich, aren't you?'

'Rich enough.'

'For what?'

He shrugged. 'I don't have to work for the rest of my life if I don't want to. Though of course I will.'

Again she shook her head. 'This place must have cost a small fortune.'

'Not quite that much. I bought it off-plan a few years ago.'

'Did you choose the furniture?'

'Lord, no. I have absolutely no taste whatever in that regard. I had it professionally decorated and furnished. Would you like to see the rest of it?'

'Yes, please.'

Scarlet quickly noted that the same colour palate had been used throughout the whole apartment, ranging from white, to white with a greyish tinge, to various shades of grey right through to black, splashes of turquoise brightening up what could otherwise have been a dull decor. Which no doubt was why the designer had chosen glass surfaces for the various tables in the living area, to lift the heaviness of the black leather sofas and chairs.

Scarlet loved the circular glass dining table—which was set in a hexagonal-shaped alcove—and had a large turquoise ceramic bowl sitting in the middle. She even loved the dining chairs, which were black leather on chrome frames. The kitchen was spectacular, the stainless steel appliances and turquoise splashback set off beautifully by black cupboard doors and white stone benchtops which had grey flecks in it. The three chrome-based stools which were tucked neatly under the breakfast bar had turquoise leather saddle-seats which had to have been specially made.

The two guest bedrooms were similarly sized and furnished, with queen-sized beds, white lacquered furniture and white shag rugs on the floor, though the bed linen was different. One had a rather masculine black, grey and white striped quilt set whereas the second one was more feminine, a white background with turquoise flowers on it. That bedroom also opened out onto the front balcony, unlike the other one. The main bathroom, situated between the two guest bedrooms, was all white with silver taps and trim, and the loveliest, thickest turquoise towels. Scarlet was rather particular when it came to bathrooms and could find no fault anywhere in that one.

When she commented on how spotless everything was, John informed her that he had the apartment serviced every few days when he was in town.

'Housekeeping,' he added, 'is not my forte.'

Scarlet didn't imagine that it would be. He was a man's man, with an outdoors job and outdoors hobbies such as surfing and camping.

The last room John showed her was the master bedroom, which blew her away even more than the kitchen. The black quilt on the king-sized bed contrasted beautifully with the white lacquered bedhead and side tables. The bedside lamps were exquisite, with chrome bases and exotic black shades which had crystal drops hanging from the bottom edges. Two rectangular white shag rugs were perfectly positioned on either side of the bed and a huge flat-screen television was built into the wall opposite the foot of the bed.

Scarlet suddenly saw herself sitting stark naked in that decadent-looking bed, propped up against a mountain of pillows whilst John was doing unimaginable things to her. It was a struggle not to blush once again—something which she seemed to be doing a lot in John's presence. Somehow, she made some innocuous compliment and took refuge by thoroughly inspecting the oversized walk-in wardrobe, before moving onto the black marble *en suite* bathroom where everything seemed to have been built for two. A spa bath *and* a shower. She couldn't look at either without once again picturing herself in there, naked again of course, with an equally naked John doing even more unimaginable things to her. And not under any covers.

Once again, heat zoomed into her cheeks.

Thankfully, her back was to John.

'You've gone rather quiet,' he said from just behind her. 'Is there something wrong?'

By the time she turned around, Scarlet had her blushing under control. She even managed a polite smile. 'Not at all. This place is lovely, John.'

'But...?'

'But what?'

'I was sure I heard a "but" in there somewhere.'

Scarlet decided to take the bull by the horns in an attempt to defuse the nervous tension which was building up inside her. 'I was wondering if you expected me to join you in here tonight.'

In spite of his earlier plans, John was tempted to say *yes, by God, of course I am*. But he could see that she wasn't ready. She was way too tense for him to achieve what he wanted to achieve, which wasn't just satisfaction for himself but satisfaction for her.

'I thought you'd be too tired,' he said, doing his best to ignore his body, which shouted in protest.

She smiled. A rather odd smile, but a smile nevertheless.

'When I'm nervous about something, I like to get it over and done with as soon as possible.'

'There's no reason for you to be nervous.'

Scarlet laughed. 'You have no idea.'

'I have no idea about what?'

Her face twisted into a grimace. 'I should have told you earlier.'

'Told me what?'

'I think I might be a little bit frigid.'

John's surprise must have shown in his eyes, for Scarlet looked away from him. 'This is so embarrassing,' she choked out.

He deliberated for a moment, then reached out to take gentle possession of her chin and turn her face back to his. He doubted very much that she was frigid—he'd seen passion in her too many times.

'Let's just take this one step at a time,' he said softly, his eyes holding hers. 'You like to be kissed, don't you? When you're with a man you're attracted to, that is.'

She blinked, then nodded.

Scarlet thought he was going to kiss her. But he didn't. Instead, he released her chin then lifted his hand to rub two of his fingertips back and forth along her lower lip, before tracing the full circle of her mouth over and over. Soon, her lips were tingling, her heart was pounding madly in her chest and she was *dying* for him to kiss her. Her mouth fell open as she struggled for breath, her tongue drying as she sucked in much-needed air. At which point he finally did what she craved: removed his fingers and replaced them with his lips.

It was a kiss such as she had never experienced before. Perversely restrained, but incredibly exciting. He cupped her face as he gently caressed her swollen lips, till a frustrated moan escaped her throat. Only then did he deepen the kiss, his lips applying more pressure, holding her lips far enough apart for his tongue to slide into her mouth.

Scarlet's head whirled. She could not think straight. Neither did she care. All she wanted was for John to keep on kissing her.

But he didn't.

She made some sort of protest when his mouth lifted abruptly from hers. A moan. A groan. She could not be sure which.

When she stared up at John she saw that he didn't seem at all rattled.

'I take it then,' he said coolly, 'that you find me attractive?'

Her stare became a glare. 'You're an arrogant bastard, John Mitchell.'

His smile widened. 'And you're incredibly beautiful, Scarlet King.'

She pursed her lips in defiance at the involuntary pleasure his compliment gave her.

'You're also not even a little bit frigid.'

'Oh!' she exclaimed frustratedly. 'You really are the most annoying man.'

'But an attractive one,' he reminded her with a perfectly straight face.

She couldn't help it. She laughed. 'Whatever am I going to do with you?' she said without thinking.

John's eyebrows arched, his eyes twinkling suggestively.

Scarlet's own blue eyes narrowed. 'Don't you dare say another thing. Now, I'm going to go unpack in one of the guest bedrooms. I'd love the one with the turquoise flowers, if it's okay with you? Meanwhile, I don't suppose there's any food about?'

'Unfortunately, cooking is not my forte either,' he returned. 'So the best I can offer you is takeaway for tonight. But I know lots of local Asian-style restaurants who'll deliver within half an hour. What would you prefer? Chinese? Thai? Vietnamese?'

'I'm not fussy,' she said. 'You choose.'

'Thai it is, then,' he said as they both turned and walked back into the living room. 'Join me back in here when you're ready. I bought some snacks and some wine in anticipation of your visit.'

Scarlet almost told him that she didn't usually drink much; that she'd just been upset that day. But she didn't want to bring up the subject of her ongoing failure to conceive a child. For a while there, she'd forgotten about that. She'd forgotten to ring her mother as well. Oh dear.

'I'll have to ring my mother first before I do another thing,' she said, feeling terribly guilty. 'Let her know I've arrived safely.'

'Fine. You do that. I'll go ring the restaurant. And Scarlet...?'

'What?'

'You can relax; I promise I won't be making you to do anything you don't want to.' His mouth curled up in a wicked smile. 'Not unless you beg me, anyway.'

CHAPTER ELEVEN

A WORRIED Janet King jumped to answer the phone as soon as it rang, relief flooding through her when she saw it was her daughter's mobile number on the display. She'd always hated flying and had been tense all afternoon at the salon, especially when the estimated time of arrival of Scarlet's flight had come and gone without a call. She'd been glad to come home where she didn't have to make polite conversation and where she could show her agitation by grumbling at the news reader on the television. Her nerve-endings were still strung out as she swept the receiver up to her ear.

'Hi, Mum,' Scarlet said before she could utter a word. 'You can relax now. The plane didn't crash and I'm safely at the hotel.'

'I wish you'd rung me from the airport,' Janet said plaintively. 'I've been worried sick.' The words were barely out of her mouth when she regretted them. She hated mothers who talked like that to their adult children. It put them in a terrible position.

Scarlet smothered a sigh. 'Sorry. I thought I'd wait till I got to the hotel so that I could tell you about it.'

'I'm the one who's sorry, darling. You've gone up there for a rest and here I am, putting guilt trips on you already. I promise not to keep on being a pain. Or to expect you to ring me all the time. But, yes, I would like to know about the hotel. Is your room nice?'

Scarlet moved over to sit on one of the huge black leather sofas, amazed at how soft and comfortable it was. 'Very,' she said as she leant back into its squashy depths. 'Has all the mod cons and a view of the harbour.'

'You never did tell me how much you paid for it.'

Scarlet winced at the lies she'd told, both directly and by omission. She hadn't realised how awkward things could become. 'Actually, I didn't just book a room, Mum. It's an apartment.'

'Goodness! It's not like you to be so extravagant, Scarlet, except perhaps when it comes to clothes. Not that I'm complaining, mind. You deserve some spoiling after all you've been through.'

It was ironic that, right at that moment, John came into the living room carrying a frosted glass of white wine which he handed to Scarlet, who mouthed, "Thank you," before lifting the glass to her lips. She had a feeling she was going to need a drink or two before this night was out.

'You'll have to send me some photos of the place,' her mother added.

Scarlet took a sip of the deliciously chilled wine whilst wondering how she could avoid doing that. Perhaps she could just send photos of the view, the guest bedroom, half the main bathroom and about a quarter of the humungous kitchen. But not right now.

'Can I leave that till tomorrow morning, Mum? I'm pretty bushed tonight. I just want to have a shower and go straight to bed.'

'Without eating anything?'

'I won't starve, Mum. There's a small stock of essentials in the kitchen,' she said truthfully. John had shown her the floor-to-ceiling pantry. 'It's lovely. There's even a complimentary bottle of very good white wine in the fridge.' She raised her glass in a toast-like gesture to John who'd settled himself on the sofa adjacent to hers. He smiled back whilst stretching his long arms along the back of the sofa, looking ridiculously sexy.

A distracting thought. It reminded her of an explicit image she'd briefly entertained last week. It was difficult for her mind not to dwell on her fantasy, when she would soon become extremely intimate with the real thing.

Though not tonight...

Was she really relieved about that?

Scarlet could not deny that, whilst she was still nervous about going to bed with John, she no longer felt afraid of it. Perversely, she was almost looking forward to it. A man who kissed as well and as imaginatively as he did would surely be a good lover. Gosh, he really did have a great body.

When she felt in danger of ogling him again, Scarlet reefed her eyes away and focused firmly on her conversation with her mother.

'So how did you cope today without me?' she asked.

'Fine. Though none of the other girls are a patch on you when it comes to colour. I suspect a few of your clients will wait till you come back before getting theirs done again. Still, you'll only be gone ten days. It's not an eternity. I'm sure they'll survive.'

'I'm sure they will. I'd better go now, Mum. I keep on yawning. I'll give you a call again tomorrow night.'

'I'd like that. You can tell me what you've been up to all day.'

Scarlet swallowed, then glanced over at John. Would he want to make love in the morning, in broad daylight? Or would he wait till tomorrow night?

'I…er… I doubt I'll be doing too much tomorrow,' she said. 'I might just walk around the city and get my bearings. Do a little shopping for food. I don't fancy going out to restaurants on my own so I'll probably cook.'

'Sounds nice. Night night, darling. Love you.'

'Love you too, Mum. Bye.' After she hung up, Scarlet took a deep swallow of the wine before glancing over at John.

'Mothers!' she said with a mixture of exasperation and affection.

'They mean well,' he replied.

'But?' Scarlet prompted with a wry little smile. 'I'm sure I heard a but in there somewhere,' she added, echoing the words he'd used earlier.

His smile carried amusement. 'I think you're the witty one here, Scarlet, not me. But, no, no buts. Mothers will be mothers, no matter how old their children get. You just have to learn how to circumnavigate their tendency to cling and control without their knowing how much you hate it.'

'But I don't hate it,' she said. 'Not the way you do. I think of my mother's concern for me as caring, not clinging and controlling.'

He shrugged his shoulders. 'Not all mothers are equal. Yours, I have to admit, is especially nice.'

'So is yours.'

'True. But mine is married to my father.'

Scarlet tipped her head slightly to one side as she searched his face. 'I've always wanted to ask you why you hate your father so much. I mean… I know he's not the happiest of souls but he's still your father.'

'Please don't go down that road, Scarlet.'

'What road?'

'The third degree road.'

'I was just curious about the relationship between you and your father. I have no intention of asking you a whole heap of questions about your life.'

'Good. Because I have no intention of answering them,' he growled as he crossed his arms in a belligerent fashion.

Scarlet added 'defensive' and 'secretive' to John's list of personality flaws, along with arrogant and rude.

'Charming,' she muttered.

'No. I'm actually not at all charming,' he admitted drily. 'I'm exactly what you called me earlier—introverted and antisocial.'

Scarlet's blood pressure began to rise. 'For pity's sake, let's not go down that road, either!'

'And what road is *that*, might I ask?' he snapped.

'The back-to-the-future childish road, where we fight all the time and end up spoiling what I came up here for. Trust me when I say I no longer wish to know the ins and out of your life story. I know I originally said I did but I've changed my mind on that score. I don't give a damn where you've been all these years, what you've done or who you've slept with, safely or otherwise. I also don't give a damn how bloody rich you are. All I care about is whether this works and we can actually make a baby!'

She was still glaring at him several seconds later when the beginnings of a smile tugged at the corners of his tightly pressed lips. Before long he was smiling broadly at her.

'You always were good at tongue lashings.'

Scarlet refused to smile back at him. She was still way too angry. Instead, she took another gulp of wine. When it went straight to her head, she realised she really needed to eat something. And soon.

As if on cue, the buzzer to the apartment's security

system went off, indicating that someone required entry to the building. Hopefully, it was someone delivering the Thai food.

'Saved by the bell,' John quipped and stood up. 'That should be dinner,' he said as he walked to the front door where he flipped a switch on the wall console and asked who it was.

'Dinner delivery for John Mitchell.'

'I'll come down and get it.'

Scarlet sat and worried a little about the future while he was downstairs, then decided she had to stop thinking. She drained her glass, then went out to the kitchen where she refilled from the opened wine bottle she found in the fridge door and returned to sit, sipping in silence, as she waited for John's return.

He arrived with some delicious-smelling containers.

'Let's go eat this in the kitchen. Unless of course you want me to set the dining table?' he added.

'I don't think we have time for that,' Scarlet said when she stood up and the room spun round. 'If I don't eat something in the next five minutes, I'm going to become seriously tipsy.'

'On one glass of wine?'

'I refilled whilst you were downstairs.'

'You drunkard, you!'

'Stop mocking me and go serve up that food!'

'Can you make it to the kitchen on your own or do you want me to carry you?'

She rolled her eyes at him. 'I think I can make it that far alone.'

'What a shame. I've always wanted to sweep you up into my arms.'

'You liar, you!'

He sighed melodramatically. 'Oh, Scarlet, whatever am I going to do with you?'

'Hopefully, you're going to feed me.'

CHAPTER TWELVE

JOHN was still sitting up in his bed, watching television, at eleven-fifteen. It was a deep-sea fishing documentary which would normally have interested him. But his mind kept wandering. The only reason he had the TV on was that he couldn't sleep. He couldn't stop thinking about Scarlet.

He now regretted his decision to leave making love to Scarlet till tomorrow. His desire had deepened with each minute he spent with her. Even when she was being sassy or actively rude, he wanted her. Actually, the sassier she was, the *more* he wanted her. It was all rather perverse. He could not wait till the morning. Yet he would have to, he supposed. He could hardly barge into her bedroom at this late hour and demand she honour their deal, particularly when she was fast asleep. That would hardly endear him to her. Which would be a shame, considering they were getting along surprisingly well, despite the sarcastic repartee which they both seemed compelled to indulge in. But what the hell? He'd enjoyed it.

Unfortunately, the evening had ended shortly after the meal was over, with Scarlet claiming total exhaustion.

He'd listened to her in the shower as he'd cleaned up the kitchen, his mind bombarded with the image of her standing there naked whilst jets of hot water streamed over her shoulders and back. Before long the image had become a fully fledged sexual fantasy. In his head she'd turned around so that the water splashed over her face and threw her head back, arching her spine so that her breasts were thrust up towards the water, gasping when it beat against her erect nipples, her belly quivering with anticipation.

Because of course in this fantasy she hadn't been alone. He'd been there in the shower, close behind her, watching and waiting. But not for long. Soon, she'd handed him a cake of soap and asked him to wash her. Which he had, oh so slowly, all over. It was deliciously decadent, the way she'd moaned. And the way she'd moved, parting her legs and inviting him in.

Unfortunately, she'd switched the shower off at that point, leaving him so damned frustrated that he could have screamed. He'd quickly headed for a shower himself, a cold one, where shards of icy water had lashed his overheated body till it was devoid of desire. But it was only a temporary solution. By the time he'd dried himself and climbed into bed shortly after eight-thirty, John had briefly contemplated doing something about the situation himself but abandoned that idea when he remembered that too much ejaculation lowered a man's sperm count. After all, Scarlet was depending on him.

No, not him especially, John reminded himself when he found himself feeling smug over this idea. Just about anyone would do. *No point in pretending you're anything special to Scarlet.*

It was perverse that this fact irked him. Male egos had a lot to answer for, John decided.

The sudden knock on his bedroom door had his heart almost jumping out of his chest. Which was ridiculous, for it could only be Scarlet.

'Come in,' he called out. 'I'm still awake,' he added somewhat unnecessarily. She could obviously see light under his door and hear the television on, otherwise she wouldn't have knocked. For a split second, John indulged in a new fantasy, one where she hadn't been able to sleep and had come to seduce him dressed in a provocative negligee.

It was a fantasy soon dashed when she opened the door and stood there in the most unprovocative nightwear he'd ever seen. Not that the pink polka-dotted shortie pyjamas she was wearing were unattractive. They were quite cute, but in the night light, with her face scrubbed clean of make-up and her hair up in a pony-tail, Scarlet looked as she'd looked when she'd been sixteen.

He'd found her indescribably sexy when she'd been sixteen. His own sixteen-year-old hormones had been raging. He'd been secretly dying to go to her sixteenth birthday party; had even planned to be nice to her. But an invitation had never arrived for him. She hadn't wanted him then and she didn't really want him now. He was just a means to an end.

'Sorry to bother you, John,' she said as she stood there, looking somewhat embarrassed. 'But I've woken up with this most awful headache. I looked in all the cupboards in the bathroom and kitchen for some pain killers but couldn't find any.'

'Really? I thought I put some headache pills in the cupboard above the fridge.'

'Oh, I didn't look in that one. It was too high up.'

'Never mind, I have some in my bathroom cupboard. I'll just go get them for you.'

Scarlet stiffened when he threw back his bed covers, suddenly afraid that he was naked. He'd *looked* naked, sitting there, propped up against a mountain of pillows, his chest totally bare right down to his waistline. But he was actually wearing a pair of black satin boxer shorts, slung low on his hips.

'What do you want?' he threw over his shoulder as he padded across the rug towards the bathroom. 'Paracetemol, or something stronger?'

'Nothing with codeine in it,' she replied. 'That makes me feel sick.'

'Paracetemol it is, then.' He returned a minute later with two tablets in one hand and a glass of water in the other. 'Drink all the water,' he advised as he handed both over to her. 'The flight and the alcohol have probably left you dehydrated.'

Scarlet did as she was told, gazing up at the television on the wall whilst she gulped down the water. It was better than ogling John, though he was well worth ogling. He really did have a great body—broad at the shoulder and slim at the hips, with a washboard stomach and just enough muscle in his arms and legs to look strongly masculine without being muscle bound. He wasn't overly hairy either, but there was a nice sprinkling of dark curls in the middle of his tanned chest—a chest which Scarlet wouldn't mind running her hands over. That was a startling thought for a girl who'd never taken the initiative in love-making in her entire life.

'Thank you,' she said when she handed the empty glass back to him. 'Sorry to have bothered you.'

'No bother. No, don't go,' he said abruptly when she turned to leave. 'Stay and watch TV with me till your headache goes.'

Scarlet had to admit that she was tempted. The thought of going back to the guest bedroom, alone, was not appealing. She suspected she might find it hard to go back to sleep, not because of the headache but because of the agitating thoughts which kept running through her head. Thoughts of John and sex. She turned back to face him, then glanced at the TV. 'Could we watch something else rather than fishing?'

'Absolutely. You can have control of the remote. There are loads of channels to choose from.'

'But where will I sit?' There was a two-seater lounger against one wall but it was under the television.

'In bed next to me, of course,' he said.

She stared at him, knowing full well what would eventually happen if she climbed into that bed.

'I promise I won't touch you, Scarlet,' he said, his eyes locking with hers. 'Not unless you want me to.'

Scarlet shook her head slowly from side to side. 'I don't know what I want any more.'

'That's because you over-think everything. Time to just let nature takes its course. You find me attractive, don't you?'

Her eyes swept over his near-naked body once more. 'Yes,' she choked out.

'And you enjoyed my kissing you earlier?'

'Yes,' she agreed again.

'How's the headache now?'

'What? Oh, er, not as bad, actually.'

'Ten more minutes and you'll feel much better, especially if you lie down in my very comfy bed and let me stroke your hair.'

'Stroke my hair,' she repeated numbly, an erotic quiver running down her spine.

'You'll have to take it down out of that pony-tail of course,' he said. 'Here, I'll do it for you.'

He moved behind her, his hands swift and sure as they removed the rubber band, letting her hair tumble free over her shoulders.

'This way,' he said, and led her over to the bed where

he threw back the covers before suddenly whirling and scooping her up into his arms.

Scarlet gasped in shock, both at the speed of his actions and the way it felt, being held hard against his naked chest. Her arms automatically lifted to wind themselves around his neck, her eyes blinking wide as they met his.

'Like I said earlier,' he said wryly. 'I've always wanted to sweep you off your feet. Now, don't say anything sarcastic, Scarlet. I know you're itching to. I can see it in your face. But this is not the time for one-upmanship. It's time for you to just trust me.'

As surprising as it was, she *did* trust him, almost as much as she desired him. It was a strange situation, one which brought a puzzled frown to her face, until she winced as a new wave of pain hit her.

'That headache is still bothering you, isn't it?' he said sympathetically as he lowered her onto the bed, her head and shoulders sinking into the layers of black pillows propped against the bedhead.

'I think, under the circumstances,' he added as he strode round the other side of the bed and climbed in next to her, 'that watching television is not a good idea.' So saying, he picked up the remote and turned the TV off. 'What you need to do is close your eyes and relax.'

He scowled when he leant over and saw her eyes were still wide open.

'Scarlet King, do you know you have a problem with obedience? Close your eyes!'

In days gone by—in fact in just hours gone by—Scarlet might have shot back some smart remark. But she was way too preoccupied to indulge in witty repartee at that moment. Way too turned on as well. She could not wait for him to touch her, even if it was just stroking her head. Because she knew that it wouldn't end there.

So she closed her eyes and held her breath, waiting in an agony of anticipation for her seduction to begin.

CHAPTER THIRTEEN

WHEN his fingers first contacted her forehead, Scarlet stiffened inside. When they slid upwards into her hair, her teeth clenched down hard in her jaw. It was a struggle not to cry out. But she managed. Just.

Her mother used to stroke her head when she'd been sick as a child, her touch soft and soothing. John's equally gentle touch might have had the same relaxing effect if she hadn't been so agitated. No, not agitated—excited. Impossible to relax when your nipples were tight and tingling. Soon, it wasn't her head she wanted him to stroke but other more intimate parts of her body. Her breasts. Her belly. Her quivering thighs. Her headache had receded, replaced by waves of dizzying desire which were as demanding and decadent as the bed she was lying in. Scarlet could not believe how much she wanted John to undress her. No longer did she care if he thought her breasts too small. She wanted his hands on them. And his mouth.

If she'd been bold, she might have told him of her cravings. But that was one thing she'd never been in the bedroom—bold.

At the same time, she was driven to say something, anything, which would indicate she wanted him to move on.

'My headache's gone,' she murmured.

John's hand stilled in her hair, but it didn't move on.

Scarlet's eyes opened so that she could work out what he was thinking.

No luck with that, however. She should have known she wouldn't be able to read his thoughts. John had never been one to wear his heart on his sleeve, or his innermost thoughts on his face.

'Maybe I should go back to my room?' she said, battling to hide dismay from showing in her face.

John let out an exasperated-sounding sigh. 'I thought I told you to stop over-thinking everything. You're staying right where you are, Scarlet.'

'I am?'

'Yes. You want this as much as I do. If you didn't, you wouldn't have stayed in the first place. You'd have told me to get lost, then walked off back to your room. If there's one thing I know very well about you, it's your stubborn nature. You never do anything you don't want to do. You *want* me to make love to you, Scarlet, so why don't you just admit it?'

Scarlet glowered up at him, his outburst firing up the urge to tear his egotistical words down in flames with some verbal lightning bolts of her own. But what would be the point? He was right. So very irritatingly right!

But that didn't mean she had to admit to *too* much. He would become insufferable if she confessed to what was really going on in her head, and in her body.

'I suppose there's no point in making you wait any longer,' she said dismissively. 'Not if you're that desperate. It's almost tomorrow, anyway. But don't go imagining I'm panting for it.'

He smiled a very knowing smile. 'We'll see, Scarlet. We'll see…'

Scarlet tried to think of something clever to retort but her brain had shut down the moment his hand withdrew from her hair and dropped down to the top button of her pyjamas. She held her breath whilst he flicked it open with one hand, grateful that his eyes were following his hand and not still looking into her frozen face. Slowly but deliberately he moved on to the next button, then the next, till all five were open, by which time she wasn't panting for it. But she *was* in danger of dying from lack of air in her lungs.

Her sucking in breath sharply brought his eyes back up to her own.

A frown bunched his dark brow together. 'You want me to stop?'

She shook her head.

'Good,' he said. 'Because I don't think I could have.'

His admission of the intensity of his own need soothed Scarlet's worry over the almost uncontrollable nature of her own. It wasn't like her to want a man this much. It was a surprise, but not an entirely unpleasant one. There was something right about enjoying the process of conceiving a baby, rather than what she'd been doing at the clinic. Not that she was likely to fall pregnant tonight. In her experience of charting her cycle each month, it was impossible. Sperm did not live for a week.

'You're thinking again,' John warned her softly. 'Have to stop that, Scarlet. Focus on what I'm doing to you and nothing else.'

He didn't have to tell her twice, especially when he parted her top, exposing her breasts to his eyes.

'So beautiful,' he murmured, cupping her left breast with his free hand and lifting it slightly before bending his head to the nipple.

John didn't suck it the way other men had sucked her nipples, like they were drinking their favourite beer through a straw which was too small. He didn't suck it at all at first. He licked it, slowly, almost lasciviously, wetting it over and over till she moaned in frustration. Even then he didn't suck it. He nibbled at it, then nipped it, then took it carefully between his teeth and tugged it, sending a dagger of dark pleasure stabbing through her entire breast. When he did it again, she twisted to one side, wrenching the burning nipple out of his mouth. She might have voiced some protest had he not pushed her roughly back against the pillow then silenced her with a kiss, which was nothing like the kiss he'd given her earlier. It was hard and hungry, obliterating all thought with a speed which Scarlet would later find astonishing. His mouth didn't abandon hers till she was way beyond anything but lying there, dazed, whilst he undressed her totally and started doing all those things she'd imagined him doing under the covers.

But there were no covers involved. There was nothing to hide her eyes from what was happening to her. She lay there, legs and arms spreadeagled, whilst his hands and lips became stunningly intimate with every inch of her body. And did she care? Not in the least. She moaned with pleasure then groaned with frustration each time he stopped, always when she was just on the verge of coming. It was a mad mixture of near ecstasy followed by sheer agony.

'Oh please,' she begged when his mouth abandoned her swollen clitoris one more tormenting, torturous time.

'Patience, Scarlet,' he said, at which point she swore at him, using a four-letter word which she rarely used. He only smiled and said, 'Soon, sweetheart.'

Her head whirled as he rose from where he'd been lying between her legs and moved up the bed to lie down next to her, propping himself on one elbow.

'Trust me,' he added, giving her a breath-stealing kiss on her parted—and, yes, *panting*—lips, before sitting up and stripping off his black boxer shorts, exposing a stunningly formidable erection. Long and thick, it stood up ram-rod straight. Scarlet couldn't stop staring at it, her mouth drying as she tried to imagine how it would feel inside her.

When he lay back down next to her, she couldn't stop herself reaching out to touch him.

It was the kind of involuntary action John had hoped eventually to evoke in Scarlet, to make her forget about babies and think only of sex. It was what he'd planned when he'd asked her to come up to Darwin a week early. He'd thought he would need a good while to totally seduce Scarlet into such an erotically charged state of mind. It seemed, however, that he might achieve his goal a lot quicker than that. She was definitely not thinking of anything but sex right at this moment.

John knew he should probably stop her doing what she was doing, but he simply could not. Her fingertips felt like butterfly wings fluttering against his engorged flesh. Never before had his penis been touched like that. So sweetly yet so sensuously. It stirred him to an almost unbearable level of arousal. Being with Scarlet was testing his willpower to the limit. He'd already lasted a long time without release… enough was enough.

'No more, Scarlet,' he said, and reached out to still her hand with his. 'I'm only human, you know,' he added with a soft smile when her rather glazed eyes lifted to his.

Scarlet could not believe she'd been so bold as to touch him like that. Or that she'd loved it—loved the feel of him, so hard and yet so soft. It came to her as John lifted her hand away that she might not mind putting her lips where her hand had been—an astonishing thought, given she'd never been keen on that particular form of foreplay. Not that she hadn't tried it once or twice. She had; men seemed crazy about it. But she'd hated the way it made her feel.

She'd never imagined for one moment that she might actually enjoy it. Or be turned on by it. But she rather suspected she would be, if she did it to John. Just the thought of doing it turned her on. So did the thought of taking him into her body. A wave of naked desire brought a frustrated groan to her lips.

'What is it?' he asked. 'What's wrong?'

'Just do it to me,' she said, her eyes as pleading as her voice.

He stared down into her flushed face as he positioned himself between her thighs.

'Lift your knees,' he commanded. 'Place the soles of your feet flat on the mattress.'

Her stomach tightened as she did so, her heart pounding against her ribs.

His entry was slow and gentle, but it still brought a gasp to her lips.

He didn't stop, pushing in further till she was filled to the hilt. But he wasn't finished. Another gasp escaped her lips when he suddenly took her by the ankles and wrapped her legs up around his waist. This new position seemed to allow him to slide in even deeper, by which time Scarlet could not wait for him to move.

When he didn't, she did.

Scarlet lifting her hips from the bed evoked something close to panic in John. Never before had a woman been able to make him lose control. Now, suddenly, he was overwhelmed by a powerful urge just to *take* her! Without finesse. Without further waiting or watching. His body began to move quite involuntarily, not slowly or gently, but vigorously, almost violently. Back and forth. Back and forth. She moved with him, squeezing him mercilessly, making his teeth clench down hard in his jaw as he tried to resist the sensations which were threatening to tip him over the edge with humiliating speed. In desperation he grabbed her hips, holding her still with a brutal grip whilst he tried to slow things down—his own body especially. But it would not be denied. There was no hope of lasting much longer, he realised with dismay. No hope at all!

CHAPTER FOURTEEN

SCARLET's mouth dropped open when she came, so astonished was she by the intensity of her climax. Never before
had she experienced spasms so powerful, or so pleasurable. Never before had she made such sounds, moaning and
groaning in a wildly wanton fashion as her flesh contracted
around his. But any sound she made was soon eclipsed
when John came. Holding her even tighter, he shuddered
violently into her, his head thrown back, eyes shut.

When his orgasm finished, his head dropping forward,
his eyes opened to reveal an expression which Scarlet could
only describe as confused. But any confusion was gone
as quickly as it came, leaving Scarlet to wonder if she'd
imagined it. By then he was smiling—though the smile
was sardonic.

'You're not even a teeny tiny bit frigid, Scarlet,' he said
in droll tones as he removed her legs from his back and let
them flop back onto the bed. 'In truth, you have the makings of a great courtesan.'

Scarlet, who was in the throes of coming back to earth,
found herself thrown down with a thud by this last remark.

'Well, thank you very much,' she said tartly. 'What a
lovely compliment, saying I'd make a great prostitute. Now,
if you don't mind...' She lifted her shoulders and wriggled
her hips in a vain attempt to eject him from her body.

A foolish move, for all it did was remind her how it felt with him inside her. Such blissful sensations did not lend themselves to her staying angry.

'I *do* mind,' he said sternly. 'It's very comfy, the way we are. So stop being silly, lie back and just relax.'

It did seem silly to keep struggling.

'Much better,' John said when she slumped back against the pillows. 'Now, how about the relaxing part?' he went on. 'Breathe in deeply and then let the air out slowly. Yes. That's the way.'

Despite doing as he suggested, Scarlet was still not totally relaxed.

'For your information,' John said, cupping her face with his hands before sliding his fingers up into the hair, 'a courtesan was not a common prostitute, but an attractive and often poor woman who made her living by using her erotic skills to ensnare herself a wealthy lover. She was much valued by her patron. He would often buy her a house, hire staff for her and pay her bills, all for the privilege of having exclusive access to her very beautiful body.'

'How interesting,' Scarlet said, finding herself perversely flattered by his words. It was somehow seductive for a girl to be told that she could be so brilliant at sex that a man would do that much to have her. Such praise was as corrupting as words of love.

'What kind of erotic skills did a good courtesan possess?' she asked, her curiosity piqued.

John positioned himself more comfortably on top of her, his bent forearms pressing into the bed on either side to ease his weight off her chest whilst his lower half remained intimately locked with hers.

'They were many and varied,' he informed her. 'But a good courtesan concentrated on discovering what her lover liked best in bed, what foreplay he enjoyed the most, what fantasies he had. And then she catered to them all.'

'So what fantasies do *you* have?' she asked.

John looked down into her wide blue eyes and considered how he should answer that.

Not the truth, of course. Most of his sexual fantasies were too decadent to be voiced aloud. At the same time, there were some fantasies which could be safely indulged in if and when the opportunity presented itself. John had often fantasised over having Scarlet at his sexual beck and call. It was a temptation impossible to resist.

'That's for me to know and you to find out, my darling Scarlet. Because you're going to become my courtesan for the duration of your stay here.'

'What?'

'You heard me.'

'That wasn't part of our deal.'

'No. It came to me when I discovered how good you were in bed.'

'Oh,' she said, and stared up at him. He really was rather wicked. And very knowing about women.

'Have you done this kind of thing before?' she suddenly asked.

'What kind of thing?'

'Don't play dumb, John. You know what I mean. Is role playing one of your fantasies?'

'No. I just thought it would be fun, that's all. Why, aren't you up for it?' he said in the kind of challenging fashion which he knew she wouldn't be able to resist. Scarlet was nothing if not competitive. Or she had been, at school with him. It had killed her whenever he'd beaten her in an exam.

Scarlet's first reaction was to fire back, *Yes, of course I am.* But hard on the heels of that pride-driven urge came the stark reality of the situation. A courtesan she was not.

John was flattering her when he said she was good in bed. She wasn't; not usually. If she'd been good just now, it was because she'd been so incredibly turned on. She didn't even know what she'd done to make him say that. Was it when she'd touched him? Or later, when she'd been writhing around under him? There'd been nothing skilled about that. She'd just gone crazy with need. Just thinking about it was turning her on again.

John sucked in sharply when he felt her move against him.

The little minx! She was answering his challenge by showing him what she could do.

'Obviously your answer is yes,' he said thickly.

'Now *you're* being silly. I don't have the experience or the expertise necessary for such a role.'

'That's a matter of opinion,' he muttered through gritted teeth.

'You can do it to me again, if you want to,' she said, her eyes having gone as smoky as her voice.

He had every intention of doing so, especially when she lifted her legs and wrapped them around him. But the moment he started moving, it happened to him again, that rush of adrenaline which heralded his earlier loss of control. He tried to slow everything down but his body had a mind of its own, and he surged deep into her with almost manic determination. Immediately, he was in danger of coming. *Immediately.* In desperation, he withdrew and flipped her over, pulling her up onto her knees under him, giving himself a few precious seconds of relief before he plunged into her again. Her instant cry of release came to the rescue of his battered pride, allowing him to stop his futile struggle. Eventually, they collapsed together onto the bed, John pulling her sideways into a spoon position so that he didn't squash her with his weight. When he wrapped his arms tightly around her and held her close she sighed a happy-sounding sigh. Soon, her breathing slowed and she slipped into that wonderfully sound sleep which often came after great sex.

Unfortunately, John wasn't so lucky, sleep eluding him as he tried to work out why he'd rocketed so out of control, not once but twice.

The only logical reason he could find was that Scarlet was *nothing* like his usual woman. Despite her age, she was a relative innocent where sex was concerned. Innocent and touchingly sweet, which could also be a factor in his uncharacteristic responses to her.

John's choice of bed partners these days were not of the innocent and sweet variety. After he'd left university—where no-strings sex was a common pastime—John had quickly found that sleeping with his female peers in the wider world was hazardous to his peace of mind. Most girls around his age didn't want one-night stands; they expected him to stay for breakfast. Expected him to ask them out again. Expected to become his steady girlfriend. In short, they wanted commitment, something John wasn't interested in. He enjoyed the bachelor lifestyle. Enjoyed being free to come and go as he pleased without having to answer to anyone, or upset anyone.

John soon realised that if he wanted to have a reasonably regular and guilt-free sex life he'd have to choose older women to sleep with, ones who weren't looking for love and marriage. Recently divorced was good, he'd found, along with the occasional career girl who was already married to her job. During the past couple of years, he'd favoured women whose only interest in him was an evening of pleasant company, usually over dinner, followed by a long night of sexual pleasure—always at their place. That way he didn't have to ask them to leave in the morning. He could do the leaving, when and if he chose.

Bianca had once asked him why he didn't bring his 'girlfriends' home. He'd told his housekeeper that *she* was the only real girlfriend he had, which had made her laugh.

His heart twisted as he always did when he thought of Bianca.

Best not think about her then, buddy. You can't change what happened.

Scarlet stirred slightly in her sleep, pulling up her knees and thrusting her very shapely bottom against his stomach, causing his till-then deflated sex to come to life once more with alarming speed.

It was impossible to sleep here now, common sense dictated, John smothering a groan as he very carefully withdrew from her oh-so-delicious body, scowling when he saw the evidence of his renewed desire for her. Truly, this was getting ridiculous!

He threw Scarlet a rueful glance as he quietly rose from the bed and dragged on his boxer shorts. *Frigid?* She was about as frigid as Darwin in the summer.

CHAPTER FIFTEEN

SCARLET woke to solitude and silence. She blinked several times, then sat up, pushing her hair back behind her ears as she cocked her head and listened for the sounds of life.

Nothing.

She had no idea what time it was, a quick glance around showing no clock anywhere. The light coming into the room from the balcony suggested it was late. Quite late, a suspicion confirmed by the urgency of her need to go to the bathroom. Scarlet was grateful for John's absence as she threw back the covers and jumped, naked, from the bed. Though that didn't stop her wondering where he was. He'd certainly been in bed with her when she'd fallen asleep.

Oh Lord!

Scarlet could not believe how incredible the night had been. How incredible *he* had felt. Maybe size did matter.

But of course it wasn't just John's size which had made last night different from any other night she'd ever spent in bed with a man. She'd been beside herself with the most dizzying pleasure long before he'd stripped off. What John didn't know about a woman's body clearly wasn't worth knowing. He was an extraordinary lover—imaginative and very patient during foreplay, but passionate and primitive when it came to the act itself. She hadn't forgotten the sounds he'd made when he'd come the first time; how they'd reminded her of a wild beast.

Had that been a subconscious fantasy of her own? she wondered as she washed her hands then stared up at herself in the vanity mirror. To be taken by a wild beast?

She would never have imagined so. But who knew what lurked in the dark recesses of one's mind?

There was one fantasy that in the cool light of day she decided definitely didn't appeal to her—that of being a courtesan. Especially John's courtesan. No way would she enjoy kow-towing to his every sexual whim and wish, Scarlet told herself firmly as she finger-combed her messy hair into place.

On the other hand, she did not regret—or resent—the degree to which she'd enjoyed his love-making. It was exciting, in a way, to discover that with the right lover she was actually highly sexed.

No doubt John was somewhat smug over his successful seduction of her, but *c'est la vie*. It would be hypocritical of her to start pretending this morning that she hadn't enjoyed every single moment. Saying so to his face, however, might prove difficult. She still hadn't overcome her shyness, not to mention her pride.

Her pride was one of the reasons she was reluctant to leave the bathroom before checking that the bedroom was still empty and the bedroom door firmly shut. As much as she hadn't worried about John seeing her naked last night when she'd been turned on, it was a different matter in the cold light of day. Hurrying back into the bedroom, Scarlet scooped up her pyjama top from where it was lying on the rug beside the bed, donning it quickly before going on a frantic search for the bottom half. She found the shorts under the covers, right down the bottom of the bed. Once they were safely on, she made the bed then, after taking a few calming breaths, went in search of the man himself.

She almost missed him, sprawled sound asleep on one of the sofas, only the sound of his deep but even breathing attracting her attention. Scarlet shook her head as she stared down at his half-naked form, amazed that he could sleep like that without a rug or a blanket for warmth. Okay, so the apartment was air-conditioned, but still…

He really did have a great body, she thought for the umpteenth time as her admiring eyes began travelling over him from head to toe, stopping abruptly when they reached the scar on his right leg, just to the side of his knee. She hadn't noticed it last night, but then she'd been somewhat distracted at the time. It was quite a nasty scar, purple and puckered around the edges, probably the result of that accident he'd had recently when he'd broken his leg. She wondered how the accident had happened and how bad it had been. If he'd been a normal man, she could have asked him about it. But John wasn't a normal man, she conceded ruefully. He had this thing about being questioned. Silly, really, but so darned typical of him. He'd always been a loner, with a loner's persona. 'Tell 'em nothing and take 'em nowhere': that was obviously his creed in life where women were concerned. It surprised Scarlet that he'd ever admitted to having this long-held desire for her. To do so must have gone against the grain.

She was still puzzling over this conundrum when she spotted an empty glass lying on the rug next to the sofa, right where John might put his foot when he finally woke up and stood up. Scarlet went round, picked the glass up and took a sniff. She didn't much care for brandy but she knew the smell well, having used brandy often when making Christmas cakes. The fact that John had left the bed and sat out here, drinking, till he fell asleep was another puzzle. Why hadn't he stayed with her?

Scarlet was standing there, trying to find an answer when she realised John was stirring.

For a split second, she contemplated bolting for the bedroom but, as she'd told him last night, when she was nervous about something, she liked to get it over and done with as soon as possible.

She waited and watched whilst John stretched and yawned first before one lid flickered upwards, then another.

'Good morning, Scarlet,' he said as he swung his long legs over the side of the sofa and sat up. 'I presume you slept well?'

'Very,' she admitted, determined to be honest. Determined to make him answer some questions as well. 'Why did you come out here to sleep?'

'For that reason,' he replied somewhat drily. 'To sleep. I was, shall we say, struggling to concentrate.'

'Oh,' she said, and blushed.

'No need to be embarrassed. It's not your fault that you're a beautiful woman. I knew, if I stayed there, I wouldn't be able to keep my hands off you. So I came out here and left you to have a good night's rest.'

'That was…very considerate of you,' she said, not sure now if she felt embarrassed or pleased. There was something incredibly seductive about a man admitting he couldn't keep his hands off you.

'My pleasure, Scarlet. But don't worry,' he added with a wicked little smile. 'You can make it up to me today.'

She gripped the glass tightly whilst trying to imagine what he had in mind. 'What time is it, do you know?'

'Time you and I had some breakfast, after which you can join me in the shower.'

'But…'

'No buts, Scarlet. We had a deal, remember?'

Scarlet straightened her shoulders. 'I don't recall agree-ing to sex morning, noon and night.'

'No?'

'No.'

'Are you saying you don't want to join me in the shower?'

'I'm saying you are not to presume that I will agree to anything and everything. You are to ask me first. And re-spect my wishes. Otherwise, this deal is off and I'll catch the first flight home.'

'Have you forgotten why you came up here in the first place?' he reminded her ruthlessly.

'I haven't forgotten,' she said with a defiant tilt of her chin. 'But that doesn't change my stance. Take it or leave it.'

Damn it but she was calling his bluff! Not that it had been a bluff, exactly. He'd thought after last night she'd be putty in his hands this morning. He supposed he should have known better. This was Scarlet he was dealing with here.

'Very well,' he conceded. 'I would love you to join me in the shower after breakfast, Scarlet. But if you don't want to, that's fine,' he added through clenched teeth.

Scarlet wasn't sure what to say now, the ease of his ca-pitulation having surprised her. She actually wanted to join him in the shower. It was his arrogant manner which had got her back up. Now that he was asking politely, it seemed rather hypocritical to say no. But she felt she had to. To give in at this early stage would feel somehow like she'd lost the battle—as though she—or, rather, her body, she hastily corrected—belonged to him. After last night, she wanted to make sure she stayed in control, and that meant setting boundaries.

'I'd rather shower by myself,' she said, trying not to

sound too prim and proper. 'I'm not used to sharing show-
ers. Or making love during the day time, for that matter.
If you don't mind, could we confine our sexual activity
to the evenings?'

'I'd be lying if I said I didn't mind. But you're calling
the shots for now, so sex will be confined to the evenings.
Until you change your mind, of course,' he added with a
wicked glitter in his bedroom-blue eyes. 'That is a woman's
privilege, isn't it—to change her mind?' And so saying, he
stood up and stretched once more, grimacing as he did so.
'Thank God I won't have to sleep out here tonight. It's hell
on my back.'

'You could have slept in one of the guest rooms,' she
pointed out somewhat tartly.

'Now, why didn't I think of that? Right, do you want
breakfast before your shower or after? Note, I'm asking
very politely and not telling you.'

Scarlet pulled a face at him. 'There's no need to be *that*
polite. I also don't expect you to wait on me hand and foot.
You showed me where everything in the kitchen was last
night. I can easily get myself some cereal and juice, which
is all I usually have for breakfast.'

'Splendid. I'll leave you to it, then. I'm off to have *my*
shower. A very long, very cold one.'

Regret consumed Scarlet as she watched him stalk off.
But she refused to back down. She needed to keep focused
on what she'd come here to do. As John had inadvertently
reminded her, this wasn't a pleasure trip, no matter how
much pleasure she might have felt last night. And, actually, Scarlet remembered reading that too much sex was
as bad for conception as too little. Couples who were having trouble falling pregnant were encouraged to chart the
woman's cycle and reserve sex for the days surrounding
ovulation. She would have to mention that to John. But

not yet, perhaps. She suspected he would not take kindly to her telling him he would have to curtail his pleasure for a couple of days early next week so that his sperm count would be at maximum level.

But tell him, she would. Eventually.

No matter what, she had to maintain some control over John. *And* herself.

Pursing her lips determinedly, Scarlet marched out to the kitchen where she swiftly set about getting herself a bowl of muesli and a glass of orange juice, all the while making plans for the day in her head. As soon as she had breakfast, she would shower and dress—in the main bathroom—after which she would ask John to take her for a walk around the CBD of Darwin, followed by a light lunch somewhere, followed by a long drive or a boat trip on the harbour, or whatever would fill in the afternoon.

She would make sure it was late afternoon by the time they came back to the apartment, leaving only enough time for them to both freshen up before going out for dinner, which should occupy a further few hours. Although usually a fast eater, she would be very slow this evening, making sure that it would be at least ten or eleven by the time they got back to the apartment, with their energy levels low after a long day of walking and sightseeing. She doubted John would be capable of making love to her more than once. Twice, at best. He did seem to have amazing stamina in that regard. But what the heck? She was sure she would survive two more ground-shaking orgasms without totally losing her willpower or, worse still, imagining that she must be in love with John simply because she was enjoying sex with him.

Her top lip curled derisively as she dismissed that insane possibility without a second thought. Only hopelessly naive romantics believed in such hogwash, and it had been some time since Scarlet had been either naive or a romantic. She supposed in one way it was rather sad to have one's illusions about love and sex dashed to the ground so emphatically. But then real life was sad, wasn't it? Real life killed off one's father when you were only nine. And real life kept you unloved and childless till you were at such an age that your dreams were almost beyond your reach.

But only almost…

Scarlet wasn't sure why, but she suddenly felt supremely confident that when she caught her flight home on Sunday week she would be pregnant with John's child. Okay, so having a baby was only half of her dreams, but it was the better half. The safer and more secure half. She would settle for that half, any day of the week.

Her heart thudded in her chest as she tried to imagine how it would feel when her pregnancy was confirmed. She would be over the moon. And so would her mother.

'Oh my God, Mum!' she exclaimed, having forgotten all about the promise she had made to her mother the previous evening to send her some photos of the apartment today.

So much to do, she thought as she started to shovel the muesli into her mouth. And so little time!

CHAPTER SIXTEEN

SCARLET ate breakfast, had a shower and got dressed in record time, choosing white capri pants and a salmon-pink top which had a not-too-low sweetheart neckline and capped sleeves. The same speed was applied to her hair, which she only half blow-dried before scooping it all up into a high pony-tail, anchored by a white elastic band. Make-up was none, other than some tinted sunscreen plus her favourite coral lipstick. She didn't spray on any perfume or don any jewellery, having resolved not to dress or act provocatively. After adding flat white sandals, she extracted her phone from her bag and set about taking photos of the main bathroom and the floral quilted guest bedroom, careful not to make either look too large or too luxurious.

Once satisfied with her snaps, Scarlet made her way out to the kitchen, half-expecting John to be in there, having breakfast. But he wasn't. She frowned. Surely he'd be showered, shaved and dressed by now? Clearly not, however, the living room proving as deserted as the kitchen. His bedroom door remained shut, she noted, so it was likely he was still in there, but no way was she going to knock, or go in search of him. Instead, she returned to the kitchen, where she took a couple of photos of just one section before moving back to the living room and shooting only a fraction of that area, getting in just one of the sofas and rugs.

It wasn't till she went out onto the balcony with the intention of snapping the spectacular harbour view that she found John sitting out there with some toast and coffee. No doubt he'd showered but he hadn't shaved, looking like a beach bum with the stubble growing on his chin and nothing on but a pair of bright board-shorts.

A very sexy beach bum.

'So here you are!' she exclaimed, doing her best not to stare at his beautifully bare chest, resentment rising with the thought that *he* was being deliberately provocative. After all, it wasn't that warm out there on the balcony. It was, in fact, quite fresh, with a stiff sea breeze blowing.

'Aren't you cold?' she asked somewhat tartly.

'I never feel the cold,' he said, his eyes lifting to run over what she was wearing. 'We inveterate campers are a tough breed. Taking photos for your mum, are you?'

'I promised her last night.'

'Yes, I heard you. You and your mum are obviously very close. Is that why you're still living with her?'

'I didn't plan to but then I also didn't plan to deliberately become a single parent,' she shot back. 'Once I made that decision, it made sense to stay on at home.'

'But you're *not* going to become a single parent. Not now. You'll have me to help out.'

'Come now, John, even if things work out and I do fall pregnant with your child, I'll still need my mother's support. You're not going to be around most of the time—it isn't part of our deal. You'll be off working in some far-flung corner of the world most of the time and only come home to visit at Christmas every year. More importantly, I *like* living with my mother. We're best friends.'

'I see. Fair enough. Get on with your photos then,' he bit out, and fell broodingly silent.

Scarlet held her tongue with difficulty whilst she took

a lot of snaps. Normally, she would have made admiring comments about the beauty of the view. But she didn't trust herself to speak right at that moment. Why she let John get under her skin so much, Scarlet wasn't sure. But he did. He always had. She had a feeling John felt exactly the same about her. It was a shame, really, given the situation. If only they could become genuine friends, it would make life so much easier.

It's up to you then, Scarlet, the voice of common sense advised her. *Don't expect John to make the move to cease hostilities between you. Men don't do things like that. It's the woman who usually makes the peace when a relationship becomes rocky.*

Not that they had a *relationship*. Up till now, all they had together was a shared childhood and one night of sex. Great sex, admittedly, but still just sex. Shared parenthood, however, would definitely change all that.

The enormity of what they were planning to do suddenly struck Scarlet like a physical blow, doubts shooting to the surface of her mind as she tried to work through what having John as the father of her baby really meant. It could become quite complicated, she realised agitatedly. And messy. Going to that clinic and having an anonymous sperm donor had been a simple plan. Lonely, maybe, but simple. No one else was directly involved. With artificial insemination, she was master of her own destiny and the controller of her child's upbringing. Could she trust John not to want more involvement once his son or daughter became a reality? A few of her girlfriends had told her how their husbands had not been so keen when they had become pregnant early in their marriages, but each had become besotted once the child had arrived. Would John have an epiphany once he became a father? It was possible, she supposed.

Scarlet stopped taking endless photographs and whirled to face him.

'I think I might have made a big mistake by accepting your offer,' she blurted out, still shaken by her thoughts.

An emotion close to panic sent John leaping to his feet. 'What?'

'You heard me.'

'I heard you, but I don't understand what's behind such a sudden turnaround. *You* contacted *me*, Scarlet, not the other way around.'

Now she looked decidedly shame-faced.

'I know. I guess I was desperate at the time.'

Desperate. John could not believe how much it hurt, hearing her say that. But then he remembered the way she'd been with him last night. That hadn't been desperation. That had been desire, pure and simple. Not so pure, either. His flesh stirred at the memory of her touching him, of her begging him to just do it to her.

He gritted his teeth as he willed his body to behave itself. This wasn't the right time to use sex to sway her mind. At the same time, if Scarlet thought for one moment he was going to let her leave, then she was dead wrong.

'Why do you think you made a big mistake accepting my offer?' he asked with forced calm as he came forward and cupped his hands over her shoulders.

She immediately clasped her phone with her two hands and held it up against her breasts, as though she was afraid of his chest touching hers.

Good, he thought.

'I just don't think it's wise for you to be the father of my baby, that's all,' she said with her usual stubbornness. 'It could become complicated.'

'In what way?'

'You might change your mind about your level of involvement. You might… Oh, I don't know what you might do, exactly. I just want my son or daughter to have a secure, happy life. I would hate there to be any conflict.'

'Well there certainly won't be any conflict if you don't have a child at all! Which could be the case if you cut and run now.'

'The clinic said I just had to be patient.'

'The clinic has vested financial interests in saying that.'

'That's a horribly cynical thing to say!'

'I'm a horrible cynic.'

'You just don't understand,' she said with a ragged sob.

The sounded affected him. He didn't want to make her cry. He just wanted to soothe her worries and make her stay with him. The thought of her leaving still filled him with alarm.

'But I do understand,' he told her gently. 'I do. You're afraid of my interfering in your role as a parent even though I promised not to. You've lost your trust in men, which includes me.'

'But how can I trust you when I don't really know you any more?'

'Ah. Back to that again.'

'I think it's only fair that you answer at least some of my questions if you're going to be the father of my baby.'

That *was* fair, John accepted grudgingly.

'Okay,' he said. 'Fire away.'

Her eyes narrowed. 'You'll tell the truth?'

'Cross my heart and hope to die,' he said. 'But only if you promise to stop this nonsense about leaving.'

Scarlet thought about that for a second, deciding that she wasn't going to let John steamroll her into anything. It had been foolish of her to come up here without thinking everything through. Uncharacteristically foolish. But of course she *had* been desperate at the time.

'I reserve the right to still leave if I find out you're not suitable father material,' she told him firmly.

'I thought you found that out last night,' he returned with a wicked little smile.

She blushed. Again.

Scarlet itched to stamp her foot in fury at herself. Blushing was hardly the way to convince John she had the upper hand.

'Must you remind me of that?' she threw at him.

'No need to be embarrassed. Now, how about you send those photos to your mum whilst I go put some clothes on? Then we'll get out of here.'

'But you were going to answer some questions.'

'You can walk and talk at the same time, can't you? Women are always claiming they can multi-task.'

Scarlet wanted to hit him. But not as much as she wanted to kiss him. Oh Lord, she was one mixed-up girl at the moment!

'Must you tease me all the time?' she snapped.

He smiled. 'Absolutely. I find you very sexy when you're angry.'

'Well it's no wonder you've wanted to screw me silly all your life, then,' she retorted, blue eyes flashing. 'Because I've been bloody angry at you since the first day we met!'

He tried not to laugh, but he couldn't help it. Neither could she. Her lips just twitched at first, then her chin started to quiver. And then they were both laughing, loud and hard.

Their laughter broke some of the sexual tension which had been steadily growing in Scarlet since she'd stepped out onto the balcony and spotted John sitting there with no shirt on. But even as she laughed she knew it would be wise to get out of this apartment as soon as possible. The physical chemistry between them was dangerously strong and extremely seductive, which was perverse, since they didn't see eye to eye about much. She was a person who valued family and community above all else. He was a loner who spurned involvement with others, even his family. She worked to live. He lived to work. Or he used to; she wasn't sure what his work ethics were now that he was rich.

These last thoughts reminded Scarlet of all the questions she wanted to ask John. Questions which had always plagued her about him. She was relieved that he'd agreed to satisfy her curiosity, because what if he hadn't? Scarlet doubted she would really have had the courage to leave. She was too close to achieving her goal of a baby. On top of that the prospect of more sex with John was a wickedly corrupting temptation, especially when she was alone in his half-naked presence. She needed to get him dressed, pronto, then get them both out of here.

CHAPTER SEVENTEEN

JOHN made his way quickly back into the master bedroom where he threw on a white T-shirt, slipped on some ancient but comfy flip-flops, then reached for a white baseball cap which he'd bought last week. He'd discovered that even in winter the sun up here in Darwin could burn, especially now that he didn't have a thick covering of scalp and facial hair to protect him.

When he returned to the living room, Scarlet was waiting for him with a roomy straw carry-all slung over her shoulder and a large-brimmed white sun-hat on her head.

John walked ahead of her to the door, opening it and waving her through before turning and locking up. Slipping the keys into his shorts pocket, he accompanied her along to the bank of lifts where they rode in companionable silence down to the lobby. Once there, he took her elbow and steered her out onto the pavement then safely across the road to the park opposite.

'The park runs the full length of the Esplanade,' he told her as they started walking along the main pathway which wound its way through the extensive lawns and gardens. 'This path will lead us to the far end of the CBD, past Government House, which is a splendid old building, then over a walkway and down a lift to the newly developed waterfront. I think you'll be impressed with what they've done to what used to be a pretty dingy area.'

'You're right—the views of the harbour from down here are incredible! And different from up on your balcony. Do you think we could go out on the harbour one day?' she asked whilst taking photos.

'Of course. I'll charter a boat. We'll go sightseeing and I'll show you how to fish. Fishing's a recent hobby of mine.'

She stopped taking photos and looked at him. 'I'm surprised. I thought you were a *terra firma* man.'

'I thought I was too. But after my accident I couldn't do too much for a few months. A friend suggested fishing and I found I loved it.'

'My dad used to like fishing. But I never went with him. I always thought it would be boring.'

'Not if you know where to fish and you have the right equipment. Then it's quite exciting. And very satisfying. They'll cook us what we catch on board the boat. If you like eating seafood, that is.'

'Love it.'

'That's one thing we have in common, then.'

Scarlet laughed. 'The only thing, I'll warrant.'

'No. Not the only thing,' he said, his voice low and knowing.

Scarlet deliberately ignored his sexual overtone by walking over to read a commemorative plaque which had a list of names on it connected with the Second World War. Darwin had been the only city in Australia ever to be bombed during any of the world wars, she'd discovered during the Internet search about the city. Scarlet took a photo of the plaque, then a few more of the view.

'What a lovely place Darwin is,' she said.

'I like it,' he said.

'So why don't you live here permanently, John? Why go

back to South America? Come to think of it, why did you choose to work there in the first place? I mean, there are jobs for geologists here in Australia. You could have just come up here, or gone to one of the many mining towns in Western Australia. There's no need to go to the other side of the world just to get away from…' The question she really wanted to ask burst out. 'Why *do* you hate your father so much, John?'

'Wow,' he said. 'That's quite a lot of questions in one hit. Look, why don't we sit down over here?' he said, directing her to a park bench that was under the shade of a tree. 'It could take me a while to answer them all.'

'Especially truthfully,' she reminded him.

'Scarlet, would I lie to you?'

'In a heartbeat,' she replied, and he smiled.

'You know me too well.'

'I know you don't like talking about yourself.'

John shrugged. 'I doubt you'll find any of this happy listening, but what the hell? You wanted the truth.'

For a split second, he wondered if he could get away with lying to Scarlet. But only for a split second.

He wasn't about to sugar-coat anything, either.

'First things first,' he said rather bluntly. 'I'm actually not going to go back to Brazil. I recently sold my house in Rio. I plan to stay and work here in Australia.'

'That's a surprise! What made you decide to return home after all these years? I got the impression you loved living in South America.'

'I did. I probably would have stayed living there indefinitely if my housekeeper—a truly sweet lady named Bianca whom I was very fond of—hadn't been killed. Stabbed to death by a gang of street kids she'd been trying to help.'

'Oh, John, that's awful!'

'It was. She was such a good woman. She used to go out every night and take food to the homeless. If I wasn't away working or out clubbing for the night, I'd go with her—not because I was a saint like she was, but because I was worried about her safety. The places she used to go were downright dangerous. I tried to stop her going out alone when I wasn't there, but she took no notice of me. She said she'd be fine. Said if she didn't help those poor kids, who would?

"When I came home early one morning to find a police car parked outside my house, I knew something bad had happened to Bianca. I have to confess I went crazy when I found out she was dead. I wanted to kill the little bastards who did it to her. As it was, I beat the hell out of a couple of them. The police weren't impressed, and gave me a warning. At the time, I didn't give a damn. They weren't doing anything that I could see to solve Bianca's murder. Anyway, I knew if I stayed there, I might do something really stupid so I sold up and left.'

'Just as well you did. Does your family know any of this?'

'Of course not!'

'But why ever not?'

'Because it's my private and personal business, not theirs.'

'So they don't know about your housekeeper being killed? Or that you've left South America for good? Or that you're going to live and work here in Australia in future?'

'Not yet. Wait a second,' he went on quickly when he saw her mouth opening. 'Let me finish before you get on your high horse and start tearing strips off me for being a secretive and unloving son. I will tell them. Well…not the bit about Bianca. Just that I've come home to Australia to live and work. Meanwhile, they're none the wiser and no one is getting hurt.'

Scarlet pressed her lips tightly together to stop herself from telling him that he was always hurting his family by his long absences, especially his mother. Carolyn had been quite upset when he'd left so soon after her party. She'd be even more upset if she knew he was up here in Darwin, holidaying, whilst she thought he was in Brazil working.

'Now, if you must know the truth, I do not actually *hate* my father. My emotions where he is concerned are not that simple.'

Scarlet blinked. What on earth could have possibly happened to sour the relationship between father and son so?

'You won't know this since my parents don't speak of it, but I was born a twin.'

'A twin!' Scarlet exclaimed, totally taken aback.

'Yes. I had a brother, Josh, born a few minutes before me. We were identical twins. Identical in genes but, as is often the case, not identical in nature. He was the extrovert; I, the introvert. He was hyperactive and rather naughty, but a real little charmer. He could talk when he was just a toddler. I was quieter and much less communicative. People thought I was shy but I wasn't. I was just…self-contained.'

Scarlet had an awful feeling about what was coming. After all, no twin brother named Josh had moved into the house opposite hers. She braced herself for bad news but it still shocked her.

'Josh drowned in our back-yard pool when he was four,' John went on. 'Mum was on the phone one day and we were playing outside. Josh pulled a chair over to the child-proof fence and attempted to climb over it. But he fell off the top of the fence and hit his head before toppling into the pool. I stood there for far too long in shock before run-

ning screaming for my mother. By the time she pulled Josh
out of the pool, he was dead.'

'Oh, John,' Scarlet choked out as tears welled up into
her eyes. 'How tragic.'

John stiffened when he saw the evidence of her sympathy. This was what he could not stand. This was why
he'd never told anyone this story. Because he didn't want
to feel what he was feeling at that moment—as though he
was somehow to blame for Josh's death. Logic told him it
couldn't possibly have been his fault, but logic meant nothing to a four-year-old seeing his mother almost catatonic
with shock and his father weeping in despair. It welled up
in him again, the guilt and the grief. Because he'd loved
Josh just as much as his parents. He'd been his twin brother.
His flesh and blood. They'd been inseparable from birth.

But no one had cared about *his* grief.

John could not believe how painful he still found the
memory. Damn it, he would not show weakness in front
of Scarlet.

'To cut a long story short,' he said abruptly, 'My father
did something the night after Josh's death which affected
me very badly. When I saw him sitting in an armchair in
our lounge, with his head in his hands, I ran up to him
and put my arms around him. He pushed me away and
told my mother to put me to bed, that he couldn't stand to
look at me.'

Scarlet sucked in sharply. What a dreadful thing for
John's father to say!

'Later that night, he did come into my room to kiss me
goodnight, but I turned my face away and refused to let
him kiss me. He just shrugged and walked away. After that,
I stopped speaking to him altogether for a very long time.
In fact I totally ignored him for years. He didn't seem to
mind or care. He was no longer the father I'd once adored.

He was just an empty shell of a man. My mother could see what was going on but she was a mess herself for ages and didn't seem to know what to say or do to make things right. She didn't recover till she had Melissa. She was the one who insisted we sell our old house and move—for a fresh start, she'd said. It made no difference to Dad. Or to me. He became a grouch and a workaholic and I became what you know I became. An angry, resentful boy.'

Scarlet had started gnawing at her bottom lip to stop herself from weeping. What a sad, sad story. Her heart went out to John as she began to understand what had made him the way he was. How incredibly hurt he must have been. No wonder he retreated into himself. And no wonder he didn't stay around his family for too long.

'I'm surprised you're as civil to your father as you are,' she said with feeling.

'He's mellowed since he retired. I can't say that I've totally forgiven or forgotten, but hatred and revenge never get you anywhere. Now that I've grown up, I can see that parents aren't perfect. They're just human beings. Josh had been the apple of Dad's eye and Josh was dead. Grief can make you say dreadful things.'

He had said appalling things to Bianca's family after she was killed, blaming them for not going with her that night. They'd been amazingly understanding of his grief and had not taken his accusations to heart. But he'd still felt terrible afterwards, once he calmed down. It was one of the reasons he'd given them his house and everything in it. To make it up to them.

'Have you ever confronted your Dad over what he said and did that night?' Scarlet asked, frowning thoughtfully.

'No.'

'At least your mother loved you and your brother equally,' she pointed out.

'I'm sure she did. But then Melissa came along, and Mum simply doted on her.'

'All mothers dote on their daughters, John. It didn't mean she loved you any less. To be fair to your mum, by then you were not the most lovable boy in the world.'

John laughed. 'Trust you to make me stop pitying myself.'

'That wasn't my intention. But do you know what, John? Things might not have been quite the way they seemed back then. I've been thinking...'

John sighed a weary sigh. 'What about this time?'

'About what your father said that night. He might have meant he couldn't stand to look at you because you reminded him of Josh. You were physically identical, after all. It might not have meant that he didn't love you just as much as your brother.'

'Pardon me, but I think his subsequent actions rather confirm that he didn't. He had every opportunity over the years to be a loving, caring father to me but he wasn't. He acted like I didn't exist. You've no idea how jealous I used to be of *your* father. Now he was what a father should be.'

'He was rather wonderful,' Scarlet agreed. 'But at least you had a great grandfather.'

'True. Grandpa was very good to me. To be honest, if it wasn't for him, I probably would have run away from home and ended up in jail.'

'Oh, surely not?' Scarlet protested.

'Why not? Jails are full of angry young men, Scarlet. Neglected sons with little self-esteem and no goals in life. My grandfather gave me back my self-esteem, plus the goal of becoming a geologist. I was shattered when he died just before my graduation. But even in death, he looked after my well-being by willing me some money. Quite a lot of money, actually. With it came a letter, telling me to travel and to see the world. So as soon as I graduated, I took off. First I went to Europe, but strangely Europe didn't appeal to me all that much. Too many cities and not enough trees maybe! I took off again and travelled all around for about two years.

"Eventually I reached South America. By that time, I had run out of money so I had to find work or go home. As you can imagine, going home didn't appeal all that much. Anyway, because I had no actual work experience, the only job I could get was with a speculative mining company who were looking for geologists to go places most people weren't prepared to go. It was dangerous work, but the money was good, and I found I rather enjoyed taking risks. Over the last decade, I discovered a new emerald mine in Columbia, oil in Argentina and natural gas in Ecuador.

"In return, I got shot at several times, fell off a mountain, almost drowned in the Amazon and was bitten by more vicious insects than you could ever count. Still, for my blood, sweat and tears I got paid serious bucks. I was able to buy myself that house in Rio and this apartment here in Darwin. I now don't have to take jobs which might get me killed!' He smiled wryly. 'I can even afford to support a child and give his or her mother enough financial freedom that she doesn't have to work for the rest of her life. If she doesn't want to,' he added.

Scarlet hadn't even given John supporting her financially a second thought. Now that he'd brought the subject up, she realised it was a tricky situation. If she accepted his money, it would give John more rights. Custody rights, maybe.

Her forehead scrunched into a frown as she once again

considered the consequences and complications which would come with John being the father of her child.

'More thinking, I see,' John said before she could voice an answer to her concerns. 'And not happy thoughts either. Look, if you don't want my money, then just say so. I won't ram it down your throat. Most women would be happy to have that offer on the table, but I should have known you're not most women.'

'I do value my independence,' she admitted.

'With my money you could buy yourself your own place. You could even employ a nanny, if you want to stay working.'

'A nanny? I don't want to hand my baby over to a nanny! As for buying my own place, I'll have you know I already have enough money to buy my own place, if I wanted to. I've been saving for a house ever since I started work. Thank you very much for your offer, John, but no; I don't want or need your financial support.'

Her stance shouldn't have annoyed him. But it did.

'Fine,' he bit out. 'I won't pay for a damned thing.'

'There's no reason to get angry,' Scarlet countered sharply. 'You should be glad that I'm not most women. Just think what would happen if I were a gold-digger. I could take you for heaps!'

In spite of himself, John's mouth quirked. She looked so disgusted by the very idea. Her anger had flushed her cheeks and made her look even more beautiful than usual. 'Fine. I accept that it's a good thing you aren't a gold-digger. Now, are there any more questions I have to answer before we can proceed with my plan for today?'

Scarlet blinked her surprise. 'You have an actual plan for today?' She'd thought *she* was the one with the plan.

'I did have. Before you put a spanner in the works and started wanting to get to know me better.'

'Well I… I…' Scarlet could not believe she was stammering when she was usually so articulate. She pressed her lips tightly together and took a deep breath before continuing.

'Okay. Fine. No more questions for now. But I might have some more later,' she added as an afterthought. *When I can think more clearly, that is.* 'So what was your plan for today?'

'A brief hour of sightseeing followed by a light lunch, followed by an afternoon in bed.'

Scarlet's mouth was suddenly bone dry. 'The whole afternoon?'

'That's a compromise. When you first walked out onto my balcony this morning looking good enough to eat, I wanted to whisk you right back into bed and keep you there all day.'

She just stared at him, the extent of his desire for her still a shock. So was the extent of her desire for him. Suddenly, her earlier resolve to restrict sex to the evenings dissolved, as she herself was dissolving.

'Also,' he went on with a sudden flare of desire in his eyes, 'this afternoon has nothing to do with babies and everything to do with pleasure. Not just mine, either. Judging on how you reacted last night, your sex life so far has been sadly lacking. I aim to rectify that, if you'll let me.'

Let him! How in earth was she going to stop him?

John rose to his feet and held out his hand to her. 'Now. Let's go sightseeing.'

CHAPTER EIGHTEEN

SCARLET was impressed by the waterfront development. It was tourist heaven, with luxury apartment blocks, a fantastic hotel, chic shops and cafés, great walkways suitable for morning jogs, a wave pool to delight children and adults alike and deep-water wharves at which cruise ships could dock. Scarlet might have made lots more complimentary comments if she hadn't been rendered uncharacteristically quiet by what was going on in her head, and in her body.

Never before had Scarlet felt such agitation. Her head whirled. Her stomach swirled. When John suggested they have some lunch at a trendy outdoor café, she was swift to agree, because it meant she could finally take her hand out of his. Not that she didn't enjoy holding hands with him. She did, more than she wanted to. But it wasn't the kind of physical closeness she was craving.

It had been wickedly clever of him to tell her what he had planned for this afternoon, she realised as they sat down opposite each other. Clever and corrupting. For she could think of nothing else now. She couldn't even make up her mind what to eat, telling him to order for her. John didn't seem to be similarly afflicted, ordering their lunches with the kind of *savoir faire* she should have expected from this new John. He didn't even consult the menu as he told the pretty young waitress to bring them two chicken-and-salad wraps on Turkish bread and two mugs of latte.

The girl's simpering smile showed she found John just as attractive as Scarlet did.

She almost made some caustic remark after the waitress hurried off to do his bidding, biting her tongue just in time. But the near-miss left Scarlet somewhat rattled. If she didn't know better, she'd think she was jealous. Which was insane! There was absolutely no reason to be jealous because some slip of a girl was dancing attention on John. After all, she wasn't going to be spending the afternoon in bed with him. Scarlet was!

She sucked in sharply at the spite-filled possessiveness behind her thoughts.

'Something wrong with what I ordered?' John asked straight away.

'No, no. It was fine. I just remembered I should have taken some photos whilst we were walking around to send to Mum,' she improvised. 'I totally forgot.'

And no damned wonder, she thought mutinously. *All I've been thinking about is having sex with you all afternoon, you wicked man!*

'You can still take some photos after we've had our lunch.'

'Yes, I suppose so.'

'But you'll have to be quick.'

'Oh? Why's that?' she asked, glancing up to the sky to see if there were any clouds gathering. But no, the sky was still clear and blue.

Some clouds had gathered in John's eyes, however, by the time her gaze returned to his.

'For an intelligent thirty-something, you can be pretty dense sometimes.' There was total exasperation and another kind of tension in his voice. 'I'm getting the sense that you don't know much about men, Scarlet.'

Scarlet decided not to take offence. She was tired of arguing with John. 'I'm well aware that I've led a narrow kind of life. After listening to all your travelling tales and adventures this morning, I would say *very* narrow. I dare say you probably think I've had a lot of boyfriends over the years but in truth I can count the number on one hand. So, no, I don't know all that much about men. I'm sorry if that disappoints you.'

John didn't want her apology. He wanted her naked in his arms. It had been hell this last hour, showing her the sights and resisting the temptation to drag her back up to his apartment post-haste. As for his being disappointed that she'd had only a handful of lovers, nothing could be further from the truth. It pleased him hugely. He loved that he could show her things in bed that she didn't know. Her lack of experience excited him. So, strangely, did her lack of feminine guile. Maybe he'd spent too many years bedding women who could read a man's needs like an open book, and who knew how to meet those needs every which way. Whatever the reason, he'd never felt such a need for any other woman.

But he would clearly have to wait a little longer. He could hardly insist that Scarlet skip the lunch he'd just ordered. Or forget taking those damned photographs for her mother. As much as John sometimes regretted the tenuous relationship he had with his family, he did not miss the demands that some parents made on their children, even into adulthood. Being a grown up, in his opinion, was being able to do your own thing without having to answer to someone all the time. Clearly, Scarlet was aghast at the lack of communication which existed between himself and his family, but he could think of nothing worse than having to ring his mother every single night he was away. Sometimes, months went by without his contacting home. He rarely felt guilty about it. Scarlet would, however. Underneath that tough exterior she liked to show to him, she had a soft, sentimental and sensitive soul.

This last realisation warned him not to say or do anything to hurt her. Now *that* would make him feel really guilty.

'Nothing about you disappoints me, Scarlet,' he said truthfully. 'I have always admired you enormously.'

'Really.' There was a trace of laughter in her voice.

'Really.'

'Even when I'm being dense about men?'

'Even then.'

'So what was I being dense about a minute ago?' she asked.

'I thought you would intuitively know that I needed to get you back to my apartment after lunch, as soon as possible.'

John saw the penny drop in her eyes, and colour flare up in her cheeks.

'Oh,' she said, then smiled a rueful smile. 'I thought it was just me suffering in silence.'

Her admission did little to soothe John's own frustration. He could not recall ever being this hard.

It was a relief that their lunch arrived at that precise moment, giving his overheated brain some well-needed respite. His overheated body as well. The wrap was excellent, though he hardly noticed, considering the speed with which he ate it.

'You'll get indigestion,' Scarlet warned him with a sweet smile. She was taking her time, he noted.

'Just eat your food and get on with those photos or I'll take them for you,' he ground out.

'Yes, sir!'

'And stop being sarcastic; I prefer the way you were a little while ago.'

'Which was?'

'Soft and sweet.'

'But I thought you said that my being stroppy turned you on?'

John spoke through gritted teeth. 'I don't want to be turned on any more right at this moment.'

'Ah, I see. Not to worry. I promise to be sweet as apple pie till we're safely behind closed doors.'

John had to laugh. 'Just get on with your food, will you?'

'I don't think I can eat any more,' she said.

Their eyes met across the table.

'Get those photos taken while I'll go pay the bill,' he said thickly as he rose to his feet.

Scarlet took only a few photos before he returned to collect her.

They hurried back the way they'd come, not holding hands this time, and not talking at all. Scarlet struggled to keep up with his long strides, her breathing heavy by the time they reached his apartment building. They rode the lift up in silence, Scarlet not daring even to look at John for fear of what he might do right there in the lift.

By the time John opened his apartment door and ushered her inside, she was desperate for him. Up against the door would have done. Or on the sofa. Or even on the floor. She imagined John would have been just as eager, so she was surprised when he didn't pounce immediately. Surprised and disappointed, especially when he stepped right away from her.

'No, Scarlet,' he said brusquely when she frowned at him. 'Not here and not yet. Now, I want you to go into the main bathroom, strip off and have a long, hot shower. I'll be doing the same in my bathroom. When you feel nicely relaxed, get out of the shower, dry yourself off then come into my bedroom. Without any clothes on, please. No towel. No robe.'

Scarlet swallowed. 'You…you expect me to walk into your room totally naked?'

'Totally. You have an incredibly beautiful body, Scarlet, and I want to see all of it, all the time.'

'All the time?' she choked out.

'Absolutely. Clothes are only going to be worn in future when we go out.'

'But…'

'No buts. This is part of my plan.'

'What plan is that?'

'A private plan.'

'But I don't see how—'

'I thought we agreed no buts,' he broke in sharply. 'And no more arguments. All I want to hear from you this afternoon is "yes, John; of course, John; anything you say, John".'

'You forgot "three bags full, John",' she snapped, but he could see the excitement in her eyes.

He smiled. 'That's my girl.'

Scarlet shook her head at him. 'You are the most infuriating man!'

'And you are the most desirable woman. Now, go and do exactly as you were told.'

He didn't wait for her reply, stalking off into the nearby master bedroom and shutting the door behind him, leaving her standing in the middle of the living room feeling totally flummoxed. But oh, so turned on. There was no question that she wouldn't do as he'd commanded. Because, deep down, she *wanted* to do it.

Doing it, however, was quite daunting. She didn't look

at herself in the bathroom mirror after she stripped off, keeping her eyes averted as she turned on the shower and waited till the water was warm enough to step into. She washed herself all over, doing her best not to linger too long on those areas which reminded her of how excited she was. Five minutes later she was out of the shower and reaching for one of the thick turquoise towels.

It took Scarlet another five minutes before she dared leave the bathroom, during which time she brushed out her hair for ages before freshening up her lipstick and spraying on some perfume. When she could not delay her emergence any longer, she scooped in several deep breaths then opened the bathroom door.

Walking naked through the apartment was the hardest thing she'd ever done, harder than showing up at that fertility clinic the first time. Which had been darned hard. By the time she reached the door to the master bedroom, Scarlet was a bundle of nerves. Steeling herself, she decided not to knock, choosing instead to open the door and go straight in.

As she entered the room, John was just coming out of his bathroom, a white towel wrapped low around his hips.

She ground to an annoyed halt, her hands in her hips. 'I want you naked too,' she threw at him.

'Not just yet,' he replied. His eyes glittered as they flicked over her from head to toe. 'You are even more beautiful standing up than lying down. Now, come over here to me. I want to watch you walk, then I want to hold you hard against me and kiss you till you beg me to just do it to you like you did last night. But not in bed—standing up with your legs wrapped around my waist and your arms tight around my neck.'

The highly erotic images his words evoked made Scarlet's head spin. How she managed to cross the room without tripping or stumbling she had no idea. But cross it she did, despite her knees feeling like jelly. He watched her closely with narrowed eyes, not saying another word. When she drew near, she could hear his heavy breathing and her own. Could feel his tension and her own. When he tossed the towel aside, she could see his arousal.

Stunningly, magnificently erect. A lethal weapon of naked desire. Her mouth dried in anticipation of his doing it to her the way he'd said he would, standing up. Her heart rate quickened, her nipples tightening.

Oh yes, she thought heatedly when he reached out to pull her into his arms, pressing her hard against him so that his erection sank deep into the soft swell of her stomach. *Yes, yes. Do it to me. Do it to me now. Don't kiss me. Don't wait. Just lift me up and do it!*

He didn't obey her silent commands. He kissed her first, hot hungry kisses which brought her to a level of frustration she could not previously have imagined. It was violent, the need to have him inside her. The need to come. When a muffled moan echoed in her throat, John tore his mouth from hers.

'Tell me that you want me, Scarlet,' he whispered fiercely into her hair.

'Yes, yes, I want you,' she choked out. 'Oh God, John, just do it. Do it the way you said.'

She gasped when he drove up into her, then again when he cupped her buttocks and lifted her right off the floor.

'Wrap your arms and legs around me,' he ground out.

After she did so, he carried her over to the bedroom wall, using it to support her back whilst he surged up into her, over and over. Her release was quick and savage, her first spasm so intense that she screamed out. He came too, just as violently, his orgasmic groans sounding more like cries of pain. His fingertips dug into her flesh whilst she clasped him just as tightly around his neck. Their climaxes lasted a considerable time, their bodies pulsing together, their hearts thudding to the same mad beat.

Finally, it was over, a wave of post-coital exhaustion bringing a heavy sigh to Scarlet's lips. John sighed also, his head lifting from where he'd buried it in her hair.

Scarlet felt absolutely drained. In fact, she was having difficulty keeping her legs where they were. They were on the verge of dropping back down to the floor when John carried her over to the bed, tipping her gently back across the black quilt before slowly withdrawing.

'See what you've done to me?' he said as he straightened and nodded downwards.

'Poor John,' she murmured sleepily. 'Perhaps you should lie down next to me and have a rest.'

'Perhaps I should. But only on condition you don't ask me any more questions.'

CHAPTER NINETEEN

'HAVE you had a lot of women?' Scarlet asked.

She was lying across the bed with her head resting on John's stomach, her face turned towards his, her left hand playing with the mat of damp curls on his chest. John was stretched out with his hands linked behind his head and his eyes on the ceiling. They'd not long returned to the bed after a rather lengthy shower.

'You promised not to ask me any more questions.'

'I did no such thing. I just let you off while you were resting. So I repeat…have you had a lot of women?'

'Yes,' he replied bluntly. 'I've had a lot of women.'

'I thought as much.'

'Does it matter?'

'I suppose not.'

'Not jealous, are you?'

'Not at all. Just curious. But when did you have time to have all these girlfriends? From what you told me, you've spent most of your adult life climbing up mountains and trekking through jungles.'

'I didn't say I've had lots of girlfriends, Scarlet. I said I've had lots of women. There's a difference.'

'Oh. Oh, I see. You're a one-night-stand type of guy.'

'Generally speaking, yes. I had a couple of steady girlfriends at uni but nothing serious. I don't have time for long relationships these days. Or the inclination.'

'But I'm sure you told me the night of your mum and dad's party that you'd just broken up with some woman.'

'I lied.'

She sat up abruptly. 'But why?'

'To avoid you asking me questions, of course.'

Of course...

As much as Scarlet wanted to know everything there was to know about John, she knew when she was beaten. He'd already told her more than she thought he ever would. To press further could spoil things. He was already glowering at her.

'Okay,' she said. 'No more questions.'

'Thank goodness. Silence is golden, you know, especially when one is totally knackered.'

Scarlet laughed, then lay back down with her head on his stomach. This time, however, she was facing the other way. She glanced down at his penis, which wasn't totally knackered. But wasn't erect, either. It didn't look quite as daunting when it was like that. She suspected, however, that she only had to take it into her mouth and it would soon be revived.

'Hey!' he exclaimed, when she took hold of his penis with a firm grip. 'What in hell do you think you're doing?'

'What do you think I'm doing?'

He groaned when she began sliding her hand up and down, her fingers tight around his flesh.

'Woman, you have no pity in you.'

'Not for you, I don't.'

'You're going to be the death of me.'

'Possibly. But what a way to go.'

He laughed, then gasped. 'Don't you dare do that!'

She didn't answer. She couldn't.

John's jaw clenched down hard at the sensations which were rocketing through his body. Damn, but she was good at that. Hard to believe her claim that she had so little sexual experience. Yet he did believe her. Scarlet was no liar. *He* was, however, when need be. His protest over her going down on him had been a lie of sorts. He'd wanted her to do just that. Wanted her to re-arouse him. Wanted her to have climax after climax.

Because that was his plan, to make her body addicted to having sex with him. And then, next Monday, two days before she entered the period when she was most likely to conceive, the sex would stop, giving his sperm count time to recover and her body time to become increasingly needy. By Wednesday, she'd be ready to fall pregnant, her mind not on babies so much but on pleasure.

It was a perfect plan, John thought as he reached down and splayed both his hands into her hair, meaning to stop her. After all, he didn't want to get her addicted to *giving* pleasure, but in receiving it. But, damn it all, it was delicious, what she was doing. His fingertips pressed hard into her scalp. Instead of pulling her off him, he found himself holding her head captive whilst he spun out of control and surrendered to temptation.

Afterwards, when she crawled up the bed to snuggle against him, he wrapped an arm around her shoulder and pulled her close.

'That was incredible,' he said, trying not to sound as shaken as he still felt. 'Thank you.'

'My pleasure,' she murmured, and pressed her still-moist lips against the base of his throat.

His heart squeezed tight as a wave of emotion washed through his body.

I'm the one who's getting addicted here, he realised. *Addicted and involved. Emotionally involved.*

The idea that he might be falling in love with Scarlet was so surprising, so startling, that John didn't know what to think or do. It seemed an impossible idea at first. He didn't do love. But gradually, once he put aside his initial shock, John began to see that it wasn't such a weird idea. He even considered the possibility that he'd been a little in love with Scarlet ever since his teenage years.

'You're going to think me very naive,' she said suddenly, lifting her head up enough to lock eyes with him. 'But I used to think that I would have to be madly in love with a man before I really enjoyed sex. I mean *really* enjoyed it, the way I have with you.' Her head lowered again to rest across his chest. 'I guess that comes from being a hopeless romantic all these years. I didn't realise that all it would take was a man who knew what he was doing in bed.'

The ironic timing of Scarlet's statement did not escape John. But her very sensible words were a relief in a way. Of course it wasn't love he felt for Scarlet. It was still lust, the same thing he'd always felt for her. Too much great sex with her was addling his brain. He needed to stop for a while.

'Thank you for the compliment, Scarlet,' he said. 'I've also made a discovery about myself and sex since going to bed with you.'

Her head lifted again. 'What's that?'

'I can't keep going for ever.'

'Neither can I. In fact, I can't even keep my eyes open,' Scarlet said as she snuggled back down, her head on his chest, her right arm flopping across his rib cage.

'I could do with a sleep too,' John said, glad she couldn't see the grimace on his face. How in God's name was he going to go to sleep with her lying all over him like that?

He didn't, of course. He just lay there beneath her, struggling to control his breathing, and his body. Scarlet fell asleep first, for which John was grateful, because it enabled him to move her off him onto the bed. She immediately curled up into the foetal position, John covering her naked body with a sheet before rolling right away from her.

Once he'd put some physical distance between them, John began to relax. But it was still quite a while before he surrendered his mind and body to the welcoming oblivion of sleep.

CHAPTER TWENTY

SCARLET was taken aback when she woke and saw that the sun was so low in the sky. She must have been asleep for a couple of hours at least!

It wasn't like her to sleep during the day. Of course, it wasn't like her to have so much sex during the day. Or any sex at all. She'd read somewhere that having a climax was the best sleeping pill in the world. No wonder she'd passed out. In fact, it was a wonder she'd woken up!

John was still out like a light, she noted as she rolled over.

All due to moi, Scarlet thought rather smugly.

'Poor darling,' she murmured, stroking his arm gently till he stirred. When he rolled onto his back and opened his eyes she sat up and smiled down at him.

'Time to get up, sleepyhead. I don't know about you but I'm starving. Is there a local restaurant you know which opens early?' she asked as she swept her hair back from her face. 'I don't think I could wait too long before I eat something.'

The sight of her bare breasts was doing wicked things to John's nicely rested body. But he checked the impulse to seduce her right then and there, reminding himself that the quicker and earlier they ate dinner, the longer the evening would be.

'The sailing club serves dinner from five-thirty,' he informed her. 'It's only a few minutes' drive from here, dress is casual, the seating *al fresco* and the sunset's worth taking your camera for.'

'Sounds perfect. Meet you in the living room in fifteen minutes,' she said. Jumping out of bed, she dashed for the door, no doubt heading for the main bathroom and guest bedroom where she'd left all her things.

'Scarlet!' he called out before she could make her escape. She turned in the doorway, no longer shy about showing him her body, he noted. That was a good sign.

'What?' she asked.

'A dress please. And no underwear.'

She blinked, then flushed.

'No buts,' he ground out. 'No arguments. No underwear.'

Her chin came up, her eyes defiant. 'No,' she threw back at him. 'I'm not going to do that.'

'Why not? You'll like it.'

'No, I won't.'

'How do you know you won't?'

'I just know.'

'Like you know you won't like camping? Or fishing? Yet you haven't tried either. Give it a go, Scarlet. No one will know but me.'

'That's one person too many. I agreed to have sex with you, John. I didn't agree to anything…kinky.'

His eyebrows arched. 'I would hardly call that kinky.'

'I would.'

'Fine. I wouldn't want you to do anything you weren't comfortable with.'

'I don't intend to. Now, I'm going to go get dressed.'

It was a rather irritated John who rose and set about getting dressed himself, pulling on fresh underwear, a pair of jeans and a black T-shirt. Obviously he had a way to go before Scarlet's mind was totally consumed by sex. *He* was the one who was plagued with that problem. His agitation was not improved when Scarlet made her appearance right on schedule, wearing a very pretty floral sundress with a flouncy skirt, tight waistline and a halter-necked bodice. Her blonde hair was bundled up rather haphazardly on top of her head, with lots of wispy strands kissing her face. She didn't appear to be wearing make-up other than some lip gloss. Even so, her cheeks glowed and her blue eyes sparkled. She looked fresh and beautiful and so sexy, it was criminal.

'You're not wearing a bra,' he said gruffly, spotting the outline of provocatively naked nipples.

She shrugged, the action bringing even more attention to her unfettered breasts. 'Some dresses aren't made for bras.'

'Whatever,' he said offhandedly, doing his best to get some perspective in the face of his escalating frustration. But it wasn't easy. He hadn't realised that his plan to seduce Scarlet into a state of permanent arousal would backfire on him so painfully. He wished now that he was wearing shorts and not hip hugging, hard-on-squashing jeans. But he could hardly change clothes at this late stage.

'I suggest you bring a jacket or a cardigan,' he advised her sharply as he headed for his front door. 'It might get cool after the sun goes down.'

'I'll go get one.'

He made no comment, not wanting to delay their departure any longer. The sooner he got her out to the sailing club, the sooner they could eat and the sooner they would be back here, at which point she would do as she was told for once!

Scarlet didn't say a word during the ride down in the lift, or the drive to the sailing club. In truth she was feeling guilty. And very uncomfortable. Because she had actually done what John had so arrogantly demanded she do, gone out without any underwear on.

Of course, no way was she about to admit it. She'd just wanted to have the experience. Wanted to see if he was right.

He wasn't, she realised very quickly. She didn't like it. The braless bit didn't overly bother her. It wasn't the first time she'd gone braless, though she didn't make a habit of it. Having her bottom bare under her dress, however, made her feel terribly vulnerable. Fearful, even. What if a wind blew her skirt up and people saw that she had no panties on?

Every muscle she owned tightened just thinking about such a horrifying and humiliating event.

By the time they arrived at the sailing club she was extremely tense. Thankfully, there was no breeze blowing. The air was still and quite warm so she didn't need her shawl, and didn't have to worry too much about any unfortunate wind accidents.

It was a smallish establishment, Scarlet saw straight away, built on a select plot of land right on the harbour. Despite its prime location, there was no pretension about the single-storey clubhouse, or the outdoor eating areas. The tables and chairs were a mixture of wooden and plastic, several of them set up right at the water's edge under the shade of tall palm trees. Because they were early, they were able to get one of the best tables where no one would be able to block out the view of the sunset. The sun was by then extremely low in the sky and beginning to turn a gorgeous golden colour. Its beauty distracted Scarlet temporarily from any concerns over her panti-less state.

'How long before it sets?' she asked John as she sat down.

'Not long. Time to start taking some photos. I'll go order

the food. What would you like? You can have steak and salad, fish and chips, a roast or Chinese.'

'Fish and chips sounds good.'

'Fish and chips it is, then.'

Scarlet got her phone out and started clicking away whilst he was gone, amazed at how the gold colour intensified as the sun sank even lower in the sky. By the time John returned, it was just touching the horizon, its colour now closer to red than gold.

'Thank you,' she said when he placed a glass of chilled white wine on the table in front of her. 'But I can't drink it just yet. I don't want to miss a moment of this.' And she turned her attention back to the sunset.

It amazed her, just how quickly the sun set. One minute the edge of the circle was just touching the horizon, the next the sun was halfway gone then, poof, totally gone.

'Oh…' she said with a regretful sigh.

'Darwin is famous for its sunsets,' John said.

'They're pretty spectacular. Mum is going to want to come up here after seeing these photos. Which reminds me,' she said as she put down her phone and picked up her glass of wine. 'I have to ring her later. Don't let me forget.'

'Are you going to ring your mother every single night?' he asked somewhat impatiently.

Scarlet took a deep swallow of wine and counted to ten before answering. She understood that John's relationship with his family was way different from hers. But that didn't give him the right to be critical of what she believed was a normal way to act.

'Yes, John,' she said at last, firmly but calmly. 'I'm going to ring my mother every single night. I love Mum very much and I know she'll be missing me. I'm sorry if you find that annoying but that's just too bad.'

She waited for him to say something sarcastic back, but

he didn't. He just nodded. 'I've always admired your spirit, Scarlet. And your honesty.'

Scarlet's hand tightened around the stem of the wine glass. 'I'm not always honest.'

John slanted her a surprised look. 'Really? Do tell.'

Talking about her mother had made Scarlet think about all the lies she'd told her before coming here. And all the lies she'd have to keep telling her every single night of her stay in Darwin. After all, she could hardly tell her the truth. Still, this train of thought did pose the question of what she would eventually tell her mother if and when she did fall pregnant to John. How would she explain it?

It shocked her that she hadn't worked out a plan concerning this problem earlier. Shocked her, too, that she'd almost forgotten about why she'd come up to Darwin in the first place. Her mind had been focused on nothing but sex for most of today. She'd gone to sleep this afternoon thinking about sex. Had woken thinking about sex. And had left off her underwear, thinking about sex.

It was worrying, this craving John had created in her to experience everything with him. Every sexual position. Every form of foreplay. Every erotic game. And, yes, even the kinky ones.

Suddenly, sitting there with no underwear on was no longer slightly embarrassing. It was seriously shameful yet at the same time so wickedly exciting that she could actually feel the heat between her thighs.

'Scarlet?' John prompted. 'What haven't you been honest about?'

'I…um… I was thinking about the lies I've told Mum. It's going to be awkward, explaining things later.'

'You mean when you fall pregnant.'

'*If* I fall pregnant,' she corrected.

'When. If. Whatever. It's a little early to start inventing stories yet. We'll worry about that when you're actually pregnant.'

'I'm sorry to be a worry-wart, John, but I need to have some story settled in my mind tonight. It's really bothering me.'

'Okay,' he said, trying to be patient. 'The way I see it, you have two possible stories to choose from. You can tell your mum the truth, or you can say you ran into me by accident whilst you were on holiday up here and we had a brief fling.'

Scarlet shook her head. 'That last idea won't fly. Mum won't believe it. Neither will your parents. Even if they did, they'd wonder what you were doing in Darwin when you were supposed to be in Brazil.'

'Then tell them the truth.'

'Which is?'

'That you told me you desperately wanted a baby the day of their party, and out of friendship I offered myself as the father, no strings attached. You can say we planned to meet in Darwin that night but kept our assignation a secret from everyone in case you didn't fall pregnant.'

Scarlet frowned. 'I suppose that seems reasonably plausible. Mum would believe it, since she knows about my failed artificial-insemination plan, but I'm not sure about your parents. After all, we've always come across as enemies, not friends.'

'Rubbish. Mum never thought that and Dad doesn't think at all. We'll go with the truth, if and when the time comes. Okay?'

'I suppose so.'

'Look, Scarlet,' he said firmly. 'I brought you up here early so that you could relax and have some fun. Forget about the future for the next few days and just think about enjoying yourself.'

'That's what I've been doing.'

'What's wrong with that?'

'I'm not sure what we've been doing is fun, exactly.'

'Then what is it?'

'Dangerous.'

'In what way dangerous?'

'I might get to like it too much.' *And to like* you *too much*, came the sudden thought.

'Sex, you mean?'

'Yes.'

'I can't see how that's dangerous.'

'You're not a woman.' Women had a long history of falling for men who were great lovers. Scarlet didn't want to fall for John. That would not be a good idea at all.

The buzzer rang at that moment, announcing that their meals were ready. John shook his head at her as he picked up the buzzer and stood up.

The food was excellent, the fish cooked in beer batter and the chips crisp and hot. The smell of the food reminded Scarlet how hungry she was and she set about eating the meal with gusto. The time it took to eat the meal was a blessing as well, for it gave her the opportunity to calm down. Of course she wasn't falling in love with John! She was just being silly and naive. Still, if she was going to keep on having sex with him—and she definitely was—then she had to adopt a more casual attitude to sex and get a grip on her emotions. Okay, so sex with him was earth-moving stuff—wasn't she a lucky girl?

Such thoughts did little to dampen her escalating desires, however. By the time they left the club for the short drive home, Scarlet was near to bursting with frustration. She suspected that John was of a similar frame of mind. His eyes kept returning to her cleavage. Which meant he was sure to pounce the moment they were alone. That would have suited Scarlet fine, except for the little matter of being butt-naked under her dress. Her pride simply would not let John discover that she'd done what he wanted after all.

'I'm going to ring my mother first,' she said the second John closed the apartment door behind them.

'Fine,' he growled. 'I've got a couple of calls I have to make, anyway.' And he marched off in the direction of the kitchen.

Scarlet scuttled off to the guest bedroom where she quickly pulled a pair of white satin panties out from her case and put them on. Once that was done, she sat down on the side of the bed with her phone in hand and punched in her home number. It rang and rang, but her mother didn't answer. When the phone clicked over to the answering machine, Scarlet thought about leaving a message but decided not to. She didn't want her mother to call her later when she was otherwise engaged. Instead, she rang off then tried her mother's mobile number, even though she knew it was probably turned off. Her mother was of that generation who only used their mobile phones for making emergency calls. She never thought to leave it turned on so that people could call her.

But, surprisingly, it was on, her mother answering after only a few rings.

'Mum!' Scarlet said with surprise in her voice. 'You actually turned your mobile on.'

'I thought I should. I knew you'd ring me tonight and I didn't want to miss your call.'

'Where on earth are you? It sounds rather noisy.'

'I'm at Erina Fair, doing some food shopping. What you can hear is the rain on the roof. It hasn't stopped bucketing down since you left.'

'No rain up here. It was about twenty-five degrees today, with just a gentle breeze blowing off the sea.'

'You're having a good time, by the sound of you.'

Good…

Now that wasn't a word which sprang to mind about today, Scarlet thought guiltily.

'I haven't been doing all that much,' she said. 'Went for a long walk around the city and down to the new water-front area which was pretty amazing. I'm just back from dinner at the sailing club.'

'The sailing club, no less! That sounds swish.'

'Actually, no, it's nothing like that at all. The club's on the small side and very casual. Where you eat is right on the water and has a great view of the sunset. I took lots of photos. Which reminds me, have you looked at the photos of the apartment I sent you?'

'I sure did. It looks lovely and the view is fantastic.'

'I've taken heaps more photos today. I'll email them to you as soon as I get off the phone.'

'Oh, don't worry about doing that, love. I'd much rather you showed me the rest of your photos when you get home. That way you can tell me all about them at the same time. So what are you going to do tomorrow?'

'I'm not sure. I haven't booked anything as yet. I might just potter around Darwin again, or sit on the balcony and read a book.'

Or I might spend all day in bed, fulfilling every single sexual fantasy I've ever had.

'You do whatever you want to do, darling. And don't worry about calling me every day. You're up there to have a complete break. And it's not like I'm lonely. I'm with the girls at the salon all day, then I'm going to my quilting meeting tomorrow night. And Carolyn has kindly asked me over to her place for dinner on Saturday. I dare say she thinks I'm missing you, and of course I am. But not in a sad way. I love it that you're having a holiday. I tell you what—leave off calling me till Sunday night. By then you'll have lots of news to tell me.'

'Okay. I'll ring you on Sunday night around seven. Bye, Mum. Look after yourself.'

'You too, darling. Love you. Bye.'

Scarlet sighed as she hung up. Her mother *was* missing her but trying desperately not to show it. Perhaps it was a good thing for her mother to learn to cope by herself for a while.

It was just as well, however, that she didn't know what her daughter was up to during her 'holiday'. She would be seriously shocked.

Scarlet could no longer pretend to be shocked. The lust which was consuming her was also obliterating both shock and shame. She could not wait to be with John again. Her heart beat quickened as she hurriedly made her way back out into the kitchen where the object of her desires was just saying goodbye to whoever he was talking to.

He placed his phone down on the kitchen counter and looked over at her.

'I expected you to talk for a lot longer than that.'

'The line wasn't good,' Scarlet informed him, amazed at how calm she sounded. 'It was raining so hard I could hardly hear her. Who were *you* talking to?' she asked, still managing to keep up her cool facade. Underneath, however, she was all liquid heat.

'That was a mate of mine. Owns a helicopter. His name's Jim. Before that I rang another mate, Brad. He owns a boat-charter business. I've been lining up our activities for the next three days. Tomorrow, we're going on that harbour cruise, the one where you learn to fish. Saturday, we're going to visit Kakadu and a few other tourist spots by air, then late in the afternoon Jim is going to set us down in a very special place where I'm going to show you that camping can be fun too. Sunday morning, Jim'll come back to collect us, then we're going to do a spot of heli-fishing before coming back here and cooking our catch. How does that sound?'

'Wonderful.' In truth, she didn't give a damn what they did tomorrow. Or Saturday. Or Sunday. All she could think about was here and now.

'John?' she said, her voice turning throaty as desire trickled like shards of hot ice down her spine, radiating out into her breasts and her belly and every other turned-on area of her body.

'Yes?'

'Could you please stop talking now?' she choked out. 'I really need you to make love to me.'

John stared at her, his gaze so hungry and hot Scarlet thought she would combust on the spot.

'In that case, I really need you to take that dress off,' he said in a low, gravelly voice. 'If you recall, I did say that no clothes were allowed when we were alone together.'

Scarlet gulped. Thank God she'd put her panties back on. As wickedly charged as she felt, she still didn't want John to know that she'd sat through dinner without any underwear on. Now that *would* be shaming. Her heart missed several beats as she reached up her back to find the zipper which anchored her dress in place. Seconds later the dress was on the floor and her pulse rate went off the Richter scale.

'Now the rest of it,' he ordered.

Her hands trembled as she took her panties off, but not through nerves. It was sheer excitement that was making her shake. Tossing the panties away, she straightened her shoulders and stood before him, totally nude, except for her shoes.

'Scarlet King,' he said as his heavy lidded gaze raked over her. 'You are one wickedly beautiful woman.'

I'm one very wicked woman, Scarlet thought, her belly tightening when he began to walk around the benchtop towards her.

Even before he pulled her into his arms, she knew that she would do anything John asked of her tonight. Anything at all.

CHAPTER TWENTY-ONE

Late Sunday afternoon

'I STILL can't believe how much I like fishing,' Scarlet said as they walked back to the apartment, John carrying a bag of provisions they'd bought at a nearby supermarket. 'I quite liked it on Friday but I really enjoyed myself this morning.'

They'd not long returned from their heli-fishing expedition, which had involved being delivered by helicopter to a special river spot where the barramundi had practically jumped onto their lines. They'd caught too many, really. They'd given Jim a few and still had five to bring home, stashing four in John's freezer and keeping out a large one which Scarlet planned to cook for them both tonight, hence the trip to the supermarket.

'I quite liked the camping part as well,' she added, though perhaps it was the place she'd loved more than roughing it in the outback. The spot John had chosen to camp next to last night had been extremely beautiful, a fresh-water billabong surrounded on three sides by rugged cliffs, and fed by a waterfall which had sparkled like diamonds in the late-afternoon sun.

He slanted her a smug smile. 'What you liked, madam, was sharing my sleeping bag.'

Well, yes, she certainly had. It had been something else, sleeping like spoons in the one sleeping bag with their arms around each other and their bodies joined, John making love to her on and off during the night. But it wasn't the amount of sex which Scarlet began thinking about now, but the quality of John's love-making. It had been different to what he'd done to her on previous nights. His love-making in the sleeping bag had been slow and gentle, and rather wonderful. It had left her feeling not ravaged, so much as loved. They'd talked at length too, exchanging memories of their childhood, laughing about incidents which had once bothered them both.

Dared she hope that their relationship was deepening? That John might care for her as she was certainly beginning to care for him?

It was impossible to pretend it was just lust she still felt for the man. She liked John's company, in bed and out. Liked his friends. Liked his surprisingly warm, easy-going way.

'I have to say I was surprised how well you took to going feral,' he said with amusement in his voice.

His comment surprised her. 'What do you mean, feral?'

He grinned. 'Once I convinced you that no one could possibly see you, you loved skinny dipping in the billabong. And sitting by the campfire naked.'

'Don't be crude,' she said sharply.

'And don't you start being a hypocrite,' he shot back. 'There was nothing crude about anything we did out there. It was fun.'

Fun? *Fun?* Was that what being with her still meant to him? Just *fun?*

It was a dismaying reality, but logical. John didn't fall in love. Even if he was capable of it, he simply didn't want to.

Unfortunately, the opposite was true of herself—she *did*

want to. Also unfortunately, she had an awful feeling that she already had. She'd foreseen this disastrous outcome the night they'd gone to the sailing club. What a fool she was to think she could stop it happening!

Dear God, how could she possibly have John as the father of her child now? At the same time, how could she not?

She was damned if she did, and damned if she didn't.

Her eyes searched his for a hint that maybe she was wrong. Maybe his feelings *had* deepened for her. But all she saw in his face was irritation and impatience. If he cared for her—even a little—he would understand that what they'd shared last night had been something special, not just *fun*!

'You're not going to start a fight, are you, Scarlet?' he asked her somewhat warily. Her heart sank. She wasn't. Of course she wasn't. But it wasn't going to be the same after this, was it? She was sure to keep hoping for more from John. Hoping and praying. And it would never happen. Yet if she had his baby he'd be in her life for ever. And she'd be secretly in love with him for ever.

'I think we should get back to the apartment,' she said stiffly and, whirling, set out purposefully along the pavement.

John shook his head as he trudged after her. Everything had been going according to his plan. Absolutely everything. She'd clearly become addicted to sex with him. Extremely addicted. And he'd been only too happy to oblige. Frankly, he'd never before felt the buzz he felt when he was with her. She could fire him up with just a look. He couldn't get enough of her. She was so damned hot, and so damned obliging.

Up till now, that was...

'What's wrong?' he asked her during their ride up in the lift.

Scarlet was still struggling with the enormity of her realisation, so she didn't have a ready or a reasonable answer for him.

'Nothing's wrong,' she bit out.

'Don't take me for a fool, Scarlet. My using the word fun upset you. I'm not sure why.'

'Yes, well, I obviously don't have as casual an attitude to sex as you do. I'm not a one-night-stand kind of girl. What we've been doing together…it's all been a bit much. To be honest, it's beginning to bother me.'

'Right. I see.'

The lift doors opened and they made their way along to his door. John extracted his keys from his shorts pocket, all the while thinking that Scarlet had just handed him the perfect excuse to put a halt to the sex till she was entering the phase when she'd be likely to conceive late on Tuesday night. Not that he wanted to stop the sex. Hell, no. He'd been looking forward to making love to her after dinner as he had every other night, a shudder of dark pleasure running through him as he recalled how total her sexual surrender was. She never said no to him any more, no matter what he wanted to do. It was going to be hard, giving that up for two days.

Under the circumstances, however, it would be wise if she spent tonight in the guest bedroom. His only problem was how to suggest it. That might be awkward. As much as Scarlet claimed she didn't like having sex for sex's sake, the truth was that she did. A lot.

John was thinking about how he could solve this problem whilst he opened the door. He didn't say a word as he walked in and headed for the kitchen with the shopping, leaving Scarlet to close the door and trail after him. The ring tone of a phone—not his—suddenly split the silence in the apartment. Scarlet ran off into the guest bedroom where she'd obviously left her mobile. John heard her answer but then she closed the door, shutting him out.

Ten minutes later, she emerged. John knew immediately that this time, something was really wrong.

'That was Joanna,' Scarlet said before he asked. 'She's one of the hairdressers at the salon. Mum had a fall on Thursday when she came home from shopping. Slipped on some wet tiles and broke her wrist. Her right wrist. The thing is, John, I have to go home.'

'Hold on a minute,' John said, his stomach instantly churning. 'What do you mean, you *have* to go home? Why do you *have* to go home? I'm sure your mother can manage. It's just a wrist, not an arm or a leg. She has good friends and neighbours. They'll all help. Have you rung her? Did she say she wants you to go home?'

'Of course I haven't rung Mum, because she'd say to stay here. But I can't do that, not now that I know what's happened. She needs me, no matter what you think. And the salon needs me. They can't operate without two of their full-time hairdressers. We'll lose clients. Joanna said it was chaos there on Friday and Saturday. Fortunately, tomorrow is a slow day. By Tuesday, however, I'll have to be there.'

'Can't they find a temp?'

Her laugh was short and dry. 'When one of the girls went on maternity leave last year, we had the devil of a time finding someone to fill in for her. No way could we get someone on short notice. Look, there's no point arguing with me over this, John. My mind is made up. I've already rung the airline and got a seat on a flight leaving first thing in the morning. I have to be at the airport no later than six-thirty.'

'What? For pity's sake, Scarlet!' John exploded. 'This is ridiculous. Three more days up here. That's all you need. Three short days. And you're going to throw it all away.

Think of yourself for once. Your mother will survive. The business will survive. Okay, so you'll lose a bit of money and maybe a couple of clients. But you'll have what you've always wanted—a baby.'

One part of Scarlet—the selfish part—agreed with him. But she could not bear the thought of her mother struggling along at home without her. Neither could she let the girls in the salon down, not now that they'd asked for her help. On top of that, there was that other critical little matter of her having fallen in love with John.

This was her way out, Scarlet realised. Her escape clause. She would never have been able to walk away from him by herself, but she could do it for other people. Strange, how calm she felt about her decision. Maybe you were always calm when you knew you were doing the right thing.

'Even if I stayed here three more days, John, there's no guarantee of a baby.'

His eyes narrowed on her, his expression fierce. 'Why aren't you more upset about this?'

'I *am* upset about it.' God, did he honestly think she *wanted* to fall in love with him?

'No, you're bloody well not. You've grabbed onto this because you *want* to leave. You don't want me to be the father of your child. That's the bottom line, isn't it?'

She almost lied again. But what would have been the point?

'Yes,' she confessed. 'That's the bottom line.'

John could not believe how furious he was.

'So what did I do to change your mind?' he snapped.

'Nothing. The problem lies with me.'

'Meaning?'

Scarlet decided that a version of the truth would serve her purpose nicely. 'As unlikely as it seems, I'm in danger of becoming emotionally involved with you. It's a flaw in some women when they have great sex with a guy. But I don't want to fall for you, John. I really don't.'

'Why not?' he demanded to know, stung by her dismissive words.

She just stared at him, not believing that he could ask such a stupid question. 'Why do you think? You don't do love and marriage. You're a committed loner who only ever comes home at Christmas and has no concept of what it is to care about anyone but yourself. I don't believe you really want to be a father. I still can't fathom why you made your offer in the first place. It never did make sense to me.'

'Or to me,' he threw at her, his temper getting the better of him. 'It was an insanely impulsive gesture and one I regretted as soon as I made it. But then *you* contacted *me*, and I thought what the heck? Like I said, I'd always wanted you. And there you were, serving yourself up on a silver platter.'

Scarlet winced. She guessed she deserved that. But it hurt, oh so much. 'Charming,' she said, her chin lifting in defiance of her pain. 'It shouldn't bother you, then, if we call it quits at this stage. After all, you've already had me.'

'I sure have, sweetheart. I've already had everything I wanted from you!'

Tears threatened but she refused to cry in front of him. 'I always knew you were a bastard. I won't be cooking any of that fish. I couldn't eat a bite. I'll also be sleeping in the guest bedroom tonight.'

'Really? You don't want a goodbye session?'

She gave him a long, hard look, fully understanding how easily hate could become the other side of love. 'Don't bother driving me to the airport,' she bit out. 'I'll order a taxi.'

He almost called her back when she whirled to walk away. Almost told her...what?

That he was desperately sorry for what he had just said? That he hadn't meant *any* of it? That he *did* care? That he *did* want to be the father of her baby?

Let her go, his conscience insisted. *She's right. You're a selfish bastard. You'd make a rotten father. Even worse than your own. Go back overseas somewhere. Africa, maybe. Get as far away from home—and Scarlet—as possible.*

Yeah, that's what I'll do, John decided grimly. *As soon as possible.*

CHAPTER TWENTY-TWO

THE plane took off shortly after seven-thirty the following morning.

Scarlet leant back in her seat and closed her eyes. It had been a long night. She hadn't slept much, of course. Impossible in the face of such deep depression.

She'd rung her mother the previous evening at seven, as promised, immediately stating that she knew about her broken wrist and that she was coming home the following day. Her mother had argued with her but Scarlet had brooked no protest, glad finally to hear relief in her mother's voice. Relief and gratitude.

It had been hard, however, not breaking down during the call. She'd broken down afterwards, crying herself to sleep, a sleep which hadn't lasted long. She'd risen around midnight and crept out to the kitchen where she'd made herself some tea and toast. John hadn't stirred, thank heavens. Hadn't stirred the following morning, either. She'd crept out of the apartment down to the waiting taxi without having to face him again. Which was a relief. She couldn't have borne that.

Tears filled her eyes once more as she thought about their argument. He'd been so cruel. Yet there'd been truth in his words. She *had* contacted him. And she *had* enjoyed every moment of the sex, even before she'd fallen in love with him.

One thing falling in love with John proved, however: she had not been truly in love with Jason. If she had, she would have been devastated by his deception. But she hadn't been devastated, not the way she was devastated at this moment. Dear God, what was she going to do? She wasn't going to go back to that clinic, that was for sure. Not yet, anyway. She wasn't in a fit state to try that again, or even to contemplate becoming a single mother. A single mother had to be emotionally stable and strong. Had to be sure. Scarlet was no longer sure of anything. In truth, she was a mess.

The tears flooded in then, hot and strong. The poor lady sitting next to her became alarmed by her sobbing and called the steward, who brought her a box of tissues, followed by a brandy. She still cried on and off all the way back to Sydney but more quietly and discreetly.

By the time they landed, she'd run out of tears. The train trip back to Gosford was spent in a semi-comatose state. She rallied herself during the taxi ride home, determined not to do or say anything to make her mother suspicious. But it took a supreme effort of will to hide her distress behind a smile. Even worse was when her mother insisted on seeing all her photos, gushing over Darwin's natural beauty and declaring that one day they would both return to have a decent holiday there together.

The word 'decent' almost pushed Scarlet over the edge. Using exhaustion from the flight as an excuse, she hurried off to have a long, hot bath after which she forced herself to cook her mother dinner before retiring for the night. Fortunately, she slept like the dead, so she probably was exhausted, both physically and emotionally. The next morning she went into the salon early, making sure that by the time the other girls arrived everything was shipshape: the accounts. The orders. The equipment.

Everyone was thrilled to see her, Joanna especially.

'Your mum was annoyed with me for calling you,' Joanna told her privately. 'But I felt I had to.'

'You did the right thing, Joanna,' Scarlet said firmly and meant it.

It was difficult, however, to keep her mind on hairdressing that day. For some insane reason she kept hoping that John might contact her, either by phone or text. A silly hope, she realised by the end of the day. Why would he bother? It was over. They were over.

By Wednesday she was back on hairdressing autopilot, which was just as well, since she remained distracted. Her mum came into the salon with her, saying she could at least answer the phone and make coffee. Her wrist was in a cast but her fingers were operational and she was learning to use her left hand.

Scarlet was grateful for her company, especially during the tedious drive home at the end of the day. She'd distractedly taken the Central Coast highway instead of Terrigal Drive, and the traffic through the roadworks was worse, if that were possible. What a relief it would be when there were two lanes both ways instead of one. It should cut the bumper-to-bumper half-hour drive back to the ten minutes it should take from Erina to Terrigal. When she complained, her mother replied that at least it wasn't raining.

'You've brought the sunshine home with you,' she said, and smiled over at her daughter.

'If you say so, Mum,' Scarlet replied through gritted teeth.

Not that the sun was shining at that moment. It had already set a good fifteen minutes earlier.

Shortly after six, Scarlet turned into the road which

led down to their street. She sighed as they rounded their corner, happy to be home. The sight of a strange silver car parked at the kerb outside their house brought a frown to her forehead. The car was very shiny and looked brand spanking new, not to mention expensive.

'Whose car's that, do you know?' she asked her mother as she swung into their driveway, barely five metres in front of the car, which she finally saw was a Lexus. So she'd been right about it being expensive. There was no one behind the wheel to recognise, but the car did carry New South Wales number plates plus the name of a Sydney dealership.

'I have no idea,' her mother replied. 'I doubt it's anyone for us.'

'True,' Scarlet said, pressing the remote which operated the garage door. She was sitting in her car, waiting whilst the garage door rolled its way slowly upwards, when something in her rear-vision mirror grabbed her attention. Swivelling her head around, she was utterly floored when she saw John walking across the road towards them, wearing an elegant grey suit with a shirt and tie. Her mouth literally dropped open as he came right up to her car and tapped on the passenger window.

'Goodness me!' her mother exclaimed. 'It's John Mitchell. Scarlet, wind my window down so that I can see what he wants.'

A wild mixture of emotions claimed Scarlet as she pressed the button which operated the window: shock. Confusion. Trepidation. But the strongest was a totally irrational joy.

'Yes, John, what is it?' her mother asked.

'Hi there, Mrs King,' he returned with a warm smile. 'Mum told me about your accident. I hope it's not causing you too much trouble.'

'I'm managing quite well, thank you, John. So what brings *you* home? I thought you'd gone back to Brazil.'

'That was my initial plan but something unforeseen happened and I've decided to come home to Terrigal to live. The thing is, Mrs King, I know Scarlet worked as an estate agent in this area for a good while and I was wondering if she might give me some advice on where and what to buy. I don't like to let grass grow under my feet so I was hoping to steal her away from you for a few hours tonight and get her advice over dinner. Mum said you're very welcome to have your dinner over at our place, so you won't have to worry about managing on your own. So what do you say, Scarlet?' he asked, glancing over at her with totally unreadable eyes. 'I have my own wheels this time,' he added, nodding towards the silver Lexus. 'You're not too tired, are you?'

What could she say when she was dying to find out what he was up to? Despite that burst of mad happiness at the sight of him, she could not believe that he seriously wanted to come back here to live. He would never do that. This was all just an excuse to get her alone. A ploy. A plan. John liked plans. But what plan was this?

A loud bell jangled in her head, warning her to be careful. Very careful.

'No, I'm not too tired,' she said, pleased that she sounded composed. 'But I would like to shower and change first. I've been at work all day. Give me half an hour, would you?'

'Fine. I'll be back, knocking on your front door, in half an hour.'

'Well that's a turn-up for the books,' Janet King said thoughtfully as she watched John retreat in the side-vision mirror. 'But not a total surprise. He always did fancy you, you know.'

'Oh, Mum, don't be ridiculous!' Scarlet said, scoffing, as she drove her car into the garage.

'I'm not being ridiculous. I have eyes. And you're not indifferent to him, either. I watched you both at Carolyn's fortieth. Play your cards right and you might not have to go back to that clinic.'

'Mum! I'm shocked.'

Her mother rolled her eyes at her. 'Scarlet King, you're thirty-four years old. Soon, you'll be thirty-five. We don't have time for shocked any more. Now what are you going to wear? Something sexy, I hope.'

Scarlet could not believe what she was hearing. She wanted to laugh at the irony of her mother virtually asking her to dress with the intention of seducing John. Little did the poor woman know that John was probably here on a mission to seduce *her*. It was the only thing which made sense. He hadn't liked it when she'd called it quits on him. He'd obviously come for more of what he'd had in Darwin.

At the same time, she could not deny that a small seed of hope had starting sprouting in her heart, no matter how illogical. This was another fatal flaw in women, Scarlet accepted wearily as she trudged from the garage to the house—their clinging to romance rather than reason. Hoping for a happily-ever-after ending as opposed to a more realistic one.

She didn't dress sexily. Her winter wardrobe wasn't sexy, though it was smart. She swiftly combined chocolate-brown wool trousers with a cream mohair jumper which had a wide boat neckline, trimmed with a row of chocolate-brown stitching. Her ankle boots were dark brown, her handbag fawn, made in imitation crocodile skin. She put her blonde hair up in a chic French roll, after which she re-made her face before slipping elegant gold and pearl drops into her lobes. Lastly, she sprayed on some of her favourite perfume, which was vanilla based and not overpowering. She was just picking up the matching brown jacket from the bed when the front doorbell rang. A glance at her gold wristwatch showed John was a couple of minutes early.

Draping the jacket over her left arm—the night wasn't overly cold—she picked up her handbag and walked slowly from her room. Her mother had by then answered the door, calling out to Scarlet that she was leaving to go over to Carolyn's and not to forget her keys as she'd probably be asleep by the time John brought her home. By the time Scarlet reached the front hallway, her mother had disappeared across the road, leaving John standing under the porch light.

Scarlet was aware of her heart thudding behind her ribs as she walked towards him; aware, too, of his eyes on her, though they were annoyingly shadowed and still unreadable. Even when she drew close she was unable to discover anything from his expression. His face was as inscrutable as ever.

'I want to know why you're here,' she threw at him. 'No more lies now.'

'I haven't told any lies,' he replied with irritating composure.

'What?' she scoffed. 'I'm expected to believe you really mean to buy a house here in Terrigal?'

'Maybe not in Terrigal, but somewhere here on the Central Coast.'

'But you always said that…that…'

He stilled her stammering with a firm hand on her upper arm. 'Scarlet, do you think we could possibly have this conversation somewhere more private?'

'Oh,' she said weakly. 'Oh, okay.'

'Lock up, then, so that we can be on our way.'

She managed to lock up without dropping the set of

keys. Just. John cupped her right elbow once she'd finished and steered her over to the passenger side of the Lexus. When he opened the door for her, she climbed in and belted up without speaking, possibly because she had no idea what to say. It wasn't often that Scarlet's mind resembled a tumble drier but this was one of those times.

'I've booked us a table at the Seasalt Restaurant in the Crowne Plaza,' John said as he climbed in behind the wheel. 'Mum assured me the food there is excellent. I've never been there for dinner myself. Actually, I haven't been anywhere local for dinner before. So this is a first for me in more ways than one,' he finished up as he started the car and drove off.

'Would you care to explain that remark?' Scarlet asked, having found her tongue at last.

'All in good time, Scarlet. All in good time.'

'I think now is as good a time as any,' she countered, unable to suppress her curiosity and her agitation any longer. 'We're alone. We're well away from our street now. For pity's sake, pull over and tell me what's going on.'

'Absolutely not. That's not how this is going to be done.'

'How *what* is going to be done?'

'I'm not going to have you tell our children in later years that their father proposed to you on the side of the road.'

'P-proposed?' Scarlet choked out, her eyes flinging wide as she stared over at him.

'You haven't heard of that word? And there I've been all these years, thinking you were highly intelligent. It means asking for your hand in marriage.'

Scarlet didn't know whether to laugh or cry. He couldn't be serious, could he?

Oh God, he *was*!

When a sob caught in her throat, he wrenched the car over to the side of the road, braking to a halt and snapping off the engine. 'Well, you've spoiled everything again now, haven't you? I was going to do this over a candlelit dinner with all the trimmings: music. Champagne. The works. But it seems some girls just can't wait.' As he turned to her he pulled a small silver box out of his jacket pocket and flipped the top open.

Another sob escaped Scarlet's lips when she saw what was nestled in a bed of dark blue velvet. Her hands came up to clasp her face, her happiness so great it was almost overwhelming.

'Oh, John,' she choked out.

'Scarlet King,' he said solemnly. 'I love you. No, that's understating things. I'm crazy about you and I simply can't live without you. Will you do me the honour of being my wife?'

Her eyes flooded, her heart too full for words.

His smile was gently wry. 'You once told me that the only use you had for a diamond was if it came atop a band of gold and with a proposal of marriage.'

Her smile, when it came, was full of a joy which had no bounds. It filled all those empty places in her heart and in her soul which had needed to be filled.

'It's so beautiful,' she murmured, reaching out to touch the huge solitaire diamond. 'Is it one of yours?'

'No. I actually don't have any truly decent diamonds in my gem collection. I bought this one yesterday in Sydney, along with this car and these clothes. I wanted to impress you.'

'I'm very impressed. But…'

'No buts. I know I told you once that I didn't do marriage; that I was a committed bachelor. But no man wants to remain a bachelor, Scarlet, once he truly falls in love. Trust me when I say all I want to do is spend every day of the rest of my life with you.'

'Oh dear,' she said, her heart having melted totally at his passionate declaration of love. Tears pricked at her eyes, tears of happiness.

'No don't say anything more till I've finished,' he raced on, perhaps worried that she was about to protest further. Which, of course, she was not.

'I dare say you're also concerned about my relationship with my family, especially my father. There's no need, Scarlet. Truly. I had a good long talk to Dad today and I found out something I wasn't aware of. Apparently, after Josh died, Dad went into a severe depression which was never properly treated. He only survived day to day by becoming a workaholic. It wasn't till he retired that Mum got him to see a more enlightened doctor and his condition was properly diagnosed and treated, which explains his change of mood lately. He told me today how sorry he was for the way he'd treated me, and Mum too. Terribly sorry.

'So you see, there's no reason for you to worry that I'm lying to you about coming to live near home. I'm actually looking forward it. I might even start up a local fishing-charter company rather than go back to mining work. After all, a family man shouldn't be travelling all over the place, doing dangerous things, should he?'

'Absolutely not,' Scarlet said, her voice thickening as her eyes welled up again.

'Hey, what's with all the tears? I thought you'd be happy.'

'I am happy. And, John…'

'Yes?'

'I love you too. Very much.'

His eyes gleamed. 'I sort of figured that out around the same time I figured myself out. Shortly after your plane took off. It just took me a while to work out what to do about it. I had to come up with a proper plan, you see.'

'Oh, you and your plans! I never did find out what your plan was for up in Darwin.'

'Mmm. Yes, well, that plan is still in operation.'

'Really? In what way?'

'I'll tell you all about it shortly. So is it a yes? Can I take the ring out of the box and slip it on your finger?'

She nodded and he did just that. It fitted her finger perfectly.

He clasped her hand tightly within both of his and looked deep into her eyes. 'I can't tell you how sorry I am for the dreadful things I said to you the other night, Scarlet. It was unforgiv—'

'Hush,' she broke in softly. 'Love is never having to say you're sorry.'

'Thank God for that,' he said with small laugh. 'Otherwise I could be apologising all night.'

'I'd rather have that candlelit dinner you told me about.'

'Me too.'

'There's only one small problem I can think of,' Scarlet said.

'What's that?'

'What on earth are we going to tell our families and friends? They're not going to believe in our engagement. It'll look much too sudden in their eyes.'

John frowned. 'You're probably right. You might have to hide that ring for a while, at least till you're safely pregnant.'

Scarlet's mouth dropped open whilst John just smiled. 'I did say that my Darwin plan is still in operation. It really was a good plan, involving great sex for days on end, followed by two or three days of abstinence till you entered your most likely to conceive phase...'

'Good grief!' Scarlet exclaimed.

'Yes, I know it sounds a bit much when you say it out

loud, but it's still a good plan. Given we've already been through an enforced abstinence phase, I didn't just book a table for dinner at the Crowne Plaza tonight. I booked us a room as well. And, before you say it, my darling wife-to-be, I know there are no guarantees of our making a baby tonight, but you have one thing going for you which is new—tonight, you will be made love to by a man who truly loves you. Tonight, you will feel safe and secure in his arms. Tonight, there will be no stress because, baby or not, we will still have each other till death do us part.'

Scarlet fought back more tears, having never been so moved in her life. She had read about the healing power of love but she'd never seen it for herself, or felt its power. But she felt it now and would never forget it.

'John Mitchell,' she choked out. 'They are the loveliest words I have ever heard. And you are the loveliest man. I think I must be luckiest girl in all the world to have found someone like you to love me.'

'I think I'm the lucky one here. But, before this deteriorates to a mutual admiration society, do you think we could move on? I haven't had a bite to eat in hours and I'm so hungry I could eat a whole barramundi all by myself!'

Scarlet smiled. She smiled on and off all night.

CHAPTER TWENTY-THREE

Fifteen months later

SCARLET tiptoed into the nursery and stood beside the rather large cot, her heart filling with joy and wonder as it always did when she looked down at her beautiful baby girls. It still amazed her to think that she and John had not made one baby that night, as they'd secretly hoped, but two.

Life had been kind to her for once. Very kind.

Any initial anxiety over expecting twins had soon been dispelled once she knew they were girls and, thankfully, not identical. John had claimed he wasn't worried at all, that he'd been thrilled to pieces by the news, but Scarlet had privately been of the opinion it wasn't a good idea to repeat a history which hadn't turned out well.

Jessica and Jennifer had been born a month early but so healthy that, after only a few days, their already besotted parents had been allowed to bring them home to the rather old but brilliantly located house which Scarlet had recommended John buy and which he had been spending all his time renovating and refurbishing. Situated between Wamberal and Terrigal beaches, it was only a short drive from both grandparents' homes, but far enough away to give them privacy. John hadn't bothered with his idea of a fishing-charter business as yet, saying he was too busy being a house husband. Not that Scarlet had returned to hairdressing. She hadn't. Looking after twins was a full-time occupation even with two doting grandmothers to help and a grandfather who, whilst not hands-on with the twins as yet—babies made him nervous—had become very hands-on helping John with the house. It made Scarlet happy to see that they were finally forging a good father and son relationship. A bit late perhaps, but better late than never.

A hand on her shoulder made her jump slightly.

'Your mum's here,' John said quietly as he bent to kiss her on the cheek. 'I told her the girls were sound asleep and to just sit down and watch TV whilst she could. Meanwhile, it's time we were off, madam. Although, before we go, can I just say how beautiful you look for an old married lady.'

'I do my best,' she said somewhat drily. Despite being madly in love, they hadn't given up their habit of verbal sparring.

'How long have we been married now? Oh yes. One year today. Twelve whole months. Three hundred and sixty-five days and you haven't divorced me yet. I think that deserves a reward, don't you?'

And there it was again, another silver box.

Scarlet's heart squeezed tight when he flipped it open. This time, it wasn't a diamond which graced the band of gold but three different stones: an emerald in the middle flanked by a sapphire and a ruby, the design curved so it sat perfectly against the large diamond solitaire of her engagement ring.

'Now these *are* from my personal gem collection,' John said as he slipped the eternity ring on her finger.

'It's a truly beautiful ring and I love it. But, John, I really didn't expect you to get me anything else. You've already filled the living room with flowers.'

'Which is exactly why you deserve more. Because you didn't expect it. Any other wife would have.'

'You're in danger of spoiling me.'

'True. But what else have I got to do with my money?'

'Yes, I can see that. But money doesn't buy happiness, John. Happiness is what we have here, in this cot. It comes from love and family. Which is why my anniversary present to you is something I can't wrap up in a box.'

'Fess up, woman. What have you done?'

'We're not just going to the Crowne Plaza for an anniversary dinner tonight. I've booked us a room.'

'But…'

'No buts, John. Mum's staying the night with our babies and we're staying the night in the honeymoon suite.'

'The honeymoon suite!'

Her shrug was carefree. 'Money doesn't buy you happiness, John, but it does buy you the opportunity for pleasure. If you recall, we haven't had any sex for at least a week.'

'Mmm. Yes. I did notice. You said you were too tired every night.'

'I lied. I was just making sure you'd be totally unable to resist me tonight.'

He shook his head at her. 'You are a devious woman.'

'And you are a magnificent lover.'

'Flattery won't get you anywhere.'

'That's what I thought. So, just to make sure, I left off my underwear.'

He stared at her, then smiled a wicked smile. 'You do realise I'll make you have dinner first.'

She smiled. 'Want to bet on that?'

He grinned. 'But of course.'
He won.

Nine months later a boy was born. They called him Harry, after John's grandfather.

* * * * *

THE PASSION
PRICE

MIRANDA LEE

CHAPTER ONE

'THE ad says the property is open for inspection every Saturday afternoon between two and three,' Dorothy pointed out. 'I'm going to drive up there today and have a look at it. What do you think of that?'

Jake put down the newspaper and looked up at the woman who'd been more of a mother to him than the woman who'd given birth to him thirty-four years before.

As much as he loved Dorothy, Jake wasn't going to indulge her in such a ridiculous idea.

'I think you're stark, raving mad,' he said.

Dorothy laughed, something she hadn't done all that often this past year.

Jake frowned. Maybe it wasn't such a ridiculous idea, if it made her happy.

Hell, no, he immediately reassessed. She was seventy-one years old. Way too old to go buying some run-down boutique winery up in the back blocks of the Hunter Valley.

Still, perhaps it would be wise not to mention Dorothy's age in his arguments. She was sensitive about that, like most women.

Not that she looked her age. Dorothy Landsdale was one of those women who had never been pretty,

5

but had grown more handsome with age. Tall, with broad shoulders and an impressive bosom, she had an intelligent face, with few lines on her perfect skin, a patrician nose and intense, deeply set blue eyes. Her silvery hair, which was dead straight, was always cut very short in a simple yet elegant style.

That was Dorothy's style all round. Simple, yet elegant. Jake had always admired the way she looked and dressed, although he sometimes wondered if she'd had her lips permanently painted red, because he'd never seen her without her favourite lipstick on.

Not that it mattered. Frankly, red lips suited her, especially when she was smiling.

Jake determined not to say anything that would wipe that wonderful smile off her face.

'Look, let's be sensible here,' he began in the same calm, cool, you-and-I-are-reasonable-people voice he reserved for juries during his closing addresses. 'You know nothing about wine-making.'

'Actually, you're wrong there, Jake, dear. You obviously don't know this, but Edward once planned on buying a boutique winery in the Hunter Valley. He fancied going up there on weekends. He collected a whole shelf-full of books on the subject of wine and wine-making at the time. Made me read them so we could talk about the subject together. But then he brought you home to live with us and that idea was abandoned. Though never entirely forgotten. He still dreamt of doing it after he retired.'

Jake experienced a dive in spirits, as he always did when the judge was talked about. He and Dorothy had both been shattered when Dorothy's husband of thirty years had died of a coronary last year, a few short months before his retirement. Jake had taken the news extra hard. If Dorothy was like a mother to him, Edward had been like a father, and more. He'd been Jake's mentor and best friend. His saviour, in fact. A wonderful man. Kind and generous and truly wise.

Jake knew he would never meet his like again.

Edward had left Jake a small fortune in his will, an astonishing document with a written request that within six months of his death Jake was to use some of his cash legacy to buy a luxury harbourside apartment and a yellow Ferrari. Jake had wept when he'd been told this. He'd confided these two fantasy purchases to his friend one night last year over a game of chess, also confessing that he would probably never buy them, even if he could afford to. He already had a perfectly nice apartment, he had explained to Edward. And a reliable car.

But Edward's last wishes were sacrosanct with Jake and he'd taken possession of the new apartment—set on prestigious McMahon's Point—just before Christmas a couple of months back. The Ferrari had come only last week. He'd had to wait ages to have a yellow one imported and delivered.

Both the apartment and the car had already given him great pleasure. But he would give them both back—hell, he'd practically sell his soul to the devil—to have the man himself sitting alive and well at this breakfast table with them.

'So that's what this is all about,' he said with a raw edge in his voice. 'You want to make Edward's dream come true.'

'In a way. But don't get me wrong. This would mostly be for me. I need a new venture, Jake. A new interest in life. Edward would hate for me to be moping around all the time, thinking my life was over because he was no longer here. When I saw that ad in the *Herald* this morning, it jumped right out at me. But it's not just the winery. I simply love the look of the house.'

Jake glanced down at the photograph of the house. 'It just looks old to me.'

'It's beautiful. I love old Australian farmhouses. Look at those gorgeous wraparound verandas. First thing I'd buy would be a swing seat. I'd sit there every afternoon with a gin and tonic and watch the sunsets. I've never had a house, you know. I've always lived in apartments. I've never had a garden, either.'

'They're a lot of work, houses and gardens,' Jake pointed out. 'Wineries, too,' he added, suddenly thinking of another time and another winery.

It, too, had been in the Hunter Valley. But not one of the boutique varieties. A reasonably large winery with acres under vine, producing tons of grapes each season that the anti-machinery Italian owner always had picked by hand.

Which was where he had come in.

Jake hadn't thought about that place, or that time

in his life, for ages. He'd trained himself over the years not to dwell on past miseries, or past mistakes.

But now that he had, the memories came swarming back. The heat that summer. The back-breaking work. And the utter boredom.

No wonder his eyes had kept going to the girl.

She'd been the only child of the Italian owner. Angelina, her name was. Angelina Mastroianni. Lush and lovely, with olive skin, jet-black hair, big brown eyes and a body that had looked fabulous in the short shorts and tight tank tops she lived in.

But it was her come-hither glances which he'd noticed the most.

As a randy and rebellious seventeen-year-old, Jake had been no stranger to sex. No stranger to having girls come on to him, either.

Yet it had taken him all summer to talk Angelina into meeting him alone. He'd thought she was playing hard to get, a conclusion seemingly backed up by the way she'd acted as soon as he'd drawn her into his arms. She hadn't been able to get enough of his kisses, or his hands. He hadn't discovered till after the big event, and her father was beating him to a pulp, that she'd only been fifteen, and a virgin to boot.

Within the hour, he'd been bundled off back to the teenage refuge in Sydney from whence he'd come. The subsequent charge of carnal knowledge had brought him up in front of the very man who'd sent him on the 'character-building' work programme at the winery in the first place.

Judge Edward Landsdale.

Jake had been scared stiff of actually being convicted and sentenced, something he'd miraculously managed to avoid during his rocky young life so far. But he'd felt his luck had run out on this occasion and the prospect of a stint in an adult jail loomed large in his mind, given that he was almost eighteen.

Fear had made him extra-belligerent, and even more loud-mouthed than usual. Judge Landsdale had seen right through him, and also seen something else. God bless him. Somehow, Edward had had the charges dropped, and then he'd done something else, something truly remarkable. He'd brought Jake home to live with him and his wife.

That had been the beginning of Jake's new life, a life where he realised there were some good people in this world, and that you could make something of yourself, if someone had faith in you and gave you very real, hands-on support.

Angelina had lingered in Jake's thoughts for a long time after that fateful night. In the end, however, he'd forced her out of his mind and moved on, filling his life with his studies and, yes, other girls.

Now that he came to think of it, however, none of his girlfriends so far had ever made him feel what Angelina had made him feel that long-ago summer.

Who knew why that was? Up till their rendezvous in the barn, they'd only talked. Perhaps it had been the long, frustrating wait which had made even kissing her seem so fabulous. The sex had hardly been memorable. She'd panicked at the last moment and he'd had to promise to pull out. Then, when she'd been so tight, he hadn't twigged why—young fool that he was. His only excuse was that he'd been totally carried away at the time.

Really, the whole thing had been nothing short of a fiasco, with her father finding them together in the winery only seconds after Jake had done the dastardly deed. He'd barely had time to zip his jeans up before the first blow connected with his nose, breaking it and spurting blood all over one highly hysterical Angelina.

Jake reached up to slowly rub the bridge of his nose.

It wasn't crooked any longer. Neither were his front teeth still broken. He didn't have any tattoos left, either. Dorothy had taken him to the best Macquarie Street cosmetic surgeons and dentists within weeks of his coming to live with her, beginning his transformation from Jake Winters, dead-beat street kid and born loser, to Jake Winters, top litigator and sure winner.

He wondered what had happened to Angelina in the intervening years. No doubt that hotheaded father of hers would have kept a closer eye on his precious daughter after that night. He'd had big dreams for his winery, had Antonio Mastroianni. Big dreams for his lovely Angelina as well.

With the wisdom of hindsight, Jake could now well understand the Italian's reaction to discovering them together. The last male on earth any father would have wanted his daughter to get tangled up with was the likes of himself. He'd been a bad boy back then. A very bad boy.

Not to Judge Edward Landsdale, though. When Edward had first met Jake, he hadn't seen the long hair, the tattoos or the countless body piercings. All he'd seen was a good boy crying to get out, a boy worth helping.

Aah, Edward. You were right, and wrong at the same time. Yes, I *have* made something of myself, thanks to you and Dorothy. But beneath my sophisticated and successful veneer, I'm still that same street kid. Tough and hard and self-centred in the way you had to become on Sydney's meaner streets to survive. Basically, a loner. Such programming is deep-seated, and possibly the reason why my personal life is not as great as my professional life.

A top trial lawyer might benefit from being on the cold-blooded side, from never letting emotion get in the way of his thinking. But how many of my girl-friends have complained of my lack of sensitivity? My selfishness? My inability to truly care about them, let alone commit?

I might be able to argue great cases and win verdicts, along with massive compensation payments for my clients, but I can't keep a woman in my life for longer than a couple of months.

And do I care?

Not enough.

The truth is I like living alone, especially now, in my fantastic harbourside apartment. I like being responsible for no one but myself.

Dorothy, of course, was a responsibility of sorts. But Dorothy was different. He loved Dorothy as much as he had loved Edward. That was why he visited her every Friday night, and why he sometimes stayed the night. To make sure she was all right. Edward would have wanted him to look after Dorothy, and he aimed to do just that.

Not an easy task, Jake reminded himself, if she was living way out in the country.

He really had to talk her out of the ridiculously romantic idea of buying this winery.

But talking Dorothy out of something was not always an easy thing to do…

When Jake's eyes glazed over and he kept idly rubbing his nose, Dorothy wondered what he was thinking about. Edward, probably. Poor Jake. Edward's death had really rocked him. They'd become so close over the years, those two. The crusty old judge with the heart of gold and the cocky street kid with no heart at all.

Till Jake had met Edward, that was.

Impossible to remain completely heartless around Edward. Dorothy knew that for a fact. The day she'd met her future husband, she'd been forty years old. Overweight and on the frumpy side, way past her prime. Edward had been five years younger at thirty-five, tall and handsome and beautifully dressed. He'd come to her aid when she'd been knocked over in Market Place by some lout on a skateboard. He'd taken her for a cup of coffee to settle her nerves and swiftly made her forget that she was a dried-up old spinster with a dreary office job and a bitter cynicism about men, especially the good-looking ones.

She'd fallen in love with Edward that very first day. Why he'd fallen in love with her, she had no idea. He'd claimed it was the heat in her eyes. Whatever, she'd lost those extra pounds she'd been carrying over the next few weeks. In her few spare hours, she'd also smartened herself up. Bought some decent clothes. Had her hair styled by a good hairdresser. And started always wearing the red lipstick Edward had admired.

They'd been married six months later, to predictions of doom from relatives. But their marriage had proved to be a great success, despite their not having any children.

Other men might have resented that. But not Edward. When she'd tearfully questioned him over his feelings about her infertility, he'd hugged her and said he'd married her for better or worse, and that resenting realities was a waste of time. But that was when he'd started working with charities that helped underprivileged boys, and where he'd lavished all his unused fatherly love.

Still, he hadn't become too personally involved with any of the boys till Jake had come along. Jake, of the ice-blue eyes and serious attitude problem.

When Edward had first brought Jake home to live with them, Dorothy couldn't stand the boy's smart mouth and slovenly ways. But gradually, a miracle had happened. Jake had changed and maybe she had changed a bit, too, becoming more tolerant and understanding.

Whatever, they'd both ended up genuinely liking each other. No, *loving* each other. Like mother and son.

Dorothy knew that if she bought this winery Jake would come and visit her up there as much as he did here, in Sydney. The Hunter Valley wasn't all that far away. A two-hour drive. It would do him good, she thought, to get out of the city occasionally. To relax and smell the flowers, so to speak. He worked way too hard. And it wasn't as though there was any special girl to keep him here in Sydney at the weekends. He'd broken up with that last one he'd been dating. A bottle-blonde with a flashy smile and a figure to match.

Why Jake kept choosing girls for their sex appeal alone, Dorothy couldn't fathom. When she'd complained about this side of Jake to Edward a couple of years back, he'd said not to worry. One day, Jake would meet the right girl, fall head over heels, get married and have a family.

Dorothy wasn't so sure about that last part. She didn't think having a family would ever be on Jake's agenda. Damaged children often veered away from having children themselves.

No, she wasn't holding her breath over that ever happening.

'Penny for your thoughts,' she said gently.

Jake snapped back to reality with a dry laugh.

'Not worth even ten cents. So when do you want to leave?'

Dorothy smiled. 'You're going to drive me up there?'

Jake shrugged. 'Can't let my best girl go careering all over the countryside by herself. Besides, I've been dying for an excuse to give my new car a proper spin. Can't do that on city roads.'

'Jake Winters! I have no intention of dying at the hands of some speed-happy fool in a yellow Ferrari.'

Jake laughed. 'And this from the wild woman who's planning to buy some run-down winery in the middle of nowhere! Don't worry, I won't go over the speed limit. And hopefully, once you see this dump for real, you'll be happy to stay right where you are and take up pottery.'

'Pottery! What a good idea! There's sure to be room for a kiln at the winery. The ad says there are ten acres of land, and only five under vine.'

Jake gave up at this point. But he was sure that Dorothy *would* see the folly of her ways and change her mind once she saw the place, and where it was.

'If we leave around ten,' Dorothy said excitedly, 'we'd get up there in time for lunch. Lots of the larger wineries have great restaurants, you know.'

Jake frowned. Mr Mastroianni had been going to build a restaurant at his winery. And guest accommodation. He'd also been going to change the name of the winery from its present unprepossessing name to something more exotic-sounding. Angelina had told him all about her *papa*'s grand plans, but Jake's mind had been on other things at the time and he couldn't remember what the new name was. Or what the old name was, for that matter. Though it hadn't been Italian.

According to Angelina, the winery had belonged to her mother's family. Jake did recall her telling him that her mother had been middle-aged when her father married her. She'd died having Angelina.

'I looked up a few of the restaurants on the internet last night,' Dorothy was rattling on. 'There's this really interesting-looking one on the same road as the place we're going to inspect. It's at a winery called the Ambrosia Estate. Isn't that a wonderful name for a winery? The nectar of the gods.'

Jake's mouth dropped open. That was it! *Ambrosia!*

'What is it?' Dorothy said. 'What did I say?'

'Did Edward ever tell you the story of how I came to be in his court?'

'Yes. Yes, of course. You…' She broke off, her eyes widening. 'Good lord, you don't mean…'

'Yep. The scene of my crime was the Ambrosia Estate.'

'Goodness! What an amazing coincidence!'

'My thoughts exactly.'

Dorothy gave him a sheepish look. 'I—er—I've already made us a booking at the restaurant there for twelve-thirty.'

Jake couldn't help being amused. What a crafty woman she was. 'You were very confident I'd drive you up there myself, weren't you?'

'I think I know you pretty well by now. But honestly, Jake, if you want me to change the booking to somewhere else, it's easily done.'

'No, don't worry. I doubt I'd be recognised. I've changed somewhat since my bad-boy days, don't you think? Though it's just as well *you* made the booking. If old-boy Mastroianni knew Jake Winters was eating lunch in his restaurant, I'd be fed hemlock. Italians have long memories and a penchant for revenge. He might not know my face but I'll bet he'd remember my name.'

Oh, yes. He'd bet the name Jake Winters was burned into Antonio Mastroianni's brain. And whilst Jake really didn't want another confrontation with Angelina's father, the possibility of running into Angelina again sparked an undeniable surge of excitement.

She would be what age now? Thirty-one? Thirty-two? Had to be thirty-two. She'd been two years younger than him and he was thirty-four.

Logic told Jake that a thirty-two-year-old Italian girl would be long married by now, with a brood of *bambinos* around her skirts.

At the same time he reasoned that even if she was married, she'd probably still be living at the winery, with her husband working in the family business. That was the way of Italians. No, she was sure to be there, somewhere.

The desire to see Angelina again increased. Was it

just curiosity, or the need to say he was sorry for what he'd done? She'd been terribly upset at the time.

But what would an apology achieve after all these years? What would be the point?

No point at all, Jake decided with a return to his usual pragmatism. Best he just have his lunch and leave. Maybe he'd catch a glimpse of Angelina. And maybe he wouldn't.

Who knew? He probably wouldn't recognise her. It was sixteen years ago after all.

CHAPTER TWO

'YOU can look for your father when you turn sixteen,' Angelina promised.

'But that's not till November!' her son protested. 'Why do I have to wait that long? It's not as though Grandpa's around any more to get upset. I mean…Oh, gosh, I know that sounded bad. Look, I miss Grandpa as much as you do, Mum. But this is important to me. I want to meet my dad. See what he looks like. *Talk* to him.'

'Has it occurred to you that he might not want to meet you? He doesn't even know you exist!'

'Yeah, I know that, but that's not his fault, is it? No one ever told him. He's got a right to know he has a son.'

Angelina sighed into the phone. She still could not come to terms with Alex's sudden obsession with finding his biological father. Every time she rang her son at school, and vice versa, it was his main topic of conversation.

Of course, when his grandfather had been alive, the subject of Jake Winters had been forbidden. In Antonio Mastroianni's eyes, the tattooed lout who'd seduced and impregnated his daughter was nothing better than a disgusting animal, not worthy of discussion. Alex's birth certificate said 'father un-known'.

When Alex had been old enough to ask questions, his grandfather had told him that his father had been *bad*, and that he was lucky not to have anything to do with him. He, Antonio Mastroianni, would be his father as well as his grandfather. In return, Alex would carry the Mastroianni name and inherit the family estate.

To give her father credit, he had heaped a great deal of love and attention on Alex. The boy had adored his grandpa in return and, in accordance with his grandfather's wishes, Alex's father was never mentioned.

But within weeks of his grandfather's tragic death late last year, Alex had started asking his mother questions about his real father, wheedling Jake's name out of her, then every other detail about him that she could remember, before finally demanding that they try to find him.

Just the thought of coming face to face with Jake again after all these years had put Angelina into a panic, which was why she'd initially come up with the 'wait-till-you're-sixteen' idea. But since then, she'd thought about the situation more calmly and stuck to her guns.

Because heaven only knew what Jake, the grown man, would be like. The last she'd heard he'd been going to be charged with carnal knowledge and would probably go to jail, something which had given her nightmares at the time. Till another night-mare had consumed her thoughts, and her life.

At worst, Jake might now be a hardened criminal. At best, Angelina still doubted he'd be the kind of man she'd want her son to spend too much time around. She didn't agree with her father that Jake had been born bad. But maturity—and motherhood—made her see Jake in a different light these days. He *had* been from the wrong side of the tracks, a ne-glected and antisocial young man, something that time rarely fixed.

'I don't want to discuss this any further, Alex,' she stated unequivocally. 'That's my decision and I think it's a fair and sensible one.'

'No, it's not,' he grumbled.

'Yes, it is. By sixteen, hopefully you'll be old enough to handle whatever you find out about your father. Trust me. I doubt it will be good news. He's probably in jail somewhere.'

Silence from the other end.

Angelina hated having to say anything that might hurt her son, but why pretend? Crazy to let him weave some kind of fantasy about his father, only to one day come face to face with a more than sobering reality.

'You said he was smart,' Alex pointed out.

'He was.' Street-smart.

'And good-looking.'

'Yes. Very.' In that tall, dark and dangerous fash-ion that silly young girls were invariably attracted to. She'd found everything about Jake wildly exciting

back then, especially the symbols of his rebellious-
ness. He'd had studs in his ears, as well as his nose,
a ring through one nipple and a tattoo on each upper
arm. Lord knew how many other tattoos he'd have
by now.

'In that case, he's not in jail,' Alex pronounced
stubbornly. 'No way.'

Angelina rolled her eyes. 'That's to be seen in
November, isn't it? But for now I'd like you to settle
down and concentrate on your studies. You're doing
your school certificate this year.'

'Waste of time,' Alex growled. 'I should be at
home there with you, helping with the harvest and
making this year's wines. Grandpa always said that
it was crazy for people to go to university and do
degrees to learn how to make wine. Hands-on experience is the right way. He told me I'd already had
the best apprenticeship in the world, and that I was
going to be a famous wine-maker one day.'

'I fully agree with him. And I'd never ask you to
go to university and get a degree. I'm just asking you
to stay at school till you're eighteen. At the very
school, might I remind you, that your grandfather
picked out for you. He was adamant that you should
get a good education.'

'OK,' he replied grudgingly. 'I'll do it for
Grandpa. But the moment I finish up here, you're
getting rid of that old fool you've hired and I'm going to do the job I was brought up to do.'

'Arnold is not an old fool,' Angelina said. 'Your

grandfather said he was once one of the best wine-makers in the valley.'

'Once, like a hundred years ago?' her son scoffed.

'Arnold is only in his sixties.' Sixty-nine, to be exact.

'Yeah, well, he looks a hundred. I don't like him and I don't like him making our wines,' Alex stated firmly, and Angelina knew her son's mind would never be swayed on that opinion. He'd always been like that, voicing his likes and dislikes in unequivocal terms from the time he could talk. If he didn't like a certain food, he'd simply say, 'Don't like it.' Then close his mouth tightly.

No threat or punishment would make him eat that food.

Stubborn, that was what he was. Her father had used to say he got it from him. But Angelina sus-pected that trait had come from a different source, as did most of Alex's physical genes as well. His height, for one.

Alex had been taller than his grandfather at thir-teen. At fifteen he was going on six feet, and still growing. And then there were his eyes. An icy blue they were, just like Jake's. With long lashes framing them. His Roman nose possibly belonged to the Mastroianni side, as well as his olive skin. But his mouth was pure Jake. Wide, with full lips, the bottom lip extra-full.

He'd probably end up a good kisser, just like his father.

'I have to go, Alex,' she said abruptly. 'I'm needed

up at the restaurant for lunch. It's always extra-busy on a Saturday when the weather's nice.'

'Yeah. OK. I have to go, too. Practise my batting. Kings School are coming over this afternoon to play cricket. We're going to whip their butts this time.'

Angelina smiled. For all her son's saying he wanted to be home at the winery, he really enjoyed life at his city boarding-school. He'd been somewhat lonely as an only child, living on a country property.

Located on Sydney's lower North Side, St Francis's College had come highly recommended, with a sensible balance of good, old-fashioned discipline and new-age thinking. Their curriculum included loads of sports and fun activities to keep their male students' hormones and energy levels under control.

This was Alex's fourth year there and he was doing very well, both in the classroom and on the sports field. He played cricket in summer and soccer in winter, but swimming was his favourite sport. The shelves in his bedroom were chock-full of swimming trophies.

'Good luck, then,' Angelina said. 'I'll give you a ring after you've whipped their butts. Now I really must go, love. *Ciao.*'

She hung up, then frowned. Cricket might distract Alex from his quest to find his father for the moment, but she didn't like her chances of putting her son off till his birthday in November. That was nine long months away.

Nine months…

Angelina's chest contracted at the thought that it was around this time sixteen years ago that she'd conceived. Late February. Alex's birthday was the twenty-fourth of November.

Today was the twenty-fourth, she realised with a jolt. And a Saturday as well. The anniversary of what had been the most earth-shattering day of her life.

Angelina shook her head as she sank down on the side of her bed, her thoughts continuing to churn away. She did not regret having Alex. She loved him more than anything in the world. He'd given her great joy.

But there'd been great misery to begin with. Misery and anguish. No one could understand what it had been like for her. She'd felt so alone, without a mother to comfort her, and with a father who'd condemned her.

Antonio Mastroianni hadn't come round till the day Alex had been born, the day he'd held Angelina's hand through all the pain of childbirth and finally realised she wasn't just a daughter who'd disappointed him, but a living, breathing human being who was going through a hell of her own.

After that, things had been better between them, but nothing would change the fact that she'd become a single mother at the tender age of sixteen. By the time Alex had been born, she'd long left school, plus lost all her school friends. When she'd come home from the hospital, there had just been herself in the house all day with a crying, colicky baby and her father, who tried to help, but was pretty useless.

Some days she'd wanted to scream at the top of her lungs. Instead, often, she'd just sat down and cried along with Alex.

Meeting Jake Winters that summer sixteen years ago had sure changed her life forever. And the thought of meeting him again scared the living daylights out of her.

Not because she felt in danger of falling in love with him again. Such an idea was ludicrous. But because of the danger of Alex falling under his father's possibly bad influence. She hadn't sacrificed her whole life to raise a secure, stable, happy boy, only to surrender him to someone she didn't really know, and possibly couldn't trust. Alex needed good male role models now that his grandfather wasn't around to direct him, not some rebel-without-a-cause type.

Angelina tried to imagine what Jake would be like today. Could he possibly have come good, or had he gone down the road to self-destruction? Was he even alive? Maybe she should start looking for him herself, do a preliminary reconnoitre. She didn't have to hire anybody, not to begin with. She could ring all the J Winters in the Sydney phone book first.

Yes, that was what she would do. She'd get on to that tomorrow. She would try in the evening. Most people were home on a Sunday evening.

Another thought suddenly popped into her mind.

What if he was married, with a wife and a family?

Angelina knew the answer to that as surely and instinctively as Alex had known that his father was not in jail.

No way!

The Jake who'd chatted her up that summer had been a hater of all things traditional and conservative. Marriage would never be for him. Or family life. Or even falling in love. She'd grown up sufficiently now to see that Jake hadn't cared about her one bit back then. All their intimate conversations whilst grape-picking together had been nothing but a way for him to get into her pants.

Which he had. But only the once. And even that must have been an anticlimax, for want of a better word.

Looking back, it was ironic that she hadn't enjoyed the actual event that had ruined her life at the time. She might have borne the memory better if she'd been carried away on the wings of ecstasy to the very end.

Jake's lovemaking had promised well to begin with. He'd been more than a good kisser, actually. He was a *great* kisser. His hands had been just as effective, with a built-in road map to all her pleasure zones. Her breasts. Her nipples. And of course the white-hot area between her legs. Soon she'd been all for him going all the way, despite some last-minute panic over getting pregnant. But the sharp pain she experienced when he penetrated her had swiftly brought her back to earth. All she'd felt during the next ten seconds or so was a crushing wave of disappointment.

Even if her father hadn't watched over her after Jake like a hawk, Angelina had steadfastly refused to become one of those single mums whose son woke up to a different man in his mummy's bed every other week. She'd made her bed, as her father had often told her, and she'd bravely resolved to lie in it. Alone.

To be honest, however, her opportunities for having even a brief fling hadn't exactly been thick on the ground to begin with. As the stay-home mother of a young child, she'd rarely been in the company of eligible men. Her weekly shopping trip to the nearby town of Cessnock had been her only regular outing. In fact, Angelina hadn't been asked out by a single member of the opposite sex till three years ago.

Two things had happened around that time to greatly change her life circumstances. Alex had gone off to boarding school and she'd enrolled in a computer course at the local technical college. She'd known she had to do something to fill the great hole in her life created by her precious son going off to school.

Once she had some computer skills under her belt, Angelina had felt confident enough to try working on the reception desk at the resort. To her surprise, she'd taken to the service industry like a duck to water. Soon, she'd been also escorting groups of guests on tours of the property, serving in the cellar and helping out at the restaurant at lunchtime on the weekends, its busiest time. She just loved talking to people, and they seemed to like talking to her.

Before this, she'd only done behind-the-scenes

jobs around the resort such as cooking and cleaning, hardly esteem-building activities. Not that she'd had much self-esteem by then. Her stay-at-home years when Alex had been a baby and a toddler had gradually eroded her confidence and turned her from an outgoing girl into a reserved, almost shy woman.

Now, suddenly, she had blossomed again, thoroughly enjoying the social interaction and yes, the admiration—however meaningless and fleeting—of the opposite sex.

She'd begun taking care with her appearance again, exercising off some of the extra pounds which had crept on over the years and paying more attention to her hair, her clothes and her make-up.

Of course, her father had noticed her transformation, plus the attention of the male tourists and guests. And yes, of course, he'd commented and criticised. But this time she'd put him firmly in his place, telling him she was a grown woman and he was to keep out of her personal and private life.

Not that there'd been one. Despite her father suspecting otherwise, she *hadn't* taken up any of the none too subtle offers she'd received from the many men who now asked her out. She didn't even want to go out with them, let alone go to bed with them. Maybe it was crazy to use her teenage experience with Jake as a basis for comparison, but none of these men had made her feel even a fraction of what she'd felt when she first met Jake.

Of course, Angelina understood that the intensity of her feelings for Jake had largely been because of her age. He'd represented everything that a young, virginal girl found wildly exciting.

Angelina had no doubt that if Jake himself walked back into her life at this moment, she would not feel anything like she had back then. She no longer found long-haired, tattooed males even remotely attractive, for starters. The sight of him might make her heart race, but only with fear, fear of the bad influence he might have on her highly impressionable and very vulnerable son.

Thinking of this reminded her that, sooner or later, she *would* come face to face with Alex's father again, possibly sooner rather than later, if she started those phone calls tomorrow evening.

The thought bothered her a great deal.

'Damn you, Jake,' she muttered as she stood up and marched across her bedroom towards her *en suite* bathroom. 'Sixteen years, and you're still causing me trouble!'

CHAPTER THREE

THE yellow Ferrari caught Angelina's eye the moment it turned from the main road into the Ambrosia Estate. She stopped what she was doing—opening a bottle of wine at one of the outdoor tables—and watched the brightly coloured sports car crunch to a halt in the nearby car park, her lips pursing into a silent whistle when a dark-haired hunk in designer jeans, pale blue polo shirt and wraparound sunglasses climbed out from behind the wheel.

What a gorgeous-looking guy!

Angelina's gaze shifted over to the passenger side. She could see another person sitting in the car but couldn't make out any details. The sun was shining on the windscreen. But Angelina was willing to bet on it being a pretty blonde. Men like that invariably had pretty blondes on their arms.

The hunk hitched his jeans up onto his hips as hunks often did. Not because his clothes really needed straightening, she'd come to realise during her recent people-watching years. It was a subconscious body-language thing, a ploy to draw female attention to that part of his body.

And it worked. Angelina certainly looked, as did the two middle-aged ladies she was serving. Both widows, their names were Judith and Vivien. They were on holiday together and had been staying at the Ambrosia Estate for a few days.

'Cocky devil,' Judith said with a wry smile in her voice when the hunk started striding round the front of the yellow Ferrari in the direction of the passenger side.

'He has every right to be,' Vivien remarked. 'Just look at that car.'

Judith snorted. 'Don't you mean, just look at that body?'

Angelina had actually stopped looking at the hunk's broad-shouldered, slim-hipped, long-legged body and was frowning over his walk. It was a most distinctive walk, somewhere between a strut and a swagger. He moved as if he was bouncing along on the balls of his feet.

'Jake…'

The word escaped her lips before she could help it, and her two lady customers immediately looked up at her.

'You *know* the guy with the yellow sports car?' Judith asked, grey eyes narrowed. She was the sharper of the two ladies.

'No,' Angelina denied, dismissing the crazy notion that the man could possibly be Jake. 'But his walk reminded me of someone I used to know.'

'A sexy someone, I'll bet.'

Angelina had to smile. 'Very.' She pulled out the cork on the bottle of chilled Verdelho and poured both ladies a full glass. Each one immediately lifted their glass to their lips. They did like their wine, those two.

The emergence of a grey-haired lady from the passenger seat of the Ferrari surprised the three of them.

'Good lord!' Judith exclaimed. 'Not quite what I was expecting. So what do you reckon, girls? His mother? Or do we cast lover boy in the role of gigolo?'

'Oh, surely not,' Vivien said with a delicate little shudder.

'You're right,' Judith went on. 'She's much too old to be bothered with that kind of thing. But she's not his mother, either. Too old for that as well. Possibly a great-aunt. Or a client. He might be her financial adviser. She looks as rich as he does.'

'I'll leave you two ladies to speculate,' Angelina said as she placed the bottle in the portable wine cooler by their table. 'Wilomena will be over shortly to take your orders. Enjoy your meal.' And your gossiping, she added silently.

As she made her way back inside, Angelina threw another glimpse over her shoulder at the man and woman who were now walking together along the path that led over the small footbridge, past the outdoor dining area and along to the main door of the restaurant. The hunk was holding the woman's arm but his head was moving from side to side as though he was looking for something. Or someone.

Angelina found herself hurrying out of his line of sight, tension gripping her insides. Her actions—plus her sudden anxiety—really irritated her. As if it could possibly be Jake! How fanciful could she get?

That's what you get when you start thinking about ghosts from the past, Angelina. You conjure one up!

She resisted the temptation to watch the hunk's approach through the picture-glass windows of the restaurant, though she did go straight to the counter where they kept the reservation book, her eyes dropping to run over the names that had been booked for lunch. There was no Winters amongst them.

Of course not. Why would there be? The hunk just walked like Jake, that was all. OK, so he *was* built a bit like Jake as well. *And* he had similar-coloured hair.

Dark brown hair, however, was hardly unusual. On top of that, this guy's hair was cropped very short, almost in a military style. Jake had been proud of his long hair. He would never have it cut like that. Not that the short-all-over look didn't suit the hunk. It was very…macho.

Jake had been very macho.

It couldn't be him, could it?

Once he came inside and took off those sunglasses, Angelina reassured herself, there would no longer be any doubt in her mind.

And if he *did* have eyes like chips of blue ice? came the gut-tightening question. What then? How did you deal with such an appalling coincidence? What sick fate would send him back to her today, of all days?

The restaurant door opened and Angelina forced

herself to look up from where she was practically hiding behind the front counter.

The hunk propped the door open with one elbow and ushered his elderly companion in ahead of him. The lady was not so fragile-looking up close, her face unlined and her blue eyes bright with good health. But she had to be seventy, if she was a day.

And the hunk? It was impossible to tell his age till he took those darned sunglasses off. He could have been anywhere between twenty-five and forty, although there was an air of self-assurance about him that suggested he'd been around a while.

The grey-haired lady stepped up to the counter first. 'I made a booking for two for twelve-thirty,' she said with a sweet smile. 'The name's Landsdale. Mrs Landsdale.'

Angelina was highly conscious of the hunk standing at the lady's shoulder. Was he staring at her from behind those opaque shades? It felt as if he was.

'Yes, I have your booking here, Mrs Landsdale,' she replied, proud of herself for sounding so polite and professional in the face of the tension that was building inside her. 'Would you like to dine inside, or alfresco? It's really lovely outside today. No wind. Not too hot. And not too many flies.'

The lady's smile widened. 'Alfresco sounds wonderful. What do you think, Jake? Shall we sit outside?'

Angelina froze. Had she heard correctly? Had the woman really said that name?

Angelina stared, open-mouthed, as he finally took

off his sunglasses, her whole world tipping on its axis.

It *was* him. Those eyes could not possibly belong to anyone else.

'Jake,' she blurted out whilst her head whirled with the incredibility of this scenario.

'Hello, Angelina,' he said in the same richly masculine voice he'd already had at seventeen. 'I'm surprised you recognised me after all these years.'

If it hadn't been for the eyes, she might not have. He was *nothing* like the boy she remembered, or the man she'd imagined he might have become. This Jake was smooth and suave and sophisticated. More handsome than ever and obviously no longer underprivileged.

'Goodness, you mean *this* is Angelina,' the greyhaired lady piped up before Angelina could find a suitable reply. 'Jake, you naughty boy. Why didn't you say something earlier?'

He lifted his broad shoulders in an elegant shrug. 'I spotted her through the windows, and decided if she didn't recognise me back I wouldn't embarrass her by saying anything.'

Well, at least that meant he hadn't deliberately come looking for her, Angelina realised with some relief. Still, this was an amazing coincidence, given she'd been thinking about him all morning. She could feel herself trembling inside with shock.

'I—er—didn't recognise you till you took off your sunglasses,' she admitted whilst she struggled to pull herself together. *Think,* girl.

'You do have very distinctive eyes, Jake,' she added, bracing herself to look into them once more. This time she managed without that ridiculous jolt to her heart.

'Do I?' he said with a light laugh. 'They just look blue to me. But now that you *have* recognised me, I must ask. Is your father around?' he whispered. 'Should I put the sunglasses back on, pronto?'

Angelina opened her mouth to tell him that her father was dead. But something stopped her. Some sudden new fear...

This man before her, this grown-up and obviously wealthy Jake might present more of a danger than the loser she'd been picturing barely an hour earlier. This man had the means to take her son away from her, in more ways than one.

She had to be very, very careful.

'You're quite safe in here,' she said, deciding she would tell him absolutely nothing of a personal nature till she'd found out more about him.

But she was extremely curious. What woman— what *mother*—wouldn't be?

The questions tumbling round in her head were almost endless, the main one being how on earth had he come to look as if he'd win the bachelor-of-the-year award in every women's magazine in Australia? And who was this Mrs Landsdale? What did she mean to Jake and how come she knew about *her*?

Despite—or perhaps because of—all these mysteries, Angelina resolved to keep her wits about her. And to act as naturally as possible.

Picking up a couple of menus, she said 'this way' with a bright smile, and showed them to what she'd always thought was the best table outside. It was to the right of the ornamental pond, with a nearby clump of tall gum trees providing natural shade. All the outdoor tables had large umbrellas, where required. But this table never needed one.

'Oh, yes, this is lovely,' Mrs Landsdale said as she sat down and glanced around. 'What a beautiful pond. And a lovely view of the valley beyond too.'

'Papa chose this spot for the restaurant because of the view. And the trees.' Too late, she wished she hadn't brought up her father.

Swiftly she handed them both menus, doing her best not to stare at Jake again. But it was hard not to. Her gaze skimmed over him once more, noting his beautifully tanned skin and the expensive gold watch on his wrist. He had money written all over him. Lots of money.

'The main-meal menu is on the front,' she explained. 'The wine list and desserts are on the back. We don't have a vast selection at any one time, but the chef does change the menu every two weeks. I can recommend the Atlantic salmon, and the rack of lamb. For dessert, the coconut pudding is to die for. I think you—'

'If you're not too busy, Angelina,' Jake interrupted, 'could you find the time to sit down and talk at some stage?'

She wanted to. Quite desperately. But pride—and common sense—refused to let her appear too eager.

'Well, we are pretty busy here on Saturdays.'

'We can't linger too long over lunch either, Jake.' Mrs Landsdale joined in. 'The property is only open for inspection between two and three. Maybe we could come back here afterwards for afternoon tea and you could catch up on old times with Angelina then. Do you serve afternoon tea here, dear?'

Angelina didn't answer straight away, her mind ticking over with what the woman had just said about a property inspection. Was Jake a real-estate agent of some kind? Or an investment adviser? What kind of property was the woman talking about?

There were quite a few wineries for sale in the valley at the moment, from the boutique variety to the very large. Arnold's old place was on the market just up the road. But he was having dreadful trouble selling it. He'd really let the house and garden go since his sister passed away.

There was only one way for Angelina to have all her questions answered. And that was to ask them. Given she'd been going to try to contact Jake anyway in the near future, it seemed silly to pass up this opportunity.

Yet some inner instinct was warning her to do just that, to not let this man back into her life. Not till Alex gave her no choice.

She searched Jake's face for a hint of the man he'd become, then wished she hadn't. The sexual power of his eyes was as strong as ever.

There was no use pretending she could just coldly send him away. She had to at least talk to him.

Fortunately, she wouldn't be alone with him. This Mrs Landsdale would be there as a buffer. And a safeguard.

'We don't actually serve afternoon tea,' she said. 'But the restaurant doesn't close for lunch till four. You are quite welcome to come back after you've inspected this property, if you like. We could have a chat over coffee.'

'I'd like that,' Jake returned. 'Give me an opportunity to find out what you've been up to all these years.'

'Same here,' she replied, pleased that she could sound unconcerned, when inside she was severely agitated. 'Now, since time is of the essence, perhaps you might like to have a quick look at the menu and give me your full order straight away. Either that, or I could take your drinks order now, then send a girl over in a couple of minutes for your meal order.'

'No, no, we'll order everything right now,' the grey-haired lady said and fell to examining the menu. 'Jake, you decide on the drinks whilst I make up my mind on the food. You know my taste in wine.'

'I see you have a suggested glass of a different Ambrosia wine with each course,' Jake said as he examined the menu. 'You know, Angelina...' he rested the menu on the edge of the table and glanced up at her '...I've never seen any Ambrosia wines in bottle shops, or on Sydney restaurant wine lists. Why is that?'

'Oh. We—er—export most of our wine. Here in Australia, we've only been selling bottles at the cellar door. Up till now, that is. Ambrosia Wines does have a booth at next weekend's food and wine expo at Darling Harbour, so hopefully we will be in some Sydney restaurants soon.'

'I see.' Jake dropped his eyes and picked up the menu again. 'These suggested glasses should suit you, Dorothy. You like to try different wines. But I won't indulge myself. Not when I'm driving. So just mineral water for me, thanks, Angelina.'

'Flat or sparkling?' Angelina asked crisply, having extracted her order book and Biro from her skirt pocket.

'Sparkling, I think,' he replied. 'To match my mood.' And he threw her a dazzling smile that sixteen years ago would have rattled her brains and sent her heartbeat into overdrive.

Angelina's heart was still going pretty fast behind her ribs, but her brain hadn't gone to total mush. She flashed him back what she considered was a brilliantly cool smile, the sort of smile she could never have produced at fifteen.

'Sparkling mineral water,' Angelina murmured as she jotted it down. 'Now, what about your meal order?'

When she glanced up from her notebook again, she found Jake staring at her left hand—her *ringless* left hand. Her fingers tightened around the notebook.

'You're not married,' he said, his tone startled.

'No,' she returned in what she hoped was a crisp, it's-really-none-of-your-business tone. 'I'm not.'

'I can't believe it! I thought you'd have half a dozen kids by now.'

'And I thought you'd be in jail,' she countered.

Mrs Landsdale laughed. 'That's telling you, Jake. Now, stop badgering the girl and just tell her what you want to eat for now. Keep the third degree till later. But I must warn you, dear, he's the very devil when he starts questioning people. Not only is he not in jail these days, but he's also a lawyer. And a very good one, too.'

Angelina wished her mouth hadn't dropped open at this news. But Jake Winters…a *lawyer*?

'Yes, I know,' he remarked drily. 'I don't blame you for being surprised. Sometimes I'm a bit surprised myself. But Dorothy's right. We'll keep all this till later.'

Angelina digested this astonishing revelation with mixed emotions. Was this good news or bad news? She supposed it was a lot better than the father of her son being in jail. But a lawyer? She couldn't think. Too many shocks in too short a time. Best she just get on with what she was doing and think about it later.

'Have you made up your mind yet, Mrs Landsdale?' she asked the grey-haired lady.

'Do call me Dorothy,' the woman returned with a warm smile. 'And yes, I'll have the Atlantic salmon. No entrée. I'll save some room for that coconut pudding you mentioned. I'm very partial to coconut.'

'Me, too,' Angelina concurred. 'And you, Jake? Made up your mind yet?'

'The same. I'm easy.'

Angelina wanted to laugh. Easy? If there was one thing Jake Winters would never be, it was easy.

CHAPTER FOUR

SHORTLY after three, Jake jumped into his pride and joy and headed back towards the Ambrosia Estate.

Under normal circumstances, he would never leave Dorothy alone in the clutches of an eager real-estate agent on the verge of making a sale. But he could see within five minutes of Dorothy walking into that darned house that she was determined to have it. On top of that, his objections to her buying a property up here in the Hunter Valley had begun to wane.

The main reason for his change of heart lived less than a mile down this road.

Angelina Mastroianni. Unmarried, and more beautiful than ever.

Like a good wine, Angelina had only improved with age. Hard to believe she was thirty-two. She looked about twenty-five. If that.

Jake smiled when he thought of the way her big brown eyes had widened at the sight of him. Shock had mingled in their velvety depths with something else, that certain something which could not be mistaken.

She was still attracted to him, as he was still attracted to her. The sparks of sexual chemistry had flown between them all during lunch.

Frankly, Jake hadn't wanted to leave. He'd enjoyed just looking at her as she served other people, her lush Italian figure straining seductively against the crisp white blouse and hip-hugging black skirt she was wearing, especially when she bent over a bit, which was often.

As he'd sipped his mineral water, he'd imagined removing that black clip from the back of her head and watching her glossy black waves tumble in glorious disarray around her slender shoulders. Between mouthfuls of Atlantic salmon, he'd thought about slipping open the pearly buttons of her blouse and peeling it back to reveal her full breasts, those breasts which had once filled his hands. More than once he'd stared at her plum-coloured mouth and wondered if she would still be as susceptible to his kisses as she'd once been.

He'd eaten all the food she'd brought him but couldn't remember much of what it tasted like. His mind—and his appetite—had been elsewhere. Dorothy had raved about her meal and the wine afterwards, giving them both five stars. She'd raved about Angelina too, saying what a lovely girl she was and hadn't he let a good one get away all those years ago!

Jake had to agree. Angelina left all the girls he'd dated over the past few years for dead. Where they'd all been entrants in the plastic-beauty parade, Angelina Mastroianni was the real thing. Everything about her was real, from her hair to her breasts to the artless way she'd tried to hide her responses to him.

She'd failed brilliantly, making her even more attractive to him.

He was already planning to ask her out. And he wasn't going to take no for answer.

The only fly in the ointment was her father.

Jake scowled his displeasure at the thought of having to tangle with that old Italian dinosaur once more. But surely, at thirty-two, Angelina could date whomever she pleased.

If she was *free* to date, of course. Just because she wasn't married didn't mean there wasn't some man in her life.

Jake swiftly dismissed the notion of any serious competition. No woman who'd looked at him as Angelina had during lunch was madly in love with another man.

The Ferrari crested a rise and the Ambrosia Estate came into view on its left, stretching across several rolling hills, most of which were covered in vines.

There was no doubt Antonio Mastroianni had made good on his grand plans for the place. The restaurant was fabulous, positioned perfectly on the property's highest point. The guest accommodation, Jake had noted earlier from the vantage point of the restaurant car park, was further back from the main road. A modern-looking, motel-style complex, complete with swimming pool, tennis courts and lush gardens.

Sixteen years ago, that area had been nothing but bare paddocks.

The huge, barn-like structure that housed the winery itself was still on the same spot, not far from where the restaurant stood. But there were several new sheds, Jake noted as he whizzed along the road towards the main entrance. Possibly packaging and storage sheds. There was also a large dam that hadn't been there before, no doubt providing irrigation to stop the vines from becoming too stressed during droughts.

The summer he'd picked grapes here sixteen years ago had been very dry and hot, and old-man Mastroianni had talked endlessly about how stressed the vines were from lack of water. Jake had thought the notion that plants could be stressed was funny at the time. Of course, he'd been a complete idiot back then, in more ways than one.

Hopefully, Angelina would give him the opportunity to show her that he was no longer such an idiot.

His heart quickened as he turned into the restaurant car park for the second time that day. An odd happening for Jake. His heart rarely beat faster, except when he was working out or about to address a difficult jury. It rarely beat this fast over a woman.

Was he worried she might say no to him?

Yeah. He had to confess he was.

Now, that was a first.

Angelina knew the moment Jake arrived back in the car park. She'd been watching out of the corner of her eye, and that bright yellow was hard to miss. This time, thankfully, Vivien and Judith were no longer there in the restaurant to make any comments. They'd not long left after a very leisurely lunch, planning to have naps in their rooms before returning for dinner. Drinking and eating made up the mainstay of their holiday.

There were only two couples left in the restaurant, lingering over coffee. But they were seated inside. Angelina could sit outside with Jake and Dorothy, and be in no danger of being overheard, or interrupted.

She was taking a few steadying breaths and pretending to tidy up behind the counter when Jake walked in, alone. Momentarily rattled, she restrained herself from commenting till they were seated safely outside, having instructed a highly curious Wilomena to bring them both coffee and carrot cake.

'Where's Dorothy?' she asked once they were alone.

Jake took off his sunglasses and relaxed back into his chair with a sigh whilst Angelina fought the temptation to stare at him once more.

'I suspect putting a deposit down on a property up the road,' he replied drily. 'A boutique winery which has certainly seen better days. I would have stayed and tried to talk her out of it if I could. But Dorothy is one stubborn woman once she sets her sights on something. And she's set her sights on this place. The house, anyway. I left her having a second viewing and finding out the ins and outs of everything. The real-estate agent said he'd drop her off here after they were finished. He said he had to pass by on his way back to Cessnock.'

Angelina tried not to panic at this unexpected development. 'Is this house...um...white, with wide verandas?'

'That's the one.'

'Good lord, that's Arnold's place!' If Dorothy bought Arnold's place there was no hope of keeping Alex's existence a secret. The vineyard community up here was like a small town. Everyone knew everything about everyone.

Her exclamation sent Jake's dark brows arching. 'You know the owner?'

'He...um...he works for me. He's my new winemaker.'

'I thought your father was the wine-maker here,' Jake said with a puzzled frown.

Oh, dear. Impossible now to keep secret that her father was dead. Still, everything was going to come out, sooner or later. She might as well start with the lesser revelation.

'Papa died last year,' Angelina said, and tensed in anticipation of Jake's reaction.

He said nothing for several seconds. Perhaps he was mulling over why she hadn't told him about this earlier when she had the chance.

'I'm sorry to hear that,' he said at last. 'Truly. I know how hard it is to lose someone you care about. A very good friend of mine died last year. Dorothy's husband. You don't realise how much you miss someone till they're not there for you any longer.'

Angelina was touched—and somewhat surprised—by Jake's sentiments. But at least she'd had one of her questions answered. In part. She now knew who Dorothy was. The wife of an old friend.

'How did your father die?' Jake asked. 'Had he been ill?'

'No. He was as healthy as a horse. It was quite tragic, really. He was bitten by a snake. A King Brown.'

'Good lord. That is tragic. But isn't it also unusual these days? To die of snake-bite? Don't they have antidotes?'

She nodded whilst she struggled to get a grip on herself. She hated talking about that awful day. After all, it wasn't all that long ago. Three months and a bit.

'He might have lived if he'd been bitten on the hand,' she explained. 'Or a foot. But he must have been bending over and was bitten on the chest, not far from the heart. He…he stopped breathing before the ambulance arrived. They tried to revive him but it was too late.'

Tears flooded her eyes as all the turmoil and torment of that day rushed back. Jake's reaching over the table to cover her hand with his catapulted her back to the present, and made her hotly aware that she'd been wrong this morning. Jake, the man, still had the same effect on her as Jake, the boy. When his long fingers started moving seductively against hers, a charge of electric sensations shot up her arm.

'Don't,' she snapped, and snatched her hand away from under his, clutching it firmly in her lap with her other hand.

He searched her face with thoughtful eyes. 'What's wrong, Angelina? Are you still angry with me for what happened sixteen years ago? I wouldn't blame you if you were. I was thinking earlier today how much I wanted to say sorry to you for how things turned out that night, so if it's not too late, I'm truly sorry.'

'No need for an apology,' she bit out. 'I was as much to blame as you were.'

'Then what's the problem? Why snatch your hand away like that?'

Angelina could hardly tell him the truth. That just the touch of his hand fired up her hormones as no man had in the past sixteen years. Not even close. Even now, she was looking at his mouth and wondering what it would feel like on hers again; wondering what making love would be like with him, now that he was older and so much more experienced.

Jake would be only too happy to accommodate her, she knew. Angelina had seen the way he'd looked at her during lunch today. She'd been on the end of such looks from men a lot lately. Invariably, they were followed up by some kind of pass.

She wouldn't mind betting Jake had organised leaving Dorothy behind for a while so that he could be alone with her. The realisation that he thought he could just take up with her where he'd left off all those years ago infuriated Angelina.

'You look as if you've changed, Jake,' she said sharply. 'But you haven't changed at all. You still think you can have any female you fancy.'

He smiled the most heart-stopping smile. 'It would be hard not to fancy you, Angelina. You were a gorgeous-looking girl, but you're one stunning-looking woman.'

Angelina gritted her teeth to stop herself from smiling back at him. Damn the man, he was incorrigible. And almost irresistible.

Wilomena arriving with the coffee and cake was a godsend. But she was gone all too soon.

'This is great cake,' Jake praised after his first mouthful.

'Glad you like it,' she remarked snippily.

He took another mouthful, followed up by some coffee. She watched him, her own appetite nil, her frustration growing. Who did he think he was? It would serve him right if she upped and told him right now the result of his last encounter with her. Finding out he had a fifteen-year-old son was sure to wipe that satisfied look off his far too handsome face.

But she didn't tell him. She couldn't be sure of his reaction, and there was no way she was going to upset Alex this year. Angelina aimed to delay Jake finding out about his son as long as possible.

'So!' Jake exclaimed, dabbing at his mouth with a serviette after polishing off his slice of cake and most of his coffee. 'Is there a current man in your life, Angelina? Or are you footloose and fancy-free?'

Here comes the pass, she thought irritably. Well, he was in for a surprise because she intended to head him off at the pass. As much as Jake still had the power to turn her head—and turn her on—Angelina wasn't about to fall for his smooth but empty line of patter twice in one lifetime.

'Yes, of course there's a man in my life,' came her blithe reply. Alex was almost a man after all.

Jake muttered something under his breath before searching her face again with those hard, sexy blue eyes of his. 'So what's the score? Is it serious? Are you living with him?'

'Sometimes.'

'Sometimes.' Jake looked puzzled. 'What does that mean?'

'He lives in Sydney most of the time. Comes up here for holidays and the occasional weekend. And I go down there to see him every once in a while.'

'What about next weekend? Will you be seeing him next weekend?'

'Nope. I'll be attending the food and wine expo at Darling Harbour.'

'You mean you'll be in Sydney and you're not going to see each other, not even at *night*?'

Angelina couldn't decide if she found Jake's shock amusing or annoying. Clearly, his priority in a relationship was still sex.

'Alex will be away next weekend,' she said coolly. Actually, Alex was going to a special swimming training camp in preparation for the big interschool swimming carnival the following weekend. He was the captain of the team. 'I'll be seeing him the following weekend.' At the swimming carnival.

'Where are you staying this weekend in Sydney?'

Angelina almost laughed. Obviously, Jake didn't aim to go quietly off into the sunset. She should have known.

'I've booked a room at the Star City Casino for Saturday night,' came her composed reply. 'It's the closest hotel to the expo.' In truth, she wasn't strictly needed at the expo. The marketing agency who now handled the Ambrosia Estate account had hired professional sales people for the weekend. But she thought it wise to check personally on how her money was being spent. This venture hadn't been cheap.

But Angelina knew you had to invest money to make money these days. It had been her idea for the winery to get a web site two years ago. Her father had argued against the idea, but she'd had her way and it had brought them in a lot of business.

'Are you planning to marry this Alex one day?' Jake asked abruptly.

'No.'

Jake shook his head, his expression bewildered. 'That's what I don't get with you, Angelina. Why *haven't* you got married? I thought marriage and children were a must with Italian girls.'

'Not with me. I have other priorities.' *Like our son.* 'Now that Papa's gone, I'm solely responsible for the running of this place. That's a lot of work. But enough about me. What about you, Jake?' she asked, swiftly deflecting the conversation away from her own personal life and on to his. 'Are you married?'

The corner of his mouth tipped up in a wry smile. 'Come, now, Angelina. I told you way back when I was seventeen that I would never get married. I've had no reason to change my mind on that score.'

Her heart sinking at this news annoyed her. What had she subconsciously been hoping could happen here? That he would fall madly in love with her this time, marry her and they would live happily ever after, the three of them?

Dream on, Angelina.

'What about children?' she couldn't resist asking. 'Haven't you ever wanted a son? Or a daughter?' she added quickly.

'God, no. I'd be a simply dreadful father. Just the thought of being responsible for a child's upbringing gives me nightmares.'

Oh, great, she thought. He's going to be thrilled when he finds out about Alex. It was as well Alex was almost grown up, if that was Jake's attitude.

'Why do you say you'd be a dreadful father?' she asked, though she suspected it had something to do with his childhood. He'd never told her specifics all those years ago, but she'd been left with the impression of serious neglect.

Angelina's father had always been a right pain in

the neck, but he'd never left her in any doubt that he loved her.

'I'm way too selfish for starters,' he confessed. 'And damaged, Dorothy would say. You know the theory. An abused child often becomes an abusive parent. But let's not talk about life's little nasties,' he swept on, brushing aside any further explanation. 'Let's talk about you instead. OK, so you don't want the traditional role of wife and mother. I can accept that. I guess you have got your hands pretty full running this place. A lot of women these days are into the business scene. And careers. Don't go imagining I'd ever judge you harshly for that.'

'How generous of you,' came her caustic retort.

He just smiled at her again, as though amused by her impertinence.

'So when are you going to dump that loser you've been seeing and go out with me?'

Now Angelina did laugh. The man had the hide of an elephant. Exasperated, she decided to prick his ego some more. 'Alex is no loser. He's just as good-looking as you are. And just as successful, I might add. In fact, he's the only son and heir to a veritable fortune.' Besides being worth millions—property-wise—the Ambrosia Estate ran at a tidy profit each year, with their resort and restaurant very popular, and their wines in high demand over in America and Europe. If Angelina's plans for expansion into more markets bore fruit, profits could be even higher in future.

'Not impressed,' Jake countered confidently. 'Money

is nothing. Attitude is everything. He's a loser. Because
if you were my woman,' Jake said, and leant closer to
her across the table, 'I'd make damned sure I wasn't
away if you were going to be in Sydney next weekend.
You wouldn't be staying at some hotel on Saturday
night, either. You'd be staying at my place.'

His eyes locked on to hers and for the life of her,
she could not look away. In the end, she laughed
again. It was the only way she could safely draw air
into her suddenly starving lungs.

'But I'm not your woman, am I?'

He leant back in his seat again, still holding her
eyes firmly captive with his. 'What if I said I wanted
you to be, more than anything I've wanted in a long
time? What if I told you to tell this Alex he's history?
What if I asked you to stay at my place next weekend
instead of the Casino?'

She should have protested at that point. But she
was too enthralled with thinking about what it would
be like to spend next weekend with him, staying at
his place.

'I have this wonderful harbourside apartment with
all the mod cons and only a short ferry ride to
Darling Harbour,' he went on when she foolishly
stayed silent. 'We could paint the town red on
Saturday night, or stay in, if you prefer. Then on
Sunday we could have lunch down on the waterfront
somewhere. You must surely get a lunch break.
Unfortunately, I have to be in court first thing

Monday morning, or we could have made it a long weekend.'

Angelina finally found her voice. 'What is it you expect me to say to these extraordinarily presumptuous suggestions?'

'Right now? Nothing. I wouldn't like to be accused of rushing you into anything, like last time. I'll call you later this week. Or you can call me earlier than that, if you'd like. Here…' He whipped out his wallet from his jeans and extracted two business cards. 'You got a pen on you?'

She did, in fact. She kept one in her skirt pocket. She fished it out and gave it to him. He flashed her a quick smile before bending to the task of adding some numbers to the first card before handing it over. 'That first number is my private and unlisted number at home. The second is my cellphone. Now, write yours down for me on this…' And he handed her a second card, along with the Biro.

She stared down at the white card which said simply 'Jake Winters, Lawyer' in bold black letters, along with an office address and phone number in smaller lettering underneath.

She turned it over and jotted down both her numbers, all the while thinking to herself, what *was* she doing?

She wasn't going to say yes to his invitation. How could she? OK, so she was tempted. She was only human. What woman wouldn't respond to what Jake was making her feel at this moment? As if she was the most beautiful, most desirable girl he'd ever met.

What had he said? That he wanted her to be his woman more than anything he'd wanted in a long time.

The devil would be proud of him!

Sixteen years ago, she'd fallen for such a line, hook, line and sinker. Well, she *had*, hadn't she? But sixteen years had taught Angelina to recognise the signs of a dedicated womaniser. You didn't have to have jumped into bed with that type to recognise their trappings. Jake had them all. The car. The clothes. And the charm.

Angelina knew beyond a doubt that being Jake's woman was only a temporary position, whereas her being Alex's mother was forever. Allowing herself to be seduced a second time by Alex's father was just not on.

At the same time, she *was* curious to learn a little more about him, and his life. This was the man she was going to have to entrust her son to, possibly sooner than she'd anticipated. After all, once Dorothy moved up here and found out dear Angelina at the Ambrosia Estate was a single mum with a fifteen-year-old son who just happened to be the dead spit of Jake, the cat would be out of the bag. And as much as Jake might try to abdicate his responsibilities where Alex was concerned, Angelina knew that her stubborn son would not let him get away with that. No, Alex would force himself into Jake's life whether Jake wanted it or not.

'I'm not promising anything,' she remarked coolly as she handed back the card. 'But you're welcome to ring me. I might agree to have lunch with you. Alex wouldn't mind my having lunch with an old friend.'

'I'm sure he won't,' Jake said as he tucked the card back into his wallet. 'It's hardly a grand passion between you two, is it?'

'You know nothing about my relationship with Alex.'

'I know enough,' he stated with an arrogance which was as unsettling as it was wickedly attractive. Why, oh, why did she have to find him so exciting?

Maybe she shouldn't agree to lunch with him. Even lunch might be a worry, especially down at Darling Harbour, with its air of away-from-home glamour and glitz. Sydney could be a very seductive city. Angelina often found herself losing her head a bit when she was there and spending more money than she should. Especially on clothes. She had a wardrobe full of lovely things she rarely wore.

She would have to weigh up the pros and cons of lunching with Jake before his call. If she thought there was any danger of making a fool of herself, she would not go.

'I'll look forward to ringing you,' Jake said, and slipped his wallet into the back pocket of his jeans. 'Meanwhile, surely you have some questions for yours truly? Don't you want to know how come I'm a lawyer and not in jail?'

Angelina shook her head at him in frustration. He was like a rolling bulldozer, difficult to stop.

'I'm sure you're going to tell me, whether I want to hear or not.'

'You *want* to hear,' he said cheekily. 'You know you do.'

So Angelina listened—yes, in rapt silence—whilst he told her everything that had happened to him since that fateful night. She marvelled at his good fortune, and couldn't help feeling a bit proud of him. Both Dorothy and her husband had clearly been wonderful, but Jake must have worked very hard to accomplish what he had.

Not that she intended telling him that. He was smug enough as it was.

'And to think I worried myself sick that I'd been responsible for your going to jail,' she said when he finished his tale of miracles.

'Did you really? Oh, that's sweet. But you were sweet back then. Very sweet.'

'Don't count on my being so sweet now, lover-boy. I've grown up. I might not live in the big bad city but a number of Sydney's more successful swinging singles have stayed at the Ambrosia Estate over the years. I know all about men like you.'

He laughed. 'Tell me about men like me.'

'You work hard and you play hard.'

'True.' He picked up his coffee-cup again.

'You like your own way and you don't always stick to the rules.'

'Mmm. True, I guess.' And smiled at her over the rim of the cup.

'You're all commitment-phobic sex addicts who change girlfriends as often as you do your cars.'

Jake almost choked on the last of his coffee. 'Now, wait here,' he spluttered. 'That's not quite true.'

'Which part is not quite true?' she asked tartly.

'I've only had two cars in the last few years. A navy Mazda and the yellow Ferrari I'm driving to-day.'

'Surprising. OK, so what's the girlfriend count during that time?'

He looked a bit sheepish. 'I don't have that many fingers and toes. But what about you, Miss Tough Cookie? Or shouldn't I ask?'

No way could she let him find out there hadn't been anyone since him. His ego would probably ex-plode. And his predatory nature would go into full pursuit mode.

'You can ask, but I'm not into the kiss-and-tell scene,' she tossed off. 'Let's just say I'm a big girl now and I run my own race.'

'Even when your father was alive?'

'After my not-so-successful rendezvous with you, I learned to be more sneaky.'

'You'd have to be with a father like yours around,' came his rueful remark. 'So! Did your dad *like* this Alex of yours? Or didn't he know about him?'

'He adored Alex.' Too late, Angelina wished she hadn't started that silly subterfuge.

'An Italian, is he?' Jake said drily.

'Half. Now, no more questions about Alex, please. Aah, Dorothy's back,' she said, spying the lady herself walking along the path towards them, accompanied by a portly, grey-haired man in his fifties. 'She seems to have brought the real-estate agent with her.' Fortunately, not one Angelina knew personally.

But when Dorothy swept in with the news she had secured the property and that she was here to get the owner's signature on some papers, a panic-stricken Angelina jumped to her feet and offered to find Arnold for them.

'But why don't you want them to know about Alex?' Arnold said when she cornered him in the barrel room of the winery five minutes later.

'The man with the woman who's buying your place is Alex's father,' Angelina explained reluctantly. 'All right?'

Arnold's eyes rounded. 'Heaven be praised! Just as well Antonio isn't here, or there'd be hell to pay. But he's not here, Angelina, so why keep the boy a secret?'

'Only for a little while, Arnold. I will tell Jake. But in my own good time. OK?'

'Has this Jake turned into a decent kind of chap?'

Decent. Now, decent was a subjective word.

'He's a lawyer,' she said.

'Nothing wrong with lawyers. At least he's got a job. Things could be worse.'

Angelina nodded. 'You're so right. Things *could* be worse.'

But not much.

CHAPTER FIVE

'YOU don't look too pleased,' Dorothy said within seconds of leaving the Ambrosia Estate. 'Did the lovely Angelina surprise you this time by saying no?'

Jake's hands tightened on the steering wheel. 'Things didn't go exactly according to plan. But I haven't given up yet.'

'Good.'

Jake's eyes slanted over towards Dorothy. 'You mean my old flame has your tick of approval?'

'She's a big improvement on your last few girl-friends,' Dorothy said in her usual droll fashion. 'And she'd be very convenient, considering where I'll be living soon. I'll have no worries about seeing you regularly if you start going out with a local girl.'

'I have to get her to drop some guy named Alex first.'

'You've never had any trouble getting your girl-friends to drop their old boyfriends before.'

'This one sounds formidable. A poor little rich boy. Very good-looking. Lives in Sydney. Too bad I didn't find out his last name. I could have had him investigated. From the sound of things, they don't get together all that often. He's probably two-timing her with some city chick. Guys like that are never faithful.'

'You'd know.'

'Dorothy Landsdale, I'll have you know I've always been faithful to my girlfriends!'

'Oh, I don't doubt it. They don't last long enough for you to do the dirty on them. Every few weeks it's out with the old and in with the new.'

Jake didn't like the flavour of this conversation. Dorothy was making him sound as if he was some kind of serial sleazebag where women were concerned. Angelina had inferred the same thing.

'I can well understand Angelina not jumping at the chance of being next in line,' Dorothy went on before Jake could defend himself. 'She might like a bit more security in her relationships. And a possible future.'

'I'll have you know she's no more interested in marriage and having a family than I am. She told me so. She's a career girl.'

'What? Oh, I find that hard to believe. That girl has marriage and motherhood written all over her.'

'You're just saying that because she's Italian.'

'Not at all. I've known enough career women in my life to recognise one when I meet her. If Angelina Mastroianni is a career woman, then I'm…I'm Marilyn Monroe!'

Jake laughed. 'In that case, perhaps I should be relieved that she said no to me.'

'Perhaps you should.'

But he wasn't relieved. He was annoyed. And frustrated. And jealous as hell of this Alex bloke.

Angelina belonged to *him*. She'd always belonged to him.

The sudden primitiveness—and *possessiveness*—of his thoughts stunned Jake. This wasn't him. This was some other man, some caveman who believed that his taking a female's virginity gave him the rights to her body forever.

Logic told Jake this was crazy thinking. But logic wasn't worth a damn beside the passion and determination that was firing Jake's belly at this moment. She was going to be his again. That Alex guy was going to be history, no matter what it took!

Angelina watched the yellow car till it disappeared from view, then she turned and walked with slow steps back down the path to the restaurant.

Wilomena—who had no doubt been waiting with bated breath to collar her alone—pounced immediately. A tall, rake-thin brunette, the restaurant's head waitress had sharp eyes to go with her sharp features.

'All right, fess up, Angelina? Who was that gorgeous hunk in the yellow Ferrari?'

'Just a guy I used to know. No one special.'

'Just a guy you used to know,' Wilomena repeated with rolling eyes. 'Did you hear that, Kevin?' she called out to the chef, who was the only other staff member left in the restaurant at this hour. The rest of the evening's waitresses wouldn't arrive till five-thirty, which was almost an hour away. 'He was just a guy she used to know. No one special.'

Kevin popped his bald head round the doorway that connected the body of the restaurant with the kitchen. In his late thirties, Kevin was English and single and a simply brilliant chef. He'd been on a working holiday around Australia a few years ago, filled in for their chef, who'd been taken ill, and never left. Since his arrival the restaurant's reputation had gone from good to great.

'Amazing how much he looked like Alex, isn't it?' Kevin said with a straight face. 'If I didn't know better, I would have said he was Alex's father.'

Angelina groaned. It was no use. She had no hope of keeping Jake's identity a secret, not even for a minute.

'It's all right,' Wilomena said gently when she saw the distress on her boss's face. 'We won't say anything. Not if you don't want us to.'

'I don't want you to,' Angelina returned pleadingly. 'Not yet, anyway. The other girls didn't notice, did they?'

'No. They're too new. And too silly. All they can think about on a Saturday is where they're going tonight, and with whom. So! Does he know about Alex? Is that why he was here?'

'No. He has no idea. He just dropped in for lunch by sheer accident and he…he…. Oh, Wilomena, it's terribly complicated.'

'Why don't you sit down and tell me all about it?'

Angelina looked at Wilomena, who at thirty-eight had a few years on her. Divorced, with two teenage girls, she lived in Cessnock and worked long hours at the restaurant six days a week to support herself and her kids. Angelina realised she could do worse than confide in Wilomena, who was both pragmatic and practical. And she needed someone to confide in. The only friends she had now were the people she worked with. Her father had been her best friend. Still, this little problem wasn't something she'd have been able to talk to him about. He'd been totally blind when it came to the subject of Jake Winters.

'OK,' she said with a sigh. 'Let's have a glass of wine and I'll tell you all.'

Wilomena smiled. She was really quite attractive when she smiled. 'Fantastic. Let's go into the kitchen so Kevin can hear. Otherwise, I'll just have to repeat everything after you've gone.'

Angelina laughed. 'You two are getting as thick as thieves, aren't you?'

'Yeah,' Wilomena said with a twinkle in her quick blue eyes. 'We are.'

Half an hour later, Angelina made her way slowly along the path that ran from the restaurant and past the cellar door before branching into two paths. One led to the winery, the other followed the driveway that led to the resort proper, a distance of about a hundred metres. She headed for the resort, her shoes crunching on the gravel, her head down in thought as she walked down the gentle incline.

Kevin had advised her to tell Jake the truth as soon as possible, especially since Alex himself wanted to meet his father. He'd said he would want to know if he had a son and would be seriously annoyed if such news was held back from him.

'And that's bulldust about this Jake saying he'd be

a rotten father,' Kevin had pronounced. 'Lots of men talk like that. You wait till he finds out he has a son for real, especially a great kid like Alex. He'll be falling over himself to be the best father he possibly can.'

Wilomena hadn't shared Kevin's optimism. There again, she had more jaundiced views about the opposite sex and their ability to be good fathers.

'What fantasyland do you live in, Kevin?' she'd countered tartly. 'Obviously, you've never been a father. From my experience, lots of men these days soon get very bored with the day-to-day responsibilities of fatherhood. Guys like Jake, especially. He admitted to Angelina he was selfish. And damaged, whatever that means. I think Angelina's right to be careful. I don't think she should tell him anything for a while. If nothing else, it gives Alex time to grow up some more. It'll be weeks before this Dorothy lady moves up here. Meanwhile, Arnold's not going to say anything.'

They'd argued back and forth, with Angelina a bemused onlooker. In the end, Kevin had thrown up his hands and told Wilomena it was no wonder she was still single, if she was so distrusting and contemptuous of men.

Angelina had done her best to smooth things over between them but by the time she'd left, there'd been a chilling silence in the kitchen. She was relieved she wasn't working there tonight. Or on the reception desk. She'd already planned to take the evening off, to do some female things, like have a long bath, shave her legs, put a treatment in her hair and do her nails. It would be good to be alone, to think.

'Angelina, Angelina!'

Angelina turned to find Wilomena running after her.

'Sorry about the ruckus in there,' Wilomena said on reaching her. 'Don't worry about it. Kevin will be fine later tonight. And yes, before you ask, we are sleeping together.'

'I...I wasn't going to ask.'

Wilomena frowned. 'No, you wouldn't, would you? You're not like other girls. It almost killed you to tell us what you told us in there, didn't it? I mean, you're not one to gossip, or to confide.'

'No, I...I guess not.' When you spent the amount of time *she* had spent alone, you lost the knack of confiding in other people. You tried to solve your problems yourself.

'Look, I just wanted to say that I think you should go out with Jake, but without telling him about Alex. Aside from having a bit of long-overdue fun, you can go see where Jake lives, and how he lives. See what kind of man he is.'

'But how did you...?'

'Yeah, I know, you didn't tell us he'd asked you out. But I didn't come down in the last shower, honey, and I watched you two today. Both times. He asked you out all right and you said no, didn't you?'

'I haven't actually given him an answer yet.'

'What does he want you to do?'

'Stay at his place when I go to Sydney for the expo next weekend.'

'Wow. He's a fast mover all right. It took Kevin two years to ask me out, then two months to get me in the sack.'

'It took Jake about two minutes the first time,' Angelina said drily.

'Ooooh. That good, eh?'

'His kisses were. The sex itself was not great. I froze, and he just went ahead.'

'But you wouldn't freeze this time,' Wilomena said intuitively.

Angelina stiffened. 'I have no intention of finding out if I would or I wouldn't. And I have no intention of staying at his place next weekend.'

'But why not? I wouldn't be able to resist, if it were me. The guy's a hunk of the first order.'

Angelina didn't need to be told that. Jake, the man, had even more sex appeal than Jake, the bad boy. And *he'd* had oodles.

'If it was anyone other than Alex's father, I would.'

'If it was anyone other than Alex's father, you wouldn't want to,' Wilomena said. 'I've known girls like you before, Angelina. You're a one-man woman. And he's the man.'

'That's romantic nonsense!'

'Is it?' Wilomena probed softly.

'Yes,' Angelina said stubbornly whilst secretly thinking that Wilomena could be right. Why else hadn't she accepted dates with other men? It wasn't as though she hadn't been asked. She couldn't even claim to be protecting Alex any more, now that he was at boarding school most of the time.

Wilomena shrugged. 'Have it your way. So, you're really not going to see Jake next weekend? Not at all?'

'I…I might go to lunch with him.'

The look on Wilomena's face was telling.

'Just lunch!' Angelina insisted. 'As you yourself said, I need to find out some more about him.'

'Sounds like an excuse to gaze at him some more.'

'I didn't gaze at him today. I was just shocked at how much he looks like Alex.'

'Who do you think you're kidding?'

Angelina groaned. 'I did stare, didn't I?'

'Don't beat yourself up over it. The man was worth a stare. I ogled myself. So did every other woman in the place.'

'Which is why I can't risk being alone with him again. The man's a right devil where women are concerned. He always was.'

'Mmm. But aren't you curious over what it would be like with him now? I mean, he's sure to be very good in the sack. If what you say about him is true, he's had plenty of practice.'

'Too much practice. No, I'm not curious about his lovemaking abilities,' she lied. 'Only about his character and whether he's going to be good for Alex.'

'You know, Angelina, you're a woman as well as a mother. Do you ever think of your own needs?'

'Yes, of course I do.'

'But I've never known you to go out on a date. Not during the time I've worked here, anyway.'

'Dating is seriously overrated. And so is sex.'

'Don't knock it till you try it.'

Angelina flushed. 'Who says I haven't?'

'I have eyes, honey. And ears. If you'd slept with someone around here, I'd know about it. Look, your father's gone now and Alex is almost grown up. Time for you to live a little.'

'Maybe. But not with Jake.' *I'd probably fall in love with him again and then where would I be?*

'Yeah, perhaps you're right. If you slept with him, it could be awkward once he finds out about Alex. He might think you were trying to trap him into marriage.'

'I'd be more concerned over what Alex thought.'

'I dare say you would. You're a very good mother, Angelina. You put me to shame sometimes.'

'Nonsense. You're a great mother.'

'I try to be. Talking of kids, I have to go and ring mine. See what the little devils are up to.'

'And I have to ring Alex and see how he did at cricket today.'

'Being a mother just never stops, does it?' And with a parting grin, Wilomena hurried off.

Angelina sighed and made her way down the rest of the path and through the covered archway that provided protection for arriving guests. A green Jaguar was parked there, with a middle-aged couple inside booking in. Angelina slipped through a side-gate just past Reception that led into a private courtyard attached to the manager's quarters, a spacious two-bedroomed unit with an *en suite* to the main.

She and Alex had moved in there two years ago after Angelina had started doing night shifts at the reception desk. The excuse she'd used for the move was that the old farmhouse where they'd been living, and where she'd been born and brought up, was a couple of hundred metres away, far too long a walk for her at night. Or so she had told her father. Papa had not been happy with their move at first, but he'd got used to it. Besides, when Alex came home on holiday, he'd often stayed with his grandfather in his old room.

Angelina rarely ventured back there, the house not having all that many good memories for her. She'd been a lonely child living there, and an even lonelier single mother. She much preferred her memoryless apartment with its fresh cream walls, cream floor coverings and all mod cons. She liked the modern furniture too, having never been fond of the heavy and ornate furniture her father had preferred. Now that her father was gone, Arnold was living in the old farmhouse, free accommodation being part of his contract as Ambrosia's wine-maker.

Of course, Alex hadn't liked that at all, having someone else living in his grandfather's house. But that was just too bad.

Another sigh escaped Angelina's lips as she let herself in the front door. What a day it had been so far. And it wasn't over yet.

She moved straight across the cream carpet to the

side-table where she kept the phone, sitting down on the green and cream checked sofa and calling Alex on his cellphone. He should have finished playing cricket by now.

'Yes, Mum,' he answered after the second ring.

'You lost,' she said, knowing that tone of voice.

'I don't want to talk about it,' he grumped.

'Never mind. You'll wallop them at the swimming carnival.'

'We'd better. They'll be insufferable if they win that, too.'

Alex had a killer competitive instinct. He was the one who would be insufferable.

'So how's things up there?' he asked.

'Everything's fine. Arnold sold his place today.' *And your father showed up out of the blue.*

Alex groaned. 'Does that mean we're stuck with him forever?'

'Alex, I'm not sure what your problem is with Arnold. He's a really nice man. You could learn a lot from him. Your grandfather said he was brilliant with whites. You know Papa was not at his best with whites. He was more of a red man. But no, we're not stuck with him forever. He said he's going to buy a little place over in Port Stephens with what he gets for his place, with enough left over for his retirement. He's well aware how keen you are to take over and is more than willing to stand aside when you feel ready to take on the job of wine-maker.'

'Good. Because I intend to do just that as soon as I finish my higher-school certificate.'

A prickle ran down Angelina's spine. He sounded like Jake had today. So strong and so determined.

'I won't stand in your way, Alex,' she said. 'This place is your inheritance, and the job of wine-maker is your right.'

'And I'm going to find my father, too. Not in November. I can't wait that long. I'm going to start next holidays. At Easter.'

Angelina grimaced. Easter! That was only a few weeks away. Still, maybe it was for the best. She couldn't stand the tension of such a long wait herself.

'All right, Alex. You'll get no further argument from me on that score. Come Easter, we'll go find your father.'

'Honest?' Alex sounded amazed. 'You're not going to make a fuss?'

'No.'

'Cool. You're the best, Mum.'

'Mmm.'

'Got to go. The dinner bell's gone. Love ya.'

'Love you, too,' she replied, but he'd already hung up.

Tears filled her eyes as she hung up too.

'Lord knows what you're crying over, Angelina,' she muttered. 'Things could be worse, as Arnold said.'

But she wasn't entirely convinced.

CHAPTER SIX

JAKE paced back and forth across his living room, unable to eat, unable to sit and watch television or work or do any of the other activities that usually filled his alone-time.

The sleek, round, silver-framed clock on the wall pronounced that it was getting on for half-past eight. He'd dropped Dorothy off at her place in Rose Bay at seven-thirty, an hour earlier. The drive back from the Hunter Valley had taken a lot longer than the drive up. They'd been caught up in the Saturday-night traffic coming into the city, slowing to a crawl near the Harbour Bridge.

'I won't miss this when I move to the country,' Dorothy had declared impatiently, which had rather amused Jake at the time. She should see how bad the traffic was in peak hours on a weekday. If there was an accident on the bridge, or in the tunnel, the lines of traffic didn't crawl. They just stopped.

But that was city living for you.

Jake had declined Dorothy's invitation to come in for a bite to eat, and now here he was, unfed and unable to relax, becoming increasingly agitated and angry. With himself.

He'd handled Angelina all wrong today. He'd come on to her way too strong, and way too fast.

That might work with city babes in wine bars on a Friday night, but not girls like Angelina. Even when she was fifteen, she hadn't been easy. She'd made him wait, forcing him to make endless small talk that summer before finally agreeing to meet him alone.

He could see now that her still being attracted to him in a physical sense wasn't enough for her to drop her current boyfriend and go out with him. She claimed she was a modern woman who'd been around, but he suspected—like Dorothy—that Angelina was not as sophisticated as she thought she was. She had an old-fashioned core.

She was going to say no when he finally rang her. Nothing was surer in his mind. And the prospect was killing him.

He had to change his tactics. Hell, he was a smart guy, wasn't he? A lawyer. Changing tactics midstream came naturally to him.

Go back to square one, Jake. Chat her up some more. Show her your warm and sensitive side. You have to have one. Edward said you did. Then you might stand a chance of winning, if not her heart, then her body.

And don't wait till tomorrow night to call. Do it now. Right now, buddy, whilst she can still remember how it felt today when you touched her hand, and looked deep into her eyes and talked about spending a whole weekend together.

If it was even remotely what you felt—what you are *still* feeling—then she has to be tempted.

Jake's hand was unsteady as he took out his wallet

and extracted the card where she'd written down her telephone numbers. He had it bad all right. It had been a long time since he'd felt this desperate over a woman. Damn it all, he'd *never* felt this desperate before!

Except perhaps that summer sixteen years ago. He'd been desperate for Angelina back then too. No wonder he'd been hopeless by the time he'd actually done it with her.

Jake craved the opportunity to show her he wasn't a hopeless lover now.

But first, he had to get her to say yes to seeing him again. Even lunch would do. She'd said she might go to lunch with him. It wasn't quite what he had in mind but it was a start.

He dragged in several deep breaths as he walked over to sweep up the receiver of his phone. His hand was only marginally steadier as he punched in her number but he consoled himself with the fact she could not see it shake.

As long as he sounded calm. And sincere. That was all that mattered.

Angelina was sitting on the sofa and painting her toenails, her right foot propped up on the glass coffee-table, when the phone rang. The brush immediately zigzagged across her second toe onto her big toe, leaving a long streak of plum nail-polish on her skin.

The swear-word she uttered was not one she would

have used if Alex had been home. Or if her father had been alive.

By the time she replaced the brush in the bottle, poured some remover on a cotton-wool ball and wiped off the wayward polish, then leant over to snatch up the phone from the nearby side-table, it had been ringing for quite a while.

'Yes?' she answered sharply. She hoped it wasn't Wilomena with more advice. She was all adviced out. Besides, she'd already made up her mind what she was going to say to Jake when he finally rang.

'Angelina? It's Jake. Have I rung at an awkward moment?'

Jake. It was Jake!

'You weren't supposed to ring till later in the week,' she snapped, hating it that just the sound of his voice could make her stomach go all squishy.

'I couldn't wait till then to apologise,' he said. 'I wouldn't have been able to sleep tonight.'

'Apologise for what?' Her voice was still sharp.

His, however, was soft and seductive.

'I was out of line today.'

'Were you really?' Now her tone was dry, and sarcastic.

No way was she going to be all sweetness and light. She was still seriously annoyed with him for turning up in her life at this particular point in time and making her make difficult decisions.

'I was pushy and presumptuous, as you said. My only excuse is that I didn't want to let you get away from me a second time. I really liked you sixteen years ago, Angelina, but I like the woman you've become even better.'

She laughed. 'Wow, you've really become the master of the polished line, haven't you? But you can save the flattery for another occasion, Jake. I've already decided to have lunch with you on Saturday.'

The dead silence on the other end of the line gave Angelina some satisfaction that she'd been able to knock him speechless. Unfortunately, now that she'd voiced her decision out loud to him, the reality of it shook her right down to her half-painted toes.

But the die had been rolled. No going back.

'Great!' he said, sounding much too happy for her liking. 'I'm already looking forward to it. But does—er—Alex know?'

'I spoke to him earlier this evening. We talked about you.'

'What did you say? I'll bet you didn't tell him how we first met.'

'Alex already knows all about you, Jake. There are no secrets between us.'

'And he *agreed* to your going to lunch with me?'

'Why should he object to a platonic lunch between old friends?'

'Old *flames*, Angelina. Not old friends.'

'Whatever. A lot of water has gone under the bridge since then, Jake.'

'I'll bet you didn't tell him everything I said to you today.'

What could she say to that?

'You didn't, did you?' Jake continued when she

remained silent. 'No man—not even your pathetic Alex—would willingly let his girlfriend go to lunch with another man who'd declared his wish to make her *his* woman.'

Angelina could not believe the passion in Jake's words. And the power. How easy it would be to forget all common sense and tell him that she had changed her mind, that she would not only go to lunch with him on Saturday, but she would also stay at his place on the Saturday night.

Dear heaven, she *was* going to make a fool of herself with him again. Or she might, if she went to lunch with him on Saturday as things stood. If he could do this to her over the phone, what could he do to her when she was alone with him in the big bad city?

She had to tell him about Alex. Right here and now. It was the only way she could protect herself against her susceptibility to this man.

'Jake, there's something I have to tell you,' she began, then stopped as she struggled for the right words. He was going to be shocked out of his mind. And furious with her for playing word games with him. How she could possibly explain why she'd done such a thing? She was going to look a fool, no matter what she said, or did.

'Alex doesn't know you're going to lunch with me at all, does he?' Jake jumped in.

'Er—no. He doesn't.'

'You realise what that means, Angelina. You're

finished with him, whether you admit it or not. You're not the sort of girl to two-time a guy.'

'I don't consider lunch a two-timing act,' she argued, panicking at the way this conversation was now going. Instead of finding sanctuary in the truth, she was getting in deeper. And deeper.

'It is when you know that the guy you're having lunch with wants more than to share a meal with you,' Jake pointed out ruefully.

'But what *you* want is not necessarily what *I* want,' she countered, stung by his presumption.

'That's not the impression you gave me today. We shared something special once, Angelina. It's still there. The sparks. The chemistry.'

'Men like you share a chemistry with lots of women, Jake. It's nothing special. Which reminds me, is there some current girlfriend who should know that you've asked another woman out to lunch?'

'No.'

'Why not?'

'I'm between girlfriends at the moment.'

She laughed. 'Am I supposed to believe that?'

'You sure are. I'm a lot of things but I'm no liar.'

'Such as what? What are you, Jake Winters, that I should worry about before daring to go to lunch with you?'

'You don't honestly expect me to put myself down, do you? I'm no saint but I'm not one of the bad guys, either. I don't lie and I don't cheat. There is no other woman in my life. But I *am* a confirmed bachelor. And I aim to stay that way. Which should please you, since you're not into wedding bells and baby bootees. Or did I get that wrong?'

'No. No, you didn't get that wrong.'

If I can't marry you, then I don't want to marry anyone.

The thought burst into her mind. Shocking her. *Shattering* her. This couldn't be. This wasn't fair. Not only that, but it was also crazy. He'd only been in her life a few short hours this time.

She couldn't be in love with him again. Not really. She was being confused and corrupted by the romance of the situation. And by desire. His, as well as her own. She wasn't sure which was the more powerful. Being wanted the way Jake said he wanted her. Or her wanting him.

Angelina still could not believe the feelings which had rampaged through her when he'd simply touched her hand.

Wilomena was probably right. She was a one-man woman.

And Jake was the man. Impossible to resist him. She could go to lunch with him next Saturday, pretending that it was a reconnaissance mission to find out what kind of man he was. But that was all it would be. A pretence.

'Tell me about your job,' she said, valiantly resolving to put their conversation back on to a more platonic, getting-to-know-you basis. 'What kind of lawyer are you?'

'A darned good one.'

'No, I mean what kind of people do you represent?'

'People who need a good lawyer to go in to bat for them. People who've been put down and put upon, usually in the corporate world. Employees who've been unfairly dismissed, or sexually harassed, or made to endure untenable work conditions. I have this woman client at the moment who's in the process of suing her boss. She worked as his assistant in an un-air-conditioned office with him for years whilst he chain-smoked. She repeatedly asked him to put her in a separate office but he wouldn't. Yet he was filthy rich. She now has terminal lung cancer and she's only forty-two. We're suing for millions. And we'll win, too.'

'But she won't,' Angelina said. 'She'll die.'

'Yes, she'll die. But her teenage children won't. She told me she'd die happier if she gets enough money to provide for them till they can provide for themselves. Her husband's an invalid as well. That's why she had to work and why she stayed working for that bastard under such rotten conditions. Because the job was within walking distance of her house, and she didn't have a car. She couldn't afford one.'

'That's so sad. I hate hearing stories like that. Don't tell me any more, Jake.'

'All right,' he said gently. 'You always did have a soft heart, Angelina. I remember the day we found that bird with the broken wing caught in the vines. You cried till your dad promised to take it to a vet.'

He was getting to her again. 'I only have a soft

heart for poor birds with broken wings,' she countered crisply. 'And poor people dying through no fault of their own. Not smooth-talking lawyers who go round trying to seduce old flames just for the heck of it.'

'Is that what you think I'm doing?'

'Come, now, Jake, you ran into me today by sheer accident. You haven't given me a second thought all these years.' Unlike herself. Even if she'd wanted to forget Jake, how could she when his eyes had been staring back at her on a daily basis for years? 'Your dear old friend Dorothy is buying a place up here,' she swept on. 'You spotted me again today, liked what you saw, and thought I'd be a convenient lay during your weekends up here.'

'That's a pretty harsh judgement.'

'I think it's a pretty honest one. Please don't try to con me, Jake. I won't like that. Be straight with me.'

'OK, you're right and you're wrong. I admit I haven't actively thought about you for years. But that doesn't mean I'd forgotten you. When I realised where I was going for lunch today, everything came flooding back. The way you made me feel that summer. The things that happened. I really wanted to see you again. I told myself it was just curiosity, or the wish to say sorry for being just a chump back then. But when I actually saw you, Angelina...when I saw you I—'

'Please don't say the world stopped,' she cut in drily.

He laughed. 'I won't. It actually sped up. At least, my pulse-rate did. Do you know how beautiful you are?' he said, his voice dropping low again. 'How sexy?'

Don't fall for all that bulldust. Keep your head, honey.

Angelina could almost hear those very words coming from Wilomena's mouth.

'You're not the first man to tell me that, Jake,' she said in a rather hard voice.

'I don't doubt it.'

'City men are amazingly inventive, especially when they're away from home. The Ambrosia Estate has become a popular venue for conferences,' she elaborated. 'Lots of them pass through all the time.'

'You sound as if you've been burnt a few times.'

'Who hasn't in this day and age?' came her off-hand reply. If he thought she'd jumped into bed with her fair share of such men, then all well and good. No way did she want him thinking he was the only man she'd ever known.

'I'm sorry but I really must go, Jake. I was in the middle of something important when you called. I'll see you on Saturday at the expo. I'm sure you can manage to find the right booth. Shall we say twelve-thirty?'

'Noon would be better.'

'Noon it is, then. Bye for now.' And she hung up.

Jake was grinning as he replaced his receiver.

Alex, old man, he thought elatedly, come next weekend, you're going to be history!

CHAPTER SEVEN

ANGELINA couldn't stop titivating herself. If she'd checked her make-up and hair once, she'd checked it a hundred times.

Not for the first time this morning, she hurried into the hotel bathroom so that she could stand in front of the cheval mirror that hung on the back of the door.

The dress she was wearing was not casual. But she knew she looked good in it, which was the most important thing to her right at that moment.

Light and silky, the sleeveless sheath skimmed her curvy figure, making her look slim yet shapely at the same time. Its scooped neckline stopped just short of showing any cleavage, the wide, softly frilled collar very feminine. The hem finished well above her knee on one side and dipped down almost to mid-calf on the other, as was the fashion this year. The print on the pale cream material was floral, the flowers small and well-spaced, their colours ranging from the palest pink to a deep plum, her favourite colour. She'd matched the dress with open-toed cream high heels and a plum handbag. Her lipstick and nail-polish were plum as well. Strong colours suited her, with her olive skin and dark hair and eyes.

Her hair—which had been up and down several

times so far this morning—was finally down, its natural wave and curl having been tamed somewhat with a ruthless blowdrying, but it still kicked up on the ends. Shoulder-blade-length, it was parted on one side and looped behind her ears to show her gold and pearl drops. A gold chain with a single gold and pearl pendant adorned her neck. The floral scents of her perfume, an extravagant one she'd bought during her last shopping trip to Sydney, was only just detectable on her skin. Angelina didn't like it when a woman's perfume preceded her into a room like a tidal wave.

She stroked the figure-hugging dress down over her hips before turning round and looking over her shoulder at her back view. Her scowl soon became a shrug. Nothing she could do about her Italian lower half. She had wide hips and a big bottom, and that was all there was to it.

Angelina turned back and looked with more approval at her front view. At least she had the breasts to go with the backside. They were a definite plus. Just as well, however, that her nipples were hidden by the wideness of the collar, because she could feel them now, pressing against the satiny confines of her underwired bra, making her hotly aware of how excited she was. How incredibly, appallingly excited.

A small moan escaped her lips, Angelina stuffing a closed fist into her mouth and biting on her knuckles in an effort to get some control over her silly self. But she was fighting a losing battle. The truth was she was dying to see Jake again. She wanted to see that look in his eyes once more, the one which made her feel like the most beautiful girl in the world.

Oh, she knew that he'd probably looked at a hundred different girls that way over the years. There were no end of lovely-looking girls here in Sydney, model-slim girls with more sophistication and style than she had. But no matter. She could pretend she was the only one, just for one miserable lunch.

Surely there was no harm in that. Lunch was safe. They wouldn't really be alone. Impossible for him to get to her sexually during lunch, no matter what his secret agenda might be. Sharing a meal was also a good opportunity to find out more about him.

Her eyes went to her wrist-watch. It was ten-past ten, still almost two hours to go before noon. The minutes were dragging, but then, she'd been up since dawn.

She hadn't slept well, and she couldn't even blame the hotel bed. She hadn't slept well all week, her mind never giving her any peace. She'd been tormented by regrets and recriminations.

Of course, in hindsight, she *should* have told Jake about Alex straight away last Saturday when he'd come back to the restaurant. And she shouldn't have begun that silly charade, letting Jake think Alex was her boyfriend. No, not boyfriend. Lover. It had only made Jake even more determined, it seemed, to win her. She'd become a challenge.

By Friday her nerves had been so bad that she hadn't felt capable of driving down to Sydney, let alone coping with the inner-city traffic. Whenever

she came down to visit Alex at weekends, she always
stayed at the Rydges Hotel in North Sydney, which
was near his school. There was never any need for
her to drive over the Harbour Bridge. If she wanted
to go shopping in the city during her weekend trips
down, she caught the train over the bridge. She never
attempted to drive. For a country-raised girl, driving
in that congestion would be a nightmare.

But getting to the expo, and the Star City hotel,
would require her to go over the bridge and negotiate
all those confusing lanes that went off in myriad different directions. Her father had brought her down to
a show at the Star City theatre last year, and even
he'd taken a wrong turn. Much easier to catch the
train down and get a cab from Central. Much easier
to come down on the Friday, too, rather than wait till
the Saturday morning.

Arnold had kindly driven her into the station yesterday morning and she'd arrived in Sydney just after
two, giving her enough time after booking in at the
hotel to go for a walk and locate where the weekend
expo was being held. It was down on a nearby wharf,
in a building that had once housed the old casino.

The finishing touches on the Ambrosia Estate
booth were being made when she arrived and she'd
been very impressed. It looked like a little piece of
Italy, with vines climbing over a mock-pergola, from
which hung big bunches of grapes—not real but very
lifelike. The right side of the booth was dedicated to
white wines, with the red wines on the left. Each side
would have its own team of pretty female demon-

strators for wine-tasting, she'd been informed by the man running the show. Cheese would be offered with the reds, slices of fruit with the drier whites, and exotic sweets with the dessert wines.

The only negative during her inspection tour was this man himself. He was a typical salesman. Thirtyish and suavely handsome with a moustache and goatee beard, he just couldn't help flirting with her. Not too strong for a first meeting. But Angelina had had plenty to do with salesmen at the resort, and she knew as sure as the sun was already up and shining that morning that today would be a different story. Today, he was going to come on much stronger. Today, he was going to be hands-on.

Which created a dilemma for Angelina. She didn't want to encourage the guy by turning up again today. At the same time, she didn't want Jake to think her presence wasn't required at the expo. She needed to actually be there at the booth, doing something constructive, when Jake showed up. Which meant she'd have to leave the sanctuary of her hotel room soon and make an appearance.

Angelina sighed. She hoped that Wayne—he must have told her his name ten times—didn't think she'd dolled herself up for him. Yesterday she'd only been wearing jeans and a simple white shirt, and he hadn't been able to stop eyeing her up and down.

The telephone suddenly ringing startled Angelina. As she hurried from the bathroom, she wondered who it would be. Unlikely to be Alex. The team wasn't allowed any outside calls during their weekend camp. The focus was to be all on swimming. Angelina had called him last night from the hotel and they'd talked for simply ages. Mostly about the expo. Alex was all for advertising their wines, unlike his grandfather, who'd been old-fashioned in his ways.

No, it couldn't be Alex, she thought as she crossed the hotel room and scooped up the receiver. Hopefully not the dreaded Wayne, wanting to know where she was.

'Yes?'

'Do you always answer the phone as if it's bad news?'

Jake. It was Jake. Angelina's stomach started to swirl.

'How did you know to ring me here?' she said.

'I was just talking to the chap running your booth at the expo and he mentioned you'd arrived yesterday. You yourself told me where you were staying, Angelina.'

'But what are you doing at the expo this early? You said noon. It's only just after ten.'

'I didn't want to risk not being able to find you later, so I thought I'd do a preliminary sortie. I'm glad I did. This place is a madhouse. You should see it. Which reminds me. Why aren't you down here, selling your wares? It wouldn't be because you don't really need to be here, would it? You couldn't possibly have lied to me about that too, the way you lied to me about when you would be arriving in Sydney?'

Angelina didn't know whether to be annoyed with

him, or charmed. 'I didn't want you pestering me any more than necessary.'

'Pestering! Wow, you really know how to take the wind out of a guy's sails, don't you?'

'Sorry. That was a bit harsh. But you know what I mean. Is there a purpose to this call, Jake, or is it just a softening-up trick?'

He laughed. 'I can see I'm going to have to be very careful with you.'

'Yes, you are. I'm fragile.'

He laughed again. 'You're about as fragile as Dorothy. OK, so I won't confess I just wanted to hear the sound of your voice. That would probably go down like a lead balloon. The second reason for this call is to check that you don't get seasick.'

'Seasick,' she repeated blankly. She was still thinking of his wanting to hear the sound of her voice.

'Yep, I'm planning on booking us a luncheon cruise on the harbour. That's another reason for my early arrival over here. I wanted to find out what was available.'

'Oh. Oh, how…lovely,' she finished, having almost said how romantic.

'I thought you might never have done that, living where you do.'

'No. No, I haven't. That's very thoughtful of you, Jake.'

'I cannot tell a lie. It wasn't thoughtful. It was my next best softening-up trick. After this phone call.'

Angelina smiled. 'You really are shameless.'

'And you really are beautiful. Yes, I know, I shouldn't have said that, either. I can't seem to help myself with you. My mouth has a mind of its own. Have you told Alex about us yet?'

'There is no *us*, Jake.'

'About lunch with me, then?'

'No.'

'You're only delaying the inevitable.'

'Yes. I know that.'

She heard his sharp intake of breath. 'Does that mean what I hope it means?'

'Let's just take one day at a time, Jake,' she said.

'Fair enough.'

'See you at the booth at noon,' she said, and hung up before she could say another single silly word.

CHAPTER EIGHT

JAKE watched her from a safe distance, Angelina totally unaware of his presence. He was a good thirty metres away from the Ambrosia Estate booth, with the milling crowds providing the perfect cover for his observation post.

She looked even more beautiful today than she had last Saturday. That dress was a stunner. But then, Angelina would look stunning in anything.

Woman was the right word to describe Angelina. So many girls these days were like stick insects. But not her. She was all soft curves and lush femininity. The two skinny blonde demonstrators working next to her in the booth looked positively anorexic by comparison.

Jake had been thinking about Angelina all week. She'd constantly distracted him at work and disturbed his sleep with dreams of the most erotic kind.

Last night had been especially erotic. He'd woken and reached for her in the bed—so real was the dream. But where he'd anticipated finding her warm and naked next to him, there'd only been a cold emptiness.

And to think she'd actually been *here*, in Sydney, last night, staying at the Star City hotel! This revelation had frustrated the hell out of him. If he'd known, he could have persuaded her to at least have dinner with him.

And she would have come. She'd virtually admitted to him over the phone this morning that she'd decided to give Alex the brush-off in favour of him.

Unfortunately, she'd also made it clear that he was still on probation. One day at a time, she'd said. He could not afford to rest on his laurels just yet. Or presume that she would say yes to more than a meal or two today.

Never in the last ten years had Jake had to be this patient with a woman. And never had he felt *less* patient.

His body was on fire, aching to be with her in the most basic way.

As his eyes roved over the silky dress she was wearing, his loins stirred alarmingly. He shifted away from the wall he was leaning against, taking several deep breaths and willing his flesh back to a semblance of control, and decency.

Suddenly, Angelina's eyes started to search the crowd as though she was looking for someone. Despite it only being ten to twelve, Jake instinctively knew she was looking for him. With rather anxious eyes, he thought. Perhaps because that Wayne fellow was being a pest. Ever since Jake had taken up his vantage point five minutes earlier, the sales rep had been chatting away to Angelina, his slimy dark eyes all over her.

When the sleazebag actually had the temerity to reach out and lay a hand on Angelina's bare arm,

Jake decided that waiting till noon was not on. He forged forward, amazed at the wave of fierce emotion which had consumed him.

Not jealousy. He didn't think for a moment Angelina fancied the guy. Jake had read her body language. He just couldn't bear for any man to touch her like that. Or to undress her with his eyes the way that guy had been doing.

The thought that *he'd* been doing some undressing with his own eyes was a sobering one. Though Jake quickly dismissed any guilt with the added thought that it was different with him. He *cared* about Angelina. It wasn't just a question of lust.

Her eyes lit up at the sight of him, making him feel almost ten feet tall.

'Ready to go, darling?' he said, firmly staking his claim.

Fortunately, Angelina didn't give him one of those don't-go-getting-carried-away-with-yourself looks she'd bestowed upon him last Saturday.

'I just have to get my handbag,' she replied eagerly.

Within thirty seconds, he was shepherding her away through the crowd, his hand resting possessively in the small of her back. Once they were out of sight of the booth, he rather expected her to tell him to keep his hands to himself.

But she didn't.

Angelina knew she was being foolish. But ooh…the touch of Jake's hand on her body was electric. His palm was like a hot iron, burning its way through her dress to her skin beneath. Heat radiated through her, making her feel as if she was glowing all over.

'Thank you for rescuing me from that creep,' she said as he steered her through the throng towards the exit.

'My pleasure.'

'I can't stand touchy-feely men.'

'Oops!' His hand promptly lifted away.

'Not you,' she hastily assured him with an upwards glance. 'I didn't mean you.'

Their eyes met and Angelina knew she'd just crossed a line, that line which she had taken such pains to draw earlier, but which was now in danger of disintegrating entirely.

Her eyes ran over him, and she thought how utterly gorgeous he was looking in his trendy city clothes. No jeans for him this time. But not a suit, either. His trousers were a bone colour, not dissimilar to the cream in her dress. Very expensive by the look of their cut, and the lack of creases. His shirt was made in black silk, worn open-necked, with its long sleeves rolled up to his elbows. Casual, yet sophisticated and suave, the epitome of the man about town, such a far cry from the Jake whom she'd ogled just as shamelessly sixteen years ago.

Only his eyes were the same. Still that same hard, icy blue, and still with the same intent. To get her into bed.

'That's a relief,' he said, and his hand settled right back where it had been.

A shiver ran down Angelina's spine. How would it feel if she had no clothes on at all? If she was lying with him, naked, in a bed, and he was sliding his hand down her back whilst the other was…?

She gulped the great lump which had formed in her throat and tried to find reasons for why his making love to her should never be allowed to happen. But none came to mind at that moment.

'Did that guy say or do anything really offensive?' Jake asked as he guided her out onto the wharf and into the sunshine. 'Do you want to me go back and sort him out?'

Angelina drew in some blessedly fresh air and tried to get herself back on to an even keel. 'Lord, no. No, that's not necessary. Wayne's harmless, really. Just too full of himself. And it's not as though I have to see him again.' Too late, she realised she'd made another blunder.

Jake pounced on it immediately. 'You don't have to go back to the booth today?'

'Not if I don't want to.'

'And do you want to?'

'Hardly.' Silly to say that she did. 'I thought I might do some shopping after our lunch,' she added, hoping to retrieve lost ground.

'Shopping for what?'

'Clothes.'

His gaze travelled slowly up and down her body. 'More clothes to drive men wild with lust?'

She flushed. 'That's not my intent when I buy a dress.'

'It might not be your intent,' he said drily. 'But the result's the same. I have to confess I do understand where poor Wayne was coming from. You'd tempt a saint, looking as you do today. And not many men are saints. But I doubt you'll have much time for shopping after our luncheon cruise. The one I've booked takes three hours. Most shops close at four on a Saturday. Besides, I was hoping you'd agree to come back to my place for a while. I live over in that direction there on MacMahon's Point,' he said, pointing straight across the expanse of sparkling blue water at the distant skyline of high-rise, harbour-hugging apartment blocks. 'I've already organised for the boat's captain to put in at the wharf there and let us off afterwards.'

'That was presumptuous of you, Jake,' came her surprisingly cool-sounding remark. Inside, she felt far from cool.

He shrugged. 'I didn't think you'd mind. I thought you might like to see where I live. I'm happy to drive you back to the hotel later in the afternoon. If you want to change for dinner, that is. But you look perfectly fine to go out with me exactly as you are.'

She laughed. 'You have today all planned out, don't you?'

'Being a lawyer has taught me that it's always wise to have a plan.'

'And do things always go according to your plans?'

'On the whole. But there are exceptions, of which

I suspect you might be one,' he finished with a rueful sigh.

She smiled, gratified that he thought she had more will-power and character than she actually possessed at that moment.

'You said one day at a time,' he reminded her. 'This is just one day, Angelina.'

He was right. It was. But she knew how Jake aimed for this day to end. All she could hope was that, when the time came, she had the courage to say no to him.

CHAPTER NINE

'YOU hear people saying how spectacular Sydney Harbour is,' Angelina said as they leant against the deck railing of the cruiser. 'I've admired it from afar many times. In movies and on television and from hotel-room windows. But it's not till you're on the water itself that you appreciate its beauty, and its size. Thank you so much for this experience, Jake.'

'I thought you might enjoy it.'

She truly had. Every bit of it. The views. The food. But especially the company.

Jake had to be one of the most intelligent and interesting men she'd ever talked to. Even if he wasn't drop-dead gorgeous and she hadn't been madly attracted to him, she'd have enjoyed his company these past three hours. They'd chatted about so many different topics, getting to know each other as the adults they'd become, not the teenagers they'd once been. She'd discovered they had similar tastes in books and movies, thrillers being their entertainment of choice. After agreeing to disagree on what kind of music was best, they'd argued happily about politics, discussed the world's leaders failing with peace and the environment, and in general had a great time, solving everything themselves with sweeping words of wisdom.

None of this would have been possible, Angelina realised, but for the other people on the cruise. Mostly tourists, with cameras which were whipped up at every opportunity to snap pictures of the bridge, the opera house and the shoreline. Their constant presence had allowed her to drop her defences and be more relaxed with Jake than she had been since he'd walked back into her life. It had been good to forget the threat of being seduced for a while and just enjoy Jake, the person, and not Jake, the sexual predator.

She was even beginning to reassess that judgement of him. Maybe she'd been harsh in thinking he was that shallow when it came to relationships. Just because he didn't want marriage and children didn't mean he wasn't capable of caring, in a fashion. Of course, his track record with women wasn't great. Even he'd admitted to that. But even men like Jake could change, couldn't they? Maybe he was getting to that age when he was ready for commitment.

But was he ready for a ready-made son, complete with mother attached?

Angelina felt that was too large a leap of faith.

No. Jake, the man, would still not be pleased when she finally told him the truth. Which was perhaps why she couldn't tell him yet. For one thing, she didn't want to spoil today. Surely she deserved one day of being totally selfish, of just being Angelina, the woman, not Angelina, the mother? It was so nice to be squired around by Jake, to have him lavish attention on her, to feel desired and wanted.

Of course, it was risky. But it was worth the risk to feel what she was feeling at the moment. Not in sixteen years had she experienced anything like it. This fizz of excitement dancing along her veins and through her head. Her very *light* head, she suddenly realised.

Her laugh sounded rather girlish, even to her own ears. 'I think I've had too much to drink.' The white wines served up with the buffet lunch had been excellent, and so easy to swallow.

'I'll make you some coffee when we get up to my place,' Jake offered. 'It's just a short walk from the wharf. Come on, this is where we get off.'

He hadn't lied about the shortness of the walk. But it was still far too long with her hand warmly encased within Jake's. By the time they'd strolled up the hill to his apartment block, and ridden up in the lift—alone together—to the fifteenth floor, Angelina was desperate to put some physical distance between them. She was glad when he dropped her hand to unlock and open his front door. But that was only a short respite. She needed longer.

'I—er—have to use your bathroom,' she said as soon as Jake shut the door behind them.

He gave her a sharp look, as though he knew exactly what she was doing. And why.

'This way,' he said crisply.

Her five-minute stay in the bathroom helped, although not the sight of the bathroom. How many people had bathrooms which had black marble right to the ceiling, not to mention real gold taps and corner spa baths big enough for two?

Angelina recalled that the living room—which she'd followed Jake across on her way to the bathroom—also had black marble tiles on the floor, not to mention thick white rugs, red leather furniture, sexy steel lamps and a television as big as a movie screen. Then there was the far wall, which was all glass, beyond which was a wide terrace and a view to die for.

The place had 'seduction palace' written all over it!

'This is a very expensive apartment, Jake,' she said when she finally joined him in the kitchen. It, too, had the same black marble on the bench-tops, and the latest in stainless-steel appliances. Above the double sinks was a wide window that overlooked the terrace and caught some more of the brilliant view of the harbour, and the bridge.

'It was all Edward's doing,' he said as he spooned the coffee into attractive stoneware mugs. 'He insisted I buy a flashy harbourside apartment with some of my inheritance.'

'Well…this is flashy all right.'

He looked up from his coffee-making, his expression disappointed. 'You don't like it.'

'No, no, I do. What's not to like? It's just… well…it does have "bachelor pad" written all over it.'

'True. But then that's what I am, Angelina. A

bachelor. I thought that was one of the things you liked about me. I fitted in with your priorities in life.'

She looked away before he glimpsed the truth on her face, walking over to slide open one of the glass doors that led out onto the balcony. 'Could we have our coffee outside?' she threw back at him, deliberately directing the conversation away from her priorities in life.

Jake shrugged. 'Whatever you fancy.'

Leading words, and one which Angelina struggled to ignore. If only he realised how much she fancied *him*. So far, she'd done a good job of keeping her desires hidden, but the fact she was even here, with him, alone, had to be telling.

She was standing against the glass security panels that bounded the terrace, her hands curled tightly over the top railing, when he joined her with the two steaming mugs.

'I remembered how you liked your coffee from last Saturday,' he said. 'I hope I got it right. Black, with one sugar?'

'Perfect,' she said, and went to take it from him. Stupidly, not with the handle. On contact with the red-hot stoneware, her hand automatically jerked back. At the same moment, Jake let the mug go and it crashed to the terrace, splintering apart on the terracotta tiles, some of the near-boiling black coffee splashing onto her stockinged legs.

Her cry of pain was real, Jake's reactions swift. Shoving his own mug onto a nearby table, he scooped Angelina up in his arms, and carried her with long strides back inside and over to the kitchen. There, he sat her on the marble counter, stripped off her shoes and swivelled her round to put her stockinged feet into the larger of the two sinks. Turning on the tap, he directed the cold water over her scalded legs.

'That water's freezing!' she cried out, and stamped her feet up and down in the sink.

'That's the idea,' he replied. 'It'll take the heat out of your skin and stop it from burning. Now, stop being such a baby.' And he kept swivelling the tap back and forth across her lower legs.

'You're getting my dress all wet,' she complained.

'I have a drier. Besides, there's coffee on that very pretty skirt, anyway. You'll have to take the dress off and soak it, if you don't want the whole thing to be ruined.'

Take her dress off! If she did that, then she'd be a goner for sure.

'Was this part of your plan for today? Spill hot coffee all over me so you could play knight the rescue and get my dress off at the same time?'

His blue eyes glittered with amusement. 'I'd love to say that I thought of it. In fact, I might put it away in my mental cupboard of plans for seducing difficult old flames. But given you dropped the mug, Angelina, might I ask you the same thing? Was this *your plan*,' he countered, his voice dropping to a low, sexy timbre, 'to spill coffee all over yourself so you could take off your dress in order to seduce *me*?'

If only he hadn't been so close, or his hands hadn't

been on her legs as well, or his eyes hadn't been searching hers.

'Could be,' she heard herself say in a faraway voice, her head whirling. But not with the wine this time. With desire. For him. 'Has it worked?' she murmured, her eyes drowning in his.

His hands stilled on her legs. Then slowly but surely, he turned off the tap and scooped her back up into his arms.

'Absolutely,' he said.

Jake's heart pounded as he carried her down the hall-way towards the master bedroom.

This was the moment he'd been waiting and hoping for. There was no stopping him now.

Yet her eyes slightly bothered him. They seemed kind of dazed. Was she still tipsy from the wine she'd drunk over lunch? Surely not. She'd hadn't consumed that much.

He angled her through the bedroom door and carried her across the expanse of white shag carpet towards the king-sized bed with its gold satin quilt and matching pillows. Her calling the apartment flashy popped back into his mind. If she'd thought the rest of his place flashy, he wondered what she'd make of this room.

But she wasn't looking at the room. She was just looking at him. With those huge, liquid brown eyes of hers. Still dazed, they were. But also adoring.

Had there ever been a woman look at him quite like the way she was looking at him?

Only her, all those years ago, when she'd been just a girl. His heart flipped over at this realisation. Dear God, let him do this right this time, he thought, and laid her gently down across the bed.

She sucked in sharply when his hands slid up under the damp hem of her dress.

'Just taking your wet stockings off,' he explained softly, and made no attempt to do anything else as he peeled them off her and draped them over a nearby chair. Despite his own intense need, Jake knew instinctively not to go too fast. Or to do anything even remotely crude. Or aggressive.

Angelina was not like any other woman he'd known. She was different. Special. Fragile, she'd called herself this morning. He'd laughed at the time but he could see that she was right. She *was* fragile.

'Do you want me to take your dress off?' he asked. 'Or do you want to do that yourself?'

She just stared up at him for a few moments before rolling over and presenting her back to him.

The naivete behind this trusting gesture touched him, and reaffirmed his new assessment of her. His very first instinct about Angelina had been right after all. She might talk tough, but she wasn't tough. Or all that experienced, either. He suspected she hadn't had as many lovers as she'd implied. How could she have, with that eagle-eyed father of hers?

The thought made him even more determined to do this right.

The zipper on her dress was long, opening up the back right down to the swell of her buttocks. The sight of nothing but a thin white satin bra strap and the beginning of what looked like a matching thong did little for his resolve to take this as slowly as possible.

'Roll over,' he ordered a bit abruptly.

She did so, and those eyes were on him again. Wide now, and dilated. Her lips fell apart as her breathing quickened appreciably.

He tore his eyes away from hers and bent to ease the dress off her shoulders and draw it down her arms and over her hips, down her legs and off her feet. He tried to remain cool and in command, but the sight of her soft, curvy body—encased in sexy satin underwear—was unbearably exciting.

Hell, how *was* he going to control himself in the face of such temptation?

His hands were unsteady as he reached to unhook the front bra clip, hesitating for a moment before exposing her breasts to his increasingly lustful gaze.

They were as perfect as he'd known they'd be. Full and lush, with dusky-tipped aureoles and large, hard nipples seemingly begging to be sucked.

But he knew that would have to wait. If he started sucking her nipples now, he would become hopelessly lost in his own desires. Hers were the ones he wanted to satisfy this first time. His male ego demanded it. And something else, some part of him which he couldn't quite grasp yet.

'I have to sit you up for a sec,' he said, and did so with a gentle tug of her hands. The action had her breasts falling deliciously forward, twin orbs of erotic promise that he steadfastly ignored as he eased the bra off her body.

'You can lie back down,' he suggested as he moved over to put the bra on the chair with the dress and stockings.

She did, her face now flushed, her eyes still wide.

The decision to leave her with her G-string on was more for his composure than her comfort.

Her eyelashes flickered wildly when his hands went to the buttons of his shirt. Her lips fell further apart.

He undressed slowly, seemingly casual and confident in his actions, but inside he was going through hell. Never had a woman watched him so intently as he removed his clothes. There again, never had he done such a deliberate strip for a woman.

Jake knew he had a good body. Mostly God-given, but also because he looked after himself, having always worked out regularly. There was a gym and a swimming pool in the apartment complex which allowed him to keep fit nowadays with the minimum of effort. So he had no reason to be embarrassed once he was in the buff.

He had to confess that he could not recall being this turned on before. Yet he hadn't even kissed her.

Drawing on protection at that point was premature on Jake's usual standards, but it seemed a good idea to be prepared. Jake had an awful feeling that once he started any form of foreplay with Angelina, he would enter the danger zone. It proved strangely awkward, with her watching him with those almost awestruck eyes of hers.

He was relieved to join her on the bed, stretching out beside her and propping himself on one elbow so that he had one hand free. His right hand.

'Wait,' she whispered, and before he could stop her she wriggled out of her panties and tossed them away, her face flushed by the time she glanced back up at him.

He didn't dare look down there. Or to think about how much he wanted to slide over between her legs and just do it. Now. *Without* preliminaries. He ached to be inside her, to feel her hot wet flesh tight around him.

At least he could touch her there. And his free hand stroked down the centre of her body and slid between her legs.

Her moan echoed his own feelings. Already she was panting, her legs growing restless, her hips writhing as a woman's did when release was near. The selfish part of Jake wanted to stop so that he could be inside her. But experience warned him that things didn't always work out that way for a woman. Better he give her a climax this way first.

'Jake,' she cried out, her eyes dilated and desperate.

His mouth crashed down onto hers, smothering her cries as she came apart under his hand. He kissed her with a desperation of his own, his tongue echoing what he would rather be doing to her with his body. Its job done, his hand moved to play with her breasts, his still wet fingertips encircling her taut nipples. Jake kept kissing her, and playing with her nipples, elated when in no time her back began to arch away from the bed in that tell-tale way. Moaning, she clung to him, her left leg lifting up onto his hip, inviting him in.

Jake needed no further invitation, groaning as his flesh slid home to the hilt. The sensations as he pumped into her were a mixture of agony and ecstasy, for he could not possibly last very long. Yet he wanted to, wanted to feel her come again with him inside her.

Her muffled moans were encouraging, as were the movements of her body. She followed his rhythm, her hips rising with his forward surge and sinking back when he withdrew. He stopping kissing her and cupped her face instead, looking deep into her glazed eyes.

He didn't say a word, just concentrated on her, slowing his rhythm appreciably but going deeper with each stroke.

She gasped, then groaned.

'Good?' he asked.

She nodded, then grimaced.

He was in his stride now, no longer balancing on that dangerous edge, determined to make her come again. She drew in more sharply with each successive stroke, her mouth falling even wider apart. Her hands tightened around his back, her nails digging into his flesh.

He felt no pain, only pleasure. The pleasure of pleasing her.

Her climax was imminent. He could feel it, deep inside. The tightening. The quivering. The rush of heat that always preceded the first spasm.

'Jake. Oh, Jake,' she cried out, and then she was there. But so, astonishingly, was he. Instantly. Brilliantly.

Poets often spoke of stars exploding when two people in love made love. Jake always thought that was just so much crap.

But this time, it *was* not unlike stars exploding. His body trembled and his head did cartwheels. His mouth found hers again and he knew that this was where he wanted to be for the rest of his life. With her. No one else. Just Angelina. And he didn't mean living together, either. He wanted her as his life partner. His wife.

Angelina Winters. Till death them did part.

It didn't occur to Jake till much later, when he was lying quietly with her sleeping form in his arms, that Angelina might not be altogether cooperative in his achieving that goal.

'I might not want what you want, Jake,' she'd said to him earlier that day.

Jake thought about all she'd told him about herself so far. Her insistence that she was independent-minded career woman. Her claim to not want marriage and children.

And then he thought of her eyes today as he'd carried her into this bedroom.

Bulldust, he decided. All of that other stuff. Dorothy was right. Angelina had marriage and motherhood written all over her. She'd been burnt, that was all, by the wrong kind of man. Some sleazebag, probably. All it needed was the right kind of guy to come along, someone who really loved her.

'*Me!*' he pronounced out loud.

Jake still wasn't sure about becoming a father, but heck, he hadn't thought till now that he'd ever fall in love, or want to get married himself. But he did. And when Jake wanted something, he made it happen.

Angelina Mastroianni was going to be his wife, no matter what she thought she wanted. Because Jake knew what she really wanted. He'd seen it just now. And felt it. What he needed to do was make her feel it again. And again. And again. He had one weekend to cement his position in her life, and in her heart. Given that was a pretty short time span, Jake decided that the best way he could achieve that was through her body; her warm, luscious, possibly neglected body.

That pathetic boyfriend of hers hadn't been doing the right thing by Angelina. Jake was sure of it. Which was fine by him. It gave him an advantage.

Just thinking about making love to her again turned him on. Retrieving a condom from where he'd shoved a few under the pillows, he slipped it on, amazed but pleased to see that he was as hard as he'd been earlier, confirming his belief that this was a once-in-a-lifetime relationship.

Scooping her naked body back against him in the spoon position, he gently stroked her breasts till she stirred in his arms, then his hand slid slowly further down her body.

'Oh,' she gasped when his fingers started softly teasing the centre of her pleasure.

But there was nothing soft, or gentle, in Jake's mind. It was full of hard resolve, as hard as his desire-filled flesh.

As soon as she moaned, and began wriggling her bottom against him, he eased himself inside her from behind.

Angelina stiffened for a second, only to melt as soon as he started rocking back and forth inside her. She would never have conceived of making love like this, on their sides, with him pressed up against her back and his hands on her front, playing with her.

It was nothing like last time; that tender and romantic position where Jake had kissed her all the while and held her like a true lover. This was entirely different. This felt…decadent. Yet oh, so exciting.

Her head whirled as a wanton wildness overtook her.

'Harder, Jake,' she bit out in a voice she didn't recognise. 'Harder.'

He groaned, then increased his tempo.

'Yes,' she groaned, her body immediately rushing towards the abyss. 'Oh, yes. Yeesss!'

CHAPTER TEN

ANGELINA knew she was in trouble the next morning. Deep, deep trouble.

It was not long after sunrise, Jake was still fast asleep in the bedroom and she was curled up on the red leather sofa, her naked body wrapped in Jake's bathrobe, her hands cradling a not-too-hot mug of coffee, her eyes taking in the sun-drenched terrace, and the bridge beyond. The traffic on it was only light at this early hour, she noted.

But not for long. The day promised to be as bright and warm as yesterday.

Yesterday...

She took the mug away from her lips and sighed. Dear heaven, what had she done?

A small, dry laugh escaped her lips. What *hadn't* she done? more like it. Her behaviour in bed was bad enough, but it hadn't been confined to Jake's bed, had it? She'd been bad in the spa bath as well, and in the kitchen whilst he'd been microwaving them a meal. And here in this very room, on the rug, in front of the television.

It was as though Jake's making love to her that second time had released something in her, and suddenly she was hungry for it all. Every experience possible with Jake.

He hadn't minded, of course. Though she'd had the impression he was a bit surprised at one stage. Not with what she did. Perhaps he was just surprised that *she* would what she did, and with such avidness.

But as much as Angelina was worried sick by where this would all end, she could find no real regrets in her heart for the actual events of last night. How could you regret something that made you feel the way she felt this morning? Like a real woman for a change. A desired and desirable woman who had been made love to very, very well.

At least now she knew what Wilomena meant by having fun. It *had* been fun. At least, it had been with Jake. The man was the very devil with women all right. If she'd shocked him once, he'd shocked her a dozen times. Thrillingly, though.

The memories made her quiver with remembered pleasure.

'What are you doing up this early?'

Angelina almost spilt her coffee again, her whole body jumping at Jake's sudden appearance behind her.

As she glanced up over the back of the sofa at him, he bent to kiss her, one of his hands sliding down the front opening of the robe at the same time.

Angelina didn't know how she *didn't* spill the coffee this time.

'Mmm,' he murmured by the time he'd straightened. 'I know what I'm going to have for breakfast. Fancy a shower together?'

'Not till I've finished my coffee,' she replied with

creditable control, considering. Angelina had already decided that, whilst yesterday had been marvellous, today was another day entirely. Today, she had to start getting some control back over herself.

Watching Jake walk over to the nearby open-plan kitchen didn't exactly help that resolve, given that he was stark naked. She told herself not to look, but look she did. By the time he'd made his coffee and returned to sprawl in an adjacent chair, sipping his coffee with apparent nonchalance, her control was definitely at risk.

Gulping down the rest of her coffee, she uncurled her legs and made some excuse about seeing to her clothes, which Jake had actually popped into the washer and dryer at some stage last night. She was just hanging her fortunately crush-free dress on a coat hanger in the beautifully appointed laundry when Jake's arms went round her waist from behind.

'Methinks the lady is suffering morning-after syndrome,' he whispered as he started unsashing her robe.

'Not at all,' she lied coolly. 'I'm just a bit concerned about today, that's all. I really need to go over to the hotel this morning, change into some casual clothes and check out. Then I have to drop in at the expo and see how we're doing.' She really couldn't go home without knowing if this venture had been a success. Arnold would ask, and so would Alex.

'When's check-out time?' Jake asked, those busy hands of his not missing a beat as they drew erotic circles around her stiffening nipples.

Angelina swallowed. She really couldn't allow him to seduce her again so easily. But of course that was his talent, wasn't it? Seduction. And sex. Tender sex. Rough sex. Imaginative sex. Whatever was required. But still just sex. She had to remember she wasn't anything so special. Just more of a challenge than his usual chicky babe.

Or she *had* been.

'Ten-thirty,' she told him, swallowing again. Why didn't he stop that? On the other hand, why didn't *she* stop him? She was just so weak where he was concerned.

Was it love making her weak? Or could she take some comfort in hoping this was just sex for her as well? In a way, this made some sense. She'd lived a celibate life for so long that surely it was only natural that she'd go mad for sex, now that she'd discovered it. Maybe she wasn't madly in love with *him*, after all.

'We have plenty of time yet,' Jake said throatily, cupping her breasts and pulling her back hard against him.

She could feel his hardness through his bathrobe.

'I'll drive you over to the hotel around ten,' he murmured as he pulled the robe further open and nuzzled at her neck. 'And take you personally to the expo. Then we can go have lunch and do some shopping.'

'Shopping?' she echoed somewhat blankly, having reached that point when intelligent thought was nigh-on impossible.

'Didn't you say you wanted to go shopping?'

'Did I?' The robe slipped off one shoulder, then the other, before dropping to the floor. Suddenly, she felt more naked than she ever had been with him. And more vulnerable.

He was smiling when he turned her round in his arms.

'I dare say you've changed your mind, like a typical woman. But I have a fancy to buy you something really sexy to wear. Something…naughty.''

She stared up into his eyes, which were gleaming hotly down at her.

'You're still a very bad boy, aren't you, Jake?' she choked out.

'I haven't noticed you objecting,' he replied with a devilishly charming grin. 'Now, come have that shower with me, gorgeous.'

She went.

'Sydney really is a beautiful city,' Angelina said as they walked, hand in hand, through Hyde Park.

Jake glanced across at her, thinking how beautiful *she* looked today. Beautiful *and* sexy. Those jeans hugged her curvy body like a second skin. Too bad about that loose white shirt she was wearing over them. Though perhaps it was as well she wasn't wearing anything too revealing on top. Jake's possessiveness of her had increased overnight, along with his desire. He only had to touch her and he wanted to make love to her again.

Jake thought of what was in the plastic shopping

bag he was holding. The sexiest black corset he'd ever seen. Angelina had refused to try it on in the shop, but he knew there would be no such objections once he got her home.

'Sydney always looks great in the summer,' he agreed, very pleased with the way things were going.

'I guess the good weather is one of the reasons the expo has gone so well,' she remarked.

'Perhaps. But it always pays to have a good product. Your wines are going to be a big hit down here in Sydney, by the sound of things. Wayne was over the moon with the orders they'd already taken and the interest shown.'

'Men like Wayne are exaggerators,' Angelina said drily. 'But it does look promising.'

Jake had to admire the way Angelina's feet were firmly on the ground when it came to her business. She was no pushover, in lots of ways.

Sexually, however, she was putty in his hands. Jake couldn't wait to get her alone again.

'I work not far from here,' he pointed out. 'My office is in that tall bluish building over there. If the sun's out, I come over to the park and eat my lunch here. Right here, in fact.' And he pulled her down onto a seat under a huge tree that provided almost an acre of shade.

His arm wound round her shoulders and his lips pressed into her hair. 'Want to make out?' he whispered.

'Jake Winters, behave yourself. I don't think we

need to make out in public, do you? We've been at it like rabbits. A breather is definitely called for.'

'Not rabbits,' he said. '*Lovers.* Once is never enough for lovers.'

'Once! How about one times twenty? I didn't know it was possible to have so much sex in one weekend.'

'Amazing, isn't it?'

Angelina glanced up into Jake's grinning face and took a mental photo of it for her memory bank. He looked so handsome today. And so happy.

She doubted he'd look quite so happy once he found out about Alex.

'What?' he said, his grin fading.

It constantly surprised Angelina, the way he seemed to pick up on her inner feelings, without her having to say a word. It was almost as though he could read her mind sometimes. He certainly knew whenever she wanted him again.

Unfortunately, this was almost continuously. She simply could not get enough of him. Even now, she wanted him to take her home. She wanted him to strip her off and lace her into that decadent-looking corset and do whatever it was he had in mind to do to her whilst she was wearing it.

Hopefully, he couldn't read her thoughts. She seriously needed this breather so she could think.

'What is it?' he repeated. 'Tell me true.'

'Nothing much. I was thinking how handsome you were. And how much I like you with short hair.'

'And I like you with long.'

She flushed as she thought of what he had done with her hair on one occasion last night. He really was a wicked man.

No, not truly wicked, Angelina conceded. But seriously naughty. A very good lover, though. Very knowledgeable about women's bodies, and totally uninhibited when it came to using that knowledge. How on earth was she going to find the strength to tell Jake about Alex, when it meant she would have to give up his lovemaking?

Because it was all going to end once the truth came out. If there was one thing the last twenty-four hours had proved to Angelina, it was that Jake only had one need for a woman, and that was as his sexual partner. His plaything. Even his calling her his lover just now was telling. Why not girlfriend? Lover had that for-sex-only connotation about it.

No, Jake hadn't changed in that regard. His aim had been to sleep with her. And now that he had, any complications would have him running a mile.

And Alex, let's face it, she thought, was one big complication.

'What a shame today has to end,' she said with a sigh.

'Does it have to?'

'Time marches on. Nothing can change that.'

'You could always stay the night with me, go home tomorrow.'

She was seriously tempted. If she'd been in bed

with him at this moment, with his hands on her naked body, she probably would have said yes.

'Sorry,' she said crisply. 'No can do. I have to get back home tonight. Work tomorrow.'

'Yeah. Same here. I'm due in court first thing in the morning.'

'On that case you told me about?' Angelina asked, grateful for the opportunity to get her mind off sex. 'The lady who's dying of lung cancer?'

'That's the one. I have to deliver my closing address.'

'Are you ready?'

'I should hope so. I've been living and breathing that case for months.'

'Do you memorise your speeches?'

'Not really. I do write my ideas down. But I never try to remember them word for word. That's the sure way to go blank and stuff it up. No, I prepare well and then I talk from the heart. You do make the occasional stumble over words that way, but the jury never minds that, if they know you're being sincere.'

'I hope you win,' she said with feeling.

'Don't worry,' Jake returned with a little squeeze of her shoulders. 'We will.'

Angelina abruptly jumped to her feet. 'Come on, let's walk some more. I want to go see St Mary's Cathedral.' And she yanked a groaning Jake to his feet.

'More walking? Can't we just sit here and cuddle?'

'You've had more than enough cuddling for one weekend. *Up!*'

'Wow. I like it when you're bossy. Would you like to be on top when we get back to my place?'

'Get that bag and come on!' She was already off, walking in the direction of the cathedral, not giving him the opportunity to take her hand again.

'Oh, look!' she exclaimed when they emerged from the park directly across from the main cathedral steps. 'There's a wedding car just arriving. Let's go over and watch, Jake. I love watching weddings.' Anything but going back to his place yet.

'Why?'

'Because!'

'That's no reason from a girl who says she doesn't want to get married.'

'I don't want to be an astronaut, either,' she argued, 'but I like watching their exploits.'

'I suppose you could compare marriage to flying into space.'

'It's certainly a risky venture.'

'But risk can be exciting.'

Angelina arched her eyebrows. 'This, from a man who said *he* never wanted to get married?'

'Maybe I've changed my mind.'

Jake saw the shock reverberate in her eyes. 'You… you don't mean that,' she said stiffly.

Jake immediately regretted his possibly ill-judged words. If he rushed her, he might lose what he wanted most. After all, this was just their first week-end together. Best stick to sex for now.

'Never say never about anything,' he remarked nonchalantly. 'That's my motto.'

'For the record, I never actually said I would *never* get married. I just said it wasn't a priority of mine.'

Jake felt heartened by the carefulness in her wording.

'That's good,' he said with a smile. 'I like a girl who keeps her options open.''

Her hitting him playfully on the arm broke the tension he'd foolishly created.

'I'm just a sex object to you, aren't I?' she accused.

'Absolutely. So, do you want to go look at this wedding, or do you want to go home? Don't forget, we've only got four hours before I drive you home. We'll have to set off by eight if I want to be back in Sydney by midnight. I'm a Cinderella kind of guy when I have to be in court in the morning.'

'Decisions. Decisions.'

'Yeah, life's a bitch, isn't it? So what do you reckon? Which is it to be?'

Angelina knew he thought she'd opt to go home. And she wanted to. She wanted to so much it was criminal.

All the more reason not to.

'I think it would do you good to see that there is more to a relationship than just sex. That couple in there are about to promise to love and cherish each other till death them do part.'

'Until divorce them do part, don't you mean?'

'You're a cynic, do you know that?'

'Takes one to know one.'

'Point taken. But I still want to see the wedding,' she said firmly, and walked over to press the button that would change the traffic lights. 'Despite the fact that the bride has already gone inside.'

'Fine by me. I not only like to watch sometimes, but also to wait. Waiting whets the appetite further.'

'You have a one-track mind.'

'Where you're concerned, I have.'

'You'd better behave yourself in this church.'

'I'll be an angel.'

'Don't be facetious.'

The lights changed and Angelina launched herself across the road, Jake hot on her heels. She could hear the organ blaring out the *Wedding March* even from that distance.

'No wandering hands during the ceremony,' she warned him as they skipped up the steps.

'Definitely not. I know you. You won't be able to control yourself.''

'I will!' she countered, but blushingly.

'No? Pity. Well, let's hope this isn't one of those long ceremonies. I'm not sure I'll be able to sit on a hard pew for more than twenty minutes, max.''

She laughed, not a good idea since they'd just entered the vaulted interior of the cathedral, right at the moment when the organ stopped. Her laughter echoed up into the cavernous and unfortunately silent ceiling. Several heads whipped round to glare.

'Sorry,' Jake apologised to them. 'I can't take her anywhere.'

'Stop it,' Angelina hissed. 'Just shut up and watch.'

He shut up. But not for long.

'Hard to see much from this far back. Want to get closer?'

'No! I can't trust you to behave.'

'True. I've always been a bad boy in churches. Can't stand all the hush-hush nonsense. Makes me want to break out.'

'If you embarrass me,' she whispered, 'I won't go to your place with you afterwards at all. I'll make you drive me straight home to the Hunter Valley.'

'Don't think so,' he returned just as softly. 'You left that pretty handbag behind, remember? We'll have to go collect it. Although, perhaps not. You could always collect it next weekend.'

Angelique frowned. She'd been trying not to think about tomorrow, let alone next weekend. 'I...I have to have lunch with Alex next weekend.'

'You don't *have* to do anything of the kind. Call him. Tell him it's over by phone.'

'No.'

'I knew you'd say that,' he muttered. 'OK, go to lunch with him if you have to. But that's just on the Saturday during the day. As soon as you're finished with him...*permanently* this time...I will expect you at my place. Shall we say four? Five?'

'Make it six.' The swimming carnival wouldn't finish till five.

'That's one hell of a long lunch. I sure hope it's

going to be somewhere public. All right, all right, so I'm acting like a jealous fool. Six, it is. I'll book us a table for dinner at eight. You can stay over till Sunday night, can't you?'

Angelina swallowed. She really shouldn't let this fiasco continue. It wasn't right. She should tell him the truth.

But she just couldn't.

'All right,' she said with a sigh. 'Now hush up.'

He hushed up, but a small boy several rows up from them didn't. He started whinging and whining about wanting to go outside. Several warnings from both his parents to be quiet and to sit still had no effect. Finally, the father lost his patience, swooped the child up in his arms and headed with swift strides back down the aisle, past Angelina and Jake.

Angelina smiled a wry smile. She remembered full well the trials and tribulations of taking a small boy to church.

Jake's suddenly leaping to his feet startled her. 'Be back in a minute,' he said. 'Got to check on something.' And he was off, bolting down the aisle after the man and child.

Angelina jumped up as well, and hurried after the three of them, catching up with Jake on the cathedral steps. He was standing there, staring, an odd confusion in his eyes.

Her hand on his tensely held arm was gentle. 'You see?' she said quietly as her gaze followed Jake's to where the father was happily lighting up a cigarette whilst he watched his son enjoying himself immensely jumping up and down the steps. 'No need to worry.'

'I thought...'

'Yes, I know what you thought,' she said softly.

She actually felt the shudder run all through Jake.

'Can we get away from here?' he said, glancing around at all the onlookers who were gathering to see the bride emerge.

'All right.' She tucked her arm through his and they just walked in silence for a while, finding their way across the road and back into the park at the next intersection.

'Is that what your father did to you, Jake?' she asked gently at last. 'Hit you?'

'No, not my father. I never knew my father. He did a flit before I was born. It was my mother who did the honours. Man, she had a punch on her, that woman. Not a day went by that she didn't lay into me for some reason. Just about anything would set her off, especially when she'd been drinking. Sometimes it was just the way I looked at her. I can still remember how scared I was to go home after school, right from the time I was in kindergarten. Although weekends were the worst. No school to escape to those days.'

Angelina was both horrified and saddened by his story. What kind of a mother would do that to her son? 'But didn't the teachers notice?' she asked. 'I mean...there must have been bruises.'

He shrugged. 'I'm a boy. Boys get bruises all the time. If they did notice, they just looked the other way. Teachers weren't always as conscientious in reporting such matters back then as they are now.'

'But what about you grandparents? Your aunts and uncles? Neighbours? Wasn't there anyone who cared?'

'Not that I knew of. Mum was estranged from her family. And the neighbours we had were just as bad. It was not a salubrious street.'

'So what happened in the end? Did you run away?'

'I put up with it as long as I could. By the time I was in high school, I didn't go home much so I didn't get hit as often. I spent more and more time on the streets after school. Got into a gang. God knows how I didn't get arrested for shoplifting. I thought I was smart but I was just lucky. Anyway, one day when I was around fifteen, I came home late and Mum started swinging at me with this frying pan. Great heavy thing it was. Collected me a beauty. I'm not sure what happened next but it was Mum who ended up on the floor. Made me feel sick afterwards, I can tell you. But then…aggression breeds aggression. That was when I walked out and never went back.'

'But where did you live?'

'On the streets, of course.'

'But…'

'Look, I survived, OK, thanks to Edward and Dorothy. Let's not get into this. It's all dead and gone, even the lady herself. I looked her up last year when Edward died and found out she'd passed away

years ago. Hepatitis. I didn't grieve, but I needed to
know what had happened to her. Closure, I guess.'

Closure? The man who'd started shaking at the
sight of a father showing even a small amount of
impatience with his son was a long way from closure.
Angelina was so glad that she had never used cor-
poral punishment on her son. She'd never allowed
her father to hit Alex either, no matter what.

Poor Jake. All of a sudden, she wanted to hold
him and love him, to make up to him for everything
he'd suffered as a child.

'Let's go home, Jake,' she suggested softly.

He stopped walking to throw her a speculative
glance. 'Home, as in your home or my home?'

'Your home.'

'Now you're talking.'

But she didn't do much talking on the way home.
She kept thinking of everything Jake had suffered as
a child.

It explained why he didn't want to have children
himself. Clearly, he was afraid he'd be a bad father,
that the cycle of physical abuse would continue.
Angelina didn't believe that it would for a moment.
Not with Jake.

Still, it was what Jake thought that counted.

It was going to come as a terrible shock when she
told him about Alex. Perhaps it was as well,
Angelina realised, that their son was a teenager and
not a baby.

'You've gone rather quiet,' Jake said as he unlocked his front door and ushered her inside. 'Is something wrong?'

'Wrong? No, no, nothing wrong.'

'It's Alex, isn't it? You're worried about him.'

'Alex will be fine,' she said. And he would be, too. He was going to be thrilled to have a father like Jake. It was Jake's reaction that worried her.

'So what is it?'

'I'm worried that I might be getting addicted to this.'

'To what?'

'To being with you.'

He dropped the shopping bag, kicked the door shut behind them and drew her into his arms once more. 'There are worse addictions, you know,' he murmured as he bent his mouth to hers.

Angelina wasn't so sure. Already it was responsible for her changing her mind about telling Jake the truth. And possibly for longer than a couple of weekends.

'This is one addiction which I would happily subscribe to,' Jake muttered against her lips. 'Come on, gorgeous,' he said, taking her hand and scooping up the shopping bag at the same time. 'Your breather is up.'

CHAPTER ELEVEN

'THURSDAY,' Angelina muttered to herself as she set about making her bed.

Four days since she'd seen Jake. Four long, boring, lonely days. And two more till she saw him again.

Coming round to the other side of her double bed, she picked up the pillow on that side and held it against her cheek. This was where Jake had laid his head the other night.

Could she still smell the scent of him on it?

Angelina imagined she could.

It had been quite late by the time Jake had driven her home last Sunday. She hadn't thought he would want to come in with her; hadn't anticipated it. But he'd insisted on walking her to the door, then claimed he needed to come inside to use the bathroom before driving back.

Her panic had been instant, and intense. For how could she let him come in? The place was full of Alex memorabilia. Photos everywhere. Trophies in his bedroom. Stuff on the fridge.

She'd finally managed to stall Jake at the door, saying that the place was a mess and she'd die of embarrassment if he saw it like that.

'Just give me one minute,' she'd begged. 'Please, Jake.'

He'd seemed amused. 'Don't tell me you're not perfect,' he'd said.

'Hardly,' she'd replied. 'Who is?'

Her dash around the rooms had been like something out of a farce. She'd scooped all the photos on top of the sideboard into the top drawer. The same with the ones on her bedside chests. She almost missed the reminder for Alex's swimming carnival on the fridge door, shoving it on top, along with the magnet photo of him as a baby. Alex's bedroom was a lost cause so she just closed that door, then flung open the bathroom door so that Jake wouldn't walk into his son's room by mistake.

He hadn't. But neither had he left after his trip to the bathroom, as she'd expected him to. He'd kissed her again, and soon she was ripping at his shirt and pulling him into her bedroom—the two-hour drive enclosed in that sexy car with Jake had done dreadful things to her resolve to be good—and the last thing Angelina remembered was falling asleep in his arms.

When she'd woken in the morning he was gone.

Mid-morning that Monday, a huge arrangement of red roses had arrived, with a card attached saying, 'Next weekend can't come quickly enough. Jake.'

The flowers were still alive and utterly gorgeous, sitting on the sideboard in place of the still absent photos. She didn't dare put any of them back up yet. In fact, since last Sunday, she'd locked Alex's bedroom door, and hidden anything else that might give the game away if Jake ever showed up here again. After his phone call last night, Angelina wouldn't be at all surprised at his driving up tonight. He'd been so excited after winning that case.

And missing her terribly, he'd said.

Angelina sighed. He wasn't the only one.

Jake sat down on his favourite seat in Hyde Park, placed the banana smoothie on the grass at his feet, then proceeded to unwrap his king-sized roll. This was the first time he'd had the opportunity to eat lunch in the park this week. Not because of the weather. Sydney had continued to be dry and warm. Circumstance had been the guilty party.

Monday, he'd been too wrecked to eat lunch. He'd had to call on every reserve of strength he had to deliver his closing address in court that morning, the weekend finally catching up with him. After the jury had retired to consider their verdict, he'd gone home and just collapsed into bed. Tuesday, he'd been far too agitated to eat. The jury had still been out. Wednesday, he'd been much too elated. At eleven that morning, the jury had found for the plaintiff to the tune of fourteen million dollars.

Now it was Thursday and the bedlam of the last couple of days was hopefully behind him. If another television station showed at his office, wanting another damned interview, he was going to go bush, preferably to the Hunter Valley.

Jake loved being a litigator. Loved having victories over the bad guys. Attention from the media, however, was not one of his loves. He hated having cameras and microphones shoved in his face. Of course, the law firm he worked for didn't mind one bit. But that kind of publicity was not Jake's bag, even if it did result in his being offered a partnership.

Strangely, Jake wasn't sure if he wanted to become a partner in Keats, Marsden and Johnson. Neither did he fancy being pushed into taking on the inevitable rush of perhaps not-so-worthy clients who thought they could make a mint out of suing their bosses over supposedly adverse working conditions. He'd only won this case because his client had a genuine complaint. Copycat cases rarely had the same integrity, or sympathy.

Jake munched into his salmon and salad roll—man, it tasted good—and wondered if now was the right time for him to make a move, start up a practice of his own. He'd be free then to take on only the clients he really wanted to represent. He wouldn't be influenced by money, which a big law firm invariably was. Of course, this would mean forgoing his six-figure salary plus bonuses, not to mention his generous expense account. It would also mean a lot of work. Starting up your own business involved a lot of red tape.

On the plus side, he would be his own boss. And the temporary loss of salary wouldn't be any great hardship. He still had a small fortune in cash left over from Edward's legacy.

Maybe he'd run the idea by Angelina tonight. She

was a businesswoman. She would know what was involved. See what she thought.

Aah, Angelina…

Already, he was looking forward to talking to her tonight. Their nightly chat was the highlight of his day, something to look forward to after work. He would ring her a lot more than that, but Angelina had forbidden him to call during the day, claiming she'd never get anything done if he did that.

Possibly true. Once they were on the phone together, they sometimes talked for hours.

Of course, he *had* broken the rules and called her as soon as the verdict came in on the Wednesday. But that was a special occasion and he hadn't kept her on the line for long.

The salad and salmon roll duly disposed of, Jake picked up his banana smoothie and started to sip.

How soon, he wondered, could he tell her he loved her and wanted to marry her?

Not too soon, Jake suspected.

A couple of times last weekend, she'd fallen silent on him. Suspiciously silent. You could almost hear the wheels turning away in her brain. Yet she'd been unforthcoming when he'd asked her what was wrong.

In a way, she was secretive. She rarely opened up to him about herself in any depth. And she never talked about her feelings for him.

In the past, he hadn't been able to stop women telling him their feelings, especially how much they loved him. Angelina never went near the subject of love. She said flattering things about his lovemaking but that wasn't the same.

Already addicted to having sex with him, she'd said last Sunday.

Jake frowned. He didn't like the idea that she might be only coming back to see him this weekend for more of the same. There was no doubting she liked sex. After his initially thinking she was pretty inexperienced in bed, she'd turned into a veritable tiger.

Once his mind took that tack, the worry started up that she hadn't been totally truthful over what she was up to this coming Saturday. To put aside a whole day to tell any man she was breaking up with him seemed excessively kind.

Maybe she's not going to break up with him at all, a dark voice whispered in his head. Maybe she's going to spend the whole day at Alex's place, in Alex's bed. And then come on to *his* bed for the rest of the weekend.

The idea revolted him. But it was possible, wasn't it? She had a very high sex drive. But was she capable of that level of deception?

He wouldn't have thought so. Still, his buying that huge diamond engagement ring yesterday afternoon now struck him as being ridiculously premature. Amazing the things a man in love would do! Fools did rush in, as the saying went.

The buzzing on Jake's cellphone had him sitting up abruptly, his banana smoothie slurping back and forth in its cardboard carton. Setting the drink down, he fished his phone out of his trouser pocket, clicked it on and swept it up to his ear.

'Yes?'

'Sally here, Jake. Sorry to bother you, but if you've finished your lunch perhaps you should get back here. You have a visitor.'

'A visitor. What kind of visitor?'

'A young man. Name of Alex.'

Alex! Jake didn't have any colleagues or acquaintances named Alex, so presumably this had to be *the* Alex.

Jake frowned over Sally calling him young. Of course, Sally thought anyone under forty was young, but it sounded as though Angelina's Alex was what was commonly called a 'younger' man.

Jake tried to ignore the instant stab of jealousy and focus on what the fool was doing, showing up at *his* office.

All he could think of was that Angelina had changed her mind and broken up with Alex over the phone, plus told him the identity of the guy she'd thrown him over for.

Jake groaned. As much as he was happy to find that his paranoid thoughts about Angelina two-timing him were just that…paranoid, the last thing he wanted was a confrontation with a furious ex boyfriend.

'I gather you know who I'm talking about,' Sally said.

'Possibly. Does my visitor have a second name?'

'Mastroianni,' Sally supplied.

'*Mastroianni!*' he repeated, totally taken aback.

And then the penny dropped. Alex was some kind of relative. Angelina had said he was half-Italian. Maybe that was what she'd meant about her relationship with him being complicated. If he was a cousin or something, she would have to explain things more fully. She couldn't just dump the guy without giving him a reason.

'I think you should get back here, Jake. This is something you have to attend to personally, by the look of things.'

'OK,' Jake said with a sigh. 'Tell him I'll be there shortly.'

The offices of Keats, Marsden and Johnson were spacious and classy, occupying half of the tenth floor of the building Jake had pointed out to Angelina the previous Sunday. Their main reception area was set directly opposite the lift well, behind a solid glass wall and two equally solid glass doors. Sally reigned over the reception desk and the waiting room, and had done so for many years. Although not unattractive for her age—she had turned fifty last month—Sally was the exception to the rule that highly visible Sydney receptionists should be curvy blondes with seductive smiles.

Jake, for one, enjoyed the wonderfully pragmatic and no-nonsense atmosphere Sally brought to the firm. Actually, Sally was one of the reasons he just might stay. He'd miss her if he left.

'Well?' he said as he strode in. 'Where is he and what am I in for?'

Sally glanced up, her no-nonsense grey eyes sweeping over him from top to toe in a critical survey, as though she were meeting him for the first time. Jake found himself automatically straightening his tie and wondering if his fly was undone.

'A shock, I would think,' she said drily. 'I put him in your office to wait for you.'

Jake ground to a halt beside her desk. 'What did you do that for? And what kind of a shock? Don't tell me he's a big bruiser.'

'He's not small,' she said, her grey eyes now gleaming rather mischievously. 'But then, neither are you.'

Jake wasn't sure if he was getting the subtle meaning behind this interchange.

'Looking for a fight, is he?'

'I wouldn't think so. More likely some answers to some questions.'

'Do you know something here that I don't know?'

Her finely plucked eyebrows lifted in feigned innocence. 'Know? No, I don't *know* anything. But I am a highly observant person, and a darned good guesser.'

'Sally, remind me to have you fired when I get to be partner.'

'Aah, so you've changed your mind about going out on your own, have you?'

He just stared at her. The woman had to be a witch in disguise. He had never discussed that idea with anyone in this firm.

'How did...? No, no, I am not going to ask.'

'Like I said,' she threw after him as he strode off down the corridor towards his office, 'I'm a darned good guesser.'

Jake hesitated at his door, irritating himself when he started checking his clothes again, as if he was going in for a bloody interview. Comforted that he looked his best in one of his newest business suits— the charcoal-grey mohair-blend—Jake still slicked his unslickably short hair back from his face before reaching for the knob.

'Sorry to keep you waiting,' he ground out as he opened the door and walked in.

The only other occupant of Jake's office immediately spun round from where he'd been standing at the corner window.

He was tall, though not as tall as Jake, or as solidly built. He was very good-looking, with strong facial features and an elegantly athletic frame. His long-lashed blue eyes reminded Jake of someone, but Jake couldn't remember who. His hair, which was dark and thick, was cut very short. Short was the fashion at the moment.

The only thing wrong with Jake's visitor was that he was dressed in a school uniform.

A shock, Sally had said.

She'd been right there.

This *couldn't* be the Alex Angelina had talked about. As sexy as Angelina was, he couldn't see her in the role of conscienceless cradle-snatcher. This boy could not be a day over seventeen. Eighteen, at a pinch.

Then who was he? Her ex-lover's younger brother? His son, maybe? Alex Mastroianni junior? If so, what was he doing here? And why was he staring at *him* as if he'd seen a bloody ghost or something?

Certainly, he wasn't in the mood for this!

'You wanted to see me?' he said abruptly, and continued round behind his desk, which sat adjacent to the window. 'Sit down,' he said with a gesture towards the two upright chairs that faced his desk. Then sat down himself.

The boy just stood there, staring.

Jake sighed.

'I gather your name is Alex Mastroianni,' he said. 'I'm Jake Winters.'

'Yes, I know,' the boy said, finding his voice at last. 'I saw you on the news last night. Twice. First on Channel Nine. Then later on Channel Two.'

'Aah yes, the news. We haven't met before, have we?' he asked, his mind teasing him again with that vague sense of recognition.

'No. Never,' the boy said.

'So what can I do for you, Mr Mastroianni?'

Jake decided to play this straight, as though the teenager before him was a potential client, and his name just a weird coincidence, which it very well might be. Life was sometimes stranger than fiction.

'Are you in need of a lawyer?'

The boy smiled. And again, reminded him of someone.

'Please call me Alex,' he said with a cool assurance that surprised Jake. Having found his tongue, he seemed to have found a degree of confidence as well.

'Very well. Alex. Please, do sit down. You're making me nervous, standing over there.'

The boy laughed. 'Not as nervous as I am.'

But he did sit down.

'You don't look nervous,' Jake said.

'Yeah, well, trust me, I am.'

'You don't have to be nervous with me. You can tell me anything. There is such a thing as client-lawyer privilege. I can't divulge anything you tell me. Like a priest.'

The boy just sat there a while longer, looking at him a bit like Sally had looked at him earlier, as though he was trying to see something in his face, or perhaps in his eyes. Was he wondering if he could be trusted?

Jake decided not to press. He didn't have any appointments for a while. He had the time to be patient, and, quite frankly, he was curious. Very curious.

'Do you remember a girl named Angelina Mastroianni?' the boy asked after a minute or two of tension-making silence. 'In case you've forgotten, you picked grapes at her father's vineyard in the Hunter Valley sixteen years ago.'

Jake snapped forward in his chair, his hands reaching for the nearest object. A Biro. He gripped it tightly and prayed this kid wasn't going to say something he didn't want to hear.

'I remember,' he returned tautly as his fingers

tightened. 'So what is Angelina to you? A cousin? An aunt?'

Stupid question, that last one, Jake. Angelina doesn't have any brothers or sisters so how could she be an aunt?

'No,' the boy denied. 'Nothing like that.'

Nothing like that. Then what?

'She's my mother.'

The Biro snapped. Clean in two.

'Your mother,' Jake repeated in a numb voice.

'Yes.'

'That's impossible! Angelina isn't old enough to be your mother!' He knew for a fact that sixteen years ago, she'd been a virgin. One and one did not make two here.

'I look old for my age. I'm only fifteen. I don't turn sixteen till the twenty-fourth of November this year.'

Jake's mind reeled. Only fifteen. And his birthday was in late November. He quickly counted backwards and landed on late February as the date of his conception. If Jake had been reeling before, he now went into serious shock.

It wasn't possible. He'd pulled out that night. Sort of. Well, maybe not in time. OK, so it *was* possible. But just as possible that Angelina had gone from him to some other guy. These things did happen once a girl had lost her virginity.

His gaze raked over the handsome boy sitting before him as he tried to work out all that Angelina had told him since they'd met up again. The lies.

No, not lies. But definitely verbal sleight of hand.

She'd deliberately kept Alex's true identity secret from him, and the question was why? It wasn't as though single mothers were uncommon these days. Even Italian ones.

'And your father?'

Even as he croaked out the question, Jake saw the truth staring back at him. Those eyes. They were *his*. So was the chin. And the hairline. Even the ears.

'Why, it's you, of course, Mr Winters,' the boy said with some bemusement in his voice, as though he was surprised Jake hadn't realised already. '*You're* my father.'

CHAPTER TWELVE

ANGELINA was behind the reception desk, booking in the Williams family, when Jake's yellow Ferrari shot down the driveway and braked to an abrupt halt under the covered archway on the other side of Mr Williams's sedate navy sedan.

Her heart began to thud.

So Jake had decided he couldn't wait till the week-end, either!

'Wow!' Mr Williams exclaimed. 'I've always wanted to cruise around Australia in a car like that.'

'In your dreams, darling,' his wife said. 'Where would we put the kids for starters?'

'With your mother, preferably,' he quipped back.

Jake, Angelina noted, did not get out of the car and come inside. Instead, after glancing over his shoulder at the reception area—which was clearly visible through the mainly glass front wall—he just sat, drumming his fingers on the steering wheel. Waiting, obviously, till she was alone.

A swirling sensation began to eddy in Angelina's stomach. But she didn't let her excitement show.

'Here are the keys to your suite,' she said with a smile as she handed them over. 'If you follow the driveway round the back, you can park right outside your main door. The pool is heated and open till ten.

The tennis court is available till the same time. Dinner starts at six in the restaurant. Did you see the restaurant as you drove in?'

'Sure did. Looks fabulous,' the wife gushed.

'Breakfast is in the same place from six-thirty till nine-thirty,' Angelina went on briskly. 'We don't cater for meals in the rooms here, I'm afraid. I've booked your free tour for tomorrow, starting at nine. Best to do it early in the summer before it gets too hot. Your guide will be waiting for you at five to nine at the cellar door, which is not far from the restaurant. Just follow the signs. I think that's all I have to tell you but please, feel free to ring and ask if you have any problems at all.'

'Oh, I'm sure we won't,' the wife beamed. 'This is all just so lovely.'

'Come on, kids,' the father said to his son and daughter, who looked about eight and ten respectively. 'Let's go and find our cossies. That pool sure looks good after our long drive. Thanks, miss.'

'Angelina,' she told him, pointing to her name tag.

'Angelina. Pretty name.'

'Pretty girl,' the wife said, but without a trace of spite, or jealousy. Angelina decided she liked her very much.

'OK, kids. Back into the car.'

Angelina had tried to keep her cool during the five minutes it had taken to go through her resort spiel. But all the time, she'd been watching Jake out of the corner of her eye.

No sooner had the navy sedan moved off than he

was out of the car and striding towards the reception room.

Angelina's gaze raked over him admiringly as he approached. It was the first time she had seen him in a suit, and my, he did look well in one. He looked well in any clothes, she conceded. And even better in nothing.

Angelina groaned and dropped her own eyes to the desk. She'd accused Jake of having a one-track mind last Sunday, but she was no better where he was concerned. One glimpse, and she was aching to rip his clothes off.

The small bell on the door tinkled as he pushed it open, Angelina pretending not to have noticed his arrival till that moment.

'Jake!' she said on looking up. 'Goodness, what are you doing here?'

He eyed her quite coldly.

'Cut the crap, Angelina. You saw me drive up. I know you did. I suggest you get someone else to take over here,' he commanded in a peremptory fashion. 'We need to talk.'

Angelina felt as if he'd punched her in the stomach. What was going on here? And who did he think he was, talking to her like that?

'I…I can't,' she replied, flustered by his rudeness. There *is* no one else. Not till five.' Barbara would take over at five for the night shift.

They both glanced at their watches. Five o'clock was fourteen minutes away.

'Is your place open?' he asked abruptly. 'I'll wait for you in there.'

Angelina hesitated to let him go into her home by himself. He might start looking around.

Though why would he…unless he'd found out something…?

The arrival of another car outside Reception forced her to make up her mind.

'Yes, it's open. Go on round and I'll be with you shortly. But what is this all about, Jake? You seem upset.'

'Upset,' he repeated, as though considering the word. 'No, I'm not upset. I'm bloody furious!' With that, he marched out, leaving Angelina to stare after him.

Has he found out about Alex? came the immediate question. But if so, how so? Had Arnold let something slip in his negotiations with Dorothy?

Angelina knew that the sale of Arnold's property was going ahead at a great rate. Money had been no object and Dorothy had had her lawyers rush through the searches. Contracts were being exchanged next week and she was going to move in a fortnight later.

Fortunately, Barbara arrived ten minutes early for work, Angelina relieved to let her take over so that she could bolt round and see what Jake wanted. Unfortunately, even in that short space of time, her nervous tension had reached dangerous proportions.

She hurried in to find Jake in her kitchen, making himself some coffee and looking as if he'd lost his case this week, instead of winning it.

'I'm here,' she said, unnecessarily, since she was standing in the same room, not ten feet from him.

His head turned and those icy blue eyes of his cut through her like knives.

'How long,' he ground out, 'did you intend to keep our son a secret from me?'

Angelina sagged against the kitchen sink. He knew.

'How...how did you find out?' she choked out, then slowly shook her head. 'Arnold, I suppose. He must have let it slip to Dorothy.' Alex was right. Arnold could be a bit of an old fool.

'Alex told me himself, in my office, just over four hours ago.'

Angelina gaped at him. This she had *not* expected. Oh, Alex...

'Naturally, when I was first told I had a visitor named Alex,' Jake ground out, 'I assumed he was your ex-lover. Imagine my surprise when I encountered a schoolboy. But I won't go into that, or even try to understand your sick reasons for letting me think such a thing. I am here because of the real person, the real Alex. Our son. Seems he saw me on TV last night and realised that I was the Jake Winters his mother had said was his father. No doubt because we look exactly like each other!'

Angelina groaned. So that was what had precipitated their son's actions. If only she'd thought of something like this happening. She herself had seen Jake on the news. What an idiot she was! But, of course, her mind had been on other things since last weekend. Her son had ceased to be her top priority for once.

Her remorse was acute.

But once she saw Jake's body language, the mother tiger in her came back with a vengeance. 'If you acted like this with him, Jake,' she bit out, her eyes narrowing, 'I won't ever forgive you.'

Jake's nostrils flared. 'Do you honestly think, after what *I* went through as a child, that I would do anything remotely hurtful to *my* son?'

Angelina was taken aback by the possessiveness in his voice. And the sheer emotional power.

This was not a man who was repulsed by the discovery that he was a father. Sure, he was shocked. And yes, he was angry. But only with her.

She smiled. She couldn't help it. 'He's wonderful, isn't he?'

'Bloody hell, Angelina, how can you smile at me after what you've done? Look, I understand why you didn't tell me about Alex when he was born, and during the years since. Aside from your father's natural hostility towards me, why would you? If I'd been in your boots I wouldn't have told me, either. But after we ran into each other again the way we did and you saw that I wasn't some kind of deadbeat, you should have told me then. Why, in God's name, didn't you? Especially when Alex was already pestering you to find me. Oh, yes, he told me all about that. Not one to hold back, is Alex. Unlike his mother,' Jake bit out.

Angelina remained guiltily silent.

'I asked you a question, Angelina. I expect an answer. Why didn't you tell me on that first Saturday? You had every opportunity, especially when I came back a second time.'

'I guess I was afraid to.'

'Afraid! Afraid of what?'

'Of your not wanting Alex!' she burst forth. 'You said you didn't ever want children.'

'Alex is a *fait accompli*,' he muttered. 'That's a different matter entirely.'

Angelina winced. He was right. She should have told him. 'You…you didn't tell him about us, did you?' she asked plaintively.

'What do you take me for, a complete fool? No, of course I didn't tell him about us. You have nothing to worry about. I made all the right noises. Did a better imitation of a father thrilled to discover he had a fifteen-year-old son than you'd see in a Hollywood movie. I also told him that I would come up and see you personally and smooth things over. He was worried sick how you would react when you found out he'd looked me up, since you had a deal to wait till Easter. Though might I add he seemed chuffed to find out I wasn't the jailbird you'd told him I was sure to be. He said he told you I wouldn't be, but you didn't seem to have the same blind faith in my character.'

She flushed, but lifted her chin defiantly. 'You have to appreciate it was a one-in-a-million chance that you'd turn out to be any good.'

'I'm not blaming you for that judgement call. You

did exactly what I would have done in your position. I suppose I could even forgive you for not telling me about Alex straight away. What I find *un*forgivable is that you didn't tell me the truth by the end of last weekend. What could you possibly have been afraid of by then?'

'Well, I…I…' How could she tell him that she was afraid he'd stop wanting to make love to her? It sounded so…selfish.

His sudden paling had her panicking.

He's guessed the truth. And he's totally appalled.

'It was that incident with the kid, wasn't it?' he said, startling her. 'And my telling you about my childhood. That's why you went all quiet on me. You were worried I might hit Alex like my mother hit me.'

'No! No, nothing like that at all! I'm sure you wouldn't do any such thing!'

'What, then?'

There was nothing for it now but to tell him the truth. In a fashion. 'I…I wanted to tell you. Really, I did. But I was afraid that it would change things between us. I thought…' She bit her lip and tried to find the right words.

'What did you think?'

'All kinds of things. At first, when I agreed to have lunch with you, I just wanted to find out what you were like, what kind of man you were, *before* I told you about Alex. You have to appreciate it was a terrible shock to me, Jake, when you turned up in my life, *and* when I found myself as attracted to you as

I was when I was just a girl. I thought I could control how I felt about you. But of course, I couldn't. Then, when the sex was so fabulous between us, I didn't want it to end. I wanted you to keep looking at me the same way. And making love to me. It was selfish of me, I know, but I…I've never felt anything like I do when I'm with you.' Tears pricked at her eyes. 'I'm sorry, Jake. Truly. I didn't mean to hurt you.'

'Well, I am hurt, Angelina. Do you have any idea what it was like, finding out we had a fifteen-year-old son like that?'

'I'm sure it was a shock.'

'That's an understatement.'

'I…I don't know what to say.'

'There's nothing you can say. The damage has been done.'

Angelina's heart sank. But then defiance kicked in. And resentment. Had what she'd done been that wicked, or seriously unforgivable?

Hardly.

'Well, I happen to think there is a lot I can say,' she threw at him. 'I've stood here, like a typically pathetic female, humbly listening to your poor-little-me tale. I've even been feeling sorry for you. But you know what? I think I'm all sorried out. Where is your sympathy for me? Do you have any idea what *my* life has been like? How hard it's been for *me*?'

'I have some idea. Alex told me. In fact, he told me more about you in the two hours I spent with him today than you have in two weeks. I know the sacrifices you've made for him. I know you've been a good mother. I know you never laid a hand on him, no matter how naughty he was. I know he thinks the world of you. I also know you don't date. *Ever*.' He glowered at her. 'It seems you've become a master at deception in a lot of things.'

'What do you mean?'

'You keep secrets from *everyone*, not just me. *I* know you've had lovers. You told me so. Yet your teenage son says there's never been another man in your life after me. He thinks you're a cross between the Virgin Mary and Mother Teresa. He even has this romantic idea that when you and I meet up again this time, we'll fall in love once more and get married.'

'Oh…' It wasn't so far removed from the romantic notions she'd been stupidly harbouring this last week.

'Yes, *oh*,' Jake said drily. 'Our son has to receive a reward for optimism, doesn't he?'

'He certainly does, considering who his father is. But for your information, Mr Smarty Pants, I have not had lovers. And I never said I had. You just jumped to that conclusion, probably because you couldn't conceive of anyone choosing to lead a celibate lifestyle. Which I did. For our son's sake. Don't think I didn't have offers. I've had plenty. So Alex was right. There's only been the one man in my life. *You!*'

Now that she'd blurted out the whole truth, Angelina rather enjoyed the shocked look on Jake's face.

'You can't seriously expect me to believe you haven't had sex in sixteen years?'

'No, I wouldn't expect you to believe that. Not *you*, a man who has a different girlfriend every other month and who can't even roll over in bed without reaching for another condom. But perhaps if you think about it a little more, you'll see I'm telling the truth. Why do you think I couldn't get enough last weekend? Because I was so frustrated, that's why.'

Jake stared at her. 'Frustrated.'

'Yes. Frustrated!' Her hands found her hips. 'I deserved a break after being such a goody-two-shoes for so long, don't you think? I could do with a few more, too. But I guess that's out of the question now. I always knew that as soon as you found out about Alex, everything would change between us. I'm no longer lover material, I'm the mother of your child. The *single* mother of your child. And, as such, to be treated with suspicion. It wouldn't take a genius to know that the invitation to come to your place this weekend is off.'

He looked stunned. 'Well, I…I need some time to think.'

Her smile was laced with bitterness. 'How come I'm not surprised? You can run but you can't hide, Jake. Alex has found you now, and if I know my son he won't let go. You're his father. Get used to it.'

'It's only been half a day, Angelina. Give *me* a break, will you?'

She laughed. 'You were right. You are going to be a pretty rotten father. Oh, I don't doubt you'll give lip-service to the role, but you just don't have what it takes in here…' She patted her hand over her heart, that heart which was breaking inside.

But be damned if she was going to show it.

'Alex's inter-school swimming carnival is on this Saturday,' she announced. 'It starts at one. Can I tell him you'll be there when I call him tonight? Or do you want time to think about that too?'

'I've already told him I'll be there.'

'No kidding. You've surprised me.'

'I surprised myself,' he muttered. 'Look, I'm doing my best, all right? I don't really know the boy. And I see now that I don't really know you.'

'Men like you never know anyone, except themselves.'

'That's a bit harsh.'

'Is it? I suggest you go home and have a good look in the mirror, Jake. If you can see past the shiny, successful, sexy surface, you just might not like what you find.'

'Angelina, I—'

'Oh, just go,' she snapped, and, wrapping her arms around herself, she whirled away from him to stare steadfastly out of the kitchen window.

She felt him staring at her. Felt his hesitation. But then he started walking. 'See you on Saturday,' he muttered, leaving his coffee untouched behind him on the counter.

By the time Angelina heard the Ferrari growl into life, she was crying her eyes out.

CHAPTER THIRTEEN

'I STILL find it hard to believe,' Dorothy said during dessert.

Jake, who always lost his appetite when he was stressed, or distressed, put down his dessert fork, his slice of lemon meringue pie still intact. 'You and me both,' he said with a weary sigh. 'I didn't sleep much last night. I kept seeing Alex's face when he called me Dad. He made me feel like such a fraud. I'm no hero, Dorothy. I'm just a man.'

'You're not *just* a man, Jake. You're an exceptional man. And you'll make an exceptional father.'

'How can you say that, knowing where I came from?'

'Because I know you. There's not a violent or a mean bone in your body. Angelina more or less said the same thing.'

'Angelina! Don't talk to me about Angelina!'

'Why? Because you're in love with her?'

Jake stiffened in his chair. 'I am not in love with her. I don't fall in love with liars.'

'She explained why she lied. And I, for one, understand her reasoning perfectly. So would you, if your male ego wasn't involved. She's a mother first and foremost. She was protecting her child.'

'She deceived me.'

'For the best of reasons. She wanted to get to know you first.'

'Yeah. In the biblical sense.'

'Oh, for pity's sake, will you get off your high horse? The girl obviously fancies you like crazy. She always did. You pack a powerful physical punch, Jake. She's a healthy young woman whose hormones have never had a chance. I don't blame her one bit if she wanted you.'

'Dorothy!'

'Goodness me, who do you think you're talking to here? A nun? I'll have you know I know exactly how Angelina must have felt last weekend. I was forty years old when I met Edward. OK, so I wasn't a virgin but as good as. I went to bed with Edward the very first night and we didn't sleep a wink. *All* night. Damn, but it was good.'

Jake just stared. He would never understand women. They could look so soft and malleable on the surface, when all the while, inside, they were tough as teak. And so damned surprising.

He hadn't expected Angelina to stand up to him the way she had yesterday. He'd expected her to wilt under his anger and beg his forgiveness. Instead, she'd read him the Riot Act and given him his walking papers.

She obviously didn't fancy him that much. *And* she sure as hell hadn't fallen in love with him last weekend as he'd foolishly hoped she had.

His goal to marry her now seemed even further away than ever. Perverse, considering they shared a child. Which brought him to the problem of Alex. Not that Alex was a problem child. He wasn't. He was a credit to Angelina. *He* was the problem. The father. The pathetic and panic-stricken parent.

He didn't know what to do or what to feel.

'Just go to the swimming carnival, Jake,' Dorothy advised, 'and let nature take its course.'

Jake shook his head. That was another thing about women. They were mind-readers. And weirdly perceptive. Look at how Sally had known Alex was his son at a glance. And then there was her knowing he was thinking of starting up his own business. How had she guessed that? Maybe the whole sex was in league with the devil.

'Stop thinking about yourself and *your* feelings,' Dorothy said sternly. 'Think about Angelina for a change. And what *she's* been through. Much more of a challenge than anything you've ever faced. Being solely responsible for looking after and bringing up a child is a massive job. She might have had her father for support but I doubt he was such a great help with the day-to-day problems of child-rearing. She did it all by herself, Jake. And she did a wonderful job by the sounds of things. The reason you've fallen in love with her is not just because she's physically beautiful. You've had oodles of good-looking girls before. It's because she's a beautiful person, with character and spirit. And you know what? I think she loves you for the same reasons.'

'Yeah, right,' he said drily.

Jake winced when Dorothy gave him one of the

savage looks she used to give him when he'd first come to live with her. 'I never took you for a coward, Jake Winters, but you're beginning to sound and act like one. You *do* love Angelina. And you love your son, even if you don't know him yet. Because he's your flesh and blood. And he loves you for the same reason. The three of you should be together, as a family. The reason Angelina got so stroppy with you yesterday is because that's what she wants too and she's afraid it's not going to happen. She's afraid her son is going to be hurt. She's afraid *she's* going to be hurt.'

'Have you finished?' Jake said ruefully.

'For tonight,' Dorothy returned as she stabbed her piece of pie with her dessert fork. 'There might be another instalment at some time in the future.'

'God forbid. Did Edward know you were like this?'

'Of course. Admittedly, he hated it when I was always right.'

Jake laughed. '*I* hate it too.'

Dorothy's breath caught. And then she let it out very slowly. He did love Angelina. Thank goodness.

'So what are you going to do about it?' she asked, feigning a composure she was far from feeling.

'Back off, Dorothy. This coward is still a male animal and likes to do things his way.'

'I don't really think you're a coward.'

'I know,' Jake said more softly.

'Er—do you think I could come to the swimming

carnival with you tomorrow?' Dorothy asked. 'I would dearly love to see the boy.'

'Only if you promise not to interfere.'

'Would I do that?'

'Yes. Now promise.'

Dorothy sighed. 'I promise.'

'OK,' he agreed, and Dorothy beamed.

She rose and scooped up Jake's untouched dessert. 'Coffee?'

'Mmm. Yes, please,' he said, watching blankly as Dorothy left the room. He was wondering what Angelina was doing and if she really might love him, as Dorothy said.

'I hate him,' Angelina muttered as she slammed the plates into the dishwasher.

'Hey, watch it with the crockery there, boss!'

'Let her break a plate or two, Kevin,' Wilomena advised from where she was scraping the remains of tonight's meals into the bin. 'Better than her breaking them over a certain person's head. Besides, they're her plates. She can do with them whatever she damned well pleases.'

'True,' Angelina growled, and slammed a few more in.

None of them broke. But then, they weren't as easily broken as other things. Like her heart.

'The bastard,' she grumped. 'How dare he say he had to *pretend* to be nice to Alex? As if anyone ever has to pretend to be nice to Alex.'

'Geez, Angelina!' Kevin exclaimed. 'Give the man a break.'

'That's exactly what she'd like to do,' Wilomena said drily. 'Across that stupid skull of his.'

'You women expect too much of a guy.'

'No kidding!' both women chorused.

'He'll come round. Just give him time.'

'Like, how long? A lifetime?' Wilomena said waspishly. 'That's how long it takes for some men to come to the party. If ever.'

'I think he sounds like an OK guy. He's going to Alex's swimming carnival tomorrow, isn't he?'

'Big deal,' Angelina muttered.

'Yeah, big deal,' Wilomena echoed.

'Women!' Kevin huffed. 'Impossible to please.'

'He could please her all right,' Wilomena said after Angelina had gone home and she and Kevin were stacking away the last of the things. 'He could tell her he loves her for starters, then ask her to marry him.'

Kevin laughed. 'You think that would please her? You know what she'd do? She'd throw back at him that he didn't really love her and he was only marrying her for the kid's sake. And then she'd say no, like a typical female.'

'Rubbish! She would not! Not if she loved him. And she does. Trust me on that. Women who love guys don't say no to a proposal of marriage.'

'You know, I'm glad to hear you say that,' Kevin said, and, drawing a small velvet box out of his white coat's pocket, he dropped to one knee then flipped it open. The cluster of diamonds in the ring glittered like his eyes.

'Wilomena Jenkins,' he said, 'I love you and I want you to be my wife. Will you marry me?'

Wilomena didn't say no. She didn't say a single word. She was too busy crying.

CHAPTER FOURTEEN

ALEX stood behind the starting blocks with the rest of his relay team, nerves making him shift from foot to foot. He swung his arms in circles to keep his muscles warm, and tried to focus on the race ahead, deliberately keeping his eyes away from the stand where he knew his parents were sitting together watching him, along with the old duck they'd brought with them.

'Dorothy's an old friend of mine,' his dad had introduced her before the meet began.

Old was right. And brother, had she stared at him.

Of course, that was because he looked so much like his dad.

His dad.

Alex scooped in a deep breath and let it out very slowly. It was still almost too good to be true, finding his father like that. He'd been confident that his dad would not be in jail. But he'd never dreamt he'd be a top lawyer. How cool was that? And what about that simply awesome car he drove? The guys at school had been green with envy when he'd rocked up on Thursday in a yellow Ferrari.

He'd felt so proud, introducing his dad around to his friends and teachers. He must have gone to sleep that night with a permanent smile on his face.

Now today was his chance to make his dad proud of him. Alex knew he wasn't good enough at his school work to line up for too many academic prizes. But he was his school's best swimmer. He'd already won the hundred-metre sprint. And the two hundred. Now he was lining up for the four-by-one relay, the last race of this meet, and he was swimming the anchor leg.

Kings were in front on the scoreboard. But only by a couple of points. If St Francis's could win this relay, the cup would be theirs. The trouble was, their second-best hundred-metre swimmer had come down with a virus that morning and they'd had to bring in the first reserve, who was three seconds slower. On paper, they couldn't possibly win, not unless they all swam above themselves.

Alex wanted to win. He wanted to win so badly.

They were being called up for the start. Alex felt sick. As team captain, he'd made the decision to put their slowest swimmer first, employing the tactic that sometimes a swimmer could swim a personal best if they were chasing. Of course, sometimes the chase theory didn't work. The behind swimmer tried too hard on the first lap and went lactic in the second.

The gun went off and their first and slowest swimmer was in the water, doing his best but possibly trying *too* hard. After he'd come in to the changeover several lengths behind, Alex wished he'd made the decision to go first himself. But he soothed his panic with the knowledge that Kings had sent their second-best swimmer off first.

By the second changeover, they'd caught up a couple of lengths. But then disaster happened. Their third swimmer's foot slipped on the starting block at the changeover, losing them another precious length. By the time he turned to come down for the second lap, he was trailing the Kings boy by a good five lengths. He dug deep, however, and came towards the wall only three lengths behind.

But even as Alex readied himself for the changeover, logic told him that three lengths were still too much. Sure, he'd won the hundred-metre race earlier in the afternoon. But only by a length. How could he possibly find another two lengths?

And then the voice came to him, across the pool, loud and clear.

'Go for it, son!'

He went, with wings on his feet, making up half a length in the changeover dive alone, coming up with the Kings swimmer's feet in his sights. There was no holding back. He wasn't close enough for fancy tactics, like riding in the other boy's wash. He put his foot down, his big arms slicing through the water, his even bigger feet churning with a six-beat kick right from the start.

You have to nail the turn, he lectured himself as the wall loomed into view. His lungs were bursting. He'd forgotten to breathe. No time now. He would breathe later, after he'd turned. He tumbled. His feet hit the wall and he was surging forward under the water. Up he eventually came, gasping for air but still swimming like a madman. He had no idea where the Kings boy was now. His head was turned the other way. All he could do was go like the hammers of hell.

His arms were burning. So were his legs. He'd never known such pain. Or such determination. He was going to win, not just for his dad, but also for his mum. He wanted to make her proud as well. Alex knew she'd given up a lot for him, and he wanted her to see that it had been worth it.

Not far now. He could hear the screaming. It had to be close. Just a bit more, Alex. You can do it. Stroke harder. Kick faster. The wall was coming up. Time it right. Dip down, stretch those fingers. You've got your dad's big hands. They have to be good for something.

He touched then exploded upwards, out of the water. He looked up, towards his mother. She had her hands over her face and she looked as if she was crying. His heart sank. He'd lost. He'd given it his all and he'd lost. But then the boy in the next lane was tapping him on the shoulder and congratulating him.

He looked up again. His mum was now wrapped in his dad's arms and the old duck next to them was grinning like a Cheshire cat, with her hand held up towards Alex in a victory sign.

Alex grinned back at her, his own hand punching up high into the air as he yelled, 'Go for it, Dad!'

CHAPTER FIFTEEN

'Is IT always like that?'

Angelina lifted her head at Jake's question. They were back at his apartment, Angelina having driven there at Jake's request after the swimming carnival was over. She was sitting on the sleek red leather sofa once more, with a Malibu and Coke cradled in her hands, wondering when she could possibly get up and leave. Just being in this place with Jake, alone, was killing her. She'd thought she hated him this past week but of course she didn't. She loved him.

'Always like what?' she asked, her voice sounding as dead and drained as she was feeling.

'When your kid does something great. Does it always feel like that?'

'Like what, exactly?'

'Like your heart is going to burst out of your chest. Like you're on top of the world, a world bathed in everlasting sunshine.'

Angelina's own heart squeezed tight as all the fears which had been gathering that afternoon suddenly crystallised into one big fear.

'Yes,' she said flatly. 'Yes, it always feels like that.'

Jake sat down on an adjacent armchair with his

own drink in his hands. Scotch on ice, by the look of it.

'We have to talk,' he said, his tone serious.

'About what?' Angelina took a sip of her drink.

'You. Me. Alex.'

'Let's just stick to Alex.'

'I think we should start with you and me. After all, that's where Alex started, sixteen years ago.'

'A lot of water has gone under the bridge since then, Jake.'

'Yes. It certainly has. We're different people now, you and me.'

'One of us is, anyway,' she bit out, then took another sip.

Jake gritted his teeth. She wasn't making things easy for him. When she'd cried back at the swimming carnival and he'd taken her into his arms, he'd thought that everything was going to be all right. Alex had clearly thought so, too. *And* Dorothy. But the moment they were alone together again, she'd withdrawn inside a cold, hard little shell that he just couldn't penetrate.

Jake decided that a change of tactics was called for.

'So you're going to do it again, are you?' he said sharply.

That got her attention. 'Do what?'

'Lie to me.'

'I never lied to you,' she said defensively.

'Yes, you did. By omission. And by implication. Now you're doing it again.'

'I don't know what you mean.'

'You're pretending you don't care about me. That you don't love me.'

He watched her mouth drop open; watched the truth flash into her eyes.

'You *do* love me,' he ground out, his voice thick with emotion.

'I...I...' She shook her head from side to side, clearly unable to speak the words.

'You love me and you're going to marry me.'

'*Marry* you!' She jumped to her feet, her drink sloshing all over the rug. 'I am not going to marry you. When and if I marry, it will be to a man who loves me as much as I love him. And *not* because he covets my son. Oh, yes, I saw the way you looked at Alex today, Jake Winters, and I knew. I knew in my heart that you wanted my boy, not just for a weekend here and there but all the time. That was why I was crying so much.'

Jake snatched the glass out of her shaking hands and rammed it down on a nearby table along with his own drink before glowering at her with fury in his eyes and frustration in his heart.

'I've heard enough of this rubbish!' he roared. 'I *do* love you, woman. I probably love you even more than you love me! If you don't believe me, then come here...' Grabbing her hand, he dragged her with him into the bedroom, where he yanked open the top drawer of his bedside chest.

'I don't think that showing me how many con-doms you've bought is proof of love,' she said scathingly as she tried to tug her hand out of his. But he refused to let it go.

His producing a ring box and flipping it open to show a spectacular diamond engagement ring shut her up. But not for long.

'Good try, Jake. Good move, too. I've got to hand it to you. You're clever.'

Jake dropped the ring box on the bed, grabbed a piece of paper from the drawer and shoved it into her hands. 'That's the sales receipt. Care to check the date?'

Angelina's eyes dropped to the date. Wednesday. He'd bought the ring on Wednesday.

She looked up, tears in her eyes. 'You bought this *before* Alex went to see you?'

Jake had to steel himself against his own rush of emotion. 'I wanted to tell you I loved you and wanted to marry you last weekend. But I was afraid of rushing you. I thought you needed time. I was prepared to give you all the time in the world. But then I walked past this jewellery-shop window and saw this ring and I just had to buy it for you. When I put it in this drawer, I told myself I didn't care how long I had to wait till you wore it, as long as you eventually did.'

'Oh…' More tears rushed in, spilling over.

He wiped them away with his fingers, then curved his hands over her shoulders. 'I love you, Angelina Mastroianni. And you love me. So I'm not going to give you any more time. We've already wasted sixteen years.' He reached to extract the diamond ring from the box and slipped it on her left hand. It fitted perfectly. 'We're going to be married. Not hurriedly. Magnificently. Next spring. In St Mary's Cathedral. But that's just a ceremony. From this moment on, you are my woman, and I am your man, exclusively, till death do us part.'

'Till death us do part,' she repeated dazedly.

'Now tell me you love me.'

'I love you.'

He sighed and drew her into his arms, his lips burrowing into her hair. 'I think you should show me how much.'

CHAPTER SIXTEEN

SEPTEMBER—the first month of spring down under—
was an iffy month for weather in Sydney. Often cold.
Often rainy. But occasionally brilliant.

St Mary's Cathedral had never looked better than
it did that September afternoon, bathed in sunshine,
the nearby gardens just beginning to blossom. But
nothing could match the splendour of the bride as
she carefully mounted the cathedral steps.

Her dress was white chiffon, with a draped bodice
and a long, flowing skirt that fell from straight under
her impressive bustline. Her dark hair was sleekly
up, with a diamanté tiara as decoration. Her veil was
very long and sheer. Her neck was bare, but delicate
diamond and pearl drops fell from her lobes.

She looked exquisite. She also looked nervous,
which enhanced that glorious air of innocence that
often clung to brides, even those who were secretly
five months pregnant.

'I never appreciated till now,' she said to
Wilomena, 'just how nerve-racking weddings are. If
I hadn't had your help today, I'd never have been
ready in time.'

'That's what bridesmaids are for,' Wilomena returned, busily fluffing out the bridal veil. 'I'll be re-

lying on you for the same help when Kevin and I tie the knot later in the year.'

Angelina smiled at the girl who had fast gone from employee to confidante to best friend. 'My pleasure. And might I say that burgundy colour really suits you, despite your doubts? The style, too.'

Wilomena's dress was chiffon as well, calf-length, with a low neckline, spaghetti straps and a long, flowing scarf that draped softly around her throat and hung down to the hem at the back

'Mmm. Yes. I'm forced to agree. Kevin said he can't wait to get it off me later tonight,' she whispered.

'Come on, Mum,' Alex said, and took his mother's arm. 'Stop the girlie chit-chat. We don't want to keep Dad waiting too long. He was champing at the bit this morning.'

Angelina looked up at her son. So handsome he was in his tuxedo. And so grown up. He'd matured considerably since Jake had come into his life. The two of them spent as much time together as they possibly could, obviously trying to make up for lost time.

Angelina might have been jealous if both the men in her life hadn't been so happy. Besides, Jake still found plenty of time for her. Quality time. In bed and out.

The *Wedding March* started up, snapping Angelina out of her thoughts. Wilomena took her place in front of the bride and began the slow walk up the aisle, just as they had rehearsed. Angelina's arms tightened around her son's when her bouquet started to shake.

'Relax, Mum,' her son advised.

'How can you be so calm?' she cried.

'Well, there's nothing to be nervous about, is there? I mean…we all love each other here. Not only that, if I'm going to do Grandpa's job, I want to do it with dignity and panache, like he would have.'

Angelina's stomach tightened at the mention of her father. 'Do you think he'd mind my marrying Jake, Alex?'

'Grandpa? Nah. He'd be happy, I reckon. Especially now.'

'You mean because Jake's turned out to be such a good man?'

Alex stifled a laugh. 'Come on, Mum. This is me you're talking to. Because of the *baby*, of course! Dad told me all about it.'

'He *told* you!'

'Yeah, there are no secrets between Dad and me. He said it was all his fault, as usual.'

'Oh…'

'He also said if I ever get a girl pregnant this side of twenty-five, he's going to skin me alive,' Alex added with a grin. 'Hey, we'd better start walking. Wil's halfway up the aisle.'

They started walking, Angelina's head whirling. Jake had told Alex about the baby. And there she'd been, trying to hide her pregnancy, worried sick about what her son would think when he found out.

'You don't mind?' she whispered out of the corner of her mouth.

'Why should I mind? I always wanted a little sister.'

'You know it's a girl as well?'

'Yep. Dad's tickled pink.'

Which was true. Not that Jake had really cared if it was a boy or a girl. He just wanted them to have a baby together. He'd told her he wanted to experience fatherhood right from the start.

'Smile, Mum,' Alex ordered.

She smiled. And then she smiled some more. Alex was right. They all loved each other here. There was nothing to worry about.

Jake's heart lurched when she smiled. Then lurched some more when her smile broadened. God, how he loved that woman!

'What a babe,' Kevin muttered beside him.

'You can say that again,' Jake returned before he realised Kevin's eyes were on his fiancée across the way.

Those two only had eyes for each other. Jake knew that for a fact. Since quitting his job, he'd been spending a lot of time up at the winery, helping out there till he worked out what he was going to do, career-wise. Probably start up his own law practice. Sally had already indicated that she was for hire, at the right price.

He and Kevin had hit it off right from the start and when Angelina said she'd asked Wilomena to be her one and only bridesmaid, Jake had no hesitation in asking Kevin to be his best man.

'Angelina looks pretty good too,' Kevin added, and Jake laughed.

He caught Sally's eye in the third pew and gave her a wink. She winked back.

Then he smiled at Dorothy, who was looking just a little tense.

Dear Dorothy. *Smart* Dorothy as well. He would be forever grateful for the solution she'd come up with for a problem he had about names. The names of his children. He wanted both of them to have the same surname. *His*. But Alex was adamant about keeping Mastroianni as his surname and Jake could appreciate that. Still, with Dorothy's help, he'd sorted that all out. He hoped Angelina would be pleased, he thought as his gaze returned to his lovely bride.

Dorothy was determined not to cry during the ceremony, but she clutched a white lace-edged handkerchief in her hands, just in case. What a beautiful bride Angelina made. But what a handsome groom Jake was. Most touching of all was the way he was looking at the woman he loved as she came down the aisle. With so much tenderness. So much love.

Oh, Edward. You would have been so proud of him today.

But no prouder than she was. Maybe she wasn't his mother by blood, but she was in her heart. And now there was a baby coming as well. A dear little baby girl for her to help mind. And to love.

Oh, dear. She dabbed at her eyes.

Jake tensed when the priest got to the part which he knew would come as a bit of a surprise to his bride.

'And do you, Jake Mastroianni, take…?'

Angelina reached out to touch the priest's arm. 'No, no,' she murmured. 'You've got it wrong. It's Jake *Winters*.'

'Not any more,' Jake whispered to her. 'I had my surname changed by deed poll. With Alex's approval, of course. I'm a Mastroianni now.' And he glanced over his shoulder at his son, who nodded to his mother with a wide smile.

'You've taken *my* name?' Angelina asked, looking pleased, but stunned.

Jake sighed with relief. He'd done the right thing. After all, he had no real attachment to his own name. His poor mother had died some years back and he'd never known any of his other relatives. But it was rather ironic that he was to be called Mr Mastroianni from now on.

I'll try not to discredit your name in any way, came his silent promise to the proud Italian man who had once broken his nose.

'Please go on,' Jake directed the priest.

The ceremony was a bit of a fog after that, Angelina not surfacing till Jake lifted the veil from her face and kissed her.

His lips on hers felt slightly different this time. Softer. More tender. More loving.

She looked up into her husband's eyes, those beautiful blue eyes that could look so hard at times. But not today. And certainly not at this moment. They were soft and wet with tears.

'Mrs Mastroianni,' he choked out, and she realised, perhaps for the first time, just how much he *did* love her.

'Mr Mastroianni,' she returned softly, and touched his cheek. 'My sweet darling. My only love.'

MILLS & BOON®

It Started With…Collection!

0715_ST15

**Don't miss Sarah Morgan's
next Puffin Island story**

*Some Kind
of Wonderful*

Brittany Forrest has stayed away from Puffin Island
since her relationship with Zach Flynn went bad.
They were married for ten days and only just
managed not to kill each other by the
end of the honeymoon.

But, when a broken arm means she must return,
Brittany moves back to her Puffin Island home.
Only to discover that Zac is there as well.

Will a summer together help two lovers reunite or
will their stormy relationship crash on to the
rocks of Puffin Island?

Some Kind of Wonderful
COMING JULY 2015
Pre-order your copy today

MILLS & BOON®

It's Got to be Perfect

* cover in development

When Ellie Rigby throws her three-carat engagement ring into the gutter, she is certain of only one thing. She has yet to know true love!

Fed up with disastrous internet dates and conflicting advice from her friends, Ellie decides to take matters into her own hands. Starting a dating agency, Ellie becomes an expert in love. Well, that is until a match with one of her clients, charming, infuriating Nick, has her questioning everything she's ever thought about love...

Order yours today at
www.millsandboon.co.uk